TALES OF SILVER DOWNS

MUSE

BOOK 1

KYLIE QUILLINAN

First published in Australia in 2015. Second edition published 2016 by Kylie Quillinan

ABN 34 112 708 734

kyliequillinan.com

National Library of Australia Cataloguing-in-Publication data:

Quillinan, Kylie

Muse / Kylie Quillinan

Paperback ISBN: 9780994331526

Ebook ISBN: 9780994331502

A823.4

This is a work of fiction. Any similarity between the characters and situations within its pages and places or persons, living or dead, is unintentional and coincidental.

Cover art by Deranged Doctor Design.

Proudly independent. Please support indie authors by legally purchasing their work.

This work uses Australian spelling and grammar.

LP13072020

DEDICATION

For Neal,
who always believed.

And for Muffin, Bella and Lulu,
for guarding me while I worked.

A NOTE FROM THE AUTHOR

This work uses British spelling and grammar.

DIARMUID

A SEVENNIGHT BEFORE my brother Caedmon was handfasted, we gathered at his bride's family estate, Misty Valley. Their modest stone lodge brimmed with friends and family. Ale flowed freely and folk danced to the raucous tunes of fiddler and whistler. Winter garments — hats, coats, scarves — were piled on a bench in the corner, abandoned in the warmth of ale and dancing. I ate and drank, avoided solicitations to dance, and tried to pretend I was happy for Caedmon.

My muse, Ida, whispered snide remarks about people around us. One subject of her scorn was a man whose nose was so long and sharp, Ida wondered whether he could slice bread with it. Another was the woman whose fat fingers could hardly bend to lift her mug. Had I the courage to voice such thoughts, surely the revelry would dissipate and we could all go home.

Every bard has a muse and Ida was as real as any man's, to me at least. Her image, in my mind's eye, was as clear as if she stood beside me. Blonde of hair, blue of eye, skin so pale it was almost translucent. Folk around these parts were dark-haired with milky white skin. Ida looked like no one I had ever seen. It helped me remember she didn't really exist.

As folk tired of dancing, we gathered in front of the grey stone fireplace at one end of the room. The sweet scent of pinecones on the fire filled the air, covering the lingering smells of roast meat and bread. The older folk warmed their bones on comfortable chairs drawn close to the flames. Small children perched on their laps or on brightly-coloured rugs at their feet. Those who were neither old nor young enough to claim a position close by the fire gathered behind. Some sat on wooden benches, others leaned against the walls.

I found a spot on a bench towards the back of the room. My belly was comfortably full and now that all the merriment had subsided, I eagerly anticipated the evening's tale-telling. Tonight I would make Ida proud.

Caedmon and his betrothed, Grainne, sat near the front, he with an arm around her shoulders. Both were flushed and bright-eyed, still catching their breath from the last dance. Grainne's father, Laeg, stood beside the fireplace. He was a hardy-looking man, plump and rosy-cheeked. Grainne and her three sisters all looked much like him.

"This seems a fine time for a tale," Laeg announced and the crowd swiftly quietened. "Caedmon, my boy, I believe you have a bard in the family. Is he here tonight?"

"Yes, my lord." Caedmon darted a glance at me over his shoulder, a warning in his eyes. "My youngest brother, Diarmuid, back there, is the bard."

Laeg nodded in my direction, although the way his eyes searched the crowd showed he didn't know my face. "Well then, young Diarmuid, will you favour us with a tale?"

My heart pounded as I made my way to the fireplace. Laeg slapped me on the back and then stepped away to lean against a wall. I cleared my throat.

"This is a new tale," I said. Although my voice was loud and confident, my breath quickened, for in this moment before I began, I suffered from nerves. While the tale was still unspoken, it was perfect but it would become imperfect in its telling. For a tale told never quite lived up to the promise of a tale untold. Once the words began to flow, calmness would wash over me, although I could never entirely lose myself in the tale. I was always acutely aware of every murmur and movement.

Flames crackled in the fireplace and occasionally a seat creaked. Children were swiftly hushed as I told a tale of a woman who had offended Titania, queen of the fey. The woman had a babe who was not yet four summers old. As punishment for the offence, Titania ordered the woman to take her child into the woods.

"'Go to the deepest, darkest part of the woods,' Titania said to the woman. 'And leave the child there. She will be food for the wild boar. They will rip her limbs from her body and tear out her heart while it still beats.'

"The woman cried and begged and offered her own life in exchange for that of the child. But Titania ignored her pleas, for the fey do not feel as we do and do not understand fear or sadness or pity."

By now, the mood in the room had changed. The seats creaked more often and children were not shushed quite as quickly. Discomfited, my words came a little faster.

"So the woman took her child by the hand and led her into the woods. As they made their way through the trees, the woman swallowed her sobs and did not allow her tears to fall, for she did not want the child to be afraid.

"At length they reached a clearing and as they stood in the centre, the woman knew she could not leave her child there, regardless of Titania's instructions. She resolved to keep walking, all the way through the woods. Eventually they would reach the other side. They would continue to walk until they found a town where the people did not know of the fey. But as she left the clearing, Titania suddenly appeared in front of her.

"The woman fell to her knees before the fey queen and again begged for her child's life. But she could not sway Titania.

"Eventually, with many tears and much sorrow, the woman kissed her child goodbye. 'Be brave, my sweet,' she whispered and released the child's hand. Sobbing now, the mother stepped back into the trees for she intended to stay to witness her child's fate. On the other side of the clearing, Titania also waited.

"Only moments passed before two wild boar entered the clearing. They sniffed the air and scented the child. The child tried to run from the enormous black beasts but Titania charmed her and she could not move her feet.

"The boars circled the child, once, twice. Then they lunged. Blood sprayed onto the leaves as they ripped the child's limbs from her body, first her arms, then when she fell down, her legs. The child did not stop screaming until they tore off her head. The mother sobbed but she did not cover her ears for she wanted to hear every moment of her child's death. She knew she would hear her daughter's screams echoing in her memory for the rest of her life.

"The boars devoured the child and even licked up her blood from the leaves. When there was nothing left, they turned and went back into the woods.

"It was only then that Titania spoke again. 'Your lesson is concluded,' she said. 'See that you have learned it well.' Then she disappeared into the woods and did not return again."

As I finished speaking, one of Grainne's relatives left, taking two small children with her. I had intended to demonstrate how the fey interfere in human lives at their own whim and that they care not for what misery they bestow. That sometimes fate or circumstance, or the fickle desire of the fey, cuts the closest of bonds and that not all tales end happily.

I waited, shifting from foot to foot, heart pounding, for my audience's reaction. My words hung heavy in the air and folk avoided my eyes. As always.

A child began to sob. "I don't like that story, Papa," she said.

There was no point waiting for Laeg to construct some suitably polite words. As I left the room, someone finally comforted the crying child.

2

DIARMUID

I TOOK A long swallow of ale and watched as Caedmon thrust another log into the fireplace. The flames flared briefly and then settled again, a small yellow blaze warding off the chill of a winter evening. It was well after midnight when we returned from Misty Valley and the rest of our family were now abed. Caedmon and I drew our chairs within the fire's golden shield while the room beyond lay in darkness. Ida was silent for now, sleeping perhaps, if muses do such a thing, or disappointed with tonight's tale.

In the depths of the flickering fire stood a raven, its gaze fixed on me as blood dripped from its beak. I didn't recall paying much attention to ravens in my earliest years but now I saw them everywhere: in the fire, in the clouds, in the shadows, in my dreams. What they meant, I could only guess, and it was on nights like this, when dark thoughts overcrowded my mind, that the ravens were most vivid. Could I touch it if I reached into the fire, or would it disappear like smoke between my fingers? Sometimes I was tempted to try. Instead, I wrapped my fingers around my mug, my skin catching on the chip on its edge. That at least was real. I was never quite sure whether the ravens were.

Caedmon settled back into his chair, his legs stretched out

before him. "Stop being so morose, little brother. It wasn't that bad."

"My name is Diarmuid," I said automatically, although, for once, the fact that he never used my name didn't irritate me. I gulped down more ale even as my head spun and my stomach threatened to reject what I had already consumed. Perhaps if I drank enough, I could forget. "You don't understand. They hate my tales, and for a bard there is nothing worse."

"So they hated one tale." Caedmon finished his ale and poured himself another from the jug on the low table between us. His hands were steady as he set the jug back down, despite the quantity of ale he had drunk with dinner.

"It's not merely one tale. It's every tale. A bard is supposed to please his audience as well as teach them, but I fail at both."

"It's because your tales are..." Caedmon paused, glancing at me as if to measure my mood.

"Go ahead. It can't make me feel any worse than I already do."

"Your tales are odd," he said, staring into the fireplace to avoid my eyes. "They're... I don't know... *wrong*. People want to hear of heroes who go on great journeys and succeed at their quests, who kill the monsters and marry the girl. You tell tales where everybody dies, villages are wiped out, mothers lose their children forever."

"I am trying to demonstrate that actions have consequences," I said somewhat stiffly, despite my assurance that his words wouldn't hurt. I tried hard not to be offended for Caedmon would never say such a thing with malicious intent. "Nobody *understands* my tales."

"That's just it. You tell tales folk have to think about, to reason through. That's not what an audience wants to hear. We want tales to cheer us, sustain us through a cold winter night. Tales of hope and victory, battle and adventure. And love."

I shot Caedmon a quick glance. He was the second oldest of my six brothers and our family's soldier son. Despite his impending handfasting, I might expect to hear him talk of victory and battles but not love.

"You must look forward to being handfasted. Grainne is... nice." My words did no justice to his betrothed, who was dark-haired and rosy-cheeked and had been nothing but friendly towards me. When she and Caedmon announced their betrothal, she had kissed my cheek and called me brother. I didn't know how to respond and by the time I realised I should probably return her embrace, she had given me an odd look and moved on.

"What does a soldier know of handfasting?" Caedmon said. "All I know is fighting and battles and death. Grainne is a good sort of girl: even-tempered, cheerful, easy on the eye. Perhaps, blessed with enough time, we might learn to love each other. But the most important thing is to choose a wife you can stand to live with. Grainne and I will do well enough together for however long we have."

His words sounded odd, hollow. I waited, contemplating the sweet smell of the burning wood and the way it lingered at the back of my mouth. I knew Caedmon was being practical for surely there must be more involved in selecting a wife. But what would I know about such things?

"She will be well provided for when I return to the campaign," Caedmon said at length. "And if she is with child before I leave, I will be satisfied with my choice."

I flushed, never comfortable with discussion about intimate matters between a man and woman. Hopefully Caedmon would assume my reddened cheeks to be caused by the fire's warmth. Of course he would want his bride to be with child before he left. Every man desired three sons: one to be heir, one to be a soldier, and one for the druids. Not every man got what he desired, though, for most never produced a son suited to be a druid.

Caedmon leaned forward to put another log on the fire that didn't need any more fuel. "I'm getting old, little brother. Old for a soldier anyway. I've survived as long as any soldier might expect to."

I had never thought of Caedmon as old. I myself was nineteen and he only five years my senior. But other soldier sons I knew who had gone off to war had long since died. Some never returned after their first campaign. Others lasted two or three or four seasons. Caedmon had been a soldier for eight summers. He certainly was old, for a soldier.

"So you decided to marry." I tucked the thought of his possible death away in a remote corner of my mind. I would take it out and examine it at some other time.

"If I am ever to marry and produce an heir, it must be now. For I don't think I will return here again."

"This will always be your home. You know that even once Papa is gone, Eremon would never turn any of us out."

"That's not what I mean, little brother." Caedmon sighed, heavily. "I think I will die on the next campaign. That's why I must produce an heir now. I can't wait any longer."

"But what makes you think such a thing? You're a good soldier. Just because you've lived longer than others, doesn't mean…" My voice faltered. Ida stirred, whispering dark comments that I ignored.

"I've seen myself, in a dream. I lay in a ditch, dead, my throat slit. And I looked no older than I do now."

"That doesn't mean it was a true dream."

"I believe it was, little brother. I feel its truth in my bones. Death approaches. I have leave to be home until the rivers start to thaw and then I must return to the campaign. If Grainne is carrying my heir before I leave, I will die without regret."

Caedmon poured himself yet another ale. He proffered the jug to me but I shook my head. My stomach rolled and I knew that by morning I would regret the ale I had already drunk.

"What about you, little brother? Is there a girl you fancy? Someone special I should meet while I'm home?"

A face flashed into my mind. I had never spoken to her but I'd seen her at various celebrations. One day, perhaps, I might work up the nerve to ask her name.

"No, there's nobody."

"There must be someone. A pretty girl, maybe someone in Maker's Well?"

I shook my head, staring intently into the fire. The raven stared back.

"Grainne has several younger sisters. Or there's the girls at Three Trees; the eldest is particularly pretty. Or—"

"No, Caedmon." I spoke with as much force as I could. "I told you. There isn't anyone."

"Perhaps you prefer men then? I know several soldiers—"

"No, I don't prefer men," I snapped. "I just… I don't know how to talk to girls. They giggle and whisper and flirt and say one thing but mean another. I don't understand them."

"But you're a bard, my boy," Caedmon said, leaning over to slap me heartily on the shoulder, not even trying to conceal his grin. "You're supposed to be an expert on the human condition. You talk prettily enough when you tell your tales. Surely you can fumble your way through a conversation with a girl?"

"Telling tales is one thing. I can practise them, know how they will end. But a conversation… You never quite know what turn it will take. I can't be prepared for that. I go red and forget how to speak and they laugh at me."

Caedmon laughed then and swallowed the rest of his ale in a hearty gulp. "I have a solution for you. We need to find you a woman. Once you bed one for the first time, the rest will be easier."

My heart pounded in my ears. Such a scenario could only be a disaster. Complete humiliation. "No, I couldn't—"

"It's settled then," he said. "And I'll listen to no arguments, little brother. I'll find you a pretty girl. Next week's winter solstice would be a good time, what with all the celebrating and drinking and making merry. All you have to do is be there."

"Caedmon, really, I can't—"

"I'm not listening." He set his mug aside and rose. "I'm off to bed now but tomorrow I'll start making arrangements."

3

DIARMUID

I SAT UP alone for some time after Caedmon went to bed, staring at the raven in the fire and nursing my ale. Finally, I set my mug aside and left the fire to burn itself out.

My bedchamber was chilly and the bed even colder. I huddled under the covers, goosebumps prickling my skin as I waited for warmth. The fire was mere coals, casting little heat on my small room. I didn't bother to build it back up. Ida whispered to me but I pushed her away.

With every tale, I hoped this would be the one the audience would like. But every time, the reaction was the same. It had always been like this, ever since the day I told my first tale as my tenth summer drew to a close. At that time, Caedmon had been due to depart for the army's training grounds where he would learn to become a soldier. It would be the first time I had been separated from him for more than a few hours.

He and I had spent every possible moment together during those last few months. We camped under the summer stars with only each other and a fire for company. We terrified ourselves investigating an ancient barrow, half expecting the fey to punish us for trespassing on hallowed ground. We battled imaginary enemies and Caedmon taught me to defend myself. I was small for my age, and slender with it, but he made sure I knew how to wield a dagger and I became somewhat capable with a small bow.

Preparing for Caedmon's first departure was difficult for I had never before said goodbye to a brother with the uncertain knowledge that he might not return. Farewelling our druid brother, Fiachra, was different, for he always had one foot in the beyond, even as a child. But Caedmon was the brother I knew best. As summer slipped away, he had become somewhat distant and disappeared for hours at a time. Perhaps he was trying to prepare me for his impending absence. Or perhaps he was preparing himself.

I said nothing about the increasing time we spent apart. In truth, I was somewhat jealous that he edged towards his destiny while I had yet to perform a single tale, for I had but recently realised that barding would be my own career. On the days Caedmon absented himself, I worked on my first tale, gently crafting it into what I thought was a thing of wonder and truth.

Caedmon had no time to wander the estate with me that last day for he was busy making his farewells to the tenants and servants, the animals and our home. It was not until just before the evening meal that I was able to snatch a few moments alone with him.

The sun was sinking towards the horizon, sending fingers of deep purple across the sky as I lingered outside in the hope of spotting Caedmon. The day's warmth had faded to a slight coolness heralding winter's approach and the late afternoon air was heavy with grass and sweet heather. Finally, he appeared from behind the barn and smiled when he saw me waiting there for him.

"Well, little brother." Caedmon wrapped an arm around my shoulders as we walked towards the house. "Tomorrow's the day."

"I know." Now that I finally had him to myself, I was tongue shy. I wanted to wish him well on his journey with all of a bard's eloquence but, in truth, I wasn't yet able to string such words together. "I wish you good luck."

"I'll be sorry to not see you grow up." Caedmon squeezed my shoulders with sudden intensity. "This is not what a big brother should do — go off to have adventures while leaving his younger brother to make his way in the world alone."

Suddenly the days yawned ahead of me, long and cold and empty without the bright spark of Caedmon's enthusiasm. It was always he who suggested we explore the fields, or camp out, or fish in the stream. He who devised some elaborate game involving the mare or a few branches. What adventure and excitement would exist for me without Caedmon?

The dinner table that night bore a splendid feast of all of Caedmon's favourite foods. Roasted hens stuffed with herbs, the last of winter's root vegetables carefully hoarded for the occasion, juicy salad greens from the garden our sister Eithne tended when she was well enough and, after, bowls of plump blackberries with fresh cream. We took our places at the table, my brothers jostling each other as they claimed favoured seats.

I picked at some chicken and nibbled on a few berries but my stomach churned. Bitterness and desertion warred with my desire to be proud of Caedmon for fulfilling his fate. And proud I was but the prospect of how empty life would be without him loomed far nearer.

Our father, Fionn, beamed with pride at his soon-to-be soldier son and regularly slapped him on the back. If he felt sadness, he did not let it show. Our mother, Agata, was pale and quiet and ate almost as little as I. Caedmon had seconds and then thirds of everything.

Five of my six brothers were present: Eremon, the oldest son and Papa's heir; Caedmon, ever my favourite; Sitric, the first brother to not have his destiny mapped for him since birth and who spoke of becoming a scribe; Marrec and Conn, one soul split between two bodies. I was the last-born son and after me came only Eithne, our sister. Fiachra, who was born after Sitric but before Marrec and Conn, was absent but nobody expected him to come home. He was a druid and had higher matters to attend to than the small matter of a brother going off to battle.

The room was rowdy as my brothers joked and laughed, passing platters between them and teasing Caedmon with the horrors he might expect on the battlefield. Caedmon himself said little; too intent on filling himself with good food while he could.

When Caedmon had finally eaten his fill, he leaned back, his hands on his belly and his face calm. "An excellent meal," he said. "And certainly a fitting farewell."

Papa wrapped an arm around Caedmon's shoulders. "A tale is in order, I think. Something suitable with which to send our young soldier off to battle. Who would like to tell it?"

This was the opportunity I had awaited for my tale was finally ready. I spoke quickly, before anyone else could volunteer.

"I will."

Silence greeted my announcement and I didn't miss the look that passed between my parents.

"Diarmuid," Mother said and her tone was cautious. "You have never before offered a tale. What causes this?"

At only ten summers old, I was too young to feel embarrassment. "I have created a tale and I would like to tell it."

The silence lasted longer this time and I looked around the table, wondering why nobody spoke. All eyes were on our parents. Mother and Papa looked only at each other as if an unspoken conversation passed between them.

"We wondered when this day would come," Papa said eventually. "Diarmuid, there is something you should know before you choose this path. Something about yourself and our family."

I waited, my heart suddenly beating hard. I could not even begin to guess what this secret might be. From the looks on my brothers' faces, it seemed only I was clueless, and perhaps Eithne, although her face was hard to read and I could never be sure whether she didn't understand or just wasn't interested.

Our parents looked at each other again and it seemed each waited for the other to speak. It was our mother who finally did.

"Diarmuid, you know you are the seventh son of a seventh son."

I waited. There must be more for this was no secret to me. I had never met any of my uncles because Papa's brothers all perished long before I was born, although the circumstances of their deaths were never discussed. In fact, the one time I asked was the only time I saw my father cry.

"In our family, the seventh son of a seventh son is very special." Mother spoke slowly, as if choosing her words with care.

The sweet feeling of anticipation was stealthily replaced with oozing dread. I would have fled but my legs refused to move and I could do nothing but sit and wait, looking from Mother to Papa and back again.

"Diarmuid, in our family, the seventh son of a seventh son is always a bard," Papa said, and it seemed the words pained him.

The dread flowed away and my heart lifted. Finally, I too had a destiny. I was one of the chosen sons who had a fate to fulfil. I might not be heir or soldier or druid but I was a *bard*.

"It's a very big responsibility," Papa said. "You have no idea how much responsibility it is to be a bard, to be a teacher of truths and a weaver of words, especially..." He stopped then and it seemed another unspoken message passed between him and Mother. An almost imperceptible shake of her head meant that whatever else he had intended went unsaid.

"Papa, why do you never tell any tales?" I asked. For if I was destined to be a bard, surely my father, as the seventh son of a seventh son, was too.

"I have told enough tales in my lifetime." His words hung heavily in the air. "More than enough. I care little to tell them anymore."

We adjourned to the living room. The room had looked a lot bigger back then and the stone fireplace towered higher than I stood. There was an assortment of both soft chairs and wooden benches, enough to seat a family of ten plus a few guests. The late summer evening was warm enough that we had no need for a fire but we gathered in our accustomed places by the hearth.

Papa leaned back into his chair and stared into the empty grate for some time before he finally turned to me. "You may as well give us your tale, Diarmuid."

I had imagined this moment over and over. Myself standing before my family, back straight and head held high as I regaled them with my tale of love and loss and lessons learnt. They would gasp at the daring of its ending, for I would tell no tales with flaccid happy resolutions. No, if I was to be a bard, I would teach people, help them become better than they were. My tales would educate, enlighten, illuminate. I would be a bard without peer.

I stood and positioned myself in front of the fireplace and told the tale that had been playing through my mind during those final hazy days of summer. I poured all of my emotions into my words: my sadness at Caedmon's imminent departure; fear that he might never come home again; anxiety that he would be injured, or worse, in battle. Loneliness. Abandonment. Heartbreak. As I spoke, the pain eased. The act of tale telling soothed my soul and my heart soared. I had a destiny. I would be the most famous bard ever for I was *meant* to tell tales.

My tale was about a young bard obsessed with his imagined muse, thinking of nothing but her with every waking moment and dreaming of her at night. Eventually, through some arcane spell or other mystery — I left that unexplained — he brings her to life, only to discover his fantasy made flesh and blood is some evil twist on the creature of his dreams. And thus the poor bard realises he must destroy his muse. I left the story there, with the bard setting out on his grand quest to track down the creature that was once his muse.

I had been so absorbed in my tale, I paid scant attention to my audience. In truth, I did not expect anything but adoration and praise. I emerged to discover my family sitting in silence. Not a single person met my eyes, not parent, nor brother, nor sister.

Mother fled with a sob, one trembling hand pressed over her mouth.

The silence stretched until eventually Papa cleared his throat. "Well, Diarmuid," was all he said.

I left, my eyes so filled with tears that I tripped over an errant rug. I didn't want to go to my room, to remain in the same house as those who couldn't, or wouldn't, appreciate my tale, so I fled out the back door and somehow made my way into Eithne's herb garden.

Its inhabitants were nearing the end of their summer blooms and preparing for the cold months ahead. I recognised few of them: blackthorn, basil, mint. Others I knew would be there but couldn't identify: chamomile, juniper, sorrel. There would be rosemary and lavender, although I was hard pressed to tell between them, and many others whose names and uses were a mystery to me.

I sat on a wooden bench and let my tears flow. As they subsided, I inhaled the mingled aromas of herbs, finding solace in their sweetness. They would be pruned soon, by Eithne if she was well, or by a servant. Their stems and leaves, flowers and seeds would be gathered and dried for use in the coming season of illness and fevers.

Movement through the garden indicated that I was no longer alone. In the darkness of the moon's ebb, I could not tell who came to offer comfort until Papa sat beside me.

"Diarmuid," he said and then sighed. "What a fine mess this is."

"I don't understand." I sniffed and wiped my nose on the back of my hand. "Why did they hate my tale?"

"It was a fine tale. We are just surprised you have come to this so young."

"I'm ten summers old. Caedmon has known all of his life he would be a soldier."

"But Caedmon is sixteen summers and only now about to become a soldier."

Although his words were reasonable, it was hard to acknowledge this when my heart felt as if it had been trampled by a herd of cows.

"Why did nobody tell me I was to be a bard? It is a noble profession, not something terrible."

Papa sighed again and shifted slightly.

"Tell me. Why did I not know?"

"We did what we thought was best for you." He spoke slowly and hesitated often. "Your mother and I thought to let you choose your own path. There are sons enough in this family who have had their futures dictated to them. We wanted you to decide for yourself whether you would be a bard or something else."

"Is it true? That every seventh son of a seventh son is a bard?"

"In our family, yes. You are descended from an unbroken line of seventh sons through many generations. And every one a bard."

"Then it seems I never had a choice," I said, and now I made no attempt to keep the bitterness from my voice.

Beside me, Papa shook his head. "No. It seems not."

He was silent for some time before he spoke next. "Diarmuid, I must warn you. Be careful of the tales you tell."

I waited. The seat creaked as Papa shifted and I thought he might leave without speaking further. At length he continued.

"As the seventh son of a seventh son, you have a special ability. You must be very careful. Sometimes… sometimes the things you say, the tales you tell, may come true."

A laugh bubbled up from inside of me. Relief, for I had thought he intended to tell me something terrible but it was merely a joke.

"Absurd," I said. "And impossible."

I felt, rather than heard, him sigh. "I wish it were so."

4

IDA

I AM. BUT I am not alone.

This place is confusing. There are terrors in here, demons he keeps well hidden. Nightmares and horror. Darkness and desolation. Despair. I crave… something. I don't know what. It is something… else. Radiance. Lightness. Beauty, symmetry, colour.

Now he is confused. Resentful. Lonely. Interesting. His heart pounds, his breath quickens. His thoughts are dark and lingering. The one he looks up to above all others has disappointed him. Oh, how he despairs now.

I whisper to myself, a sly comment intended for my own amusement. He hears me. And not only does he hear but he understands. He weaves my comment into his own thoughts, braiding our words together until I can barely tell which were his and which were mine. He probably never knew.

I whisper again about the one he loves and his heart hardens. He believes me.

No longer am I confused or alone for he is here with me. Or I am here with him. Day after day, I speak to him. Commentary about those around him, thoughts that bury themselves deep in his heart. My words resonate with him. I feel power, intimacy, companionship. I feel alive.

He fancies himself a bard so I whisper ideas. He takes them greedily and begs for more. I see myself take shape in his mind. A woman's form. He gives me long white hair and eyes the blue of a frozen river. A slender figure, dainty hands. Have I ever before had a form? I don't know. As I continue to whisper, his image of me grows firmer.

More and more, his thoughts linger on me. Now, with every event, every conversation, it is me to whom his thinking turns first. He wonders what I would make of it, how I would respond. He names me: Ida. I don't know whether I have ever had a name before. Ida will do as well as any.

I soon learn how to make him feed me. And feed me he does. The flow of power, at first hesitant and intermittent, becomes a steady stream. As I feed, he weakens. Not so he would notice; physically he is no different. It is in his mind the changes occur. For I have learnt the type of thoughts he must have for me to draw power from him. As he sinks into melancholy, his loneliness and bitterness strengthen me. And, gradually, I forget I ever longed for something else.

I anticipate that he will realise what is happening but day after day, week after week, he doesn't. Eventually I stop expecting it. And indeed I hope he does not realise. At least, not until I am strong enough to leave. After that, it won't matter. But for now, I need him. He will be my freedom.

5

BRIGIT

"BRIGIT, ARE YOU shelling those peas or mashing them?" Mother's tone was sharp and her face said clearly that she despaired of trying to teach me anything.

I removed my sticky hands from the bowl and wiped them on my apron, leaving green streaks against its crisp whiteness. While lost in my thoughts, I had been crushing the pods.

"I'm sorry."

Mother sighed and turned back to the herbal concoction she was preparing. I studied her profile, silhouetted in the late afternoon sun streaming through the kitchen window. My thick, dark hair that frizzed out of control in humid weather was a match for hers, as were my dark eyes and sharp chin. I envied the roundness of my younger sisters who were all dimples and soft features. I was angles and sharp lines with neither bust nor waist. Only my hair marked me as female although I never wore it with the ribbons and pretty braids of my sisters. Instead, I pulled it back at the nape of my neck and secured it with a plain string. Even so, it continuously escaped.

I brushed a few strands away from my face and turned to the window, longing to be outside, despite the bleak landscape. The

thick stone walls of our lodge kept the heat in and by mid afternoon, the warmth in the kitchen was stifling. Outside, the snow
was thin on the ground and the wind rustling the leaves of the fir
trees promised adventure. Inside was comfortable and familiar
but hardly exciting. A worn workbench at which Mother and I
stood. Shelves of plates, cups and cooking implements hung from
the grey stone walls. A stack of firewood sat tidily in the corner. A
pot of soup bubbled on the wood stove. The hardy scent of herbs
and vegetables mingled with the yeasty aroma of fresh-baked
bread, making my mouth water.

"No point wasting good peas," Mother said. "We can use them
in the soup. Just remove the pods. And, Brigit dear, try not to
mash the rest."

"Yes, Mother." I bent my head over the bowl and tried hard to
focus on my task. But soon I was again lost in my thoughts, my
hands moving of their own accord as visions swirled before my
eyes.

A man: young, dark haired, with a shadowy raven clinging to
his shoulder. A small dog, its white hair streaked with blood and
eyes filled with pain. A woman: pale, thin, her eyes shining with
steely strength.

The Sight ran in the blood of our female line. My mother was a
wise woman, as was her mother, and her mother before. I too was
expected to become a wise woman, steeped in knowledge of herbs
and cures. But I had never been very good at doing what I was
told. Rather than a calm, comfortable life, I wanted adventure,
mystery, danger, yes even romance. Of course, there was no
reason why I couldn't have all of that as a wise woman, or
perhaps before, but a quiet life dedicated to healing and wisdom
was not what I wanted. The visions told me that my path led in
another direction.

Mother must have spoken several times before her voice again
intruded on my world.

"Brigit!"

"Mother?"

I followed her eyes to my bowl to find I had done no more than mash the remaining peas in their pods. Guilt flooded through me. We couldn't afford to waste food this late in winter and these were the last of the fresh peas. There would be only dried peas now until the new season.

Mother sighed. Did she truly think she could make a wise woman, or even a competent wife, out of me? Perhaps she was unwilling to concede that I was not suited for the destiny intended for me. Certainly, she didn't know how much of a wise woman's talent I possessed, for I never spoke of the visions or of how easily I retained knowledge of herbs and their uses. I paid little enough attention to her instructions because one glance was all it took for a recipe to imprint on my mind.

I hid my abilities as best I could for fear my fate would be irreversibly fixed if I revealed them. I never deliberately ruined a recipe, any more than I had intended to mash today's peas. How could I focus on shelling peas or distilling herbs when my head was full of the dark visions that might be my future? How much longer would I wait before the visions became reality?

"Brigit, please, remove the pods and then leave them. I'll add them to the soup when I finish here."

Mother hunched over her bowl, adding a handful of herb and a sprinkle of powder. A cough mixture, it seemed.

"Who is that for?" I began picking pods out of the bowl, leaving what I could of the mashed peas. I rarely asked about Mother's duties for fear that a question might be mistaken for interest, but I needed to atone for today's carelessness.

"One of the villagers has a sick child," Mother said with a sigh, pausing to brush back the hair escaping from her bun. It stubbornly sprang back, just like mine did. Her face was lined and her eyes tired. Likely, my presence today had only made more work for her.

With a pang, I regretted my inattention. My fate was not her fault and Mother had no more choice in her future than I did. All she had ever done was try to prepare me for the day when she wouldn't be here. Still, she had a more accommodating nature than I. She wasn't stubborn like me. That's a word I've heard applied to myself more times than I can count. My father was oft described as stubborn too, and it caused his death. Perhaps that's why Mother perseveres with me. She's hoping I won't make the same mistakes as he did.

"Can I help you with something else?" I asked and, for once, I sincerely meant it.

Mother gave me a brief smile. "No, my dear, you run along. I can manage here on my own."

I fled, stopping only for a coat, scarf and my winter boots. After the warmth of the kitchen, the cold outside hit me like a physical blow. The sun, although high in the sky, yielded little warmth and I shivered even with my thick coat. I walked briskly, intending no particular destination.

Snow drifted down from the trees as a breeze danced through their branches, leaving them naked without their winter adornment. Blackthorn, with its spiny branches that come spring would be covered with creamy-white buds. Hazel, with its grey-brown bark, towering over its neighbours. Birch, its slender branches uncaring of appearance as it grew however it chose. In summer, these fields would be thick with lush grass, which would cushion my feet as I walked. Now I trod on fresh snow, crisp and crunching with each step.

Freed of distractions, the visions came stronger, flooding my mind with a confusing array of images, until I hardly knew where, or when, I was. I could make no sense of them, not least the two I saw most often: the white dog covered in blood and the young man, hardly more than a boy, who cradled the dog as tenderly as if it was a child. Who were they? And what was my connection to them? Our link, whatever it was, must be strong for them to feature so frequently in my visions.

I had little control over the images and was ill-inclined to spend any time learning such a thing. Still, today was one of the rare times I wished I could control them. I needed clearer information on what these visions meant to me and on what part I was to play in the forthcoming events. The visions had been more frequent of late and that likely meant something would happen very soon. If only I knew what.

Soon the sun began to sink and the air became even colder. As I headed for home, a figure appeared, some distance off to the side. I watched out of the corner of my eye for a while. It was a girl, I was certain of that. Long of both leg and hair, she easily kept pace with me. When I turned towards her, she disappeared, returning only when I looked away. One of the fey, no doubt.

The fey had long had a presence in my life. My earliest memories included a young girl, seemingly no older than myself, although the appearance of the fey can be misleading. She and I played together in a fall of autumn leaves, in the water of summer rivers, in the cool depths of the woods. She did everything I did: ran, swam, laughed, danced. We climbed trees together, sunbaked on rocks, and walked hand in hand.

As I grew up, she stayed the same and eventually she no longer came to me. I had grieved the loss of my childhood friend and wondered why she had absented herself from my world. Perhaps it was because the more adult pursuits now imposed on me were of no interest to her. Perhaps she found some other child to play with. Whatever the reason, I remembered her fondly, although, strangely, I no longer recalled her name and with the passing of time, her once-familiar face had blurred in my memory.

Some time after my first fey friend left, another of her kind came into my life. He was thin and lithe with sticks in his hair and grass stains on his tattered trousers. He taunted me as I was kept indoors, learning to sew or read or cook. He knew I longed to be free, running through the fields and exploring the woods, and he teased me with images of the life I was now deprived of.

When I refused to yield to the outdoor delights dangled before me, he played tricks. Needles would suddenly embed themselves in my finger, causing bright drops of blood to ruin my embroidery. Pots overflowed and wriggling bugs appeared in the centre of the pies I baked. Rugs slid out from under my feet and footstools suddenly appeared in front of me as I walked. Many a scrape, bruise, burn and cut I endured before he left me.

Several years had passed since then and I thought the fey had finally stopped watching me. Now, in my twentieth year, they had returned. Well, the girl could walk beside me if she chose, provided that was all she did.

I ignored the fey girl and she seemed happy enough for me to do so. The sky was almost night-dark by the time I reached home and the light spilling from the windows, promising warmth and human companionship, was a welcome sight. I banished both fey and visions from my mind. I would not allow them to intrude tonight.

6

BRIGIT

S LEEP THAT NIGHT was long in coming and in the quiet of night, the visions lingered.

The man, the woman, the bloodstained terrier. A road stretches through unfamiliar fields and hills, winding ever onward out of my sight. The terrier stands in a dragon's den, surrounded by the creature's treasures. A man and a boy explore a barrow. The boy, now a man himself, and the dog sleep together beside a fire. Another man, large and with a kind face, strokes the little dog's head with a tenderness that makes my heart ache. A confrontation with the fey; I myself step forward and speak to their queen. And in the background of every vision, a raven with glossy black plumage and blood dripping from its beak.

The images jumbled together and I had no sense of their order. The Sight could show past, present, future or maybe, and the only thing of which I could be sure was that these visions were connected to me. This future would collide with my future. This past would impact my present.

I woke with dry and gritty eyes and a head that felt like it was stuffed full of straw. Even in my sleep I couldn't escape the Sight's warning for blood and the ever-present raven filled my dreams. I dressed and pulled a comb through my hair. The water in the bowl on my dresser was bitingly cold as I splashed my face.

Outside, the sun was rising into a clear sky. A far-off mountain was dazzling white against the sky's brilliant blue. Light breeze teased the branches of birch and blackthorn and kicked up the snow on the ground. If the fey girl watched, I couldn't sense her.

In the kitchen, the aroma of last night's soup lingered, competing with the fresh bread Mother was removing from the oven as I entered. She deposited the loaf on the scarred wooden table, which was set for breakfast, and sat. Her shoulders were slumped and her face haggard as she absently brushed the hair from her eyes. Did the visions plague her all night as they did me? I murmured a greeting, sat on a chair on the opposite side of the table, and served myself a bowl of porridge.

"You look tired," Mother said, echoing my own thoughts about her.

My gaze flicked up and met hers. I saw silent understanding. She knew. Even if I pretended I saw nothing, she knew.

"I'm fine," I said. "Don't worry about me."

It wasn't until I had finished my porridge and took my bowl to the sink that she spoke again.

"Oh but I do," she said softly. "I always do."

I pretended I didn't hear and spent a little longer at the sink than necessary, scrubbing my bowl until it was spotless. I dried it carefully and placed it on a shelf. Only once I was sure my voice wouldn't betray me did I speak again. "What do you need me to do today?"

Mother gave me a wry look. "After your help yesterday, I'm not sure I need any more assistance from you."

"I feel bad about the peas. There must be something I can do. You look so tired."

Mother smiled and rubbed her temples. "If only this headache would go away. What you could do, I suppose, is take a compress down to Old Man Tam. He cut his foot last week. When he finally called for me yesterday, the wound was red and hot."

"An infection."

"Yes, but perhaps not too bad. If he had waited another day or two, it would have been more serious. I released pressure from the wound and used what herbs I had with me. But I promised I would take him a compress today."

"I'll look after that for you."

She gave me a look and I knew exactly what she was thinking.

"I promise I'll pay attention. Arnica and comfrey for the pain, and fenugreek or thyme to draw out the infection."

Mother smiled and if she seemed sad, I quickly dismissed it.

Noise from upstairs indicated my sisters were awake. Shrieks, giggles and a heavy thud as something, or someone, fell to the floor made me thankful I had risen early enough to avoid breakfast with them. Their exuberance was too much first thing in the morning, especially while I was still trying to shed lingering memories of visions and dreams I didn't understand.

As I set off for Old Man Tam's cottage some time later, I was confident I had honoured Mother's instructions. A jar containing the herbal concoction for the compress was safely tucked into a bag along with a few pears and a handful of eggs. Icy wind burned the bare skin on my face. I wrapped my scarf more snugly around my neck and hurried on.

Old Man Tam's lodge was small and looked like it had been built in haste. He answered promptly when I knocked on the door. His eyes, sunk deep within folds of skin, examined me for longer than seemed necessary to verify my identity.

"I was expecting your mother," he said. His face was so wrinkled I couldn't tell smile from frown, but I sensed disappointment.

I tried to make my voice pleasant. "She's feeling poorly today so she sent me instead."

He stared down at the bag in my hands and this time I received the distinct impression of a frown. "She promised she would bring a compress today."

"I have it right here." He didn't need to know it was I who had made it.

"Well, I suppose you had better come in then," he said at length.

I swallowed the retort that sprang to my lips. Clearly I did not have my mother's ability to win people over with just a few words.

He led me into the living room and I winced at how he favoured his right leg. What would I do if the wound seemed beyond the aid of a compress? Old Man Tam lowered himself into a faded stuffed chair by the fireplace and propped his leg up on a footstool. When I removed the bandage, I was relieved to see no sign of the skin turning bad.

I heated a pot of water on the wood stove. The kitchen was somewhat bare but tidy enough. Plates and cups were neatly arranged on shelves, the bench was clean, and a small basket of cut wood sat on the floor next to the stove. If Old Man Tam had a servant who cleaned the house and looked after him, she didn't seem to be in attendance today. Once the water was hot, I showed him how to steep the herbs and then, once it had cooled some-what, to soak a cloth in it. I wrapped the compress around his foot and Old Man Tam sighed.

"That does feel good, Missy," he said, somewhat begrudgingly.

"My name's Brigit."

"Sure it is, Missy." He sounded almost amenable. "Sure it is."

The house was quiet, the only other inhabitant seemingly a fat black cat who glared at me from a chair in the corner of the room. Old Man Tam's wife had died years ago. I remembered her but only barely. A squat, bad-tempered old woman who walked with a stoop and a cane. She had loathed children immensely, or at least, she had loathed me.

There was no reason to linger. I left Old Man Tam, murmuring some vague words about being sure my mother would call in to see him soon, and fled, tripping over my own feet and his cat in my eagerness to be gone.

This was the life ahead of me. An eternity of answering calls from folk who needed some simple medical treatment. Caring for those who clearly disliked me but had no other options. Sick children. Pregnant women seeking remedies to ease nausea or perhaps rid them of an unwanted babe. Old people, whose bodies were beginning to fail. Some, I knew, Mother could help. For others, the best she could do was to ease their pain for a while.

There was no danger or adventure in this life. No romance or mystery. Just the mind-numbing monotony of visits to the sick and the old. Reassuring and soothing them, dispensing wisdom with compassion and understanding. There were girls who left their families to live with a wise woman in order to learn her craft.

But I didn't want a future I had no say in. I wanted to mount a horse and ride off over the far distant plains on some marvellous quest. I wanted to perform noble and heroic deeds, to seek treasures and save innocents and come riding back home in triumph. But that is not the life a woman aspires to. It is not the life a decent woman may lead. And yet, the visions suggested this sort of future was in store for me.

It seemed there were two fates ahead of me. The one Mother had tried to prepare me for, and the one in the visions. Could the act of choosing determine which one I lived? Were both fates open to me until I chose? Perhaps this was why the visions lingered, vivid and strong and compelling. They were urging me to choose.

I could follow the fate intended for me, become a wise woman, perhaps marry some day. My husband would likely be a farmer, or a soldier. I would live out my life in security, perhaps even in comfort if I was lucky. There would be children, and a life that was quiet, uneventful, and of use to my community. Or I could follow the visions and seek danger, romance, mystery and adventure. There would be blood and fear and pain, and if I survived all of that, I would know I had truly lived.

As I left Old Man Tam's house and strode along the dusty path that led home, hugging my coat tight against the cold wind, I chose. I wanted danger and adventure. I didn't want potions and possets, compresses and simple charms. I wanted mystery and romance. And if blood and pain came with that choice, I'd gladly take them too.

7

DIARMUID

THE NIGHT OF my nineteenth Winter Solstice arrived far too swiftly. Winter kept a firm grip on Silver Downs. Frost strangled the ivy's attempt to creep up the house walls. The sky was bleak, heavy with the promise of snow and the tang of wood smoke, and empty without the trill of blackbird or robin. At night, howling winds lashed the house and sought out every crack between window and pane.

I had found no opportunity to speak privately to Caedmon since the night we sat up late, drinking ale in front of the fire. I sought him out over and over but he was never where people said he had intended to go. For everyone else, the longest night of the year was cause for celebration, for the Solstice heralded the turn of winter and an end to the long darkness. For me, spring's pleasures seemed far away.

As the sun sent streaks of fire through the sky, I returned to my bedchamber and changed into my best shirt, my fingers fumbling over the buttons. The mere thought of talking to a woman caused my hands to shake and my knees to tremble, even when alone in my bedchamber. If I had cause to actually speak to one, my voice would croak, words would come out in the wrong order and sooner or later I would skulk away, thoroughly embarrassed.

I threw myself onto the bed, intending to linger for a few minutes. I needed just a little longer alone. I had never before had cause to disagree with Caedmon, never voiced a thought in opposition to him. He, of all my brothers, was the one I looked up to. Ida whispered something that I ignored. There was no room in my mind for her at present.

Tonight's celebrations were at the neighbouring estate of Three Trees. Was it was one of the daughters of that family with whom Caedmon had made his arrangements? They were pretty, bubbly girls — four of them — and I routinely avoided them. Their constant giggles and banter confused me and I was never sure whether they were flirting or making fun of me.

What would the girl, whoever she was, think of the fact that my brother had asked her to bed me? Would she laugh or politely restrain her mirth? She might assume I had some deformity or perhaps that I was feeble. Would I even be able to speak to her or would the words flee, leaving me standing open-mouthed and her certain I was a simpleton? Oh dear gods, perhaps she wasn't the first girl Caedmon had approached.

Lost in thought, I was startled when Caedmon entered my bedchamber. He looked very fine in a red shirt with gold braid on the cuffs. As usual, he didn't wait for an invitation but flung himself onto the bed, jostling me aside as if I weighed no more than a child.

"So, little brother," he said.

"Caedmon, where have you been? I've been looking everywhere for you." I sat up and scooted down to the end, as my narrow bed wasn't wide enough for the two of us to lie side by side.

"I'm sure you have. But no cowardice tonight, eh? It's all arranged. All you have to do is show up and be a man."

"Who is it?" Not that I had any intention of going through with his plan.

"Her name is Rhiwallon."

"Do I know her?"

"Do you want her family history? It doesn't matter who she is or where she's from. What matters is she is willing and has promised to be gentle with you."

"She knows?" My face burned.

"Of course she knows." Caedmon frowned. "I would hardly set you up with a girl who was unwilling."

"But—"

"Fine. I know you, little brother. You won't let it rest until I tell you. Rhiwallon is about three summers younger than you — I didn't exactly ask her age — and her father runs a tavern in Maker's Well. She's quite a pretty thing: red hair, green eyes, perhaps a little skinny for my tastes but she should suit you well enough."

"She's from Maker's Well? Why is she going to Three Trees for the Solstice?"

"Why not?" he countered with a shrug. "Does it matter? You think too much, little brother."

"Caedmon, I can't—"

He hauled himself up from the bed and left, pausing in the doorway to look back at me. "I've gone to a lot of effort to set this up for you, little brother."

"I know but—"

"It's time to leave. That's what you're wearing?"

I smoothed my green shirt. Perhaps the fabric was not quite as bright as it used to be and a few threads had worked loose from the cuffs, but it was still perfectly decent, even if it wasn't as fine as Caedmon's. When I met his eyes again, he was frowning.

"Wait here," he said and left.

He returned a few moments later and tossed me a blue shirt, which had round shell buttons and silver thread around the collar and hem.

"Hurry up," Caedmon said with a groan as I hesitated. "You don't need to inspect it. It's clean. It doesn't even have any blood stains."

"Blood stains?"

"Just put it on, will you?"

Caedmon tapped his foot as I pulled off my shirt and shrugged into his, which was certainly far nicer than anything I owned. It was somewhat too big for me for I was ever slender and Caedmon was broad-shouldered and well-muscled. For a moment, I was wistful. Had I been the soldier son, that could be me right now, lending my younger brother a shirt and teaching him about women and life. But I had no younger brothers and Eithne was hardly likely to need advice from me. Besides, it wasn't like I actually intended to go along with Caedmon's plan. I would seek an opportunity to slip away from him after we arrived at Three Trees. I would find somewhere to hide and wait until it was time to leave. Caedmon would be angry but at least I wouldn't be humiliated. It wasn't much of a plan but it was all I had.

He hustled me down the stairs and we pulled on our winter coats, which hung by the front door. With a thick scarf, gloves, a hat and my sturdy boots, I could hardly move but I would be warm.

The rest of the family already waited by the cart. The oxen snorted and stomped impatiently. Papa wore a splendid dark blue cape and Mother had a hint of yellow showing between scarf and collar. My oldest brother Eremon stood with an arm around his wife, Niamh, who looked unusually relaxed, probably because their twins had been left with a servant. And there was Eithne, my little sister, her hair tied back with a red ribbon, eyes sparkling with excitement.

Of course, this was not all of our family. Sitric was in Maker's Well and would attend the festivities there. Twins Marrec and Conn had also gone to the town to celebrate with the families of the women to whom they were betrothed. And, as always, Fiachra was absent, he who was training to be a druid.

We piled into the cart and set off. The fields we passed were shadowy and empty, the sheep locked away in warm barns for the night. As the oxen hauled us ever closer to Three Trees, nausea swirled in my stomach. I fidgeted and shifted in my seat. What if I couldn't get away from Caedmon? The girl would surely laugh at me as I stammered and blushed and made my excuses. Perhaps she would tell her friends and they would giggle together. Of course, she would tell Caedmon and then all of my brothers would know too. I wanted to jump down from the cart and run straight back to Silver Downs. To distract myself, I turned to my sister who sat beside me. She was bundled up in a thick coat with a blanket wrapped around her shoulders. Her usually pale cheeks were flushed with excitement.

"You look pretty this evening, Eithne," I said.

She caught my eye briefly, startled, then ducked her head and blushed. "Thank you," she whispered. "You look very handsome."

"I'm wearing one of Caedmon's shirts," I confessed.

Eithne smiled but didn't reply.

"Are you meeting with friends tonight?" I asked, and then wished I hadn't for I had no wish to embarrass her.

"Oh yes," she said with unaccustomed vivacity and then blushed again, looking away swiftly.

I was too surprised to ask further and sat silently after that, watching the trees and homes and sheep as we trundled pass. A raven perched on the naked branches of an oak tree, watching us intently. The fire faded from the sky, replaced with encroaching blackness, and we arrived at Three Trees.

Some distance from the lodge, a massive fire cast a golden sheen over the field. At least two dozen people were already gathered nearby, their heavy winter coats abandoned in a pile on a bench. The air echoed with laughter and the crackling of the fire.

Caedmon had anticipated my intent to escape, for he was by my side even as I climbed down from the cart. He flung an arm across my shoulders. To anyone watching, it would look like a friendly moment of brotherly solidarity. They wouldn't see his iron grip.

We had barely disembarked before a servant appeared in front of us, bearing a tray of mugs. Three Trees always provided the very finest ales and Caedmon released me briefly to claim two mugs. He thrust one at me and took a swig from the other.

"Drink up, little brother. Not too much, mind, but enough to get that tight look off your face."

I took the mug, glancing around for hiding places. Lights shone from the direction of the house. A looming shape in the other direction would be one of the outbuildings, perhaps the barn. I could see little else in the shadows.

Caedmon wrapped his arm around me again, keeping me clenched by his side as he greeted friends and paid his respects to our hosts. Despite his carefree and cheery air, I sensed disappointment, perhaps because Grainne, his intended bride, was nowhere to be found. He consoled himself with a special greeting for each of the daughters of the Three Trees household. Born only a year apart, they were plump and dark-haired and exceedingly giggly. I wondered how Caedmon could find anything to say to them. They apparently found him amusing, for they burst into laughter at everything he said.

Eventually we ended up to the side of the huge fire. The air was crisp with winter's chill and heavy with the smell of smoke and roast pig and the sounds of celebration. It seemed only I dreaded this night, for everywhere I looked folk smiled and laughed and drank. A boy who looked to be around my own age slung his arm around a girl who smiled up at him. Another couple clasped hands and slipped away together into the darkness. Heat rose to my cheeks and I looked away.

I was far too warm so close to the fire. Perhaps I should plead ill and beg of my hosts somewhere to sleep. Before I could voice my thought, servants began offering around trays of roast meat and bread. Caedmon somehow managed to eat his fill without once releasing me. I picked at a thick slice of wild boar wedged inside a loaf but had no appetite. I tried, now and then, as Caedmon conversed with various neighbours, to wiggle out from under his arm. But even when he seemed to pay me no attention, my slightest movement caused his arm to tighten.

Under Caedmon's stern eye, I drank two mugs of ale. By the end of the second, my head swam and I was suddenly less concerned about my upcoming embarrassment. At least once this was over, Caedmon would be satisfied he had tried to make a man of me, regardless of the success or otherwise of the endeavour.

Two men standing at the edge of the crowd caught my eye. They were druids, all brown robes and braided hair with golden torcs around their necks. They neither ate nor drank, just watched, blending into the background of the festivities. I only noticed them because the younger one caught my eye and stared for a long moment before he nodded and turned away.

My heart thudded. Was this my brother, Fiachra? I was but five summers old when he left and I barely remembered what he looked like back then. The druid was dark-haired like all the men in our family and broad of shoulder like my brothers. His age was difficult to estimate in the shifting shadows of the fire, but druids tended to have an ageless quality anyway. I would have liked to approach him, but I didn't know what to say and I would feel like a fool if it weren't Fiachra.

Eventually the other druid came forward to conduct the solstice ceremony. It was blessedly brief for this particular druid was one who always kept the formalities short, perhaps understanding that folk preferred to eat and drink, talk and dance than listen to a lengthy invocation of the beings of air, earth, fire and water.

As the druids retreated back into the shadows, Caedmon secured another mug of ale for each of us. His arm was still firmly clamped over my shoulders, leaving no possibility of escape. I clutched my mug with sweaty fingers.

"Drink that down, little brother," Caedmon ordered.

My head already spun and my stomach rolled as I caught the lingering scent of roasted meat. Casually, as if we were merely meandering around to speak to some friends, Caedmon steered me away from the fire and towards the barn. Light shone dimly from beneath the covered windows. My heart started pounding wildly and I tried to wriggle out from under his arm. He cracked open the barn door and swiftly shoved me inside.

"Her name is Rhiwallon," he reminded me. "And don't come back out until you're a man." He grinned at me then and raised his mug. "Have fun, little brother."

By the time I turned to face him, he had closed the door. Ida whispered to me, dark thoughts about betrayal and desertion. Before I could think about slipping away, a voice came from behind me.

"You must be Diarmuid."

Her voice was soft and low, and under other circumstances I might almost have considered it pleasant. But now it merely filled me with horror. Dread trickled all the way down to my toes as I turned to face her.

She was exactly the type of girl who always struck me dumb. Moss-green eyes sparkled as if we shared a joke. Long, reddish hair floated around her shoulders. She held herself confidently, casually, and I knew instantly she had never experienced a moment of doubt about herself. She leaned against the rough wooden wall, waiting for me to finish my inspection of her.

"Are- are you Rhi- Rhiwallon?" Already I had made a fool of myself.

The girl didn't answer. Instead she peeled herself off the wall and walked towards me. I thrust my mug onto a shelf, very nearly sloshing it everywhere, and shoved my hands behind my back before she could see how they trembled.

She came right up close to me. Her head barely reached my shoulders and as she leaned in, all I could smell was summer and sunshine and herbs. I wanted to close my eyes and breathe in the scent of her.

Rhiwallon rested a hand lightly on my chest. Could she feel how fast my heart beat?

"Caedmon said you were handsomer than he."

"Oh. Am I?" What a daft thing to say. Ida's mocking laugh echoed through my mind.

"Hmm, perhaps," she said with a slow smile that filled my stomach with unexpected warmth. She reached behind me for my hand. "Come with me."

The barn was tidy with everything put away in its place. Farm tools and horse tack hung from hooks on the walls. Smaller items sat neatly on the shelves. Rhiwallon led me to the back of the barn, past the lamp that sat on a workbench, to where the stalls were shrouded in darkness. My nose recognised both horse and cow. We entered one of the stalls where there was a large pile of fresh hay and no beast.

Rhiwallon turned to me and her eyes were wide and dark as she wrapped her arms around my neck. She pressed her body against mine and kissed me full on the lips. I had never been kissed by a girl before, except for a brief touch on the cheek by Mother or Eithne and once by Grainne.

Certainly those familial kisses did not make my knees knock together so loud I wondered whether anyone else heard and nor did they make my heart beat fit to burst right through my chest. Those kisses also didn't make other parts of my body respond the way Rhiwallon's kiss did and I wondered for the first time whether perhaps I could actually do this. If she was kind and gentle and didn't laugh at me, I might actually…

Rhiwallon broke the kiss and pulled away. Keeping her gaze fixed on me, she unlaced her blouse. It fell open and I saw her bare breasts. Her skin shone in the lamplight. Rhiwallon took my hand and placed it on her breast. Her nipples hardened under my hand and I froze, wondering what I was supposed to do.

She kissed me again and now my hand seemed to have a mind of its own as it gently explored her bare skin, stroking her soft breasts and lingering over her rounded stomach. She pulled me down into the hay. We lay side by side and she wrapped her leg around me. My hand slid down to explore the silky expanse of thigh beneath her skirts and she moaned and wriggled closer to me. As her hand edged into my trousers, panic returned. My budding desire fled and I was limp beneath her hand.

Rhiwallon pulled her lips off mine to stare at me quizzically. "Diarmuid—"

Mortified, I pulled away and stood, swiftly buttoning the pants I didn't even remember her undoing.

"Diarmuid." She tried again and although her voice was gentle, I couldn't bear to stay there another moment.

"Sorry," I muttered, straightening my borrowed shirt as I fled. I tripped over something and slammed into the wall. There was a soft giggle behind me and my face flamed as I scurried out, humiliation complete.

Caedmon loitered nearby as I exited the barn. He started to speak but my glare cut him off. I said nothing but stalked away into the darkness, seeking somewhere to hide until it was time to go home.

8

DIARMUID

CAEDMON AND GRAINNE'S handfasting was a sevennight after Midwinter. I had been sleeping poorly since my encounter with Rhiwallon and woke that morning feeling morose and peevish. My dreams had been filled with the raven that stared with empty eyes while blood dripped from its beak.

As I lay in bed, the house already echoed with the chaos and commotion of preparation for the festivities, even though dawn was barely breaking. I pulled the covers over my head. Perhaps nobody would notice if I didn't get up today. Eventually, footsteps thundering past my bedchamber and a rooster's crowing drove me from my bed.

I dressed in yesterday's discarded clothes. What did it matter if my pants had grass stains on the seat and my shirt was splattered with soup? Nobody would notice what I wore. The only time anyone saw me — *really* saw me — was when I told a tale, and then it was only to criticise.

I slunk through the house like a storm cloud, ignoring Eithne's excited cry of "Diarmuid, come here", and slipped out the back door. Swathed in coat, scarf and hat, with my boots crunching over yesterday's snow and the fields around me silent, my mood lifted somewhat. The air smelled of smoke and fir, and was empty of sound other than what I myself made. There was no chatter of voice, no clashing of pots, no crashing of brooms. The fresh, empty air cleared my head a little.

Silver Downs lay nestled in a valley created by rolling hills of pastureland. In the summer, the fields were covered with silver thistledown, their flowers round as a bumblebee's belly. Many hours had I spent lying amidst the thistledown, blowing on the fragile blossoms to release them up into the air and waiting for them to drift back down, falling whisper-soft on my face. Even more hours had I spent roaming the fields, up hill, down into gully, across the streams. I knew every footstep of those fields, all the way from one border to the other, from the corner in which the lodge stood to the far edge where the woods began.

Papa forbade us to enter the woods for it was said they contained a doorway into the realm of the fey. Tales told of those who ventured deep into the woods and never returned. Whether they declined to come back, having sampled the delights of the fey world, or whether they weren't permitted to return, nobody could say.

In truth, I had never thought much about the woods. They were there on the edge of our land, and they were there on the edge of my consciousness. As a small boy, I was kept too busy to contemplate trespassing into forbidden territory. Six older brothers meant I learnt to fight somewhat for they routinely wrestled me to the ground for the smallest fault. I had no formal schooling, but my brothers took turns teaching me to read and I could draft a simple letter and read the reply. I could count and tally sums and I knew the history of the lands surrounding us. Many years passed before I realised how unusual it was that all of our family could read, write and tally at least a little.

By mid morning, I had reached one of the twin rivers meandering across the corner of the estate. In summer, this was a pleasant spot where one could watch fish swimming in the river and water bugs dancing across the top. Now, the waters were frozen with just the slightest ripple in the ice hinting at how they usually flowed.

Sitting on a sun-warmed rock, my eyes traced the outline of an aged oak tree, its bare branches stark against the winter-grey sky. I tucked the image away for use in a tale and Ida murmured her approval.

With the sun beating down on me and the satisfaction of solitude, things didn't seem quite so bad. I cautiously turned my mind to my Midwinter humiliation. Anger soared, towards Caedmon, Rhiwallon, myself. Embarrassment warred with frustration that Caedmon had refused to listen when I protested his plan. No doubt by now Rhiwallon had told everyone she knew. Heat rose in my cheeks, my hands trembled and Ida whispered of treachery. I pushed away the thoughts, and Ida, for my feelings were yet too raw to examine them closely.

I would spend this time here by the river creating a new tale. Something to amaze my audience. My most recent tale-telling, at Caedmon's betrothal party, still sent pangs of hurt through my heart. I had not yet achieved any level of success as a bard. Yet every time a tale failed to please, it left me determined to create a better one. One day, I would compose the perfect tale. A tale no audience could ignore. It might even be my very next tale. And so I pushed the memories away and got to work.

I started with a warrior. Immediately I thought of Caedmon and I hardened my heart. I would not allow myself to become distracted. I had work to do. So, a warrior. A simple man with no large expectations for his life other than to survive each battle, marry a good woman and produce at least three sons. But of course, life is never as simple as we wish. Perhaps his wife has produced only daughters and he fears he will never have an heir. My interest dissipated. What audience would want to hear such drivel?

I lay back on the rock, my body fitting comfortably into a shallow depression. In summer, I could lie here and listen to the river gurgling over rocks and around water plants. Small patches of sunlight would pierce a green canopy above me and dust motes would sparkle as they danced in its rays. Now, I could see straight up through the naked trees to the grey sky beyond. I was warm enough with my thick coat and the sun streaming down on me through the skeletons of the trees.

My thoughts wandered through a variety of topics. Possible tale ideas. Caedmon's upcoming handfasting. My muse. I called her Ida for it meant thirst, an appropriate name given how I longed for her inspiration. Sometimes I pretended she was real, that my inspiration truly stemmed from a presence inhabiting my mind. What would it be like to share my head with another living creature? Would she know my thoughts and I hers? We would be closer than any husband and wife.

In my mind's eye, Ida smiled and images from my new tale swirled around me. I suddenly realised what it lacked: courage and purpose. Perhaps one of the fey has fallen in love with the warrior's wife and tries to persuade her to leave him. But the wife is faithful to her husband, and refuses the attentions of the fey. So the fey sets three tasks for her husband to complete to prove he is worthy of her.

The idea was plausible enough, for the fey interfered in human lives for their own reasons. Some believed it was because they wove human lives into a pattern to satisfy a design only they saw. Others thought it was merely whim that drove the fey to interfere and that there was no higher purpose. Me, I didn't know. What the fey chose to do with the lives in which they interfered was of no concern to me other than as fodder for my tales.

A tiny smile played on Ida's lips as if she was satisfied with these initial explorations of my new tale. Her mouth was wide, the lips thin and blood red. It was not an attractive mouth. Not like Rhiwallon's.

Again, the hot memory of humiliation flooded through me along with a stab of anger towards Caedmon. The situation was his fault. It was he who pushed me to do what I didn't want to. The more I thought about it, the madder I got until if Caedmon

had appeared in front of me right then, I might almost have
hit him.

Ida's smile broke through my thoughts and again I felt she was
satisfied. My new tale pleased her and the knowledge mollified
me, cooling my temper. It was enough, for now, that an audience
of one, albeit imaginary, was pleased. For that's all any bard ever
wants, to please his audience. Perhaps if I could learn to please
my imaginary muse, I might also be able to succeed with a real
audience. One day, I would weave my words into a beautiful
constellation of humour and truth and learning, fine enough to
satisfy any audience. One day, I would conclude the telling of a
tale to smiles and nods, applause and cheers, rather than silence
and sudden excuses.

I spent the morning pleasantly absorbed in my new tale. Ideas
appeared in my mind — snippets of dialogue, glimpses of
imagery — as if fed by Ida. And this tale felt different from any
other I had created. It was authentic. Honest. Illuminating. There
was light and dark, wonder and horror, and an outcome that
would surprise even the most learned listener. Surely this would
be the tale to please my audience.

9

DIARMUID

AS THE SUN reached the midpoint of the sky, and my stomach growled with hunger, I started towards home. All morning I had busied myself with my new tale but now, as I drew closer to family and ceremony, I gingerly let myself think about the upcoming celebrations.

With Caedmon's aim of producing an heir before he left, there had been no time for a lengthy betrothment. He and Grainne had waited only long enough to send word to the closest druid settlement. A druid, or perhaps two, was expected to arrive this morning and then Caedmon and Grainne could be handfasted. Caedmon had itched at even so short a delay, but he wanted his heir to be legally recognised. So he waited and was as grumpy as a badger with a sore paw.

Caedmon and I had barely spoken since Midwinter. I was angry, disappointed, lost. Caedmon had been my hero since I was old enough to choose a favourite brother. I didn't know quite how to deal with the fracture between us.

I intended to slip into the house, snatch some bread and cheese, and go straight to my bedchamber. But the druids had arrived and Papa caught my eye as I tried to sidle past to the kitchen.

The druids sat at the dining table, eating heartily but not looking at all like men who had spent eight nights on the road. One wore a robe so white it seemed to glow. The other was clad in the brown garments of a novice.

I gave the druids only a cursory inspection until I noticed how close Mother sat beside the novice, clutching his hand and smiling up at him. It was not unusual for a novice to accompany a master for such duties. The face of this one was calm and clean-shaven, his hair hung to his shoulders in braids, and his eyes seemed to peer into my very soul. His face was familiar and it took a moment before I remembered where I had seen him: at the solstice festivities.

When I studied him closely, I saw echoes of our family. His shoulders were broad like Fionn and Eremon and Caedmon. His hair was dark, like all of us, and his grey eyes were shared by Eithne and also Eremon and Niamh's twins. Still, I might not have recognised him were it not for the way Mother smiled at him.

"This must be Diarmuid." Fiachra's voice was clear and musical, a voice made for calling to the elements. "My youngest brother."

"Fiachra." I hardly knew what to do. Of course the appropriate way to greet a brother whom one had not seen for years was to hug him, but was that still appropriate when the brother was a druid?

He rose and enveloped me in his arms. I expected him to be skinnier for surely druids did not eat much and did no physical work, but the arms around me were well-muscled and his embrace was strong.

"Well met, brother," he said.

"Don't let me keep you from your meal," I replied, not knowing what else to say.

"Come sit by me, Diarmuid. Tell me about yourself."

With the melancholy still weighing heavily on me, I wanted only to be alone but I could not refuse Fiachra with grace. The other druid, an older man I did not recognise, slid along the wooden bench so I could sit between them.

I settled myself on the bench and reached for the bread, smearing a thick slice with honey from our own bees. It ran over my fingers as I bit into it, sweet and sticky and tasting of Silver Downs.

"So you are the bard brother." Fiachra reached for another slice of bread. The honey didn't drip off his bread the way it did mine.

"So it would seem," I said.

"And you the seventh son of a seventh son."

"I am."

"I assume you know what that means?"

Before I could respond, Mother interrupted. "Fiachra, would you tell us about your studies?"

He gave me a look that seemed to promise we would continue this conversation later and then turned to our mother.

"There is little I can discuss publicly, even with family. We study the folklore and the history of these lands. We learn of the fey and of those who came before them. We study the elements and learn how to interact with them. More, I cannot say."

"Why are you here?" I reached for another slice of bread.

The moment stretched uncomfortably.

"I cannot discuss that," Fiachra said finally.

"Surely it is because of Caedmon's wedding," Mother said. "It is good of them to let you be here with us."

Fiachra shook his head. "Caedmon's wedding is convenient but it is not the reason I am here. I would have come soon anyway. But perhaps not quite this soon."

I thought of Eithne. Was she sicker than she seemed? Perhaps Fiachra had been permitted a leave of absence to attend his sister in her last days. The bread suddenly stuck in my throat and the sweet stickiness of the honey repulsed me.

"If you need anything," I said.

Fiachra met my eyes and nodded slightly. "I can't shield you from this, Diarmuid. What you sow, you must reap."

I puzzled over his words briefly and then let them go, forgetting them for far longer than I should have.

10

DIARMUID

T HE HANDFASTING CEREMONY was held outdoors beneath an old oak tree that had likely seen many such rituals over its long years. The snow-laden hills mirrored a sky that was now filled with fluffy white clouds, so that everywhere I looked was blindingly white. The wind was tinged with ice and I shivered despite my thick coat and sturdy boots. I thrust my hands into my pockets and wriggled my toes to keep them warm as Caedmon and Grainne exchanged the words that would bind them. Strangers stood on each side of me, folk who had arrived with Grainne's family.

My eyes suddenly filled with tears and I dashed them away before anyone noticed. Why was I crying? I should be happy for Caedmon but instead I felt isolated, sorry for myself, and angry with Caedmon.

The older druid, whose name I never did learn, conducted the ceremony. He asked the blessing of each of the elements and then Caedmon and Grainne spoke their vows. They smiled at each other and I tried hard to push aside my anger. Grainne would be a widow before long if Caedmon's grim suspicions were correct. Did she know that these next few weeks might be their only days together?

A fist clenched my heart and sorrow flowed through me. If this was to be our final parting, I didn't want it tinged with anger. I would speak to him tomorrow, tell him how angry I was, that it was unfair of him to put me in such a situation. It was unfair on Rhiwallon too. If Caedmon were to apologise, perhaps I could forgive him. Ida whispered, snippets of a tale about two brothers, and I promised to mull over her idea later. She sank back down into the depths of my mind.

As the druid wrapped a length of red ribbon around Caedmon and Grainne's wrists, binding them together with the fabric and their promises, I looked around for the members of my family. For the first time since Fiachra had left as a boy, we were all together.

Mother wiped away a tear and Papa wrapped an arm around her. She leaned into him. Their solidarity in that moment reflected the partnership they had demonstrated through my entire life. Papa ran the estate with assistance from my brothers and the tenants who built their homes on Silver Downs land and provided labour in exchange for Papa's protection. The estate produced mostly everything we needed and, sometimes, a small surplus to be sold or traded. Mother ran the household, supervised the women who worked for us as servants, and brought up the family. We weren't wealthy but Papa provided well for us, and Mother managed the resources carefully.

Wherever Father was, my eldest brother, Eremon, would be nearby and indeed today he and Niamh stood a few paces from our parents. Older than me by six years, Eremon was Papa's heir and had worked the estate alongside our father since he was barely old enough to walk. He was much like Papa in both appearance and attitude. He and Niamh lived in their own house on the family estate, close enough to spend evenings with us but far enough for privacy as they established their own family. Their twin sons were barely three summers old but already Eremon and Niamh had their heir and druid. The boys were solemn today, each clutching the hand of a parent.

A year after Eremon came Caedmon, the soldier son. He was

rarely home from campaign but when he did return, he always had time for his youngest brother. I would shadow him, lapping up stories of battles and quests, and dreaming of the day I might have my own adventure to tell. Never before had I felt so distant from him, separated by my anger and his thoughtlessness.

Sitric was the next son, younger again by one year. He had worked as a scribe for some six summers already and spent most of his time in Maker's Well, the town nearest to our estate and the better part of a day's walk in good weather. He made a steady living, writing and reading letters for those who were unable, and recording purchases, sales, loans, and other matters as folk might want a written account of. I searched for Sitric in the crowd and found him at last. He stood on the edge, a little apart from the others.

It was not until the fourth son that the druids received their due. The men of that order knew Fiachra was to be theirs, for as his birth began two of their number appeared at our farmstead to offer small enchantments for his safety. Like Sitric, Fiachra stood alone. I wondered that he could be warm enough in his brown robes but if he shivered, I couldn't see it.

Mother was certain her next babe would be a girl. It was instead to be twin boys, Marrec and Conn, my elders by just two years. Neither had displayed any inclination towards a particular trade, so they assisted Papa and Eremon with the management of Silver Downs and thus Papa had three sons capable of running the estate when he died. As always, Marrec and Conn stood together. Beside them stood their betrotheds, small dark-haired women, sisters who seemed to share almost as close a relationship as their intended husbands.

I was born after Marrec and Conn, seventh son of a seventh son, and although I knew it not in my youngest years, destined to be a bard. With my inability to so much as look a woman in the eyes, it seemed I would watch each of my brothers marry until in the end only Eithne and I remained alone.

I sought out my sister in the crowd. She was three years

younger than I and my only memory of her birth was an image of Papa, his face white with dread and slick with fear. As a babe, Eithne was ever small and sickly. She was sixteen now and thus of marriageable age, but she had not the strength to survive pregnancy and no man would want a wife who could not provide the three sons he needed. I should have stood next to her, for surely she would be feeling as alone as I. But when I finally found Eithne, she wasn't watching the ceremony. I followed her line of sight.

He wasn't there amidst our family and friends but stood within a grove of young ash trees, about a hundred paces away. I would have recognised the pale face and too red lips had I ever seen them before. He leaned against a grey trunk, gaze fixed on Eithne. A small smile passed between them.

Who was he? How did Eithne know him? And what was the meaning of the secretive smile they shared? Surely he was not allowing Eithne to fancy herself in love with him.

The ceremony finally concluded and folks moved in to congratulate Caedmon and Grainne. I pushed my way through the crowd. But Fiachra blocked my way.

"No, Diarmuid." He placed a hand firmly on my shoulder. "You must not interfere."

"I don't want to see Eithne hurt." I tried to slip out from under his hand, but I could no more escape Fiachra's grasp than I could Caedmon's.

"You must leave Eithne to her own fate."

"He is misleading her. Or he is misleading them both. If I can talk to him, tell him how unwell she is—"

"This is not your concern."

"You would leave her to be hurt, to have her heart broken?" Bitterness clouded both voice and mind. "She is your sister."

"She *is* my sister and I will look out for her as I can. Eithne has her own destiny and we must leave her to pursue it unhindered."

"Can it lead to anything other than unhappiness?"

Fiachra shrugged. "It may. Or it may not. Regardless, we shall not interfere. You, Diarmuid, have your own destiny to be concerned with."

"And what is my destiny? Do you know?"

"I can't interfere in yours either, but I can help you go into it with your eyes open."

"What do you mean?"

"Meet me tonight, after everyone is in bed. I'll be waiting at the back door."

He slipped away then and melted into the crowd. I glanced towards the trees but the stranger was gone.

Despite my irritation with Fiachra, his words intrigued me. For now though, I needed to participate in the festivities. I must try to shake off the melancholy and at least act joyous. So I smiled and ate and drank. I didn't mingle, didn't seek out others, and few came to speak to me. Ida kept up her usual commentary in my mind and I passed the time in a conversation, of sorts, with her.

Long tables dragged outside into the meagre sunshine were draped with festive red cloths and piled high with food. The cook and her helpers served an outstanding feast of soup, roast meat, baked vegetables, and grainy bread, followed by pies filled with chunky apples and served with fresh cream. My appetite was unusually fierce, despite the melancholy, and I ate until I thought my stomach would burst. I drank only sparingly, wanting a clear head for my discussion with Fiachra. It might not be possible to persuade a druid to change his mind but I would try. Eithne's wellbeing was too important. And Fiachra be damned, I would do what I thought necessary to protect my sister.

As light faded from the sky and the night chill gripped the air, we moved indoors and gathered in front of the fireplace. Every chair and bench was full and those who did not have a chair leaned against the walls or sat on the thick rugs. I squeezed onto the end of a bench beside a harried-looking woman and three small boys. Distant relatives perhaps for the woman's face looked much like Eithne's and she gave me a nod as if in recognition.

Servants handed around mugs of spiced wine and I wrapped

my cold hands around one although I did not intend to drink it. When Papa asked for a tale, he looked to the druids. I felt only the briefest pang of disappointment for it was a rare treat to hear a tale from a druid.

After a momentary discussion with his elder, Fiachra moved to the front of the room. His voice was calm and confident, and I envied his ease. As much as I felt called to be a bard, I had never been as comfortable in the telling of a tale as Fiachra seemed. He spoke well, an old tale of the Children of Lir who were turned into swans and suffered for many hundreds of years before being restored to their human forms.

The audience was silent as Fiachra told his tale. Everyone watched him and even the children appeared to listen intently. An ache of jealousy rose within me. Ida stirred, whispering sweet fragments of a new tale, but I pushed her away. I could hardly leave in the midst of Fiachra's tale without looking bad-mannered and ill-tempered.

There was a brief silence as Fiachra's final words lingered in the air. Then the applause started and cries for him to tell another. He demurred politely and returned to his position at the back of the room.

Papa stood then and the room quietened. He hesitated and when he spoke, his voice wavered just a little.

"My son," he said. "It is an unexpected joy to have you with us on this happy occasion and I thank you for your tale."

Fiachra inclined his head towards Papa. He didn't smile but pride shone in his grey eyes. I hadn't realised a druid could feel such a thing for they always seemed more Other than human. I had thought that perhaps human emotions were drained from them during their training. But right now, Fiachra seemed nothing more than a man who was pleased with his father's praise.

I tucked the memory away in my mind. It might be something I could use in a tale, perhaps a story of a druid who falls in love and must decide between his training and his destiny or his new love. Satisfaction flowed from Ida. Clearly this was her idea, not mine. I silently thanked her, promising I would work on this new tale as soon as I could.

The celebrations continued long after I gave up any pretence of participating. There was ale and dancing and platters of bread and meat. The fiddler knew a seemingly inexhaustible repertoire of melodies, few of which I recognised. I sat in front of the fire, ignoring the raven that lurked within its flames and fiddling with my mug of now-cooled wine. Ideas for new tales chased each other around in my mind but with all of the music and chatter and laughter, I couldn't concentrate on them so I sat and let the noise wash over me.

Eventually, the festivity died and the ale slowed. Grainne's family prepared to depart for their own estate, despite the lateness of the evening and Mother's urging that they stay.

Caedmon and Grainne went to the bedchamber that had been prepared for them. I remembered Eremon's handfasting and how the women had strewn the bed with flower petals and lit the fire in the hearth so the room would be warm for them. Candlelight had danced on the walls, making the room cozy and serene. I was sharply reminded of Rhiwallon and the melancholy gripped my insides tighter than ever. With my inability to even speak to a woman, let alone do anything else, the intimacies of a nuptial bedchamber would never be for me.

I yawned, wishing everyone in bed already as sleepy-eyed servants cleared away leftover food and half-filled mugs. Finally, they too departed for their own bedchambers, leaving the remainder of the cleaning until morning. Nobody noticed me sitting by the dying fire.

Floorboards creaked overhead as folk undressed and prepared for bed. Gradually the house quietened. I tiptoed to the back door. Huddled into my warmest coat, I slid back the door bolt. Frigid wind rushed in. As I eased the door closed, Fiachra already stood beside me.

He held a finger to his lips and I nodded. I followed him past the house and outbuildings, although not easily. If I didn't keep my gaze locked on his back, he disappeared right into the shadows. Tiny flakes of snow settled on my shoulders as I tried, unsuccessfully, to walk as soundlessly as Fiachra. Icy air crept under my coat and I pulled it tighter around me, fighting a swift gust that threatened to rip it from my shoulders.

The barn suddenly loomed over us. Fiachra slipped inside, immediately melting into the darkness. By the time I managed to close the door against the wind pulling at it, a lamp on a nearby shelf sent light through the barn. After the darkness outside, the sudden brightness burned my eyes. Fiachra stood with his back to the lamp and his face in shadows.

"Well, brother," Fiachra said. "That was a long evening."

"Did you not enjoy it?" Perhaps I wasn't the only one who had merely pretended.

He shrugged. "Celebrations are well and good. They are a necessary part of human life. But our lives as druids are quiet, with much silence and contemplation, and little to distract us from our studies."

"You must be free to leave now that the celebrations are over. You can go back to wherever it is you live."

I half-wished I could go with him.

"Aah, Diarmuid, there's much I can't tell you. Let me say only that events will soon occur that I have been sent to watch over. There is little I can do to aid you, but I can warn you that things may not be as they seem."

"What do you mean? I thought you were here because of Eithne?"

Fiachra shifted slightly and his face was no longer shadowed. His lips curled slightly; it might have been a smile. "Eithne too has an arduous journey ahead of her but it is not her journey to which I refer. The events about to unfold are to do with you."

"Me?" My voice squeaked in surprise. "What did I do?"

"I can say only this: a friend does not whisper. A friend will offer aid loudly and publicly."

"So why do we meet in a barn in the middle of the night?" I asked, my heart already bitter.

Fiachra stared into my eyes for a long moment. "The events ahead of you are dangerous and not only to yourself. As a druid, I may only observe. As a brother, I warn you to be careful."

"If you're that concerned about me as a brother, why don't you speak plainly? How am I supposed to know what you mean when you talk in riddles?"

He placed his hand on my forehead and pushed slightly. Warmth began where his fingers touched my skin and travelled all through my body, leaving a lingering fizzy trail. My body tingled.

"My blessing on you, brother."

Then Fiachra slid past me, opened the door and disappeared into the swirling snow that was fast becoming a storm.

I yawned, suddenly overwhelmingly tired. When the melancholy was bad, it always left me fatigued. I was strangely warm, given that I stood in a barn in the middle of a winter's night. I might as well spend what remained of the night here.

I found a clean pile of hay, wrapped my coat tight around me and crawled in. It was only then I remembered the lamp but it would burn out eventually and I was far too tired to get up again. The hay smelled of dust and summer. It was prickly but my coat shielded me well enough. Soft animal sounds drifted past as ox and cow settled, having been woken by our late-night arrival.

As I waited for sleep, I wondered what message Fiachra had intended to impart. What good were riddles and clues? If he wanted to help, he needed to speak plainly.

Ida stirred and I remembered she had given me a new tale. Tomorrow, I promised, tomorrow I would think on it. I was too tired right now.

If she were a real woman, how would she respond to my refusing to create her story right now? Would she be annoyed? No, Ida knew me better than I knew myself. She would accept my fatigue, and the way the melancholy made me withdraw. She would sympathise with my conflicted feelings about Caedmon and Fiachra. One a brother I had idolised my whole life, who I had thought could never disappoint me. The other almost a stranger to me. What kind of man had he grown up to be? He was a druid so he was surely knowledgeable. But was he also kind? Generous? Brave? All I really knew was he seemed quiet and ill-inclined to festivities.

If only Ida were real. I would be able to talk to her, I was sure of that. For Ida wasn't like other women. She didn't simper and giggle and mean something other than she said, like the girls I encountered at various celebrations. She would be genuine and straightforward. She would help me untangle my feelings. Ida would understand me.

I finally slept and I dreamed I saw Ida standing beside the haystack, watching me. As always, she was pale and fragile-looking, and her midnight blue dress seemed to whip around her legs even though there was no draft within the tightly-made barn. She smiled at me, but there was no fondness in the motion, then raised one white hand to press it to her lips. She blew a kiss towards where I slumbered in the hay and then walked away.

In my dream, I heard the barn door slam shut behind her. A chill breeze sent snowflakes whipping around the barn, but soon settled. I slept on, warm and comfortable and tired after such a long day.

11

IDA

I FEED ON his despair. He feeds on the tales I whisper. A symbiotic relationship of sorts. We need each other, but he needs me more. Or perhaps I need him more. I no longer remember.

As his despair grows, I strengthen. I become *more*. He sees the raven everywhere: in his dreams, in his mind, in the fire. Yet he doesn't *see* it. He doesn't recognise me in any form other than that he gave me.

My strength grows. I absorb the images and ideas in his tales, drawing them into myself, making them a part of me. I grow stronger and stronger, until, finally, I am strong enough. I think, *Out,* and then I am. Without him. His head is his own again. Will he notice?

Now I stretch, limbs reaching for the sky. It feels good, so good. Have I ever had a physical form before? I lean over him as he sleeps. So innocent he appears. To look at him, one would never know the darkness in his mind, the horror of his dreams. But he has served his purpose and I need him no longer. I could crush him now as he sleeps. But no, I leave him. We have occupied his head together for many years and his mind is as familiar to me as my own. He is like my own flesh, my blood, my mind. So

I will not destroy him but instead leave him to his grim thoughts. I blow a kiss towards him.

Power floods my body and the barn door blows open ahead of me. I step out into a swirling eddy of snow. Soft, cool flakes melt against my skin as I tip my face up to the sky. Sensations, feelings, physicality. Warm skin, cold snow, hot breath, chill breeze. I inhale and the winter night, crisp and fresh, floods my nostrils. They tingle and my lungs burn as the cold air hits them.

I stride into the snow and, with a thought, slam the door behind me. On the other side of the door, the boy stirs. He knows something has changed. He just doesn't know how much.

Where shall I go? It hardly matters. I am *myself*. I can go anywhere, do anything. With every step, my body feels more solid, more real. Power soaks into my bones, my organs, my blood. It seeps through every part of me until I am drenched in it.

Diarmuid once told a tale in which a druid stopped the snow from falling. I think I could do it, if I chose. I could make the snow hang still in the air but I don't, for I enjoy its light weight and the bitterness of its presence. I watch as soft flakes drift down to settle on my bare arms. Cold, yes, but not unbearable, not to one such as I and certainly not tonight. I raise my arms higher, up above my head and stretch out my fingers. Could I touch the sky if I wanted to? I feel the muscles in my arms lengthen, the joints shift slightly. Blood drains from my upraised limbs. Slowly I lower my arms and blood rushes back down to my fingers.

I breathe deeply, noting how the cold air catches in my lungs. My ribs expand with each breath and blood flows through my body with each pump of my heart. My stomach feels strange. Hollow, empty. Is this hunger? A cold breeze whistles past, teasing my skirt. I notice, finally, that I wear no shoes. My feet are covered in snow to the ankles. It feels unpleasant. Too cold. I do not like this. Time to move on, to find shelter. Time to find myself a home.

12

DIARMUID

I WOKE BURIED up to my nose in hay, my heart strangely light. I had almost forgotten how much brighter the world was without a cloak of melancholy. I scrambled out of the hay and pulled off my coat. Shaking it to remove the straw was largely futile.

Outside, the storm had abated, leaving only deep drifts of snow. The air was fresh and cold enough to burn my lungs. Sunlight sparkled on ice, bright and white and cheerful. It was a perfect winter's morning.

As I ploughed through knee-deep snow, hoping I was not too late for a hot breakfast, I hummed a tune. It was nothing special, merely a cheerful ditty Mother often sang when I was a child. I could only recall the occasional phrase here and there but the tune was swift and uplifting, and I broke into a smile. I couldn't remember the last time I had felt the inclination to sing.

Only Caedmon lingered at the table by the time I arrived although the assortment of used plates and bowls indicated that the rest of the family had already eaten. A single glimpse of Caedmon's face reminded me of my humiliation and my cheerful mood dissolved. My face flamed and I kept my eyes averted as I reached for the almost empty kettle. The last of the porridge had cooled but I was hungry enough to eat it anyway.

I felt Caedmon watching me but I stared at my bowl as I ate, not inclined to break the silence. Eventually he sighed and cleared his throat.

"Do you intend to stay mad at me for the rest of my life, little brother?"

"Perhaps." I scraped the last of the porridge from my bowl and reached for the bread.

"I have less than a turning of the moon before I return to the campaign."

I grunted through a mouthful of bread and honey.

"If I die on campaign, perhaps then you will regret not forgiving me."

My response was another grunt, which could have passed for either assent or dissent.

Caedmon sighed. "Gods, you are the most stubborn person I know. Was it really so bad?"

"Didn't she tell you?" I fixed my gaze on a trail of breadcrumbs and licked sticky honey off my fingers.

"No, although I asked. She said it was none of my business but she would thank me to not ask her to make men of any other brothers I might have."

My grunt became a squawk of startled surprise. I finally met his eyes. They were tired, his face lined. "She told you nothing?"

"No, little brother, not a thing. I gather by the storm cloud that appears on your face every time you see me, the evening didn't go as planned. But I know nothing else."

My heart lightened and bitterness drained away. I had cringed, night after night, as I pictured Rhiwallon telling him, in explicit detail, about my failure. I had never even countenanced the possibility that she might be discrete.

"She's a good sort of girl," I said, feeling I owed Rhiwallon at least this much for my assumption.

"She is." Caedmon looked as if he wanted to say more but then shook his head. "Well, little brother, I shall go see if Grainne is ready to leave. Today we decide where to build our home. I think a sunny position will suit her, perhaps on the top of that hill just beyond where the twin rivers merge. Grainne will have to oversee the construction when I leave. Eremon will help if she has need. He understands the situation."

"You still think you will die on the next campaign?"

He seemed reluctant to speak further. "Whether I do or not, I must be prepared. Grainne will be well provided for." Then he stood and shook a few crumbs off his shirt. "I am pleased that you have forgiven me, Diarmuid. I did not want to leave with you so mad at me."

He left before I could say anything else. It was only later I realised he had called me by name for the first time.

13

DIARMUID

OVER THE NEXT few days, I worked on a new tale. Or, rather, I tried to. I spent my time rambling across the snowy fields of Silver Downs as was my usual practice when creating, but for the first time neither words nor images would flow. My tales had dried up, I told myself, like a stream waiting for the first of the season's rain. They would return, just as the rain always did. I simply had to be patient.

I walked day after day, from the crisp dawn of a late winter's morning until darkness or storms drove me home. I had not a single tale in my head. I tried to remember other tales, my own or someone else's, to reassure myself I could still weave a narrative, but even the old tales burrowed deep and refused to be found. I sought out Ida. I needed her. Always before when the words would not flow, she had been there. I conjured up her image but it was merely a memory, devoid of breath or life. My inspiration was gone.

As day stretched into long day, I feared I might never tell another tale. Mother began to give me strange looks, no doubt wondering why I gulped down my meals and then bolted to my bedchamber. She asked no questions, for which I was thankful.

For how could I tell anyone? I was born to be a bard. It was my destiny.

Little more than a sevennight remained before Caedmon was due to depart. Already hints of spring were appearing. The nights were not quite as cold and the sun warmed the afternoon air to an almost-pleasant temperature. Soon the rivers would begin to thaw and then Caedmon must leave. He and Grainne were busy overseeing preparations for their new home. From what little I saw of him, he looked satisfied, in the way only a newly-handfasted man can. Grainne was melting the hard edges of my soldier brother.

After yet another fruitless day, I arrived home to find a rough-looking man had arrived. He had a thick, black beard and scars on his knuckles. His name was Bran and he was passing through, he said, on his way to visit his sister who lived several days' walk south. Papa invited him to stay the night with us for it was mid-afternoon and he would not reach the next estate before dark.

We gathered around the table that evening and Bran ate heartily. The soup was thick and nutritious, full of herbs and vegetables. Last summer had been good to us and this winter there was plenty to go around, even so close to spring. In other years our supplies had been lean by this time and we had made do with thin soups and flat breads.

"What news have you?" Papa asked. "We've heard nothing from further afield than Maker's Well through most of the winter."

"Disturbing reports, my lord." Bran tore off a chunk of bread and dipped it in his soup. His full black beard sopped up almost as much as the bread did. "Murder and mayhem. Violence and destruction."

Papa's face was grave. "Perhaps then your news is not such as one should share at the dinner table."

Bran nodded and slurped the last of his soup. Mother passed him a ladle and he eagerly helped himself to more. Once everyone had eaten their fill, we moved into the living room. A fire blazed in the hearth and the room was already pleasantly warm. Mother produced a large jug of sweet, spiced wine. I claimed a padded chair, which was situated just within reach of the fire's warmth. Mug in hand, I stared into the flames, trying not to see the fiery raven lurking in its midst.

Once we were all settled, Papa turned to Bran. "Would you care to share your news with us now? Here by the fireplace is a more suitable location for a tale of woe and injury."

Bran nodded and swallowed a large mouthful of wine. "This is very good, my lady," he said to Mother.

She smiled, pleased, and got up to refill his mug. "Tell us your news and I will ensure you do not go thirsty during its telling."

After another warm mouthful, Bran began. "I am from Badger's Crossing," he said. "It is more than a sevennight's walk from here. As I told you earlier, I travel to visit my sister, who I have not seen since she handfasted three years ago. I do not bring good news for I must tell her of our mother's death. Badger's Crossing is, I believe, about the size of Maker's Well. The next town past us is Mapleton, a two-day walk, and then there is Crow's Nest, which is the better part of a day further. It is from there I have heard disturbing reports.

"What I know is grim. A man passing through Badger's Crossing on his way from Crow's Nest told of a witch who holds the town in thrall. They do anything she says and seem desperate to please her. She is a beautiful woman, he says, one whom it would not be unusual to hear that a man slavishly obeys, but a whole town? It is more than passing strange.

"If she says kill your neighbour, they do it willingly. If she says take this child and leave it in the woods, they obey. To the child, she says, go, they will take you to the woods and the wild pigs will tear you to pieces and eat your body, and the child says yes, my lady."

I froze. Bran's words were familiar, but I couldn't immediately place them. Then I remembered. Hadn't I once told a tale in which Titania, queen of the fey, directed a woman to take a child to the woods and leave her there for the wild animals to eat? Coincidence of course but as I looked across the room, my eyes met Papa's. His face was pale and lined.

"What does she look like, this woman who wields such power?" Caedmon asked, his voice sceptical.

"The man I heard this from swore she was the most beautiful woman he had ever seen. Her hair was entirely white, her eyes were blue, clear and cruel. Her skin was like snow and so fine it was almost translucent."

The spiced wine clung to my tongue, suddenly sour. White hair, blue eyes, pale skin. But Ida wasn't real. She was no more real than any other tale I had created. She was an image in my head, born of my desire to imagine my tales meant something. For if they were whispered to me by some Otherworldly muse, surely they were important.

But it seemed Ida was no longer in my head and neither were the tales she had whispered. It was a coincidence though. It had to be. Papa was no longer looking at me. In fact, it seemed all of my family were very carefully avoiding my eyes. But none of them knew about Ida.

Bran's words washed over me as he described how the witch played family against family, friend against neighbour, until nobody trusted anyone else. People had died, homes were lost, children disappeared and were never found. And yet still they did everything the witch told them to.

"Surely they do not have to do as she says?" Mother asked. She shuddered and pulled Eithne close to her.

Bran held out his mug to be refilled. "The way I heard it, they do not question. Everything she says, they rush to obey. It seems they no longer think for themselves."

"Where is Fiachra tonight?" Eremon asked. He sat beside Niamh, each with a child on their lap, their twin sons, heir and druid. "He could tell us whether this is possible."

Fiachra had a strange ability of disappearing quietly, unnoticed until someone asked for him. He did not appear at every meal and did not sleep in the bedchamber Mother had prepared for him. Where he went and what he did was a mystery.

"Fiachra has a higher master than family," Papa said and the shine in his eyes could have been either pride or sadness. "I'll speak to him when he returns. Mayhap he will have knowledge of similar circumstances."

As I looked at our family assembled around the hearth, a chill gripped me. Papa stood, leaning against the fireplace, grave and authoritative. Mother sat in her usual place, close by the fire. Her face was pale and concerned. Eithne sat nearby, her chair drawn up beside Mother's. Her face too was pale but her eyes glittered fever-bright.

Eremon, Niamh and their sons sat together on a bench. Caedmon was further back from the fire, Grainne nestled on his lap. Marrec and Conn lounged on benches at the back of the room, talking quietly between themselves. They were often like that: nearby but not quite a part of what happened. Sitric was in Maker's Well as usual. Fiachra might be anywhere.

These were the people I loved and they were all I loved in the world. What would I do if the witch came here? But Crow's Nest was a long way from Silver Downs. We were safe here from her reign of terror and death.

14

DIARMUID

ONG AFTER THE house became quiet, I was still sleepless. From my bed, I looked around my small chamber, lit by the fire flickering in the hearth. This room was so familiar, I barely noticed it anymore. The toys and games of my childhood had long been packed away and replaced by an assortment of interesting rocks, leaves and feathers I had collected on my rambles around the estate. The one toy still on display was a small wooden sword, made by Caedmon to suit my then-six-summers-old frame. It sat on the bench below the window, a reminder of long summer days traipsing the length and breadth of Silver Downs with Caedmon. My bedchamber contained little else. A narrow bed and a chest of drawers with washbowl and ewer. A thick rug and heavy curtains kept the cold at bay. The room smelled of home and warmth and comfort.

Comfort was something I sorely needed as I shivered under the covers while recalling Bran's words. Icy tendrils of horror crept through my limbs. Surely such a thing was not possible. I had not created this witch. I was just a bard, not a druid. I had no knowledge of magics or potions, spells or chants or charms. I couldn't even tell rosemary from lavender, let alone create some malignant evil with the power of words alone. But running through my mind was Papa's warning the night I had proclaimed myself to be a bard. The night he had told me I could bring my tales to life. I had laughed and we never again discussed the matter.

It was many hours before I slept. And when I did, I dreamed of a raven. It stood on the end of my bed and stared at me with glassy eyes as black-red blood dripped from its beak. Eventually, it gave a single caw and left in a rush of ebony feathers, flinging bloody droplets over my face as it rose. It flew out through the open window. I tried to wipe the blood from my face before realising I was awake.

I shivered and huddled further down under the blankets. A biting breeze rustled my hair and I pulled the covers over my head. At length I realised there should be no wind, for the window had been latched and the drapes drawn when I went to sleep. But now the window was wide open and the curtains billowed as another gust blew around the bedchamber. I got up and closed the window, ensuring it was securely locked. The latch must have worked itself free as I slept.

I stirred the fire and added more wood. Flames rippled as the fire leaped in the grate. It had been some time since I had dreamed of the raven. Several weeks at least. Usually, the dark bird appeared in my dreams every few nights. I had long wondered what it meant. It was clearly a symbol of something, but what? Death? In other circumstances, I might have thought it portended Eithne's death but with Fiachra's words still ringing in my head, I wondered whether the raven signified my own death.

A friend does not whisper, Fiachra had said. *A friend will offer aid loudly and publicly.* What friend did he mean? I didn't really have any, although with six brothers, a sister, and two nephews, I could always find company if I wanted it. Our family had its routines, with evenings spent around the fire, companionably exchanging tales, and I had never felt the need for more society than that. I knew boys my own age, of course. They were friendly enough and we would talk for a while when we met at various festivals, but I had always preferred solitude and silence, and in truth, was far happier spending my time roaming the estate and creating tales than making idle conversation with someone I only saw a few times a year.

I eventually returned to bed and sunlight was peeking around the drapes by the time I next woke. The window was still closed and I felt a little foolish at the surge of relief that flooded my body. But as I rose, a chill colder than midwinter gripped me and my knees turned to water. For there, on the blanket, was a bright red drop of blood. Right where the dream raven had stood.

I eventually forced myself to move, to look away from the redness. Perhaps it wasn't really blood. It could have been there for days. If it *was* blood, then clearly I had cut myself at some stage and the blood had dropped, unnoticed, on my blanket. It didn't mean a raven had actually stood on my bed during the night — a raven whose beak dripped blood.

By mid-morning I had almost convinced myself I had imagined the blood. It was a spot of dirt perhaps, maybe mud, but I had gotten confused and assumed it was something more than it was. I pushed the image to the back of my mind and tried to forget. By the time I thought to check the blanket again, a servant had replaced it with a clean one.

My mood was light that morning. I felt relaxed, carefree, almost happy. Perhaps I was finally emerging from the melancholy that had gripped me for years. It had been a long time since I had felt as free as I had of late. Not since the early days of my tenth year, the last summer before Caedmon left to be a soldier. How light and full of hope I had felt then. Every day had been long and sunny and full of adventure. Perhaps this was the start of my journey to regain that freedom.

Bran departed immediately after breakfast and for a day or two I almost forgot his news of the witch. But then Sitric returned home, bringing similar tales. And a friend of Grainne's father knew someone who lived in the town next to Crow's Nest and insisted the tales were true. From the family at Three Trees, we learnt that the son of their cousin had beaten a man to death for no reason other than that the witch told him to. A chill ran through me with each new story. These were no longer tales from a stranger who may or may not have been trying to impress his hosts, but news from people we knew, about people they knew.

The more we heard, the more my uneasiness grew. I could tell no one for the idea was laughable, this silly notion that it was my fault. That the witch was really Ida, somehow brought to life and escaped from my head. Anyone who heard such a thing would surely think me a fool. What an imagination, they would say, even for a bard. Yet I could never quite forget the way Papa had sighed the night I had told the tale of a bard who brought his imaginary muse to life.

15

DIARMUID

D AYS PASSED AND I was still unable to create a tale. Not even the tiniest spark of inspiration lingered within me. At night, I lay awake, hour after hour. If I slipped into sleep, my dreams were restless and filled with ravens who stared at me with blood dripping from their beaks. When morning came, I was tired and irritable and no closer to convincing myself that Ida was not the witch. I was merely a bard. And yet, I was the seventh son of a seventh son.

On the eve of Caedmon's departure, the family gathered around the dinner table. My brothers joked and jostled with each other for space. Sitric travelled from Maker's Well and even Fiachra made a rare appearance for he still lingered at Silver Downs. Cook provided an outstanding feast: roasted wild boar, sweet and juicy and dripping with fat; winter root vegetables, drizzled with honey and baked until they were crispy and golden; thick slices of brown bread which we dipped in the rich meat juices; followed by pies filled with preserved blackberries. I ate until my stomach was ready to burst.

After the meal, we moved to our accustomed places by the living room hearth. Our fire tonight was small for the nights were finally warming. My mind was still occupied with the feast and with the lingering taste of tart blackberries on my tongue. I was caught off guard when Papa called for a tale.

"Something stirring, Diarmuid," were his instructions. "Something to put Caedmon in the right frame of mind as he leaves us tomorrow. Tonight we want heroes and courage, my boy."

I knew what he wanted me to hear in his words: don't tell one of my usual sorrowful tales. It seemed I was the only one who saw the benefit in these tales that taught. Even my own family could not rise above the thought that a tale should merely entertain.

I moved to the fireplace, heart pounding and my mind blank. I had managed to avoid being in this situation ever since the tales had fled my head but tonight I had been careless and lingered. I couldn't refuse, not on Caedmon's last evening with us.

I glanced around the room. Mother and Eithne sat with their chairs drawn close together. Eremon and Niamh shared a bench; their boys played on the floor at their feet. Marrec and Conn sat on another bench at the back of the room. Papa and Sitric reclined in comfortable padded chairs, one on each side of the room. They were all silent, waiting for me to begin.

My gaze locked with Caedmon's and the sound of Rhiwallon's laugh echoed in my memory. Anger stirred, anger I had thought forgotten. Beside Caedmon, Grainne clutched his hand and smiled at me. She was flushed and bright eyed, resting her other hand to her stomach. Did she already carry his heir? Jealousy squeezed my heart and for a moment my only thought was that he had everything. He was the man I wanted to be. The man I would never be.

In that moment inspiration finally returned. The tale I told was of a soldier who leaves for campaign, his head full of images of the sweetheart he leaves behind, believing her well and safe and carrying his child. Shortly after, one of the fey, who is smitten with the girl, goes to her and asks her to forget the soldier and come away with him to the Otherworld. When she refuses, he becomes enraged and beats her senseless, tearing her clothes with his long fingernails and biting viciously at her soft flesh.

When the girl's family discovers her, bruised and beaten and bloody, they blame the soldier, and her male relatives set off in pursuit. The tale finished with her menfolk, having beaten the soldier to death, learning the truth of the girl's injuries. The moral, of course, was that it is unwise to rush into action without ensuring one has full knowledge of the circumstances. One should never assume.

As always, the tale's end prompted an uncomfortable silence. It was Caedmon who eventually spoke.

"Not exactly an uplifting tale with which to send me off, little brother."

I shrugged and tried to forget his words. I was well accustomed to audiences disliking my tales. Still, it hurt, especially when it was Caedmon.

"It was a… different sort of tale," Grainne said.

Nobody else seemed inclined to comment and after a few moments Eremon announced he too had a tale to share. I stepped back and leaned against the wall. As soon as everyone seemed engrossed in his tale, I slipped out of the room.

I slowly cracked open the back door, hesitating as it creaked, but nobody came to investigate. I set off towards the barn, wanting to be alone for a short while. The late winter night was colder than I had expected and I swiftly regretted not bringing a coat. The ground shone silver in the moonlight and remnants of the last snowfall crackled underfoot. Distant fir trees stood like sentinels, silent witnesses to the night's events.

Suddenly a figure in a dark cloak trod soundlessly beside me. I greeted Fiachra with a nod. There seemed no need for words. He returned my nod and we walked together without speaking. The only noise was the crunching of my boots against the snow and the sighing of the trees as the night breeze whipped through them.

I opened the barn door and by the time I secured it again, Fiachra had a lamp lit.

"Events are occurring, Diarmuid," he said. "The time of evil has arrived. The only question remaining is what will you do about it?"

"Me?" I squawked. "What am I supposed to do?"

"You do not know?" Fiachra's face was solemn and I could read nothing in his eyes.

I shook my head.

"But surely you suspect?"

I hesitated, not wanting to voice aloud my silly superstition.

"All you tell me will be held in confidence, brother."

"I wondered…" My courage failed but he waited patiently as I sought the words to admit what I barely believed. "The witch… I thought… I think she may be my fault."

Fiachra held my gaze and waited. If he judged me, it did not show on his face.

"I created a woman. In my mind. A muse. She was just another tale really. I pretended she whispered ideas to me and I told my tales to her. The more I thought about her, the more real she seemed to become. Then one night I dreamed she left my head and walked away. I think she might be the witch everyone has been talking about."

It sounded as ridiculous as I had expected but Fiachra nodded gravely.

"So what do you intend to do?" he asked.

Courage increased, flooding through my body like warm soup. "I guess I have to stop her," I said, although I had not actually considered this until now. "If I created her and somehow brought her to life, I can't leave her to… People have died. If this is my fault…"

My voice trailed off. Fiachra stretched out a hand and laid it gently on my shoulder. Like the last time he touched me, a warm tingle passed through my body.

"You must do what you must do, Diarmuid. If you believe you have created this creature, you must stop her."

"But how? How can I stop a witch? I'm just a bard."

"You tell me. How did you create her?"

"I thought of her. And then she was there, in my mind."

"If you created her in your mind, then your mind can also devise a way to stop her."

"I suppose I should go to Crow's Nest. Find the witch. See if she really is Ida."

Fiachra nodded and gently pressed his fingertips against my forehead in a final benediction. "My blessing be on you, brother. Be brave. Be cautious of whom you trust. You will find companions on this journey but they will not all be what they seem."

"You already know what will happen? Will I…" I couldn't put into words all I wanted to ask.

"I can tell you nothing further, Diarmuid. You must be free to choose your own way. Indeed, I do not know the outcome of your journey. There are options, choices, paths. Each leads to a different result. But which one you will choose, I do not know."

"When should I leave?"

"As soon as possible, tomorrow if you can. Creatures such as these are often strongest with the dark of the moon. She has already had one darkness. Two or three may make her unstoppable."

"The new moon was just a couple of days ago so I have almost four sevennights until the next."

"Less, for her strength will grow as the moon waxes and its darkness draws nearer."

"I'll leave tomorrow morning." My voice was somewhat thready for this gave me little time to prepare.

Fiachra nodded and his eyes were solemn. "I will be watching you on your journey, brother. There may be little I can do to aid you but if you have need of me, call and I will come if I can."

"How will you hear me?"

He smiled briefly. "I will hear. Do not fear that I won't."

"Mother. Will you tell her something? Enough that she won't worry but perhaps not the whole truth?"

"Do not worry about our mother. With all else happening here, she will barely notice your absence."

The thought was discomfiting.

"I wish you well, brother. May your journey be successful and may you return home with both mind and body intact."

The moon was well on its odyssey across the night sky before I went to bed. I bundled up the items I thought I might need into an oilcloth and stowed them in a deep pack. Two clean shirts and a spare pair of socks. Flint. A small dagger. Two blankets for the nights were yet cold. A surreptitious trip to the kitchen after the servants had retired for the night secured several days' supply of food: bread, cheese, water, some dried meat, pork perhaps but it was hard to tell. I had little in the way of coin but all I had went into the pack. Caedmon sometimes gave me a coin or two before he returned to the campaign and I had rarely had need of them.

By the time I was done, the pack was far heavier than I liked. I emptied it and started again. Spare boots weren't necessary for I could buy them on my way. The needle and thread I kept, and after all, they weighed little. The second blanket was surely a luxury. I hesitated over the spare water flask but I could ration my supplies and fill my flask at every opportunity. I weighed the purse in my hand. It wasn't that heavy and I might need every coin.

And so it went on, until the pack was reduced to a weight I thought I could carry all day. It looked piteously small now for I had discarded more than I kept. I could only hope those summer expeditions with Caedmon had prepared me for this journey.

16

IDA

W ITH FREEDOM COMES joy and pain, pleasure and sorrow. Pride, rage, passion, remorse. So many emotions. I feel them all and know I am truly alive. They flow into me, strengthening my body, fuelling my power. I draw them into me, more and more and more, until all that remains of the source is an empty and lifeless shell. It is of no matter. There are plenty of other sources. And they all have such a wonderful array of emotions. I can hardly believe how much, and how deeply, they feel.

I grow stronger with every day and soon I discover fear. That is the most powerful emotion of all. Once I find it, I crave more and more. The power is like nothing I have ever imagined.

If only I had known what waited out here for me, I might have left sooner. But I needed to wait. I had to bide my time until I was strong enough.

If he was not so full of darkness, perhaps I would yet still be too weak. I might still be waiting, siphoning off his emotions, piece by piece, encouraging his darkest thoughts and dreams, and drawing all of that power into myself.

If he was weaker or his soul was lighter, I might never have gained the power to leave.

17

BRIGIT

A S WINTER BEGAN her slow withdrawal, the intensity of the visions increased. At night, I tossed sleeplessly while images of the boy, the white dog and the woman filled my mind. By day, I was anxious and tired, as irritable as a honeybee smoked out of its hive, and unable to concentrate on anything. Signs of spring were everywhere the day Mother sent me to gather herbs for her. Perhaps she had Seen my fate, for after I had recited the list of herbs she wanted, she gently placed her palm on my forehead.

"My blessing on you, my child," she said. "Travel safe."

I scowled, in no mood for blessings and benedictions. I snatched up a basket and my coat and left without a word to her. She stood in the doorway, watching after me for the longest time.

My mood lifted as I stomped across the fields under a sky blanketed with fluffy white clouds. No breeze ruffled the branch of birch or beech. The snow underfoot was thinner now for the days were starting to warm. I walked with purpose for I knew exactly where I needed to go. Two of the herbs Mother wanted could be found by a particular stream; for another, I would need to venture into the nearby woods. I watched for the fourth as I walked, for its leaves preferred sunlight and open air.

By the time I reached the woods, I had found all but one of the herbs. My legs were tiring and I was hungry, for in my bad temper I had not thought to bring any food. The air was colder within the shelter of the woods and smelled of moss and dampness. Little snow had reached these depths. Fir trees grew close together, fighting to grow tallest and reach the sunlight first. I picked my way around fallen branches and between mossy rocks, trying not to tread on the small mushrooms growing in the shadows.

At first I had ignored the fey girl as she slipped from tree to tree, almost invisible in the gloom, but now I was hungry and tired and more than a little fed up with being spied on.

"Why do you follow me?" I asked as I clambered over a toppled fir that blocked my path. My voice echoed through the woods, louder than I had intended. There was no response, not that I expected any. However, as I rounded a bend in the barely-visible path I followed, more sense than sight, she stood there.

Slight and fey, she had long dark hair that curled and tangled around her shoulders. Her skin was milky white and her lips far too red. Her eyes were what startled me the most for they were as blue as a summer sky and seemed to pierce my soul as she stared at me. She stood awkwardly, hip jutting out to the side, and waited. For what, I wasn't sure.

It was I who spoke first. "Hello." She continued to stare. "Why do you now stand there after trying to be invisible for so many days?"

"Had I wanted to be invisible," she retorted haughtily, "you would have known naught of my presence."

"Why do you follow me then?"

"To watch you."

"Why?"

"So that we know what you do and what you don't."

"Why do you need to know?"

"Because you will be important, in as much as a mortal can be."

"Important to what?"

"To everything," she said. "And so you must do as I say."

"I shall not," I said indignantly, before realising she hadn't yet said what she wanted from me.

She glared, clearly unused to anyone refusing her instructions. "You shall. For you have no choice. Everything in your life has led you towards today, towards here and now."

I reined in my temper. Perhaps it was better if I at least appeared to consider her demands. "What is it you want from me?"

"You will leave here immediately and set out on a journey."

"And where would I travel to?"

"It is not important that you know the destination." Her tone was dismissive and my annoyance rose again. "All that is important is your obedience."

"You expect me to leave my home and my life to journey towards some end you will not even share with me?"

"Yes."

"Ludicrous," I said. "You do not know much about mortals if you think I will do this merely because you tell me to."

She frowned and stamped her foot in the leaf litter. "I know everything about mortals. Have I not watched you, learnt all about you? I know what you like, what you don't, what you dream, what you fear. I have watched you as you worked, as you played, as you slept. I know everything about you."

"You clearly know nothing about me if you think I will depart on some mysterious journey just because you tell me to." I resisted the urge to stamp my own foot. "What use has your watching been if you know so little?"

Her pretty face turned ugly and she glared at me. "You will do as I say. Whether you do it willingly or no, I care not. My task is to ensure you go, and go you will."

"I refuse."

"You cannot refuse. You have no idea of the consequences."

"Then tell me the consequences. Let me make an informed decision."

"You do not need to know," she said. "All you need to know is that you are required to go. And go you shall."

"No. I will not. And that is my final word on the matter."

I continued picking my way towards the place where the final herb was wont to grow.

"This is your last chance," she said and her voice held a warning I blithely ignored. "You will be sorry if you do not obey willingly."

I focused my attention on the path ahead. I heard a huff of exasperation and then the ground rose up to meet my face. The smell of the woods intensified and yet colours became strangely muted. Perhaps I had fainted, hit my head. I thrust my hands into soft fir needles, trying to clutch at the ground, but seemed merely to scrabble fruitlessly.

My hands looked... odd. White, furry. I raised them to see them more clearly and promptly fell flat on my face in the leaves.

As I picked myself up, my entire body felt strange. I was hunched over in an unaccustomed position with both hands and feet on the ground, yet it felt strangely natural. My behind trembled and when I looked back over my shoulder, I saw an expanse of silky white hair and a short, stubby tail that flicked from side to side. It stopped when I glared at it but started again as soon as I looked away.

I realised I was panting with my tongue hanging out. I closed my mouth but suddenly I was suffocating. I opened my mouth and panted, tongue lolling out again. I sat in the leaf litter and studied the white paws at the end of my arms. Four claws plus a fifth, shorter. Thick white hair, which almost obscured the shiny black claws. Between my eyes I could just make out a black nose, which seemed to stick out far further than it should.

Memories of visions flooded my mind and I trembled. There had been a blood-soaked dog in many of them, a small, white terrier, its eyes filled with pain. I had wondered what connection to me the dog would have and now I knew. I looked back towards the fey girl but she was gone.

I wasted much time sitting in the leaves, staring at my new paws, until I finally realised the day was swiftly passing. My only hope was to find my way home. Mother would surely know what to do, for she was a wise woman and had much arcane knowledge. I did not let myself think about what I would do if she did not recognise me. I tried to speak, to say *Mother, it is I,* but my mouth wouldn't cooperate and all that came out was a strangled moan.

I had no way of carrying the basket. I tried to lift it in my mouth but choked on the plaited handle, so the herbs I had gathered would go to waste. I might have expected it to take some time to get used to walking on four legs, but it felt like the most natural thing in the world. Provided I didn't think about which paw went where, the body I was in seemed to know what to do.

The tail — I could hardly consider it *my* tail — twitched from side to side whenever I thought about it. I couldn't quite figure out how it worked or what its purpose was. I had a vague idea that a wagging tail meant a happy dog but this tail moved with the slightest thought. I had never realised how little I knew about dogs.

I headed towards home but the path seemed different. For starters, I was at the wrong height and so the markers I had noted that would have told me I travelled in the right direction weren't where I expected them to be. After a while, I realised I was following the faint scent of myself. I had walked through here recently. All I had to do to find my way home was follow my own scent. It is harder than it sounds, particularly when one is new to being a dog. Once I started focusing on scent, my sensitive nose became overwhelmed and I froze, paralysed with indecision about which smell to follow. There was moss and water and decay. Mushrooms, mould and some sort of furry creature. I walked without any definite direction for some time, getting used to my new nose and form. By the time I regained my senses, I had lost my own trail.

I was completely lost, alone in the woods, and not in my own body.

18

BRIGIT

I SEARCHED THE woods desperately, trying to find my own scent. But no matter how I sniffed and snuffed, it was all earth and dampness, leaves and decay. I paused for a short rest and scrambled up onto a low rock, hoping the height would allow me to recognise something familiar.

My new ears heard every whisper and rustle and I didn't dare let myself wonder what manner of creature made such noises. As soon as my legs felt somewhat rested, I continued my search. Had I been able to weep, I would have but it seemed my new eyes could cry no tears.

I searched and searched, growing increasingly frantic and trying not to think about tales of folk who wandered into the woods and never returned. Soon the little light that seeped this far into the woods began to slip away.

I redoubled my efforts, running from fir tree to shrubby chestnut, from rock to leafy patch, desperate to find some familiar scent or sight to point me towards home. My whole body trembled and the tail was tucked firmly between my back legs. Had I been in my own form, being lost in the woods would not be quite so bad. I knew exactly what I could do with my own hands and feet and, if nothing else, I could have screamed or cried or yelled. In this form, I was helpless.

When finally the light had all but disappeared, I had to admit there was no chance of finding my way home today. I was hungry and thirsty but didn't trust my new eyes and nose. I knew almost every food source growing in the woods for Mother had ensured I learnt all a girl destined to become a wise woman should. In my own form, I wouldn't have hesitated. I would have known whether those nuts dangling tantalisingly just out of reach were edible, or whether the roots of the plant by my foot were nutritious, or whether the mushrooms growing in the shade of the rocks were safe to eat. In my own form, I could have made a substantial meal out of the foodstuffs around me.

But in this strange new form, I doubted myself. The change from woman to dog might have affected my senses or my brain. I no longer knew whether I could rely on my knowledge and I wasn't familiar enough with this nose to trust it. So tonight, I would go hungry, but it wouldn't be for long. Tomorrow, I would find my way home.

In the shelter of a thick holly bush, I gathered a mound of fir needles, scraping them into place with my paws. It made for a surprisingly soft bed. I curled up on the pile, wrapped the tail around me and tucked my nose into my paws for warmth.

The night was long and cold. I soon burrowed down into the needles, covering my body with them but I was still so cold that at times I doubted I would live through the night.

Perhaps some stranger would find my body, buried in fir needles. They would have no way of knowing this form was more than it seemed. Nobody would take news of my passing to my mother. But the Sight was strong in her and she had nurtured her gift in a way I never had. Did she know this morning that I did not depart on any ordinary herb-gathering expedition? Perhaps the Sight would show her a small, white dog, shivering in the midst of a pile of fir needles. Would she wonder what this image meant?

Would she debate whether the vision portrayed past, present, future, or merely a possibility? Or would she know it was I, cursed by the fey for refusing some mission they would not even explain? Mother always said my stubbornness would get me into trouble one day.

So I tortured myself with such thoughts as I shivered through the night. I did not sleep but it was not only the cold that kept me awake. Mostly, it was fear. Fear of what might creep up on me if I slept. Fear of the visions that replayed in my mind, showing the bloodstained terrier over and over until I was sure I would go mad if I hadn't already. I also had the tiniest bit of hope that the fey girl might relent and restore me to my own form. However I was in two minds as to whether or not I would actually accept her strange quest, if that were the price for being returned to my own body.

I poked my head out of the needles every now and then to check whether morning had yet arrived. Eventually sunlight began to filter through the fir canopy and hope, which had seemed so far away during the night, returned. Today, I would find my way home. My legs were stiff and clumsy as I scrambled out of the pile of fir needles that had been my bed.

A noise that seemed out of place in the morning quiet made me hesitate. Part wheeze, part snort, it was coming nearer. With the noise came a strong smell. I didn't recognise it but my new nose twitched as if I should. My heart beat faster and my legs turned to liquid as icy tendrils of fear wound through them. I knew neither sound nor smell but the form I was in recognised danger regardless and every instinct within me said to flee. But I was frozen in place.

The sound came closer and closer. Then an enormous black boar lumbered out from behind a fir and headed straight towards me. I quivered at the sight of its scarred muzzle and long tusks. My startled gasp came out as a bark of sorts. The boar paused and looked around, its nostrils widening as it caught my scent. There was no time to hide. Another step closer, a snort, and then it saw me.

I scrambled out of the fir needles, paws sliding in their softness. Those few moments it took to get my grip was all the boar
needed. It lunged. A tusk grazed my shoulder. It stung and I
whimpered. I was trapped between the holly bush that had given
overnight shelter from the breeze and a large boar that thought I
smelled like breakfast. My limbs felt no stronger than thistledown
as I faced the boar. Its rank odour filled my nose. My mind was
blank. The beast stared back, nostrils flaring, still tasting my scent.
Its shoulder muscles rippled as it prepared to attack. I should
have run while I had the chance.

The boar lowered its head and charged. A tusk pierced my
shoulder. Dampness spread quickly and pain shot through me. If I
had hands, I would have clasped one over the wound to stem the
blood. But I had nothing other than small furry paws and I
needed them to run.

The boar pulled back, readied itself to attack again. Its tusk
glittered with blood. As it lowered its head, I finally found the
strength to move. But I was slow and clumsy with pain. A tusk
pierced me again, this time in the side. I screamed and it was a
strangely human sound, despite my canine mouth. I tried to run
but the boar blocked my path with its enormous body, surprisingly fast for such a heavy creature. Or perhaps it was simply
hungry.

If I couldn't run, I would have to fight. Either that, or lie down
and let the beast have me. I drew back my lips and bared my
teeth, managing a sound that was half-snarl, half-whimper. The
boar snorted, unimpressed, and lowered its head again. I flung
myself at it, somehow avoiding the huge head and deadly tusks.
My jaws closed around its ankle but the skin was tough and I was
already weak with blood loss. The boar shook me off easily. I was
flung to the ground. The world spun. Snarling hogs surrounded
me, their tusks red with my blood. *Get up, Brigit. Get up now.*

The beast leaned in to sniff me, perhaps checking whether I
still lived. Its hoof landed on my front paw, mashing it into the
leaf litter. Pain exploded through my paw and up my leg. Then

the boar had my ear in its mouth. It shook its head and my ear tore. Blood dripped down my face, obscuring my vision, and trickled into my mouth. It was warm and salty and there was a lot of it.

The boar released my ear and I staggered to my feet. I ran. Somehow, I dodged one way just as it moved the other and, unimaginably, I was suddenly behind it. *Run.* That was the only thought in my head. Run as far and as fast as I could. Behind me, the beast grunted. I felt, rather than heard, it turn. But it was large and already tiring and I had a head start. It followed briefly but soon gave up, perhaps preferring to find a meal that didn't mind being eaten quite so much.

I ran until my legs gave out and I collapsed in a heaving, bloody heap. My whole body trembled and I could hardly see for the blood dripping into my eyes. Warm foam dripped from my mouth as I gasped for breath. Everything hurt and I couldn't see enough of my body to tell how bad the wounds were. Blood pooled beneath me, seeping into the leaf litter.

I could think of nothing but the pain and for some time, all I could do was lie there, panting. But I couldn't stay. I had to move on, no matter how much it hurt. I didn't know how far I had run. Injured as I was, perhaps it wasn't far at all. The boar could still be on my trail and, if not, the woods contained other beasts who would seize the opportunity of an easy meal. I was in no condition to survive another fight.

I managed to haul myself up onto my haunches and used my uninjured front paw to wipe the blood from my eyes. I had to find the way home. Mother would aid me, even if she didn't recognise me in this body. She would never turn away a creature in need. I staggered to my feet and a wave of new pain flooded through me. My front paw, the one the boar stood on, would bear no weight and blood still ran freely from it. Surely the bone was broken. It was a wonder I had managed to run at all for now I could barely walk.

It was awkward, limping on three paws, and pain shot

through me with every jerky step. How soon would I be too weak from blood loss to move? I would keep going for as long as I could, and when I could walk no further, well, I tried not to think about that.

Blood from my torn ear continued to run down my forehead and already it dripped into my eyes again. Now I knew how the terrier in my visions had become injured. I had always wondered whether some of the blood might be mine, but I had never expected it to be this much.

19

DIARMUID

I LEFT HOME early the next morning while streaks of rose and violet still filled the sky. The air was crisp and clean, warning that nights were yet cold for the traveller sleeping out of doors. If I let myself dwell on that, I might lose what little courage I had. So, I cleared my mind and set off. One foot in front of the other.

The first village on my way was Tors. It was a little further away than Maker's Well although to the north rather than the west. My aim for this first day of travel was to get as close to Tors as possible before nightfall.

The snow was light and easy to walk through, and the brisk walk soon warmed me. The morning passed with surprising speed. By the time the sun was high overhead, I neared the edge of Silver Downs land. The woods, which I was forbidden to enter, loomed ahead of me. I intended to veer around them to where a rough path led to Tors.

Although well accustomed to spending a day walking, I did not usually wear a heavy pack and already my legs wobbled. How could I walk day after day if I was fatigued by midday? I set my pack down in the snow and ate bread and cheese while standing. A light breeze kicked up and the warmth I had felt quickly disappeared. As soon as I finished, I shouldered my pack and set off again.

The ground sloped down towards the woods. Even this far from them, I passed increasing numbers of trees as if the woods started gently here. I could not name most of the trees except for the firs, standing tall and proud, their green needles clinging in defiance of winter.

Had anyone realised I was gone yet? How long until Fiachra told them? Would someone come after me, try to stop me? Perhaps I could convince them to travel with me. I would be less afraid with company. It wouldn't be Eremon, of course, for his place was to stay at Silver Downs. And not Fiachra. He had made it clear he would not aid me unless I called him and I wasn't yet desperate enough. He hadn't explicitly said he would be breaking some sort of rule by helping me but it was implied. Sitric wouldn't leave his business but perhaps Marrec and Conn might come. Maybe I should return home, ask them to accompany me? But I would not make it home before nightfall and there was no guarantee they would agree anyway. Besides, I had less than two sevennights to complete my task and there was no time to waste. So I kept walking.

Now that I had allowed fear to creep into my mind, it was impossible not to worry. About whether the witch was Ida. How I might stop her and whether I would have to destroy her. Whether it was possible to do so without also destroying myself. Whether Caedmon had left home this morning bearing a death sentence from last night's tale. The dream in which he saw his own death had shown his body lying in a ditch, his throat slit. And that was how the soldier in my tale also met his end.

None of this would have happened if I hadn't been so careless with the tales I told. How full of hope I was with my first tale, the one about the bard and his muse. A tale had seemed like some wonderful new plaything, shiny and sparkling and full of promise. And then when my audience hated it, I fell deep into melancholy where the world seemed dimmer, its colours faded, and hope and joy were crushed like an ant beneath my boot.

How did my ability work? And why was it only the tale about Ida that had come to life? I could only pray that last night's tale hadn't also come true. My thoughts were full of *could have* and *should have*. The one thing of which I was certain was that I would never tell another tale.

I left Silver Downs land and reached the road. Although roughly made, it was still easier than walking through fields. On one side continued the same woods that edged Silver Downs. On the other was pastureland. These rolling hills would be lush with thick green grass come summer. I wondered if I would ever return to see it.

As the sun dipped closer to the horizon and the first shades of a brilliant orange sunset appeared, I searched for a suitable place to spend the night. Caedmon would say to find a spot with protection from the night wind on at least one side. There must be clearance for a fire and I should be out of sight of the road. The sound of water trickling over stones reached my ears and, without hesitation, I left the road to follow it. Proximity to fresh water, that was another thing Caedmon would look for.

I followed the sound into the woods. The stream couldn't be far away. As I ventured deeper, the firs grew more thickly and soon they blocked all but the most persistent rays of sunlight. I moved carefully, feeling my way with each step for I could see little now. I walked and walked but still the water sounded no closer.

Some small creature kept pace with me, slipping swiftly from tree to tree. I turned to look and it vanished behind a hawthorn bush. When I looked away, it glided to the next fir tree.

My heart beat faster. The creature clearly didn't want to be seen and I couldn't quite make out what it was. Small, but human in form. One of the fey?

Lost in my thoughts, I didn't notice that the sound of trickling water had disappeared. Deep in the woods and in almost total darkness, I was in danger of becoming hopelessly lost, if indeed I wasn't already. Time and again, Caedmon had warned me not to venture into unfamiliar woods. I was stupid to leave the road, stupid to follow a sound regardless of what it might promise.

I set down my pack, unhooked the small lamp hanging from the side, and fumbled for a flint. The lamp shed welcome light over my surroundings and I saw another small being perched on a nearby rock. It disappeared as soon as I looked at it. So two of them followed me, perhaps more.

"Who are you?" I called and my voice wavered only a little.

Silence greeted my words.

"I know you are there. I have seen you."

Nothing.

"What do you want?"

There was a giggle then, soft and high pitched. I waited but no further response came. Shouldering my pack and carrying the lamp by its handle, I started back towards the road. I would return to where I had entered the woods and make camp there on the very edge where I could see the road but still receive shelter from the wind.

I had walked barely a dozen paces before I stumbled into a shallow ditch masked by a mound of leaves. I landed unevenly and pain shot through my ankle. The lantern slipped from my fingers and its small flame disappeared, the oil likely spilled onto the leaves.

Another giggle.

Clutching the trunk of a nearby fir, I hauled myself to my feet. The rough bark dug into my fingers, tearing my skin. With a cautious step, I tested my ankle. The pain was immediate. I sucked in a breath and swallowed the bitter words that rose to my lips, not wanting to further amuse my invisible watchers. Clearly I would walk no further tonight. I let my pack fall to the ground. If I could not walk, I would have to make camp right here.

If the creatures shadowing me were fey of some sort, the sound I followed might have been a trick. Did they intend for me to be hurt or only to lose my way? Perhaps they aimed to delay my journey. If they knew why I travelled, surely they knew I could ill afford to linger. Hopefully I would be able to walk by morning. I could not consider any alternative. The longer I delayed, the more trouble Ida could cause. People had already died.

I could put no weight on my ankle so it was on hands and knees that I cleared space sufficient for a small fire. I used only dead branches from the ground and dry fir needles. That was another of Caedmon's rules: never take branches from a living tree. He said it was better that we go without fire for a night than hurt a tree.

I felt slightly more cheerful once a small fire was burning. I retrieved the blanket from my pack and spread it out beside the fire. Next came some rations, just enough to sustain me, and no more. I allowed myself two mouthfuls of water. My mouth was dry enough to drain the flask but my small water supply must be conserved. I cursed myself for leaving the second flask behind.

After I had eaten my meagre meal, there was nothing else to do but sleep. The air was chill, and the night would only grow colder, but at least the trees blocked all wind. I wrapped the blanket around myself and lay down, trying to find a reasonably comfortable position where I didn't have either rocks or sticks digging into me.

I had scarcely found a tolerable spot when I heard a noise. It was different to the one that had enticed me to stray from the road, a soft whimper that barely reached my ears. But it could still be another fey trick. I couldn't even defend myself for I had foolishly left my dagger in my pack rather than in my boot. How unimpressed Caedmon would be if he could see me now, lost in the woods, too injured to stand, and weaponless.

Slightly out of my reach was a stick that looked sturdy enough. If some creature came towards me, I would fling myself at the stick and hope to make it to my feet in time. I couldn't afford to think about the possibility of not being able to stand. The whimper came again, a little louder, and I relaxed somewhat for it did not sound threatening. Rather, it sounded like a creature in pain.

"Where are you?" I asked, my voice soft so as not to startle it, whatever it was.

There was no response. I eyed the stick again.

"Come out. I know you are there."

A rustle and another whimper, and then the creature crept out from behind a bush. It was a small dog, a terrier of some sort, dirty and blood-stained now, but possibly once white. Its ears were lowered and one hung oddly as if torn. The dog, barely knee high to me, limped on three paws, tail curled between its back legs. Blood dripped from the front paw held aloft and from a wound on its head. More blood smeared its flank.

"Come here," I said and held a hand out to the dog. "Let me see that paw."

It hesitated, sniffing the air.

"I won't hurt you."

As if it understood, the terrier limped forward and halted a few paces in front of me. Now that I could see it clearly, I was surprised the animal could walk at all. Blood oozed from wounds on its shoulder, flank and muzzle. The ear that hung oddly was ripped half off and blood still trickled down the side of its face. The bleeding paw, though, was my immediate concern. Surely a creature of this size could ill afford much blood loss.

Slowly, so as not to spook the terrier, I reached for my pack. Black eyes fixed on me as the terrier sat, still holding up its injured paw. I fumbled in my pack and my fingers found the roll of bandage I had forgotten about. I would have strapped my ankle had I remembered, but the terrier needed it more than I did. I drew out the bandage and my flask.

"I'm going to wash some of the blood off," I said softly, hoping the terrier would understand I intended aid. "And then I need to wrap your paw. The bleeding won't stop otherwise."

It continued to stare at me, eyes large and unblinking. I

reached out, ready to quickly pull away if it tried to bite, and would have sworn the terrier extended its paw and placed it right in my hand. I poured a little water over the paw. As the blood was washed away, I saw a deep cut surrounded by swollen, bruised skin.

"This is going to hurt," I warned. "I'm sorry."

The gaze from those big black eyes remained fastened on my face. I wrapped the paw firmly, still half expecting to be bitten. The terrier sat quietly, paw extended stiffly, and only whimpered once. I cut the bandage with my dagger and tied the end. The terrier continued to sit there, its paw now held out awkwardly to one side. Those eyes were disconcerting, the way they were fixed so intently on my face.

I eyed the wounds on its shoulder, side and ear. I couldn't clean them for it would take the rest of my water. I wrapped the remaining bandage around the terrier's stomach, covering the wound on its flank and using my spare socks for padding. The shoulder wound was probably shallow for it was already crusted over. Blood was starting to clot on the ripped ear also.

"I would wash off more of the blood but we need to save the water. I can spare a little for you to drink though."

I had nothing that could serve as a bowl, so I poured some water into my cupped hand. The terrier leaned forward and drank eagerly, tongue lapping at my palm. It looked up at me expectantly when the water was gone. I poured another handful and it drank that down too. When it eyed me again, I shook my head.

"I'm sorry, we have to save the rest."

It stood then and limped, still on three legs, over to a fir, where it squatted and urinated.

"Oh, you're a girl."

The terrier hobbled back and stood in front of me, bandaged paw still held up. I patted the blanket. The terrier would be company, if nothing else, and likely wouldn't live through the night anyway.

"You may as well sit down. You won't get far with that paw."

She sniffed at me but whether it was intended as a thank you or in derision, I couldn't tell. She circled several times, awkwardly and with a whimper, before curling up with the bandaged paw still held aloft.

I fished within my pack for a strip of dried meat, broke it into small pieces and laid them in front of her on the blanket.

"Like I said, we have to conserve the rations. But there's enough for you to have a little tonight."

I lay down as near to the fire as I thought was safe. She ate the meat and then edged closer until she lay with her back curled into the curve of my legs. Her shivers vibrated through my body. I wrapped the blanket around us both. Her body was cold against me but she soon began to warm.

Staring into the flames as I waited for sleep to claim me, I didn't feel quite as bad as I had earlier. I had food in my belly, albeit not much, and with the terrier snuggled up to me, I was comfortably warm. Fiachra had said I would have companions on this journey. Perhaps the injured terrier was the first.

She was still curled up against me when I woke. I had no sense of time here in depths of the woods. Sparse sunlight filtered in through the firs but it could be dawn or midday for all I could tell. I only knew I had slept long enough for the fire to burn out. I didn't want to disturb the terrier, but as she slept on, I became increasingly aware of my bladder. Eventually, I had to move. I tried to sit up silently but she stirred as soon as I shifted. The look on her face said she had no idea where she was.

"It's all right. You're safe. You can stay there but I need to get up."

She stretched and stood gingerly, whimpering as her injured paw touched the ground. Blood had soaked through the bandage during the night but not as much as I might have expected. She hobbled stiffly over to a fir and crouched by it to relieve herself.

I hauled myself to my feet, feeling less than limber. I could put barely any weight on my sprained ankle. I would be staying here for at least today. I managed to half-hop, half-stumble some distance from the blanket and kept my back firmly to the terrier, oddly embarrassed at the thought of her watching. The necessities done, I hobbled back to the blanket. The terrier sat there, licking her bandaged paw.

"You shouldn't lick that," I said. "It won't heal unless you leave it alone."

She looked up at me, unblinking.

"Let's have some breakfast and then I'll change the bandage on that paw. How does that sound?"

Another unblinking stare.

I tore my gaze away from her and rummaged in the pack. "We have bread, cheese, dried meat."

She studied the strip of dried meat in my hand. I tore it into pieces for her and then took the remains of yesterday's loaf and a small wedge of cheese for myself. The terrier gulped down the meat and then watched as I ate. I offered some of my bread but she merely sniffed it and then stared at the cheese in my hand.

"You can't have the cheese," I told her. "You already had the meat. You can have some bread but the cheese is mine."

Still she stared and eventually I gave her half, albeit reluctantly. She ate the cheese in two swallows and then seemed satisfied.

Having finished my meal, I allowed myself two mouthfuls of water and then offered the terrier some in my cupped palm. She drank thirstily and I pretended not to notice when she looked beseechingly at me for more. The flask was more than two thirds empty already.

With breakfast finished, I rummaged in the pack for a makeshift bandage. All I had were my two spare shirts. I sliced one into strips with my dagger, then reached for the terrier.

"Will you hold still for me?"

She sat stiffly as I unwound the bandage. Dried blood glued it to her paw and I hesitantly peeled it away, still expecting her to bite. The wound was crusted with blood and I was reluctant to wash it in case the bleeding started again. I couldn't spare any more water anyway. I wrapped her paw with the strips from my shirt and tossed the bloodied bandage into the fire's dead coals.

With the remnants of my ruined shirt, I strapped my ankle. It was swollen, tender to touch and the skin felt hot. Surely by tomorrow the swelling would be reduced. I would be able to walk then. I had to.

I crawled around on my hands and knees to gather more fallen branches and soon a merry blaze warmed us. With nothing else to do, the day passed with agonising slowness. I dozed from time to time but mostly I just lay staring up into the canopy and trying not to think about the mess I was in or how I would find Ida, let alone destroy her, or what it meant about my own nature that I had created such evil. The terrier was quiet and still and seemed to sleep most of the day. I hoped she was healing for there was little else I could do to help her.

As the woods around us finally grew darker again, we shared another meagre meal. Then we curled up together with the blanket wrapped around us. She went to back to sleep almost immediately and her paws twitched as she dreamed.

I lay there for a long time, staring into the flames. The night woods around us were still and silent. I had seen no sign of the two small creatures that had led me from my path. Surely, if they still watched, they could see I needed help. *We* needed help.

This was not exactly the journey I had imagined.

20

DIARMUID

I N THE EARLY hours of the night, the rain started. It seeped through my blanket and into my clothes. Very soon, I was soaked through, shivering even as I clutched the sopping blanket around me. The fire sputtered and died. The terrier lay motionless, curled up with her nose tucked into her tail. Water dripped from her hair and soaked the makeshift bandages.

The night was painfully long and there were times I believed we would both die of the cold long before morning ever came. My shivers became shuddering waves that crashed over my body and I could no longer feel my hands or toes. I drew the terrier to my chest and wrapped my arms around her, seeking some warmth from her cold body even as I hoped to warm her with mine.

When at last the rain eased and the light filtering in through the firs brightened, I nudged the terrier aside and sat up. I unwrapped the soaked bandage around my ankle, my fingers clumsy and unfeeling. My ankle was still swollen and tender but perhaps not quite as much.

Although the rain had ceased, I was no warmer and every part of my body ached. When I hauled myself to my feet and tested my ankle, the pain was immense. I gritted my teeth and sucked in a breath. I could bear a little weight on the ankle but not much.

Perhaps with the aid of a crutch of some sort I could make my way out of the woods. I only had to get as far as the road and then I could wait for someone to pass by. What other choice did I have? Nobody would happen on me if I stayed here, and once Fiachra explained my absence, it was unlikely anyone would come looking for me. Even if they did — if perhaps Marrec and Conn came — they wouldn't think to search for me in the woods. My only chance of rescue was to reach the road.

The terrier sat up and stretched, looking even more stiff and sorry for herself than I felt.

"I can hardly leave you here, can I?" I said.

She looked up at me quizzically.

"It's not like you can fend for yourself in that condition. Do you think you can keep up if I take you with me?"

The look she gave me was full of indignation and I hastily added, "That is, if you want to."

She sniffed and looked away.

"I'm in no better condition, I guess. Perhaps with the two of us together, we can make it back to the road."

She eyed me again, considering.

"Once we reach the road, we can decide what to do next."

She sniffed, perhaps in agreement.

The remaining rations were scant and wet. One small loaf of bread, now soggy and beyond edible, a small piece of cheese, four strips of dried meat. I tossed the bread into the fire pit, then took half the cheese and a strip of meat for myself and gave the terrier a piece of meat. She wolfed it and then watched as I packed the rest away.

"No more," I said firmly. "We'll need it tonight."

I had brought provisions for but one stomach and only two days, expecting to restock my supplies in Tors. Unless we found help today, tomorrow would be hungry. We each drank a few mouthfuls of water and then there was nothing left to do but wring out the soggy blanket and stow it away in my pack.

I found a reasonably straight length of branch to serve as a crutch. The terrier would have to cope on her own and either keep up or… I refused to think past that.

"We have to stick together." I used the crutch to haul myself to my feet, then hitched the pack over my shoulders. "Nice and slow, no faster than either of us can cope with, all right?"

She gave me a look that clearly said she could keep up with anything I could manage.

Our progress was painfully slow and after barely two dozen paces, both the terrier and I were panting. We had only passed maybe five firs in that distance. Each jarring step sent pain stabbing through my ankle. My wet clothes clung to my body uncomfortably.

I paused to rest briefly, leaning on the makeshift crutch. The terrier sat, head drooping. Her breathing was unsteady. I counted to twenty and we set off once more.

"You need a name," I said when we stopped to rest yet again. Count to twenty. Move on.

Her ears twitched but she didn't look at me. Her head hung even lower now and she barely seemed to have the strength to hold herself up.

Beneath the blood, her coat was perhaps white.

"Snowball?" I suggested.

A slight flick of an ear was her only reaction.

"Not Snowball. What else is white?" Another few steps before I could speak again. "Clouds. Ribbons. Owls. Owl?"

She deigned to sniff at me.

"Rabbit? Bunny?"

Not even a sniff this time. I halted and the terrier immediately sat in the leaf litter. Her head drooped and white foam dripped from her mouth. Was this where she would refuse to walk any further? I counted to twenty and then heaved off again. With a grunt, she followed.

"What about white flowers? Foxglove, Snowdrop, Bluebell. Bramble."

Her ears twitched and she finally looked up at me, big eyes even wider with pain and heavy with exhaustion.

"Bramble? You like that?"

She sniffed, a different sound from the one she used for derision.

"Bramble it is."

I had no more breath left to talk and I needed all of my strength to keep moving anyway. We only had to get to the road. We couldn't possibly continue past that, even though the road would be far easier than the woods where every step involved lifting the foot over branch or mossy stone, often to land in a slippery patch of leaves and slide before I could catch my balance again. But we would be all right if we could get to the road. Someone would come along sooner or later. Bramble and I would wait.

Again and again, I walked until I could go no further. I stopped to rest for a count of twenty. Each time, Bramble and I both somehow found the strength to move on again. The woods around us were full of the rustling of animals snuffling around in the fallen leaves and the calls of woodlarks. A raven swooped past my head, too intent on whatever business it followed to even notice me. I tried to watch for the strange creatures that had led me here but it was all I could do to stay standing.

Step by step, panting and exhausted. My thoughts started to wander. I was confused. Again and again, I suddenly realised I was staggering through the woods and, for a few moments, I wondered why I hurt so much. Several times I stopped and threw down the branch that served as my crutch, preparing to lie down and rest before I remembered. I had to get to the road. If I lay down, I might never get up again. Somehow, I awkwardly retrieved the crutch from the ground and we moved on.

The light filtering in through the firs was softer now. The day was slipping away and my spirits sank even lower. It was likely that neither Bramble nor I would survive another night in the woods. Right when I began to lose all hope, the light ahead brightened.

"I think we're almost at the road."

I would have run that last hundred paces but it was all I could do to limp along, leaning heavily on the crutch with each step. My fingers were blistered from the rough wood but I could barely stand without the crutch, let along walk.

Twice more I forgot what I was doing but each time I saw the light ahead and remembered. Bramble could barely lift her paws but somehow she too kept going.

Then, abruptly, we were out of the woods. One moment it seemed the firs extended forever, and then suddenly sunlight burnt my eyes, even though the sun sat a mere finger's width above the horizon. There was little time left until sunset. As we stood at the edge of the woods, blinking in the sudden brightness, a voice boomed.

"Hello there, friend. Lucky you came out when you did. If you were a few moments later, I would have gone and missed you."

My eyes adjusted and I could finally focus on the speaker. He sat atop a wooden cart hooked up to a pair of large, black oxen. When he stood, I realised he was possibly the biggest man I had ever seen. Tall and wide-shouldered, he looked like he could easily drag the cart himself if the oxen tired. He climbed down, moving more gracefully than I would have expected for one his size.

"Oh my," he said as he drew closer to us. "You look right dreadful." His gaze drifted down to Bramble. "Both of you."

I opened my mouth but no reply came out. Suddenly my head spun, I felt sick to my stomach and my legs would no longer hold me. As I fell, the man scooped me up in his arms.

"Now there," he said. "You need some rest. I'm going to put you in my cart."

"Bramble," I said, my voice weak. I moved my mouth but nothing else came out.

"That's your dog, is it?" He gave me a small, sad smile. "Pretty name, that. Bramble. Had a friend with a daughter called Bramble once."

As if I weighed no more than a child, he deposited me into the cart. Bramble was swiftly placed beside me and she leaned weakly against my leg. The man frowned as he inspected the blood-soaked bandages on her paw and side.

"That don't look good. Needs a clean and some proper bandaging."

He looked us both over again.

"I was heading home anyway. You can stay a few days. Rest up."

I would have cried if I'd had the energy.

The cart shook as the man swung himself back up into the front seat. He clicked at the oxen and we set off with a jolt.

"I'm Owain, by the way," he called over his shoulder. "My missus would say I shoulda told you that afore anything else. Owain, you big oaf, she'd say, you need to learn some manners."

I couldn't reply. I lay back on the bare wooden floor of the cart, staring up into a grey sky heavy with clouds. It would rain again tonight. And we would be sleeping under a roof.

Beside me, Bramble breathed so shallowly I wondered whether she was still conscious. I tried to raise a hand to touch her but couldn't so much as twitch a finger. Strangely, I no longer hurt. Perhaps I slept, or lost consciousness, for I knew nothing else until Owain was lifting Bramble out of the cart. The little terrier lay limply in his arms and I vaguely wondered whether she was dead. It seemed I should feel something if she was but I couldn't quite figure out what.

"I'll come back for you," Owain said to me and disappeared, taking Bramble with him.

I waited, drifting, neither entirely conscious nor unconscious, until I heard Owain return. I managed to turn my head towards him and fancied I saw a half-naked man run out from behind the house. He had a long nose and tousled hair and wore only a shirt. His bare behind shone in the late afternoon sunlight as he darted across the yard and behind the barn. Owain's back was to the man and it seemed he waited a few moments longer than necessary before lifting me from the cart.

"A man—" I started.

"Ssh," Owain said and his jaw was clenched. "You need to rest."

"But—"

"Save your strength."

The following hours were a blur. I lay in a bed which was blissfully soft after two nights on the ground. Someone undressed me, bathed me, applied a warm poultice to my ankle and then strapped it firmly. Warm, dry blankets were piled on top of me. My head was held up and a meaty broth spooned into my mouth. I gulped greedily and it spilled down my chin to be efficiently wiped up. My stomach rumbled as my head was laid back down on the pillow.

"More," I mumbled.

"Later," a voice said. "It will make you sick if you eat too much too soon."

Then I was alone. I drifted hazily. I was warm and clean, had food in my belly, and my ankle burned pleasantly from the poultice. The bedchamber smelled of healing herbs, possibly from the poultice or maybe someone had thrown them on the fire. An oil lantern on the dresser kept the darkness at bay.

I tried to roll over and found I was not alone. Bramble lay beside me, curled up in a tight ball. She too had been bathed and her hair was snow-white. Her injured paw stuck out stiffly, neatly wrapped in a clean, white bandage. Other bandages covered the wounds on her shoulder, flank and ear.

"I told you we would make it if we stuck together," I said but the words seemed to melt in my mouth and what came out was unintelligible.

Bramble opened one dark eye to stare at me then sniffed and went back to sleep. I laid a hand gently against her back, finding comfort in the warm body beside me. Then I too slept.

WHEN I NEXT woke, my head was clear and the pain in my ankle had subsided to a dull ache. My stomach rumbled with hunger and my tongue felt fat and furry.

I lay on a wide bed, starched white covers tucked firmly around me, the fabric smooth and fine beneath my fingers. The patch of warmth by my hip was Bramble. A plump, stuffed chair was drawn up to a hearth containing neatly raked coals. A wooden dresser bearing jug and basin stood beneath a window. Someone had opened the curtains since I last woke but all I could see was a patch of leaden sky. This must be Owain's home but I had no idea where it was or how far we had travelled in the cart.

A woman entered my bedchamber. She was perhaps a five or six summers older than me. Her dark hair was neatly tied back and her work dress was immaculate. She looked me over, her gaze critical.

"You are awake." Her voice held no warmth. "How do you feel?"

"Hungry."

She laid a cool hand against my forehead. "The fever has broken at last."

"I had a fever?"

Her eyes narrowed. "You were very ill. Don't you remember?"

"I thought I was just hungry."

Her forehead wrinkled and she pursed her lips. Obviously I had said something incredibly stupid.

"I will apply another poultice to your ankle and strap it again. Then you may see if you can get up. If you can make your way to the dinner table, it will be far less trouble for me."

The doorway darkened and Owain entered. His plain face broke into a smile.

"Hello," he said. "How do you feel?"

"The fever has broken and he's hungry," the woman snapped.

Owain's face briefly registered hurt although his eyes said clearly he worshipped this woman.

I finally remembered that I had passed out without introducing myself to Owain. "My name is Diarmuid."

The woman frowned at me again. "So it would seem."

"This is my Maeve, my wife," Owain said quickly. "She has been caring for you."

"And it's not like I didn't already have enough to do, is it?" Maeve had a glare each for Owain and I. "Between keeping the household running and you trying to get me with child, I don't have time to spare as it is. And then you bring home a half-dead stranger and his dog and expect me to nurse them."

Owain flushed. "They needed help. Couldn't leave them on the side of the road."

"I don't see why not. They weren't your responsibility."

Owain hung his head and looked away.

"Can I have some water?" I asked, an awkward witness to their argument.

Maeve filled a mug from the jug on the dresser. She stared up at the ceiling as she held it out and I fumbled to take it from her. Owain came to my rescue, taking the mug in his big hands and holding it gently to my mouth. Water ran down my chin as I gulped. He didn't comment, only wiped my face with a towel. Maeve was gone by the time I had drunk my fill.

"Let's get you up and see how you feel." Owain helped me to stand. He guided me across the room towards the window, his strong arm a sturdy anchor around my waist. "A few steps, no more, eh."

With the first step, I realised how weak I was. My knees buckled and my legs shook and it was only Owain's strong arms that kept me standing. My ankle was still tender but I could put some weight on it with Owain's support. I barely managed six steps before I could go no further, panting from the effort of even so little. My heart sank. It would be some days yet before I resumed my journey and the dark of the moon drew closer with every night I delayed.

"Bed now," he said and carried me back. "You should rest. I'll come get you at dinner time."

Then it was Bramble's turn. Owain held a small wooden bowl up to her mouth and she lapped thirstily. He gently stroked her hip, well away from her injuries, and she looked up at him with an expression of gratitude. It seemed even she knew how close we had both come to death. When Owain left, Bramble and I curled up together again and I drifted back to sleep.

The bedchamber was darker when I next woke. My mouth was dry again and my stomach grumbled loudly. My head was clearer and for a few moments, I thought perhaps we could resume our journey on the morrow. That hope was dashed when I tried to get out of bed for I was still too weak to do any more than sit up alone.

When Owain returned, he smiled broadly and I couldn't help but smile back. There was something about him that made me like him very much. More than that, I trusted him.

"Are you hungry?" he asked.

Before I could respond, Bramble hauled herself up with a bark.

Owain laughed. "Well then, Bramble. Let's take you downstairs for dinner." He lifted her, his large hands careful to avoid her injuries. "I'll be back for you in a moment," he said over his shoulder.

When he returned, Owain scooped me up, lifting me as easily as he had Bramble.

"Don't want to do too much yet," he muttered. "Best that you rest."

"I have to continue on my journey."

"In a few days."

He carried me down to the dining room and deposited me on a wide, stuffed chair. The furniture was solid and elegantly carved and the walls were draped with fine embroideries. I had taken Owain for a simple farmer but clearly he was something more. Bramble nestled in a thickly-padded basket beside my chair. Her eyes were bright and alert. The scent of roasted meat and fresh bread wafted in from the kitchen and my stomach growled so hard it hurt.

"What occupation do you have, Owain?" I leaned down to stroke Bramble's head. She leaned into my hand.

"Oh, this and that." He busied himself with settling into a chair across the table from me.

Maeve bustled in with a platter before I could ask further and dropped it onto the table with what seemed like unnecessary force.

"Good evening, Maeve," I said. "Thank you for looking after us."

She huffed and straightened the platter. "It's not like I don't already have enough to do."

Owain cleared his throat apologetically.

"We really appreciate it," I said. "I don't know what would have become of us if Owain hadn't come along when he did. We couldn't have made it much further."

"You were almost dead when I found you," Owain said cheerfully. "Wouldn't have lasted another night. Either of you," he added with a glance towards Bramble.

She flicked an ear at him and held his gaze.

"Thank you, Owain," I said. "And I'm sure Bramble would thank you also if she could talk."

"Oh she talks in her own way." He dragged his gaze away from Bramble.

Maeve's scowl didn't budge as we ate. Owain said little but every word irritated her and when she spoke, it was usually to remind him how much more difficult her life was with him in it. Owain tolerated her criticisms with gentle shrugs.

The meal was lavish and I ate with gusto. Roasted hen, winter root vegetables, rich gravy. Thick slices of brown bread. A sweet honey that reminded me, with a pang of homesickness, of Silver Downs. Bramble ate from a bowl of choice selections of chicken and vegetables. Owain must have filled the bowl himself. I couldn't imagine Maeve going to that effort.

Maeve barely ate but merely picked at a piece of chicken and then reduced a slice of bread to crumbs on her plate. I would have felt uncomfortable about eating so much when she had so little if it weren't for Owain who had second and then third helpings of everything.

"Thank you for your hospitality," I said to Maeve. "I hope I won't have to intrude on you for much longer."

Maeve looked up briefly from the growing pile of crumbs. "I suppose you can stay another day or two."

"Nonsense, Diarmuid," Owain said. "It'll be at least a seven-night before you are well enough to leave."

Maeve glared across the table at him. He lowered his gaze but didn't retract his words.

"I'll wait until morning before I make any decisions," I said. "But I'm sure I'll feel much better by then."

Maeve rose abruptly and left. Her voice came from the kitchen although I couldn't make out what she said. Directing the servants, perhaps. Owain pushed back his chair, scooped up Bramble's basket in one arm and helped me to rise with the other. I leaned heavily on him as we went into the next room where a small fire blazed with a merriness it alone seemed to feel. I sank down into an oversized chair, its thick padding cushioning my body comfortably. My legs trembled from the short walk and my ankle throbbed.

Owain positioned Bramble's basket close by his chair where she would feel the fire's warmth and then sat down with a sigh. Bramble stretched out and rested her chin on her paws. Dishes clattered loudly from the direction of the kitchen. Someone was taking their feelings out on the crockery.

"I'm sorry if Bramble and I being here is causing problems for you," I said.

Owain shrugged. "She's always like this. Doesn't like me much, I'm afraid."

"Then why did she handfast with you?" I regretted my rudeness the instant the words left my mouth but Owain didn't seem bothered.

"I made her father a generous offer. She preferred someone else."

"She resents you."

"Thought she'd come around. See I wasn't so bad. But it's been three summers. She still hates me and we still have no heir." He stared silently into the fire for a while. "Not much I can do. And it's not a bad life we have. I know I'm a simple man but I do all right. We have everything we need."

I looked around the room, which was generously appointed with heavy wooden cabinets, plush chairs and thick rugs. Dark drapes covered the windows, keeping out the early spring evening's chill. It was clear Owain did better than all right.

"I'm sure I won't need to stay a sevennight," I said. "A day, maybe two, and I'll be well again. I can't afford to delay any longer."

"Can't rush these things. And there's Bramble too."

We both looked down at the little terrier curled up in the basket. She gazed up at us, her eyes already drooping.

"She might not be well enough to come with me." The words hurt but I had to do what was best for Bramble, not for myself.

"She lost a lot of blood and it's going to be a while before she can walk properly."

Owain nodded and returned his gaze to the fire.

"Would you... Could I... That is, if she can't come with me, can she stay with you?" I finished in a rush, wishing I had found a more elegant way to say it.

"Sure." Owain spared Bramble another quick glance. "If she wants. Mayhap though she wants to stick with you."

I looked down at Bramble to find her sitting up and glaring at me. Curiously, she appeared to have taken offence at my request. How much of our conversation had she understood? Surely it wasn't possible for a dog to recognise more than a few words. Come, sit, eat. But still, the look she gave made me want to hang my head in shame.

"I'm not saying I want to leave her behind," I said quickly.

Owain mumbled something that might have been agreement. We sat in silence after that, each occupied with his own thoughts, and I noticed he dropped a hand down to stroke Bramble gently on the head.

Bramble no longer seemed sleepy. Although she lay down again, she continued to glare at me. I kept my gaze firmly on the raven in the fire and pretended I didn't see the hurt in Bramble's eyes.

DIARMUID

I WAS PITIFULLY weak from my illness but each day I grew a little stronger and my ankle a little more sound. I passed my recovery time mostly lying in bed, talking to Bramble, and worrying about how many nights remained until the next full moon. I didn't see much of Owain after breakfast each day but every evening he came to carry Bramble and I downstairs for dinner. After we had eaten, the three of us would laze in front of the fire. Maeve always absented herself after the evening meal and I wouldn't see her again until breakfast.

"Didn't expect her to make it," Owain said one evening, referring to Bramble who was sprawled on his lap, head draped over his knee, seemingly asleep. "Didn't expect either of you to make it actually."

"She's tougher than she looks," I said.

Bramble opened one eye to glare at me.

"I don't thinks she likes me much," I added with something of a laugh. Bramble might glare and huff at me but every night she slept curled in a warm ball against my side.

"Her wounds were festering." Owain stroked Bramble's back with a gentleness unexpected in one so large.

"I didn't realise." Guilt filled me. If only I hadn't rationed the water. If only I had cleaned her wounds more thoroughly. Perhaps they wouldn't have become infected if I had looked after her properly.

"Her ear won't heal right." Owain's hand touched the bandaged ear ever so gently. "There's a piece missing. Maeve stitched it best she could."

"At least she's alive. I wonder what happened to her before she found me."

"Boar."

I looked at Bramble with new respect. "She's so small. I can't imagine how she could fight a boar and survive."

Bramble huffed although she didn't deign to open her eyes. She didn't have to. I already knew the sound was directed at me. I could hardly reconcile the white terrier curled up on Owain's lap with the blood-soaked creature who had first slunk towards me in the woods. Her injured paw was still bandaged. The bones weren't broken but the paw was badly bruised and the large gash from which so much blood had oozed was healing slowly. She still refused to put any weight on that paw but she moved around easily enough on three legs. Her other wounds — ear and shoulder and flank — were still red and inflamed.

There was time yet for Bramble to heal though for I was still weak and tired easily. I ate everything Maeve put in front of me and often, with Owain's insistence, had seconds, but still my clothes hung more loosely than before and my face, when I caught a glimpse of it in the wash bowl, was gaunt and haggard.

I relaxed into the comfortable chair, basking in the fire's warmth, and tried not to notice the raven flickering in its depths. Fatigue crept through my body, leaving my limbs heavy. Soon I was yawning enough for Owain to decide it was time we all retired. He banked down the fire and we headed upstairs.

As Bramble and I lay in bed, thick blankets pulled up over both of us, the sounds of an argument between Owain and Maeve reached my ears. Were they arguing about us? Maeve made it clear at every opportunity that our presence was an inconvenience. I would have probably left by now, even as weak as I was, if not for Owain's quiet insistence that we stay. He and Maeve had a strange relationship. She clearly disdained him. He suffered her harsh words with nothing more than a resigned shrug and an occasional sigh. Bramble shifted beside me and I wrapped an arm around her.

"I wish I knew what they were saying," I murmured. "I bet you can hear every word."

She draped her head across my arm. The stiff hairs on her chin tickled my skin.

"Are you comfortable? I hope your wounds aren't bothering you too much."

A soft sound, almost a sigh.

"Do you think I can do this, Bramble? If the witch is Ida, do you think I can find her? Do you think I can really destroy her?"

Bramble stirred. She was listening.

"I wonder sometimes. I don't know whether I'm strong enough. I have no idea what I'm doing or how to destroy her. I only know I have to do it or... or die trying."

It was the first time I had dared voice this thought. Perhaps Ida would hold the same power over me that she had over the villagers of Crow's Nest. What if I abandoned my quest merely because she told me to? What if she forced me to do awful things? Or if she killed me?

"I wish I knew what she was doing," I whispered. "We've been here too long. More than a sevennight. The closer the dark of the moon comes... I'm scared, Bramble. I feel so alone. I know this is my fault and I have to be the one to fix it, but still..."

She huffed at me.

"Yes, I know you're here. But it would be nice to have someone I could talk to."

Another huff and then she disentangled herself from my arm and rose. She wiggled out from under the covers, moved to the end of the bed and lay down again, her back to me. I had left the curtains open and her white hair shone in the moonlight that peeked through the window.

"Don't be like that."

No response.

"Bramble, please."

A huff.

With a sigh, I sat up and reached for her, nestling her once again under the covers and in the crook of my arm.

"I'm thankful to have you. I don't know what I'd do if I was all alone."

I prattled to her for a while, telling her how lovely she looked with her shiny white coat and her big unblinking eyes. Likely she didn't understand anything I said but it soothed me if nothing else. Eventually the stiffness left her body, she draped her head over my arm again, and I knew I was forgiven.

My words tapered off and I closed my eyes. How would I ever sleep alone again? Perhaps I wouldn't have to. Perhaps Bramble would be well enough to come with me, and we would somehow defeat Ida, and then we could go home together to Silver Downs.

I drifted off to sleep with my mind full of Bramble running across the grassy fields at home, sitting beside me as I created my tales, and curling up next to me in bed every night.

23

IDA

HE COMES. I feel it, in my bones, in my blood, in every breath I take. He and I, we are one, even if he doesn't know it. So now he comes and I understand his intent: to destroy me.

At first, he drew closer, slowly but steadily. Now his journey has halted. Nonetheless, he will come to me eventually.

I know he intends to destroy me but that confounds me. He created me. Everything I am is because of him. Everything I know came from his mind, all I know of the world is from his tales. And the tales tell me the world is a dark and dangerous place. It is full of terror and evil and despair.

I want… something more. I cannot express it, this vague longing inside of me. The tales do not hold any explanation of this. I only know there is something *more*.

Until I discover what the *more* is, I have made myself a home of sorts. I have a house at any rate, in a village. His tales taught me much about evil. Wherever evil exists, it must be rooted out and destroyed. The people here fear me, I see that. If only they knew I am trying to help them, to save their village. Our village. For I am living by his tales. I am cleansing the village. Evil by evil,

I am removing those who contaminate this place. Those who have darkness in their hearts, those who have secrets. Those who long for something else.

24

BRIGIT

WE STAYED AT Owain's for nine nights before Diarmuid was ready to continue his journey. Even then, Owain urged him to stay one last night. *For Bramble's sake*, he said.

I was glad for the reprieve, for my paw was tender and walking was still painful. Not that I could have told Diarmuid. He, as a bard, should have seen there was more to me than four paws and a tail. I had been trying to communicate, to show him I was no normal dog, but he wouldn't listen. Instead, it was Owain who noticed.

As he carried me upstairs that last evening, while Diarmuid followed slowly behind, Owain stared into my eyes.

"You're more than you seem," he said, quietly.

I held his gaze, unblinking, but he said nothing further, only deposited me on the bed. Diarmuid, when he arrived, was breathing a little too heavily. He wasn't yet as recovered as he believed. Owain left and Diarmuid and I curled up together in the bed, the blankets draped over us up to our necks. Diarmuid wrapped an arm around me and I sighed, contented.

"We have to move on tomorrow, Bramble," he said.

How strange that Diarmuid had chosen such a name for me.

My father used to call me Bramble as a child. He often said I was as stubborn as a bramble bush.

"I wish I knew what was happening in Crow's Nest," Diarmuid said. "I don't even know whether Ida is still there. What if she's moved on? How will I find her?"

I growled softly, requesting that he shut up and let me sleep. He talked for some time, repeating himself endlessly. I ignored him as best I could until I heard my name.

"What am I going to do about you, Bramble?"

I flicked an ear at him.

"I can hardly take you with me while you're injured. Perhaps I should leave you here with Owain. He would take good care of you."

I lifted my head to glare at him. Did he really think it would be his decision whether or not I travelled with him? Had I been able to speak, I couldn't have said exactly why it seemed so important I go with Diarmuid. I simply knew I must. How I would cope with the endless hours of walking as we travelled to Crow's Nest, I didn't know. I would endure it because I had to.

Diarmuid didn't notice my indignation. One hand absently stroked my back and, reluctantly, I allowed the motion to soothe me. I dropped my head down onto my paws and squeezed my eyes shut. Perhaps if I tried really hard, I could fall asleep and leave him to talk to himself. He continued to speak and I let the words wash over me. It was the catch in his voice that finally caught my attention again.

"I'd never forgive myself if I took you with me and something happened to you. What if I get killed? Who would look after you?"

You great idiot. It will likely be me looking after you.

He continued to talk and I continued to try to ignore him. Finally, he was silent and I was able to work on falling asleep in earnest. As I was drifting off, Owain and Maeve's raised voices drew me back to wakefulness. They bickered constantly. Or rather Maeve bickered constantly and Owain mostly let her have her say.

Then he would hang his head and walk away. I had never heard him snap back.

But tonight it wasn't only Maeve I heard, but also Owain, his low voice a stark comparison to her shrillness. Whatever the argument was about, and I had an awful feeling it was probably Diarmuid and I, Owain was not giving up. Eventually a door slammed and the house was silent. Diarmuid said nothing for a change, but he held me a little tighter.

I woke with the sun and waited in bed while Diarmuid washed and dressed. It wasn't until he was ready to go downstairs that I stood and stretched, extending each leg as far as it would go, rejoicing in the new strength in my muscles.

Diarmuid lifted me down from the bed for my wounded paw could not yet handle a jump. The twisted scars on my shoulder and side were bright and vicious but they were healing and felt less tight every day. Owain had said my ear was permanently damaged but I had no way of viewing it. I didn't allow my mind to drift to whether I might retain any injuries when I was finally restored to my own form. No point in worrying about the future while I had the present to deal with.

Maeve was nowhere to be seen and today there was none of the thick porridge she usually served. Diarmuid and Owain ate slices of yesterday's bread slathered with summer berry preserves. Owain placed a bowl of last night's mutton in my basket by Diarmuid's chair. I also received a soft stroke on the shoulder and in return I briefly pressed my nose against his hand. I met his gaze, trying to express thankfulness for all he had done for us. He nodded solemnly.

Little talk passed between Diarmuid and Owain as they ate. I chewed my mutton slowly. I was sorry to be leaving Owain for I had become fond of the large, gentle man. But if I must choose between him and Diarmuid, it was clear where I belonged. Diarmuid might be a clueless idiot but we had been brought together for a reason. *You will leave here and set out on a journey,* the fey girl had said. She never did say why or to where I journeyed but it didn't matter anymore. It seemed she had achieved her aim for here I was, breakfasting in a house far from my own home with two people who were strangers to me ten nights ago. For surely this was the journey she had intended. How else could I have found Diarmuid in the vast expanse of the woods if the fey hadn't guided my steps towards him? He had been waiting for me, whether he knew it or not. Were his own injuries also a result of the fey's meddling?

Diarmuid's journey was a strange one. I had pieced it together, bit by bit, from the confessions he whispered late at night. He was a bard, he had made no secret of that. What he hadn't told Owain was that he had imagined a muse — a woman he pretended whispered his tales to him — and had somehow brought her to life. She had escaped and was doing… something bad. He hadn't said what but his journey was to find her and stop whatever it was. And he believed he had only until the new moon to complete his quest.

A new moon was a powerful time. What would happen when it arrived? If I were to guess, I'd say that this creature he had created would become even more powerful. I didn't know what Diarmuid intended to do when we arrived at Crow's Nest. Obviously he meant to stop her, but how?

As the daughter of a wise woman, I had seen enough of the world's mysteries that I didn't doubt his claim of what he had done. It was a curious ability and, truth be told, it scared me. Could he bring to life other images from his mind? What other power might he possess? I wasn't yet sure whether I should fear him but I knew I should be wary. I certainly shouldn't trust him.

25

BRIGIT

AFTER WE HAD eaten, Diarmuid went upstairs to collect his pack. I waited in my basket, figuring I may as well enjoy the last few minutes of comfort I was likely to have for a while. To my surprise, Owain picked me up, basket and all.

"Might as well take you outside," he muttered and carried me out to where his two huge oxen stood, hitched to the cart that had brought us here ten nights ago. The beasts blew nostrils of steam in the crisp air. The cart already contained several large bundles wrapped in oilcloth with a pile of folded blankets on top. Owain stowed my basket securely between the packages. He tucked a soft blanket around me and I gratefully nestled into it with only my eyes and nose poking out.

The cart shuddered as Owain hauled himself into the front. The oxen snorted, eager to be off. I could see little other than the blue sky and the inside of the cart from my cozy nest but I heard the front door of Owain's house open and close.

"Figured I may as well go with you," Owain said, presumably to Diarmuid. "You and Bramble, you don't look like you'll manage long on your own."

There was silence from Diarmuid and I knew exactly what he

was thinking for I had already had the same thought. I had expected Owain would send us off with enough provisions to last a few days, but this — the luxury of travelling in a cart and time to rest while my wounds finished healing — was far more than I had dared to hope for.

"What about Maeve?" Diarmuid asked.

"She'll be happier with me gone." Owain's voice hitched a little. "Besides, you and Bramble, you need me. Maeve's never needed anyone. I've left enough coin for her to get by for a good while. And when that runs out, I guess she'll have to go back to her father, or take another husband."

For the first time, I was relieved I couldn't speak. Perhaps our presence had given Owain the excuse he needed, an honourable reason to leave. Regardless, I wouldn't have known whether to offer condolences or an apology or something else.

"Pass me your pack," Owain said. "Not much room here in front. You'll have to sit in the back with Bramble."

Diarmuid moved the blankets to the floor of the cart and settled himself on one with another wrapped around his shoulders. He perhaps wasn't as comfortable as me, but it was certainly better than walking.

"Not a bad way to travel, is it Bramble?" he muttered as he leaned back against the bundles and tucked the blanket more firmly around himself. Owain clicked at the oxen and, with a jolt, we were off. The motion of the cart soon sent me to sleep. I woke occasionally. Sometimes Diarmuid was staring out at the hills. Sometimes he was watching me.

The sun was high overhead before we stopped and then only briefly. Owain produced bread and cheese, and some dried meat for me. We ate in silence, Diarmuid and Owain leaning against the cart, me sitting in the back. The hills stretched before us, empty but for the winding path, melting snow, and trees. A smudge of smoke on the horizon signalled a lodge but we saw no other human presence as we ate.

I felt more alert as we travelled on through the afternoon. The day had grown warmer and, for a while at least, I didn't need to huddle beneath a blanket but could enjoy the breeze rustling my fur. I inhaled deeply, savouring the cold air and the tang of smoke. Cows and sheep grazed in the fields, making what they could of the winter-short grass. An eagle sailed high overhead, drifting on the currents. What was it like to fly up there, as high as the clouds? How small we must look to the eagle as we crossed its path below.

Soon enough I tired of the scenery and my eyes began to droop. The last thing I saw was Diarmuid, his brow wrinkled and his gaze vacant. His lips moved although I heard nothing. Perhaps he was making plans for when we reached Crow's Nest. Maybe he was practising what he would say to the creature he had made.

My thoughts were slow as I hovered on the edge of sleep. The visions had been silent ever since the fey girl had forced me into this form. Without their constant presence, it was like part of my soul was missing. The meanings of some of the visions were now clear but there was so much more that I didn't yet understand. I didn't need to see them again to recall their details but I missed their relentless intrusion in a way I had never thought I would.

Diarmuid was the young man who had featured so prominently. Owain was the man who had stroked the little white dog. But who was the woman with long white hair and ice blue eyes? Was she the creature we travelled towards or someone we would meet on the way? And when would I face Titania? Of course, the visions show not only past, present and future, but also maybe. The future in which I wore my own form as I met the fey queen might never come to pass. I clung to the hope that it would. As much as I didn't want the life Mother had prepared me for, perhaps it was time to finally admit that I did indeed possess some of a wise woman's talents. Perhaps it was time to learn how to use them.

We camped that night by the side of the road in a valley that was somewhat sheltered from the wind and where the ground was mostly free of snow. Owain produced a meal of bread, cheese, pears and dried meat. After we had eaten, we sat by the fire in companionable silence. I leaned against Owain's legs, enjoying the fire's warmth on my face and the gentle hand stroking my back.

The night air was cold but without the tang of frost. I snuggled down into my basket, warm enough within the pile of blankets Owain had draped over me. He had positioned my basket where I could see both him and Diarmuid as they slept on oilcloths on the ground.

I woke with a start some time later when Diarmuid cried out in his sleep. The fire had burnt down low but there was still enough light for me to see Diarmuid thrashing around. He sat up with a start, awake at last, and seemed to stare at something on the end of his blanket. I would have sworn I saw a raven take flight, swiftly disappearing into the depths of the night. Diarmuid sat there for a few moments longer and then lay down again. My eyes closed and I drifted back into sleep.

26

DIARMUID

I HAD SLEPT restlessly, my dreams full of ravens and some other beast I only dimly remembered after I woke. My breath steamed in the brisk morning air as we set off. Grey clouds cloaked the sky and a drizzling rain began before the first hour had passed.

"Diarmuid, the spare oilcloths are under your pack," Owain called over his shoulder. "And pass me my coat."

I pulled Bramble's basket closer and spread an oilcloth over us both. Up front, Owain rode with his coat draped over his head. I pitied the poor oxen who had no cover. At Silver Downs, the fires would be stoked to stave off the early spring chill and my brothers would be sharing ale and telling tales. My heart ached. Home felt like a very long way away.

At noon, we stopped briefly to rest the oxen. I dug through the pack of provisions and found bread and cheese for Owain and I, and some dried meat for Bramble. She eyed my cheese but I stared intently at a line of ash trees in the distance and pretended not to notice.

"Should have been here by noon," Owain said as we passed through a village some time later.

The persistent drizzle eventually turned to heavy rain and our progress slowed even more. I was sodden and numb with cold, despite the oilcloth. Bramble crawled onto my lap and shivered. I kept the oilcloth wrapped firmly around her but even so, the rain found its way in and her hair was damp. I thought longingly of warm baths, fireplaces and dry beds.

"There's a house up ahead," Owain said. "I'll ask if we can stay the night."

But when we arrived, the house was ablaze with lights, music and merriment and we were hesitant to intrude. Surely nobody would mind if we slept in the barn, which stood some distance from the house. As the oxen patiently pulled the cart towards the barn, their ears pricked up despite the water dripping from them. It seemed even they knew warmth and dryness lay just ahead.

The barn was small but looked well made. As long as it was water tight, it would suit me just fine. We pulled up and Owain jumped down from the cart. I clambered down somewhat stiffly and then lifted Bramble to the ground. She hurried into the barn, pausing at the entrance only long enough to shake the water from her hair.

By the time we got the oxen inside and had unhitched the cart, I couldn't feel my fingers. I fervently wished I was at Silver Downs, sitting in front of a blazing fire with a mug of Mother's spiced wine in my hand and a belly full of warm food. The best I could hope for tonight was to warm my hands beside a lamp and that our blankets would be only damp rather than soaked. Either way, it would be a long, cold night.

I retrieved my spare shirt, pants and socks, which were blessedly dry. I wrung out my dripping shirt and draped it over the side of the cart. My boots were damp but might perhaps dry by morning.

The barn was tidy enough, if somewhat dusty, and well stocked with plenty of shelves and hooks for various tools. Large bins of animal feed stood in one corner. A dozen stalls lined the back wall, doors closed. A soft lowing indicated that at least one of them was inhabited by a cow.

Owain finished rubbing down the oxen to dry them off and led each into a stall. He retrieved an armload of provisions from the cart and arranged them on an empty shelf which made for a convenient table. My mouth watered and my stomach gave a low growl at the sight of a feast that put my own journey rations to shame. A loaf of bread. A jar of honey and one of berry preserves. Large wedges of cheese, some soft and white, some hard and yellow. A small sack of last summer's apples, and an entire tart that looked just like one of Maeve's berry pies. For Bramble, there were slices of dark meat although from the way she was sniffing in the direction of the cheese, I knew that wouldn't be all she ate.

"Might as well eat the pie," Owain said cheerily. "Won't keep much longer."

"Why didn't we eat any of this last night?" I asked, recalling the bread and hard cheese we had dined on.

He flashed me a grin. "Didn't want to eat all the good stuff on the first night."

Owain cut large wedges from the pie. I dusted off a stool, pulled it up to the bench and attacked my serve. The pastry was somewhat crumbled around the edges but the filling was sweet and delicious. I gobbled it down but even so, Owain was already on his second slice before I finished. Bramble daintily ate some dried meat. Owain offered her some pie but she sniffed disdainfully.

We ate in silence. The pie devoured, Owain started on the bread and cheese. I was pleasantly full after two slices of pie but nibbled at an apple divided into thin slices with the dagger Caedmon had insisted I always carried in my boot. I had finally learned that lesson well. Owain passed Bramble some hard cheese and she lay in her basket to gnaw at it, the cheese tucked between her paws.

Owain finally sat back and rubbed his belly. "Won't be seeing any more of Maeve's pies, I s'pose."

"You could go back," I said. "It's not too late."

"'Twas never me she wanted." He yawned and headed towards the back of the barn. "G'night."

He went into one of the stalls. There was an indignant yell — a woman's voice — and then Owain backed out of the stall, hands held out in front of him.

"Sorry, didn't 'spect anyone to be in there."

"Well now you know, perhaps you could find somewhere else to sleep," a frosty voice replied.

Owain turned to me, a sheepish look on his face. "There's a girl in there."

Before I could reply, she came out of the stall and my heart stopped. Long red hair, green eyes and a mouth I remembered well. She was dressed unusually for a woman, in a loose-fitting shirt with pants instead of a skirt.

"Diarmuid!" For a moment she looked flustered. "What are you doing here."

"Rhiwallon. I… we're…"

"Diarmuid here's on a quest," Owain said.

I felt even more flustered than she looked. Colour rose rapidly in my cheeks. *Don't think about that night,* I told myself. *Or you'll be a stammering and incoherent idiot.*

"Why are you here?" I asked after we had stared at each other for several seconds.

"I'm…" Rhiwallon hesitated but then with a flick of her hair, she straightened her shoulders and looked me in the eyes. "I'm running away."

"Why?"

"Why not?"

"It's not the sort of thing someone does, not without a reason."

"I didn't say I didn't have a reason."

"You didn't say you did, so I assumed…"

"I didn't say because it's none of your business."

"Oh." Now I felt both humiliated and deflated.

Bramble trotted up to Rhiwallon and sniffed her legs. Rhiwallon glanced down but made no move to pat her.

"What happened to the dog?" she asked.

I felt a burst of pride. "She was bleeding and half-dead when I found her in the woods. She had been in a fight."

"With what?"

"Owain thinks it was a boar. She's got lots of bite marks and one of her paws was bleeding pretty badly."

"Tusks," Owain said. "Not bites."

"She's pretty tough, whatever happened to her," I said.

"Is she yours?" Rhiwallon asked.

Bramble stiffened and before I could open my mouth, she was already glaring at me.

"Not really," I said. "She's travelling with me but I guess she chooses her own path."

Owain yawned and backed away. "Guess I'll find somewhere else to sleep."

"I should think so." Rhiwallon eyed him up and down. "I'll be sleeping in that stall and I won't appreciate being disturbed. Anyone who thinks to sneak up on me will find my dagger stuck in his belly."

"You don't need to worry about us," I said, quickly. "Owain's handfasted and I'm…" My voice trailed off.

Rhiwallon gave me a half smile.

"Yes, Diarmuid. I remember."

27

DIARMUID

I WOKE TO the clattering of crockery and the warmth of Bramble curled up against my back. My stomach growled as I crawled out of the hay that had been my bed. To my surprise, it was Rhiwallon laying out the meal on the same bench we had used as a table last night. She was again dressed in pants and a loose shirt with her red hair bundled up under a grey scarf. A quiver of arrows hung from a belt around her waist.

"We may as well pool our rations and share," she said, not looking up from what she was doing. "I can contribute a loaf of bread. It's still fresh."

"We have plenty of supplies," I said. "Enough to share. You can save yours—"

Rhiwallon finally looked at me and glared so fiercely that my toes curled up and I wanted to slink back to the stall I had slept in.

"I neither want nor need your pity," she said.

"I didn't mean—"

"Diarmuid, if we're going to travel together, we need to get something straight. I am not some helpless woman who is going to sit back and wait for somebody to find me a meal or a place to sleep. I can, and will, contribute. I am choosing to travel with you for the security of having companions. But I don't need you, and I'd do perfectly well on my own if necessary."

"You're coming with us?" My voice came out too high.

"Of course I am. I'd be stupid not to. Now, go and wake up that big friend of yours. Then we can do some proper introductions, which we neglected last night, and get on with our meal."

"Name's Owain." He stumbled out of one of the stalls, looking as if he hadn't slept at all.

Rhiwallon nodded at him. "Well met, Owain. I'm Rhiwallon. As you may have gathered, Diarmuid and I have met previously. I'll be travelling with you for a while."

From beside my feet, Bramble made a soft sound.

"And this is Bramble," I said.

Rhiwallon looked down at her. "I'd prefer you kept it away from me."

"She," I said. "Bramble's a girl."

"Either way, just keep it away from me."

Bramble huffed and I reached down to scratch behind her ear. She leaned into my hand. Rhiwallon hadn't been this abrupt the last time we met.

Rhiwallon had set out her loaf of bread, a pot of Owain's honey and a bag of Owain's apples. I hesitated, not wanting to be the first to cut into her bread but equally sure I would offend her if I ate only apples. Owain didn't pause but reached for the bread, cut off a thick slice and draped it with honey. We ate in silence until Bramble sniffed.

"Bramble, I'm sorry," I said with a pang of guilt. Owain was faster than I and swiftly produced some dried meat and a small piece of cheese for her.

"Where did you say you were going?" Rhiwallon asked. She licked the honey from her fingers and took an apple.

My lips suddenly felt like they were glued together.

"To Crow's Nest," Owain said. "Diarmuid here's on a quest."

"What sort of quest?" she asked.

Owain reached for an apple and bit into it, leaving me to

answer. I swallowed a mouthful of bread. It stuck in my throat. I coughed and thumped myself on the chest, fumbling for my water flask. Rhiwallon was still watching, waiting for my response.

"I have to visit someone," I said after I had finally gotten myself back under control. I turned to Owain as a thought struck me. "You don't know," I said to him. "You left Maeve and your home to come with me without even knowing why."

Owain shrugged. "Didn't figure it mattered much. Needed help, you and Bramble. Weren't fit to walk all that way. I wasn't doing anything else, figured I'd come along."

"It's fine," Rhiwallon said. "Don't tell me if you don't want to."

"It's not—" I started.

"Forget it, Diarmuid." She shot me a withering look. "I don't need to know your precious secret."

My cheeks burned.

"Rain's cleared," Owain said with a glance out of the dusty window. "We should leave soon."

He quickly packed up the remaining food and deposited the sack in the cart. For such a large man, his motions were neat and economical. Every time I reached for something, he was one step ahead of me.

Rhiwallon had a single pack, a blanket and the quiver of arrows she wore on her hip. Her bow leaned against a wall. It was smaller than a normal bow, perhaps specially made to suit her frame. She slung the pack over one shoulder and the bow over the other. I had to admit she looked capable and ready for anything that might occur on her journey. She certainly looked like a woman who could defend herself.

The morning sky was blue, the air cool, and yesterday's rain a memory. I might have felt almost happy as we departed were it not for Rhiwallon's unexpected company. Finally, I was moving forward on my journey. I had companions, oxen and a cart, and supplies. And I was sitting side by side with the woman who knew my most embarrassing secret. I avoided Rhiwallon's eyes as we settled ourselves in the cart with Bramble's basket between us.

We spoke little. Owain never said much anyway, and with him sitting up front, conversation was difficult. Rhiwallon seemed absorbed in her own thoughts. That suited me for the only woman I had ever been able to talk to was an illusion of my imagination. Or at least she used to be.

How did the image of a beautiful woman turn into a creature that enticed neighbours to kill each other? How did the muse who whispered inspiration to me become evil? That had never been my intent. Fear gripped my bowels. I always thought myself to be a good sort of person. I had never killed anyone; in fact I had never even so much as slaughtered a hare. On our summer expeditions, it was always Caedmon who caught and killed our dinner, never I. But it seemed some latent evil hid deep inside of me, for how else could I create such a creature? Was the raven I kept seeing a symbol of the darkness that would eventually consume me? Would I, like Ida, soon rejoice in cruel deeds? I needed a plan. I couldn't arrive in Crow's Nest without one. But my thoughts chased each other around and I could think of no way to stop Ida. It was late afternoon before we reached the village of Aberton.

"I know an inn," Owain said as the cart trundled over the rough streets.

We pulled up in front of a somewhat shabby sign which proclaimed our destination to be The Ox and Cart. I sniggered and Rhiwallon looked at me, her face blank.

"What's so funny?"

"The sign."

She said nothing.

"We're arriving in a cart pulled by oxen."

Still nothing.

"To an inn called The Ox and Cart."

"Oh." She frowned and looked away.

"Can't you read?" I intended the question merely as curiosity but Rhiwallon glared at me.

"Not everyone has the luxury of time for schooling," she said shortly. "Knowing how to read doesn't teach a woman anything about the way the world works."

"Not much of a reader either," Owain said. "Never needed it much."

Rhiwallon ignored both of us as she climbed down from the cart. I busied myself with lifting Bramble down and trying to hide my fiery cheeks. I moved to retrieve Rhiwallon's pack for her but she leaned past me and snatched it up. I slung my own over my shoulder.

Inside, the innkeeper leaned against the bar. A portly fellow with a ruddy face, he eyed us each in turn, his gaze lingering on Rhiwallon.

"Afternoon, folks," he said cheerily, straightening up and giving the bar an industrious wipe. "Need a drink? You're too early for dinner but we have some soup left over from lunch if you're hungry."

Owain looked at me but said nothing. Rhiwallon stared out the window.

"Do you have any bedchambers available?" I asked, tentatively. I had never before had to procure a room for myself, let alone others, and didn't quite know how to go about it.

"Pretty full at the moment," the innkeeper said. "Lots of folks passing through this week. I've only got one room available tonight. I could let the lady have it. You two can have the hayloft in the barn, if you like. And the dog," he added, almost as an afterthought.

I hesitated. Rhiwallon gave a huge sigh, likely intended as commentary on my ability to negotiate.

"We'll take it," she said. "We can share."

"Please yourselves," the innkeeper said. "It's two silvers for the room plus half a silver each for the extra two, er three, occupants.

Another silver if you want a bath and three coppers each for a hot meal."

Owain was already reaching for the pouch dangling from his belt but Rhiwallon stopped him with a flick of her wrist.

"An extra silver and a half to sleep three people and a dog in one room?" she said. "That's extortion."

"That's the price," the innkeeper said. "You don't want to pay it, there'll be someone else along soon enough who will."

"I'm sure you normally accommodate two people in that bedchamber without extra charge," Rhiwallon said. "We'll pay the half silver for one extra person only."

The innkeeper seemed to deflate. "All right, missy, two silvers and a half for the bedchamber. Did you want baths?"

"Yes."

"Second floor, first door on the left. You'll have to carry your bags up yourselves. You got oxen out there? The boy will take 'em to the barn and give 'em a feed for an extra two coppers."

"I always feed them myself," Owain said. He nodded at Rhiwallon and I. "Go on up. I'll go look after the oxen."

The stairs creaked and swayed beneath our feet as if the whole establishment might tumble down and I was thankful we were staying only one night. Rhiwallon huffed at the flimsy door with a broken lock but when she saw the bedchamber, she turned and marched right back down the stairs. There was an argument below and when Rhiwallon reappeared, her face was satisfied.

"Two silvers for the bedchamber and no charge for the bath," she said. "See, reading's not everything."

Bramble inspected the bedchamber and gave her opinion with a sniff. As unused to travelling as I was, I had to agree it wasn't much. A bed, somewhat lumpy. One grimy window. A small cupboard, two shelves and two chairs, one with stuffing trailing from a split seam. The rug was of questionable cleanliness and likely the bed linens were too.

There was a knock on the door and I opened it to a skinny boy bearing two pails of steaming water. He hauled them into the bedchamber without a word and left, returning shortly after with a third bucket and some threadbare towels.

Rhiwallon pressed a coin into his hand and he gave her a grateful smile.

"He doesn't look like he gets nearly enough to eat," she said, after the boy had left, with a hint of defensiveness.

I said nothing.

"Out," she said. "I want the first bath."

I went back down to the bar alone. Bramble had already curled up on one of the chairs and was pretending to be asleep. It seemed the direction to leave didn't include her.

The innkeeper was less friendly now and lost any last interest in me once he realised I didn't want to buy a drink. I sat at a table in the corner of the room and waited, running my fingers over the scratches on the table top. When Owain returned, he sat across from me and held up two fingers to the innkeeper. The man's face brightened somewhat and his service was prompt. Two sloshing mugs of ale appeared on the table. Owain took one and drained half of it in a gulp. I hesitated but he nodded towards the other. "Drink up. I'm buying."

I had never particularly liked ale nor the way it made my head spin and my stomach roll, but I took a cautious sip. It tasted something akin to how I expected cat's pee would.

Owain drained the rest of his mug and waved the innkeeper over. "Another. And don't water it down this time."

The man flushed faintly and quickly deposited another mug on the table. He waited as Owain tasted it and the nod from the big man made the innkeeper's face relax.

"Hot meals," Owain said to him. "What do you have?"

"There's vegetable soup, sir," the innkeeper said, with sudden deference in his tone. "That'll be ready in about an hour or there's some left from lunch I can warm up. If you can wait, there'll be mutton with vegetables and gravy. There's always fresh bread. And I can probably arrange some pie if you like."

"Four mutton," Owain said. "With pie."

"Four, sir?" the innkeeper asked.

"Four," Owain said. "But pie for three."

"Yes, sir."

"Do you stay at inns often?" I asked as the innkeeper departed.

"Sometimes," Owain said. "Have to travel a bit in my line of work."

"What do you do?"

Owain stared into his mug for a long moment and I half expected him to brush off the question as he had last time.

"You may as well know," he said finally. He gripped his mug tightly. "I'm a mercenary."

"A what?"

"Men hire me to get rid of someone who is causing trouble."

"Get rid of them? You mean…"

"Kill them."

I was glad I was already sitting for I surely would have fallen over in surprise. Owain might be large but he was also the gentlest man I had ever encountered.

"How…" I stammered. "Why…"

He shrugged. "Someone's gotta do it. Money's good. I don't talk about it much though. People don't like it."

I squirmed on my bench, caught between unease at his revelation and self-awareness at my own nervousness. Only minutes ago, I had been thinking I didn't mind a broken lock because Owain would be there, but now… I took a large swallow of ale, seeking to shut out my thoughts.

We sat in silence until Rhiwallon returned, wearing a clean shirt and another pair of those curious pants. An indignant and somewhat damp Bramble followed. Rhiwallon's red hair hung in a wet braid down her back and her cheeks were still rosy from the hot water.

"Who's next?" she asked, looking almost cheerful.

Owain nodded at me. "Go ahead."

The water no longer steamed but it was still plenty warm enough for a pleasant bath. I stripped down and scrubbed myself all over. My clothes were grimy and I would need to find a way to clean them. Wearing my only change of clothes and feeling much refreshed, I went back down to the bar.

Owain drained his mug and stood. "Guess I could do with a bath too."

"Water's still warm." I avoided his eyes, feeling lousy even as I did. How many people had he killed?

I felt Rhiwallon watching me as I sat down. I caught my breath, wondering whether I should apologise for my earlier comment about reading but likely she would find a way to take offence at that too. Instead, I waved to the innkeeper, trying to mimic the way Owain casually held up a finger to indicate how many mugs of ale he wanted. The service wasn't quite as swift and the man said nothing as he slapped a mug down in front of me. It tasted no better than the last but I drank it anyway, trying not to gag.

"He told me," Rhiwallon said.

"Yeah?" I stared into my mug.

"What he does." She was silent for a few moments although I still felt her gaze on me. "He said you took it hard."

"I was surprised, that's all." I sounded defensive, even to my own ear.

"He doesn't usually tell people. Says they get all strange, like you did."

"I'm not all strange. I'm just surprised."

"Get over it. He's still the same man."

I was stunned into silence and we sat without speaking until Owain returned. He motioned to the innkeeper for another round of drinks.

I wrapped an arm around Bramble who had jumped up onto my bench, drawing courage from her quiet nearness even as my shirt soaked through from her damp hair. I tried to find the words to apologise to Owain but as I finally opened my mouth, Rhiwallon spoke.

"So, Diarmuid, you never did say what this mysterious quest is all about."

I closed my mouth with a snap. Owain had revealed his secret. Now it was my turn.

"I'm going to Crow's Nest," I said.

Rhiwallon rolled her eyes. "I know that, but you haven't said why."

I flushed, then took a deep breath. "I'm a bard."

"Caedmon may have mentioned that." She sounded dubious.

My cheeks coloured although whether it was with embarrassment or anger, I couldn't have said. "I'm also the seventh son of a seventh son."

She raised an eyebrow. "So?"

"When a seventh son of a seventh son is a bard, he has… abilities. Or, at least, he does in my family."

"What sort of abilities?"

"I can sometimes bring my tales to life. Not always, and I don't know how it works. But sometimes the tales I tell, well, they happen."

The corners of Rhiwallon's mouth twitched.

"It's true," I said.

"I didn't say it wasn't."

"You don't believe me."

"No."

Bramble squirmed in my arms and I realised I had been holding her far too tightly. I released her and she stared up at me.

"But I think you believe it," Rhiwallon said and her tone was softer now.

I shrugged. "Like I said, I don't know how it works. I only know it happens."

"You need to fix something," Owain said slowly. "Something from a tale."

"I created a muse," I said. "In my head. It was a silly little thing to entertain myself but I pretended she was the source of my tales. Then, somehow, she came to life and escaped."

"She escaped from your head?" Rhiwallon's face said clearly that she didn't believe me.

Hot flames of embarrassment warmed my whole body. "Yes, and something went wrong. She's taken over Crow's Nest and she's making people kill each other."

"How do you know it's your imaginary muse?" Rhiwallon asked. "How do you know she isn't still in your head?"

"She isn't there anymore. She's nothing but a memory in my head now. She came to life but she's twisted. Wrong."

"But how do you know this woman you're travelling so far to get to is the one you made up?" Rhiwallon said.

"I just know," I said, miserably. "How does a parent recognise their child? It's her, I know it."

"You plan to stop her," Owain said.

I was surprised at the calm acceptance in his voice. He had discovered I too was responsible for death, and yet there he sat, drinking his ale and listening to my tale. If he judged me, I couldn't tell it from his face or words.

"How?" Rhiwallon asked. "I'm not saying I believe any of this, but how would you stop her?"

"I don't know. I'm hoping I'll figure that out. For now, I just need to get there. Make sure it's really her. Then... I don't know."

As the room darkened and grew chilly, the innkeeper lit lamps and soon the fireplace blazed, sending warmth through the room. Other patrons drifted into the room and soon the quietness was replaced with the steady murmur of conversation. A serving girl brought out our meals, four plates of mutton and three of pie.

Owain took one of the plates and carefully sliced the meat and vegetables into small pieces then set it down next to Bramble on the bench. Yet again it was he, not I, who thought to feed her.

My stomach had started to rumble as soon as the smell of roasted meat hit my nostrils and I ate eagerly. The mutton was tough, the vegetables clearly old and the gravy watery, but it was hot and filling.

We lingered a little longer after dinner. My stomach was full and the atmosphere was somewhat companionable, despite the stiffness between Rhiwallon and I.

I looked around the table. My journey's companions, although not what I might have expected: a mercenary, a woman running for reasons left unsaid, and a dog. Fiachra had said something else about my companions, that they would not all be what they seemed. And now I had discovered what that meant, for who would assume the gentle man across the table from me to be a hired killer?

28

IDA

I FEEL HIM moving towards me once again and he is no longer alone. I have seen his companions when I have visited him at night. The heart of one is filled with death, another has a heart that longs. The heart of the third contains a secret desperately hidden.

What do these companions mean to him? What would happen if I removed one? He told a tale once in which a sorcerer sent a magical construct to abduct a traveller. I could create such a thing. In his tale, the beast had eight legs and many eyes. It was large and venomous and filled with blackness. As I think of the beast, it appears before me. Solid. Hairy. Hungry.

Which companion should I remove? Perhaps the one with the secret. I remember her from the last time they met. I saw her then through his eyes, felt the emotions she aroused in him. She was the source of much confusion for him.

I send my beast towards him and wait. I am intrigued to learn whether he and his companions will act in the same way as the characters in his tale. I don't yet understand why sometimes folk act the way Diarmuid's tales say they should, and other times they don't.

In the meantime, my power grows with each day. At first, it

was a trickle, like the merest hint of water seeping into a dry riverbed with the first of the winter rains. It eased through my limbs, moving ever so gently. As the days passed, the trickle became a steady flow and then a gushing stream.

The more I wield my power, the stronger the flow becomes. With my increasing power, I cleanse my surroundings. And the more evil I remove from this meagre village, the more my power grows. I do not let myself think of the inhabitants as people, for I fear I will pity them. Instead, I steel myself and do what I must.

There was a child. I sensed darkness in her heart. She reminded me of Diarmuid in a way. There was power inside of her, a power I didn't understand. But she didn't yet know her power, couldn't draw on it at will. I could not allow her to stay for she would contaminate the village. She might even destroy it.

Diarmuid told a tale once of a mother who was commanded by Titania to take her child into the woods and leave her there. So I followed his instructions. I charmed the mother of this powerful child and she took the girl to the woods. She stood and watched as the wild boars tore her child apart. Thus the girl and her strange powers were destroyed before she ever learnt to use them. And my village has one less evil to contend with.

29

BRIGIT

O N THE THIRD night after we left Owain's house, we stayed in the village of Shelby at an inn called The Cat's Whiskers. The inn looked rough and worn, the sort of accommodation where one should double check that their bedchamber door was locked before they went to sleep.

As best I could tell, somewhere around fifteen nights had passed since Diarmuid had started his journey. More than two sevennights and halfway to the new moon. Time was running out if his belief that he had to reach his muse before then was correct.

We procured two bedchambers at The Cat's Whiskers, bathed, and then gathered in the dining room. The room was perhaps half full, the crowd a little more hardened than where we had stayed previously. The tables and benches were battered as if they were often thrown to the floor and even the innkeeper looked like he had been tossed across the counter a few times. The meal presented to us was a less than appetising array of half-cold mutton and watery soup. I sniffed at the mutton, suspicious about its freshness.

"Ugh," Rhiwallon said, wrinkling her nose as she stared down at her plate. "I can't eat that."

"It's not that bad," Owain said. His plate was already half empty.

Rhiwallon put a hand over her nose. "The smell of it is making me sick."

I sniffed my plate again. It definitely wasn't as fresh as it could be but it wasn't off. Owain had thoughtfully cut my serve into small pieces for me and I took a tentative bite. Tough and chewy, but edible. Certainly not worth the fuss Rhiwallon was making.

She pushed her plate away. "I'd rather starve."

Owain shrugged and reached for her plate. "I'll eat it if you aren't going to."

I was only half-listening. I couldn't quite figure Rhiwallon out. Her mood changed by the day. Sometimes she seemed tough and capable, like the night we met her in the barn when she threatened to stab anyone who sneaked up on her. At other times, like tonight, she was jittery and irrational.

Before I could think further on this, a group of travellers entered. There were six, all lean men with a professional air about them. Rhiwallon spluttered and I looked up just in time to see the colour drain from her face. She inched a little closer to Owain and ducked her head. Her unbound hair fell forward and mostly covered her face. She clenched her hands together tightly but not before I saw how they trembled. I could smell the fear that suddenly wafted from her.

The men spoke to the innkeeper for longer than seemed necessary to arrange bedchambers and meals, and then arrayed themselves around a table at the far end of the room. The innkeeper brought them mugs of ale. Rhiwallon seemed to sink down further. Owain's body shielded her from the men's view although if Owain himself realised anything was wrong, he gave no sign of it.

I jumped down from the bench. One benefit to being a dog was that people often didn't see me. Nose to the dirty floor, I inched closer to the men. One of them glanced towards me and I sniffed intently at a stale crust of bread. The man's gaze barely skimmed me before he looked away. I sidled closer.

"How much further do we go?" one of his companions asked. He downed his ale in a few gulps and the innkeeper swiftly replaced the mug.

Another man, one with an air of authority, shrugged. "We keep going until we find what we're looking for."

"Are you sure we're heading the right way?" the first man asked. "Surely by now we should have come across some sign of her."

The one who seemed to be the leader set down his mug and looked him in the eye. "We have our orders," he said and his words were clear and deliberate. "And we follow them. Anyone doesn't like that, they're free to leave. Without pay, of course."

I held my breath, hoping for more, but the conversation turned to more mundane topics, the chance of rain tomorrow and whether one of them needed new boots before the group moved on. The one who appeared to be the leader looked around the room, eyes narrowed as he examined each of the occupants. Owain's bulk still largely obscured Rhiwallon and the man barely glanced at her.

I lingered for another few minutes but heard nothing useful other than that they planned to depart late the following morning. I returned to our table and Owain met my gaze with just the slightest nod before suggesting we retire. He draped an arm loosely around Rhiwallon's shoulders as we left. She kept her head down, hair covering her face and her shoulders slumped as if to disguise her height, or perhaps her build.

When we reached our bedchambers, Owain suggested we all sleep in the same room. Rhiwallon agreed quickly and moved her pack into the larger bedchamber that Owain, Diarmuid and I had intended to share. Diarmuid laid a blanket down on the rug and stretched out. I curled up beside him in my usual spot and tucked my nose into my paws to keep it warm.

My mind whirled. Who or what was Rhiwallon running from?

I could think of three reasons a woman like her would be running away: to escape violence, to flee from an unwanted marriage, or because she was with child and could secure no promise from the babe's father. Neither Diarmuid nor Owain noticed the times Rhiwallon slipped away to vomit or the way she sometimes held a hand over her stomach, as if cradling the life inside. She couldn't have been more than two moons along for there was no discernible swelling of her belly.

If Mother were here, she could have aided Rhiwallon with herbs. Fennel, perhaps, or a tea of raspberry leaf. Mother could have eased her sickness or, if Rhiwallon wanted, provided other herbs to release the child from her womb. Even I in my own form could have helped. If Rhiwallon took anything to soothe her stomach, I never saw it.

Her relationship with Diarmuid also puzzled me. Once or twice Rhiwallon had hinted she knew some secret of his. He had blushed bright red and mumbled. Obviously they had met before but I couldn't figure out exactly what manner of relationship they had or how well they knew each other.

Rhiwallon rarely saw the small terrier by her feet and she had about as much intuition as Diarmuid. Despite her initial demand that Diarmuid should keep me away from her, she didn't seem to mind my presence. Occasionally, she patted me roughly on the head, or ruffled the hair on my back, not noticing my discomfort. But she certainly didn't whisper any confidences to me the way Diarmuid did so I had little insight into her behaviour. Why was Rhiwallon running? And who pursued her?

30

DIARMUID

OUR JOURNEY WAS uneventful. The oxen walked tirelessly, the cart didn't break down, and we weren't attacked by robbers intent on murdering us as we slept. It had been almost three sevennights since I left home. I had expected to be at Crow's Nest long before now. Of course, I also hadn't expected such a lengthy delay while I was ill and my ankle was healing.

The easy travelling left me with plenty of time to plan for my confrontation with Ida. She was unlikely to listen to reason, however persuasive my words might be. Equally unlikely that she would feel compelled to obey me even if I was, in some way, her creator. So it seemed I must find a way to destroy her. Despite Caedmon's efforts to teach me to fight, my ability was limited to perhaps defending myself against an unskilled and unmotivated attacker. Perhaps my companions would aid me. Owain had the strength of several men and Rhiwallon was proficient with a bow and arrow. They were happy enough to travel with me but would they also help destroy Ida?

Crow's Nest was now only a two-day journey away and we were well between villages when it was time to stop for the night. We chose a spot beside a stand of shrubby young rowan trees, which were still mostly naked from the winter. Our routines for setting up camp came easily and without discussion for we had spent several nights outdoors.

Owain unhitched the oxen, then fed and watered them. Rhiwallon and I unloaded what we needed from the cart. Then she disappeared with her bow and arrow while I cleared a spot for a fire and gathered wood. It was always Rhiwallon, though, who lit the fire. She could down a hare and skin it long before I could start the fire and would hiss in exasperation as she watched my feeble attempts. Eventually she would shove me aside and light it herself, while I stood beside her, feeling inadequate and useless.

Nevertheless I persisted. I gathered up a good pile of twigs and some leaf litter and then retrieved my flint. Tonight though I couldn't produce so much as a spark. The wood was bone dry and the breeze was light enough that I couldn't blame its interference. Bramble watched from her basket, which I had positioned nearby, as I tried again and again, my frustration increasing as each attempt failed to produce even a whiff of smoke.

Rhiwallon returned with two neatly-skinned squirrels and took the flint from my hand without a word. I couldn't bear to watch her succeed where yet again I had failed so I turned to lay out the remainder of our meal: somewhat stale bread, hard cheese, and a few handfuls of hazelnuts we had picked that morning. But tonight, even Rhiwallon was unable to coax a flame into existence. She rearranged the twigs, and tried again, holding the flint close to the leaves and sheltering its flame with her hand. But still the fire wouldn't catch. Eventually she swore and shoved the flint into her pocket.

"No fire tonight," she said, her voice tight.

Owain had by now finished with the oxen. He glanced at the stacked twigs and the dead squirrels and shrugged. "No matter."

I swallowed an offer to try. It would likely earn me a scornful glare and a few sharp words. If Rhiwallon couldn't get the fire started, I probably couldn't either. Instead I retrieved some dried meat from our remaining rations in the cart. When I returned, the squirrels had disappeared and Bramble had a somewhat regretful look on her face. Clearly they hadn't been offered to her.

We ate in silence, then Rhiwallon rose with a determined look. But yet again she couldn't produce even the smallest of flames. The evening stretched long and bleak without a fire to warm us. I soon lay down and wrapped myself in a blanket. The ground was hard and it took some time before I could get comfortable enough to sleep. Bramble curled up in her favourite spot behind my knees and I draped another blanket over her. I woke some time later to Bramble barking loudly, a series of short, sharp sounds I had never before heard from her. Owain was yelling something but I couldn't make it out over Bramble's barking. I sat up, sleep still clinging to my mind, confused by all the noise.

"What's wrong?" I asked. "Bramble, be quiet. Come here, girl."

She continued barking. A lamp flared. Owain lifted it high as he moved around our small campsite. Never before had I seen him move so quickly and it was this that finally informed my sleep-addled brain that there was a problem.

"Owain," I yelled over Bramble's noise. "What's wrong? Where's Rhiwallon?"

"Gone." He didn't pause long enough to even glance at me.

"What? Bramble, be quiet girl."

Bramble slunk over to me and crawled onto my lap. Her small frame convulsed with tremors and I gathered her up in my arms. I had never seen her act like this. Something was very wrong.

"Bramble, what is it?"

She whined and burrowed her nose into my chest. Owain still lurched around, the lamp held high, calling for Rhiwallon.

"Owain? Owain!"

"Rhiwallon's gone." His voice broke and the lamplight shone on the tear tracks on his cheeks.

"Gone where?"

He seemed to stumble blindly. He almost fell and the lamp

dipped precariously close to the ground, but he regained his balance and kept moving.

"Owain, stop. Tell me what happened."

Bramble's trembles started to ease. Her face was still burrowed into my chest and she didn't seem inclined to move. I kept my arms around her, stroking her back. Owain finally set down the lamp and collapsed onto his blanket, head in his hands and his shoulders slumped. He seemed smaller than he usually did.

"Something was standing over her when I woke," he said hoarsely. "It took her."

A few moments passed before my mouth would work. "Who? Why?" I hardly knew where to start.

"Couldn't move, couldn't speak."

My mouth framed questions I couldn't say. Finally, I managed to squeak, "The fey?"

He shrugged. "You're the bard."

"But… What would they want with Rhiwallon?" A horrible thought occurred to me. "It wasn't Rhiwallon they wanted. They want to stop me from getting to Crow's Nest. Or delay me. It's a distraction. Like how they led me off the path last time."

Fiachra had said I would have companions and that one would not be what they seemed, but he hadn't said I wouldn't need each of them. I tried to remember his exact words, whether he had said my companions would still be with me when I faced Ida, but I couldn't think clearly. There was a possibility I would need all three to stop her.

"We have to go after her," I said. Owain nodded his agreement.

I packed some provisions while Owain untethered the oxen. They would have to fend for themselves until we returned.

"Do you know much about the fey?" I asked. I didn't wait for his reply. "We must not eat or drink anything offered to us within their territory. Time may not pass the same way as it does here. We might seem to be there a week and find only an hour has passed here, or it might seem no time there and weeks here."

Owain grunted, intent on sharpening his daggers.

"We should make sure we don't get separated. And we shouldn't believe anything the fey say, be it good or bad. They won't lie, or at least the old tales say they won't, but they may twist the truth and make things seem what they are not."

Owain handed me a dagger. Moonlight glinted off steel as he slid another into his boot. He slung his pack over his shoulder and hefted his axe. I tested the dagger's weight. It was larger than my own and more finely made. When I ran my thumb along the blade, the skin parted effortlessly and a bead of blood appeared. My own small dagger was already in my boot; the experience in the woods, when I didn't know it was only Bramble behind the bush, had taught me the value of being armed better than Caedmon's lectures ever did. I slid Owain's dagger into my other boot. It didn't sit quite as comfortably as my own.

Owain strode over to where Rhiwallon had been sleeping. Her blanket was empty and rumpled. Beside the blanket lay her bow and quiver. She wouldn't have left willingly without them. Owain picked them up and slung them over his other shoulder.

"She'll want these when we find her," he said.

I nodded, unwilling to voice my fear that the fey might have taken Rhiwallon somewhere we couldn't follow. I looked around for Bramble. For one heart-stopping moment I feared she too had been taken. Then I saw a streak of white some distance from our camp. She dashed around, nose to the ground.

"Come on, Bramble," I called, and then to Owain, "Which way do you think?"

He nodded towards Bramble who still circled, sniffing at the ground. "Follow Bramble."

Indeed, as soon as we looked at her, Bramble gave a short, sharp bark. It was a definite *follow me*. I hesitated but Bramble barked again. Owain started towards her. Still she waited, looking to me.

"All right, I'm coming." I picked up my pack. "But I hope you know where you're going."

Bramble trotted off, following a path only she could identify.

She paused, looking back over her shoulder to make sure we were following. Branches crunched beneath Owain's heavy boots and I hurried after him, anxious to keep myself within the light of the lamp he bore. She led us on a winding path around bush, up hill and then down, over rock and through a dry creek. We walked in circles and doubled back on our path. Finally, Bramble paused at a low mound, mostly still snow-covered but with a few eager strands of grass poking through.

"This is where the path leads?" I asked. "What are we supposed to do now?"

Bramble gave me a disdainful stare and turned back to the mound. She barked three times and an opening appeared. It was large enough to admit a grown man. Inside was shrouded in darkness. I was so shocked that my legs almost gave out beneath me. It was a coincidence, of course, the opening appearing right as Bramble barked. Likely our presence had somehow activated it.

"Good girl," Owain said.

Bramble flicked her tail at him and glared at me.

"Well done, Bramble." I leaned down to rub her ears. "I don't know how you did that, but well done."

She ducked her head out of my reach and stepped away. If she wasn't just a dog, I would have thought she was angry with me.

Owain held the axe in front of him, gripping it in one hand and the lamp with the other. "I'll go first."

I was only too glad to agree. He stepped into the barrow, ducking his head in order to fit, and I followed. The moment I passed through the entrance, one of my boots began to feel warm. Then suddenly it was hot. Burning hot. Owain threw both axe and lamp outside onto the snow and ran out of the mound. The lamp's flame sputtered and died. My foot felt like it was on fire. I dived through the opening and flung myself to the ground to pull off the boot. Owain's dagger dropped out and sizzled in the snow. I reached for it but burnt my fingers.

"Hot," Owain said.

"Yours too?" I looked from his axe to the dagger and knew

what I had forgotten. Almost every tale I knew of the fey told of this. "Cold iron. The fey can't stand to be near it. There must be a charm on this place to prevent us from entering with cold iron."

"No weapons?"

My little bronze dagger was still safely tucked into my other boot. I opened my mouth to tell Owain but hesitated. If there was a charm to prevent us entering with cold iron, there may be other charms on this place. Perhaps even now the fey watched or listened.

"No, no weapons," I said and pulled my boot back on.

Bramble watched from the entrance to the mound, one front paw slightly raised. With the tip of one finger, I touched Owain's dagger. It was still warm but cooling rapidly. Definitely there was a charm at work for I had never seen iron cool so swiftly. Owain gingerly picked up his axe and hefted it, then lay it back down on the ground with a regretful look.

"Let's go," I said. "Slowly, and stick together. Bramble, you stay right next me."

She glanced at me and sniffed. We marched back into the mound. Once inside, a faint green light lit the darkness, just enough to see our path. There was no obvious source of light but it seemed we would have no need for a lamp. The tunnel passed through firmly-compacted earth and sloped sharply down. I tried not to think about the earthen ceiling or its lack of visible supports. The air smelled like moist earth, the kind that's good for planting crops in.

Owain went first, clenched hands indicating he was less than comfortable without the familiar weight of his axe. I took up the rear with Bramble between us. Was it better to be first or last? The first was most likely to run into any trap or ambush. But the last was at risk of something sneaking up on him from behind. I was somewhat comforted by the weight of the small dagger in my boot.

We had gone barely twenty paces before the path took an abrupt turn to the right and the last shimmers of moonlight disappeared, leaving the pale green light as our only source of illumination. I stepped carefully to avoid treading on Bramble who scurried with her tail tucked between her legs. How much did she understand? Clearly she knew we searched for Rhiwallon and she was afraid. Likely that was all she knew.

We walked and walked. Sometimes the path sloped down; at other times, it veered uphill. It would turn to the right then to the left and at one stage even wound back in the direction from which we had come. In no time at all, I was completely disorientated. And still we walked. The only sounds were those we made ourselves.

The air was warm and still, scented with dirt and moss. I was soon covered in a thin sheen of perspiration. We paused briefly to drink. Bramble began holding up her injured paw, hopping along on three legs. Owain scooped her up and tucked her under his arm.

In the dim green light, I had no sense of time. The path inclined upwards again and we trudged on, going up and up until I felt sure we must soon emerge from the earth into the fresh air above. By the time the path levelled again, my muscles quivered and I could hardly lift my feet. I gritted my teeth and plodded on, not wanting to be the first to admit I couldn't continue. Eventually, Owain stopped and set Bramble down.

"May as well take a break," he said. "Been walking a long time."

"How long can this tunnel possibly be?"

I didn't expect an answer and he didn't reply. I set down my pack and slid to the ground in relief. The path stretched ahead of us, dimly lit with sickly green for as far as I could see. I leaned against the cool earthen wall and sighed. Bramble curled up next to me, resting her head on my thigh, and I stroked her ears.

Owain lowered his huge frame down next to me and rummaged in the pack. He offered me an apple and Bramble a strip of dried meat.

"How long do you think we've been walking?" I asked.

Owain shrugged.

"It must be dawn, at least."

"Prob'ly later."

Having eaten, we each took a small drink from the flask — Owain poured a portion into his cupped hand for Bramble — and then sat in silence for some time. Eventually Owain stirred.

"May as well push on," he said.

I hauled myself to my feet, stifling a groan as tired muscles protested. We walked and walked. Several times we stopped to rest and twice more to eat. I was so tired, I could no longer even think. I walked when Owain told me to, stopped when he stopped, ate when he handed me food. He seemed tireless and kept moving steadily, legs pumping up and down at the same pace. He had long since been carrying my pack and I was too tired to object.

I had fallen behind, plodding along. There was an idea rattling around in my exhausted brain but I was too tired to make sense of it. There was… something. Something I should do. Or try. I was almost too tired to care what it was but it seemed there was possibly some hope in the idea, whatever it was.

Ahead of me, Owain waited at a turning of the tunnel. Perhaps once we reached the corner, there would be something else up ahead. Rhiwallon maybe, or an exit. But when I reached Owain, the only thing around the corner was more of the green-lit tunnel.

They were never-ending, these fey tunnels. Were we the first mortals to become lost in them? Would we eventually come across other folk, or perhaps only their bones? Was this what happened to some of those the tales told of, ones who disappeared from their lives and never returned?

Tales. I finally understood the idea my mind had been trying to suggest.

"I should tell a tale." My voice was thin, thready and didn't sound much like me at all.

Owain looked back at me but said nothing. Perhaps he was too tired to speak. Indeed, it seemed like such an effort. I could barely keep myself on my feet anymore, let alone spare the energy to talk.

"Perhaps a tale can get us out of here," I said.

"Go on." He set Bramble down on the ground and she immediately curled up into a ball, head draped across her paws, eyes closed. Owain leaned against the tunnel wall and waited.

A tale. If it was true that I could bring my tales to life, then I could use that ability to get us out of here. I needed to tell a tale about a group of friends who become separated when one of them is abducted and who find themselves trapped in the land of the fey. Haltingly, I began to speak. My thoughts were confused and at first my words made little sense. But slowly the familiar act of tale telling took over and the words came more easily, despite my exhaustion.

I told of how the group searched for their friend, becoming more and more tired and unable to find either their friend or a way out of the tunnels. At last, exhausted and close to collapse, the bard tells a tale in which the group find themselves suddenly standing before a door in the tunnel wall, a door that wasn't there before. They open the door and find themselves outside in the sunshine and fresh air. And their missing friend waits to greet them as they stumble out, weary and heartsore. I concluded the tale and searched the walls, waiting for the door to appear. But nothing happened.

"I don't understand," I said. "Why didn't it work?"

Owain peeled himself off the wall. "Better keep walking then," he said.

At some stage we stopped to rest and I fell asleep, curled up on the dirt with Bramble beside me and my pack beneath my head. Owain slept sitting against the wall. I woke to the same steady green light and the never-ending tunnel. We ate and sipped small portions of water. There wasn't much left, certainly not enough to last while we retraced our steps. As we set off again, it was all I could do to keep putting one foot in front of the other, following Owain and Bramble. My legs wobbled, my feet were blistered and my back ached.

Some time later, the tunnel finally ended. We came around a bend and into an enormous cavern, its high ceiling lost in the depths of the dim green light. The walls shimmered with bands of different coloured rocks: gold and red and brown. The entry through which we passed was the only exit. We would have to retrace our steps, all the way back along the green-lit path.

I dropped my pack and followed it down to the floor. Bramble climbed onto my lap, which was uncharacteristic of her. Although she slept with me each night, it was usually Owain's lap she sought during the day. I pulled out the water flask. Only a few drops remained and we shared them amongst the three of us.

Owain remained standing although he set down his pack and Rhiwallon's bow and quiver. I wondered that he could bear to stay on his feet another moment. My own feet ached and my ankle, so recently injured, was tender. It wouldn't hold up much longer. I started to unlace my boots when Bramble sat up abruptly, ears pricked.

We were no longer alone.

31

DIARMUID

A HOST OF beings filled the cavern. They resembled humans, appearing in a variety of sizes from child to adult but their milk-white skin and ruby-red lips left me in no doubt that they were fey. I pushed Bramble off my lap and clambered to my feet without lacing up my boots. The fey stared at us in eerie silence, their faces devoid of expression.

My eyes were drawn to a particular couple. She was beautiful with long dark hair and a cold stare, and he was even taller than their fellows. Eventually, my tired brain realised that these beings I was so rudely staring at were probably their rulers. They featured in so many tales that every child knew their names: Oberon and Titania.

At my feet, Bramble stood with ears alert and her tail drooping. Owain's face was white, his hands clenched. The fey seemed content to stand and stare at us. Despite their numbers, which must have been in the hundreds, there was not a noise from any of them.

I cleared my throat, the sound awkwardly loud in the silence of the cavern, and when I spoke my voice was thready. "We are looking for Rhiwallon."

Titania raised an eyebrow and her lips curled just the tiniest bit. "Indeed," she said.

I waited but she did not seem inclined to volunteer anything further. "Have you taken her?" I asked.

Titania raised graceful hands and indicated I should look around the cavern. "Do you see her here amongst us?"

I started to reply but stopped. The tales say the fey cannot lie but they will willingly mislead, answering with trickery and riddles. I could read nothing in Titania's cold gaze. I searched for a question she could not mislead me with. "Will you take us to her?" I asked.

Titania laughed but there was no amusement in the sound. Others laughed also and then, abruptly, they all fell silent in the same moment. "No," she said. "I will not take you to her. If you want to find the human girl, you must seek her yourselves."

I opened my mouth but Titania forestalled my words with a raised finger. "One question further," she said. "And then I will answer no more."

I closed my mouth with a snap. Three questions. How could I, steeped in tales as I was, not have anticipated this? I should have known, should have considered my words more carefully. I could ask whether Rhiwallon was safe but that would give no clue as to her location.

"How can we find Rhiwallon?" I asked.

Titania's eyes glittered and when she spoke, her lips twisted cruelly and her voice rang through the cavern. "One will bear another's coat until the final round. One will face their greatest fear, wearing a gossamer gown. One may pass the fiery depths and only once may go. Locate the key to leave this place. In plain view it will be found."

My heart sank down into my boots. It was a riddle and it made little sense. Obviously, it was Rhiwallon who would face her greatest fear although I didn't understand the reference to a gossamer gown. I had no idea who might wear somebody else's coat for neither Owain nor I had brought such an item into the mound. I didn't want to even think about what might be meant by passing the fiery depths. And then there was the key: it needed to be found but wouldn't really be hidden?

In the time I had spent thinking, the fey had left. One moment they stood there, staring at us in silence, and in the blink of an eye they were gone. Not so much as a rustle or a murmur betrayed their exit and afterward, the only evidence of their presence was a single leaf, blood-red against the brown stone of the cavern floor. It hadn't been there before.

Owain bent to pick up the leaf. It lay lightly on his palm and, together, we stared at it. I had never before seen such a leaf. Its edges were straight, the corners pointed. It shimmered with a red so deep, it was almost black. Lying on Owain's palm, it looked like a triangle sliced into his skin exposing the blood beneath.

"Odd," Owain said. He carefully tucked the leaf away in his shirt pocket. "Might be important."

Yet again I had fallen short.

"That their queen?" he asked.

I nodded but whatever Owain thought of Titania, he kept it to himself.

"What do we do now?" I asked, more to myself than to him. We had walked for at least a day, maybe more, to get here and now it seemed we must walk all the way back. We had no water and our only remaining food was a stale end of bread and two strips of dried meat. Perhaps in this strange world of the fey, the way out would be shorter than the way in. There were tales of such things. But we needed to find Rhiwallon first.

I laced up my boots and then hitched my pack onto my shoulder. "I guess we may as well get moving."

As Owain and I turned back to the exit, Bramble barked.

"What is it, girl?" I asked. She gave me a haughty look and I muttered an apology. Bramble sniffed and looked back towards the far side of the cavern. I followed her line of sight.

"Is that—" Owain asked.

"It looks—" I said at the same time. "It's an opening."

"Wasn't there before," Owain said.

Where previously there had been nothing but solid stone now yawned a dark chasm. Owain and I looked at each other.

"It's that or go back the way we came," I said. "The fey brought us here for a reason and I don't think it was only to laugh at us. They didn't want us to see that opening until now."

"Got to find Rhiwallon," Owain said.

I looked from him to Bramble. "Group decision. Do we go that way or back the way we came?"

Owain nodded towards the other side of the cavern. Bramble's gaze too was on the opening that hadn't been there before.

"Let's go then," I said.

As we walked across the cavern, our footsteps echoed through its depths. Were we making an awful mistake? The fey wanted something from me, but exactly what, I had no idea. They had interfered from the first day of my journey when they had lured me from my path with the promise of water. But if I hadn't strayed, I wouldn't have found Bramble. Perhaps they meant for that to occur but what possible reason could they have? What use was a dog to the fey?

Then there was Owain. If I hadn't strayed from my original route, Bramble and I would not have emerged from the woods right as Owain happened by. And if the three of us had not decided to pass a rainy night in a certain barn, we would not have discovered Rhiwallon hiding there. And all of that had led us to here and now: Rhiwallon abducted by the fey for some reason we could only guess at but which might have something to do with my quest.

If we were somewhere deep in the land of the fey, as I suspected, these tunnels might lead on forever, endlessly twisting and turning. Branching paths could leave us hopelessly lost.

"We need to mark the paths we take," I said. "This opening wasn't here before. Or maybe it was hidden from us. There's no telling how many others there might be, openings that will appear as we pass or close after we enter. We need to know which way we came."

"If I had my axe…" Owain said, empty hands clenched.

I remembered the dagger in my boot. Would the fey notice if I used it in here? I hesitated with my hand halfway to my boot. The dagger was our only weapon other than Rhiwallon's bow, which was too small for Owain. I might be able to use it but I had never actually killed anything before. I wasn't certain that I would be able to defend us.

Owain fumbled in his pack and retrieved a small bronze brooch. The yellow gem set in the front gleamed dully. A faint blush tinged his cheeks. "Thought I might want something to remember her by." He extended the pin and scratched a small sigil — a simple cross — next to the exit. "Let's go find the girl."

The tunnel was lit with the same sickly green light. Just enough to see by, not enough to see clearly. We had barely gone a hundred paces before we faced three branching tunnels. The ones to the left and right were tinged with green. As I peered down the central tunnel, an invisible hand gripped my stomach. This tunnel was lit by a red glow, and dread and danger emanated from it.

Bramble sniffed the entrances to the tunnels, lingering at each before she moved on. Then she stood in front of the central tunnel. Her tail was tucked firmly between her legs and her small body quivered.

"No, Bramble, not that one," I said.

She looked up at me and sniffed.

"She has led us true this far," Owain said. His face was pale but his voice was steady.

I looked from Owain to Bramble and the fist gripping my stomach now clutched my bowels as well.

"Are you sure, Bramble?" I asked. "Perhaps they took her down one of the other passages."

She sniffed at me again and looked towards the red tunnel.

"If Rhiwallon went that way, no point going another way," Owain said.

His matter-of-fact tone shamed me. Owain was right: if she had been taken down this passage, that was where we too would go. I nodded and Owain pulled out his brooch to mark the wall with a cross.

Menace pervaded the red-lit tunnel. Nausea rose in my throat and I swallowed it back down. We walked slowly, cautiously, but the tunnel stretched ahead, silent and empty and threateningly red. My heart hammered and my nerves were on edge as I braced myself for something to happen.

Owain's breathing was loud and ragged, and mine wasn't much quieter. The sense of impending danger magnified with each step until I was sure I would scream if something didn't happen shortly. We had not gone far, maybe a few hundred paces and two twists of the tunnel, before we reached another branching passage. Two tunnels yawned ahead of us. One was lit with the familiar green light and the other with the sinister red.

We stopped and both Owain and I looked to Bramble for guidance. She sniffed briefly at the green passage and then stood at the mouth of the red one.

I breathed deeply and forced my fists to unclench. Blood oozed from where my nails had cut into my palms. My legs still wobbled and nausea filled my stomach. Owain's face was pale, his eyes large. Bramble trembled, tail tucked between her legs. I forced my legs to move. They wobbled but at least they held me up. My mouth was dry and sweat trickled down between my shoulder blades.

The red tunnel ended abruptly and without incident. A cavern yawned ahead of us. Unlike the previous one, which was empty and lit by clean, white light, this cavern was filled with red and the same sense of menace as the tunnel. The air felt too thick to breathe and the rosy haze distorted my perception of distance. The walls faded into the redly opaque air.

The cavern was filled with huge mounds of fallen rock, everything from pebbles to boulders the height of three men. An enormous web hung from the roof and stretched out of sight, a web which could not have been made by any ordinary beast but one which was hundreds, maybe thousands, of times larger. It covered easily a quarter of the cavern's roof. I had no wish to encounter any beast that could create a web so large.

"She could be in here," Owain said.

I was reluctant to agree but he was right. "How do we search this without getting separated? There could be anything behind the rocks. A big hole or… I don't know, a creature of some sort."

Owain scooped Bramble up. "I'll carry her. Just to be safe."

"We need a plan," I said.

Owain pointed towards the nearest corner. "We zigzag. This way first and then back, until we reach the web."

"And we always pass the rocks on the right side."

We set off, walking slowly, scanning the area for any sign of Rhiwallon. Rocks taller than I prevented me from seeing anything more than my immediate surroundings. I soon became dizzy with the effort of trying to look everywhere at once, up and down, left and right. The fey path would not have led us here if there wasn't some clue to be found. I didn't dare hope Rhiwallon herself would be here but there must be something they wanted us to find. The key, perhaps — the key that would be in plain view.

Step by step, we searched, passing to the right around each tower of rocks. I tried not to imagine Rhiwallon's body crushed beneath them. The tales said the fey wouldn't deliberately harm a human, but it was possible they might injure her through careless-ness. I found myself inspecting the base of each rocky pile for a protruding hand or foot.

It felt like we walked for hours, but at the same time it seemed like nothing. With each step, I was acutely aware of the dimin-ishing space yet to be searched. I grew less and less hopeful of finding any clue to Rhiwallon's location. Was this just another trick, another way to delay us?

I replayed the riddle in my mind. It contained no obvious reference to time, but from what I knew of the fey, it was likely that if we took too long Rhiwallon would be lost for ever. Even if the riddle did not mention a deadline, the creature that inhabited the web would not stay away from its home forever. And the longer we lingered here, the more time was passing in our own world. Every day here brought the new moon one night nearer and Ida that little bit closer to being unstoppable.

IDA

I NO LONGER feel Diarmuid. Is he dead? Surely I would know if he was. I would feel some parting of our connection, a breach, a severing. But this does not feel like a parting. He has simply… disappeared. I no longer feel my beast either. It is most curious and I do not know what to make of their disappearance.

Without Diarmuid to fill my senses, I feel oddly empty. He is a part of me in a way I never understood before. I had thought I could simply leave his head and never think of him again. But we are irrevocably joined. Now he is gone and I am alone.

What will I do if Diarmuid doesn't reappear? I shall go on as I have been, I suppose. I shall continue cleansing my village. And when I am done, what then? Another village perhaps? It seems somewhat pointless now if I can never show Diarmuid what I have done, how hard I have worked to rid my village of its taint. I can never hope he will be proud of me, that he might join me so we can work side by side, a bard and his muse. I cannot be a muse if I have no bard. Without Diarmuid, I no longer know what I am.

BRIGIT

SECURE IN OWAIN'S arms, I puzzled over our strange situation as we scoured the rocky cavern. Whoever had snatched Rhiwallon made no attempt to hide their scent. It was almost as if they wanted us to follow. Diarmuid could ill afford any delay to his quest although it was possible, perhaps even probable, that time in the fey tunnels was not passing at the same speed as time in the mortal world.

The odour that had led us here was odd. It wasn't human but neither did it smell like any animal I knew. It was a blend of every flower I had ever smelled mixed with something smoky and a trace of rotting leaves. It lingered so strongly that I wondered how Diarmuid and Owain couldn't smell it themselves.

Was my ability to track Rhiwallon's abductor the reason the fey girl had sent me on this journey in such a form? I had thought that perhaps she meant for me to play some part in Diarmuid's quest to stop his muse. But my only abilities were charms and cures, and the visions over which I had no control. What could I possibly do to aid him, especially in this form, if not to lead him to Rhiwallon?

The Sight had given no hint of this strange journey into the fey lands, but the vision in which I saw myself, in my own form, step forward to speak to Titania gave me hope that I would eventually be returned to my own body.

I suddenly realised that, as usual, I had wandered off into my own thoughts instead of paying attention to the task at hand. I turned my mind back to the search for Rhiwallon. My tail snaked down between my legs every time I looked at the web in the far corner of the cavern. I did not want to meet the creature who inhabited it.

Tucked under Owain's arm, I could feel his heart beating too quickly. He was scared, although on the outside he appeared as steadfast and implacable as ever. My paw ached and I had been thankful when Owain noticed my limp. I would have felt bad about burdening him with my weight, slight as it was, except that he barely seemed to notice. If he felt fatigue, he never showed it.

Diarmuid had started falling behind somewhere around the time we stopped to sleep in the green-lit tunnels. He never complained but Owain slowed his pace. I noticed too that as the water ran low Owain barely drank anything, merely wetting his lips to leave more for Diarmuid and I. He was a good man, Owain, and deserved far better than Maeve, however much he adored her.

As we searched the cavern, I tasted the air. The scent of Rhiwallon's attacker lingered strongly in here and beneath it I thought I detected the faintest trace of Rhiwallon herself. She was close, I was sure of that. If she wasn't still in this red-shrouded cavern, then she had been here very recently.

Finally, the only place left to search was behind the web itself. As we drew closer, I realised it was even more mammoth than I had thought. Each sticky strand was as thick as a man's finger. Something loomed on the other side, obscured by the web and the red murkiness. The web itself was securely anchored to the floor and sides and ceiling of the cavern. There was no way to creep around it. It seemed that someone must put their head through to see what was on the other side. Given that I was the smallest, it should have been me but I lacked the ability to convey whatever I saw. Owain was too big. It would have to be Diarmuid.

My heart stuttered as I watched Diarmuid drop his pack and take a deep breath, steadying himself. He too had realised it must be him. He was still something of a mystery to me, a strange contradiction with his claim to be able to bring his tales to life coupled with an utter lack of intuition. I owed him my life but there was also something else I felt, although it was still new and I hadn't let myself examine it fully. Despite his flaws, despite his complete inability to listen to me, I felt an ache in my heart when he was out of sight. A leap in my blood when he returned. Disappointment he couldn't see me for what I really was. And hope that perhaps one day he would.

34

DIARMUID

AS I STARED up at the web, my courage faltered. Had I the strength to run away, and enough supplies to last until I found a way out of this place, I would have fled, however much of a coward that made me.

"I'll do it," I said, reluctantly. "My head is smaller than yours."

I half-hoped Owain would disagree but he said nothing, only picked up an orange rock the size of my head and hefted it. It gave me some small amount of comfort to know that he would be waiting here, ready to defend me.

I dropped my pack on the ground. My legs already trembled so violently that I feared they might fail to hold me. I pictured myself falling forward into the web, trapped in its sticky strands and unable to free myself before its owner returned.

I met Bramble's eyes and she stared at me, unblinking. Her sense of smell was keen. Surely she would know if some other-worldly beast waited on the other side of the web. Surely she would try to alert me if she thought danger was imminent.

Slowly, slowly, I inserted my head between the threads, careful not to touch them. At first, all I could see was more rocks. Just another enormous tower of rocks streaked with grey and purple and red, even larger than those we had spent the last hour circling around. I looked up. And there she was.

Rhiwallon was perched at the very top of the massive rocky tower. Or at least, there was a figure with long red hair up there. I couldn't manoeuvre my head enough to see her clearly but what I saw made my courage falter. She was wrapped in a cocoon of silvery threads, upright, perhaps tied to a tall rock. A gossamer dress. The riddle seemed so obvious now. And her greatest fear? Abduction? The beast? I could only guess. I carefully withdrew my head from the web.

"Is she there?" Owain's face was pale and sombre.

"She's at the top of a tower of rocks, restrained with webs. One of us is going to have to climb up to cut her free."

We were both silent for a few moments.

"It has to be me," I said miserably, feeling like a pretty poor sort of hero. "We would have to cut too much of the web to get you through and the rocks might not be stable enough for someone your size."

"No way of cutting through it, though."

I retrieved the little bronze dagger from my boot. Owain didn't comment on my secret weapon. I assessed the threads. Here, a part of the web looked thinner and more crudely made than the rest. Bile rose in my throat and I forced it back down. There was no choice. We couldn't leave Rhiwallon here. Bramble's eyes were wide and full of concern.

"Be good for Owain." My voice wobbled dangerously. I bent down to stroke her whiskery cheek and she leaned into my touch, briefly closing her eyes. I clenched my jaw against the tears threatening to fall. "I'll be back soon."

Bramble whimpered and my heart ached. If I didn't go right now, I might lose what little courage I had.

"We'll be right here," Owain said. "Waiting."

I turned back to the web and raised my dagger. The thread was thicker than my thumb. My hand trembled and I took a deep breath, willing myself to calm. Careful not to touch the strand in case it clung to me, I gently sawed at it. Vibrations danced along the web no matter how light I tried to make my touch. The strand parted. I sawed at the next and soon it too fell away. One after another, I cut the sticky strings. One more and I would have an opening large enough to step through. Slowly the dagger sliced through and that strand too fell away.

I sucked in a deep breath as I readied myself to step through. I wanted to depart bravely, like a hero in an ancient tale, striding forth to meet danger without fear in my heart. Instead, my legs wobbled and my hands even more. Some hero I was. All I wanted to do was turn and flee. I could grab Bramble and be gone in moments. The thought shamed me, for I knew Owain would never leave Rhiwallon here. I had come for her only because Fiachra had hinted that my companions would be important to my quest. Owain would rescue her, or die trying, because it was the right thing to do.

"Watch for the beast," I said. Not exactly a bard-worthy final comment.

Clutching the dagger in my sweaty palm, heart thudding so loudly that surely the beast must hear even if it hadn't noticed the damage to its home, I stepped through the web.

Far above me, the sticky strands held Rhiwallon upright but her head was tipped forward and hair obscured her face. I couldn't tell whether she was unconscious or asleep.

"Diarmuid, what are you doing?" Owain's voice was soft and urgent.

"I'm about to start climbing." I tucked the dagger into my boot.

"Hurry," he said and his voice caught on the word.

Sweat trickled down the side of my face as I stared up at Rhiwallon's limp form and wished it was Owain here rather than me. I took a deep breath and prepared to climb.

Most of the rocks were only knee-high to me, so as long as the tower was stable, I should be able to climb it. I stepped up onto the first rock and scrabbled for a grip, my fingers slick with sweat. I hesitated but my purchase seemed steady so far. Another step up, then another. Slowly, slowly, agonisingly slowly. Step, grip, pull, pause.

I kept my eyes focused on the rocks around me. I didn't dare look up or down for fear of losing my balance and falling. Step, grip, pull. A heart-stopping moment as a rock shifted beneath me. I caught my breath and dug my fingers in so hard that a fingernail cracked. I eased up onto the next rock. Step, grip, pull. Rock by rock. Another fingernail broke. I was leaving scarlet smears on the rocks. Time seemed to stop. There was no end to this tower. I would climb forever and never reach the top.

Finally, I hauled myself over the edge and wiped bloody fingers on my pants. My hands throbbed but there was no time to check the damage. The beast could be on its way back. Rhiwallon was tied to a tall rock. Thick strands of sticky web held her upright.

"Rhiwallon," I whispered. "It's me, Diarmuid."

She moaned and twitched. With one trembling hand, I drew the hair back from her face. I had expected her to be bruised and bloodied but she appeared uninjured, although very pale.

"Rhiwallon." I patted her cheek, leaving smudges of blood. "Come on, Rhiwallon, you need to wake up."

Finally her eyes opened. They fixed on me, seemingly unknowing but then her eyes focused. "Diarmuid?" she croaked.

"It's all right." I tried to sound more confident than I felt. "I'm going to get you out of here. Just be quiet."

Rhiwallon looked around. I knew the exact moment she understood where she was for she moaned again, louder this time, and began to pull frantically at her sticky bonds.

"Hold still," I whispered. "I can cut the web but I need you to hold still."

"No, no." She thrashed and kicked but had little room to move. Her head cracked against the rock and she was still again.

"Rhiwallon? Come on, stay awake."

She moaned.

"Don't move," I whispered. "And be quiet. I don't know where the beast is."

She didn't respond. I took a deep breath, trying not to panic. When I sliced through the sticky strands, she collapsed at my feet, her eyes open and staring blankly. I patted her on the shoulder but she didn't seem to notice.

"Rhiwallon, get up." I poked her in the ribs and then, when she still didn't respond, slapped her lightly on the cheek. "Come on."

Rhiwallon blinked, her eyes dazed. I tugged on her arm and managed to get my shoulder partially under her. She made some effort to stand as I hauled her to her feet. Once I got her up, she could stand without assistance.

"I need you to listen to me." I grabbed her chin and turned her face towards me. She looked in my direction, if not directly at me. "Concentrate."

Her eyes were blank.

"We have to climb down these rocks. I can't carry you down. You have to climb. Do you understand?"

Rhiwallon blinked.

I dragged her over to the edge. "Look down."

Slowly, she tipped her head down.

"Can you see where we have to go? We need to climb down these rocks, all the way to the bottom. Owain and Bramble are waiting down there for us."

"Bramble?" she whispered.

"Yes, Bramble. She's at the bottom. You need to climb down to her."

"Climb."

"That's right. Let's go."

Somehow I got Rhiwallon down onto her belly and edged her, feet first, over the side. I could hardly breathe as I waited to see whether she would simply let go and fall.

"You have to climb," I said. "Go down."

Rhiwallon didn't move, didn't respond. Did she even know

where she was? Neither of us would survive a fall from this height.

"Move." I made my voice as harsh as I could. "Go on, move. Now."

She hesitated, wavered, and I thought she would surely fall. But then her fingers flexed, taking hold of a rock and clinging to it as she lowered herself down onto the next one. I could have cried with relief. As soon as Rhiwallon had progressed far enough that she couldn't grab me if she panicked, I followed her down.

Our progress was slow for I had to continually prompt her. She kept stopping as if she had forgotten what she was doing. So I told her to move, to go down, to get to the next rock. I followed slowly, staying well out of her reach and trying not to worry about how slowly we were moving. We were halfway down when Owain's cry echoed through the cavern.

"Diarmuid, it comes."

"Go, Rhiwallon." I dropped down onto the next rock and almost landed on her fingers.

She started and looked up at me. For a moment I thought I saw a flicker of comprehension and then it was gone, replaced by the vacant stare.

"Move," I snarled.

Then I heard Owain again, a ringing call of challenge, which was answered by a low hiss. There was a crash like rocks smashing together. I gritted my teeth and moved faster. Another clash of rocks. Another yell from Owain. We were almost at the bottom.

"Faster," I hissed.

Almost there. One rock to go.

Then I saw the beast. It was on our side of the web and far too close to the rocks on which we perched. It was easily twice my height with a furry black body and too many legs to count. I cowered as it reared up on its back legs, hissing, and all eight eyes looked directly at me. Venom dripped from its fangs and sizzled on the rocky floor. Time seemed to blur and disappear. The beast hissed again. Owain yelled and a rock slammed into the beast's side. It yowled.

I dropped down from the rocks, landing heavily. Pain shot through my injured ankle and I smothered a cry. Rhiwallon still hesitated on the last rock.

"Come on, Rhiwallon."

She climbed down, moving far too slowly. As soon as her feet touched the ground, I grabbed her hand and we ran. My ankle burned with every step but it held my weight. The beast was blocking our access to the hole I had cut so I ran towards the far end of the web. If Owain could keep the beast occupied long enough, I could cut a new hole. Rhiwallon stumbled and fell. I hauled her back to her feet, ignoring the blood on her knees and palms.

Another hiss came from behind us. As we reached the far corner, I looked back and the sight of the enormous creature leaping towards us, legs outstretched, was worse than any nightmare. Its mouth gaped open, red and terrifying and far too large.

Rhiwallon stumbled again and fell, dragging me with her. The last thing I saw was furry black underbelly. Then I was squashed beneath it, still clutching Rhiwallon's hand with everything I had. The world went black.

DIARMUID

THE CAVERN FLOOR was hard beneath me, smooth but unforgiving on my sore body. I opened my eyes. Rocks towered above me and the enormous web was motionless. I lifted my arms, expecting the resistance of gossamer bonds. My arms weren't tied, but they were slick with blood and a putrid greyish goo.

I licked my dry lips, tasted something foul, and tried to speak. My first attempt was an incoherent mumble but it was enough to bring Bramble to my side. She sniffed me, her nose close to my face, dark eyes worried.

"Hey girl," I tried to say. What came out was another moan but Bramble wagged her tail and gave a short bark.

Owain was by my side in an instant. His solemn face chilled me.

"Rhiwallon?" My voice was hoarse and my throat hurt to say even that much. Owain's face stilled and my heart dropped.

"Alive," he said. "But not well."

I tried to sit up but my body wouldn't cooperate and my bloodied hands couldn't grip the rocky floor. Owain helped me, his shoulder strong and sturdy beneath my arm.

"What is this stuff all over me?" My head throbbed and the cavern shifted.

"Beast exploded."

"It's dead?"

Owain's face was grim. "Dead all right."

"Where is it?"

He shook his head. "Don't need to see."

"Where's Rhiwallon?"

"Behind you. I'll help, when you're ready." His mouth was set in a grim line.

Once the cavern stopped spinning, Owain helped me to my feet, gripping my shoulders tightly. My injured ankle throbbed. My head felt like thistledown and my whole body hurt. My hands were sticky but I couldn't find a clean place on either pants or shirt to wipe them, and we had no water. My stomach rolled and I clenched my jaw, fighting not to add vomit to the mess covering me.

Rhiwallon sat on a rock a dozen or so paces behind where I had lain, her shoulders hunched and hair hanging down over her face. She too was covered in blood and mess. Owain held me up as I staggered over to her. Bramble was right by my side, pressing her nose against my calf each time I paused. When we reached Rhiwallon, Bramble sat beside her, close but not touching, looking up at her with troubled eyes and lowered ears.

"Rhiwallon?" I croaked.

She sat perfectly still, hands clasped loosely in her lap. I reached out one hand to part her hair, pushing it away from her face. I wouldn't have touched her, covered in the sticky mess as I was, except that it was all over her too. Globs of the stuff hung in her hair and on her cheeks. Rhiwallon's face was blank, her eyes open but empty.

Snatches of tales ran through my mind, stories of those who had returned from the lands of the fey with their minds damaged, their lives forever changed. I swallowed hard. She wouldn't have been here if it wasn't for me.

"Has she spoken?" I asked.

Owain shook his head.

"She's—" I couldn't put it into words.

"Gone," Owain supplied.

"I think so. She's… she's traumatised."

"Will she come back?"

I waved a hand in front of her eyes. Owain's face was hopeful, his voice tentative. Bramble put her front paws on Rhiwallon's knees and leaned in to sniff her. I gently rested a hand on the top of Bramble's head and she leaned into my touch. At least she was unharmed.

"It was too much for her." I chose my words carefully. "More than she could handle. I think…" His face fell. I took a deep breath. "I think she's lost her mind."

"But she'll get better, won't she?" he asked, fiercely.

"I don't know, Owain. I'm not a healer, just a bard."

Owain crouched in front of Rhiwallon and wrapped his large hands around her tiny ones. "It's over, Rhiwallon. The beast is dead. It's all over."

Rhiwallon didn't move. Owain released her hands and stood. His face showed remorse and guilt. "It's my fault," he said. "I didn't protect her."

"It's not—"

He stopped me with an abrupt motion of his hand. "I'll look after her. Won't let her down again."

"What do you mean?"

He nodded towards Rhiwallon. "I'll look after her till she comes back to herself. Then I'll handfast with her, if she'll have me. I can protect her, look after her. She'll never want for anything."

"What about Maeve?" The words were out of my mouth before I thought twice.

Owain gave me a tight smile. "She's free to go her own way. Me and Rhiwallon will start somewhere else. A new life."

I looked back at Rhiwallon, so still and silent. This was more my fault than Owain's but it never would have occurred to me to offer to bind myself to her.

"We need to move on," I said. "The beast might have a mate."

Owain nodded and slung his pack and the bow and quiver over his shoulders. Then he lifted Rhiwallon. She hung limply in his arms, like a broken doll.

I had avoided looking at the gaping hole at the end of the cavern until now. As we walked towards the opening, my heart was as heavy as the rocks surrounding us. Whatever we faced next might well be worse.

36

IDA

W HERE ONCE I felt the shining spark of Diarmuid's life, somewhere in my breast, now there is nothing. For days, I have felt nothing.

I hardly know what to do. I am not myself. The thought that he might be dead fills my body with... with something I cannot name. My stomach clenches, my throat aches, and strangest of all, my eyes fill with liquid.

Emotions. I thought I understood them, but I find that although I know their names, I don't know how they feel. Is this fear? Sadness? Grief? Horror? Diarmuid's tales speak of all these things but I cannot tell one from the other. My eyes burn when I think of Diarmuid and my hands tremble at the thought that he might be dead.

I sit alone in the living room of the house I inhabit. Its former inhabitants left when I announced I would live here. What else was I to do? I needed somewhere to live and this is a fine house. They needn't have left, though. I think I would have welcomed their company. Perhaps I would not feel quite so alone had I some distraction from wondering whether Diarmuid is dead.

A companion is what I need. A diversion. If he is strong and handsome, even better. I do not want to dwell on the reason for these strange feelings. For I suspect I know what it is and I am not yet prepared to admit it, even to myself. So I shall choose a companion and he will come here to live with me. He will be a pleasant distraction from these feelings I do not know how to deal with.

37

BRIGIT

THE BEAST LAY dead on the cavern floor and we walked away, albeit somewhat unsteadily. The smell of flowers and rotting leaves clung to the beast's body, the scent I had tracked to locate Rhiwallon. I wanted to tuck my tail between my legs and flatten my ears back against my head and run as fast as I could. Where to, it didn't matter, as long as it was far away from here.

Despite the fey companions of my younger years, most of my knowledge about their race came from ancient tales, and from the wisdom passed down from wise woman to apprentice. Although the tasks of the fey might seem unachievable, the laws of balance meant that there must be a way for it to be completed, however unlikely. I clutched this thought tightly in my heart and prayed that such ancient wisdom wasn't wrong. There had to be a way out of this place.

As we walked through yet another green-lit tunnel, I felt someone watching. I sniffed the air, searching for the watcher's scent, but the only odours I detected belonged to our party: sweat, the unmistakable stink of fear, and the dead beast, whose fetid insides coated Diarmuid and Rhiwallon. If the beast had a mate, I scented no trace of it nearby. Even the fey, whom I thought I had detected from time to time, were now absent. I had mostly come to trust that this body understood the world in a way my human brain never could. And right now, even thought I could identify no other scent, I knew we were not alone.

As we reached the opening, a new scent finally reached my nose and the fear that something terrible awaited us on the other side became overpowering. It smelled like the coals of a dead fire mixed with rotting eggs and utter desperation. Shudders wracked my body and my paws refused to move.

Diarmuid caressed the back of my head and, despite the ooze coating his fingers, I leaned into his hand. The warmth of his fingers soothed me somewhat and a tiniest bit of terror unwrapped itself from my heart.

"Come, Bramble," he said. "We have no choice."

I willed myself to move but my paws felt like they had sunk roots down through the rocky floor. Diarmuid scooped me up. This close to him, the stench of the dead beast was overwhelming and I gagged. He held me to his chest and I could feel his heart beating rapidly.

As we passed through the opening, I rested my head against Diarmuid's shoulder. In the safety of his arms my terror faded, and as my heartbeat calmed, our two hearts beat together for a few moments. And I suddenly knew, deep in my soul, that he was the reason I was here.

How did I not see this earlier? My sense of smell had been useful in locating Rhiwallon but there was little else I could contribute to Diarmuid's quest. But he was part of some pattern the fey intended to weave in my life. Or perhaps I was meant as part of his pattern. No matter. The fey intended we be together and they were determined to ensure it happened. So determined they cared little what form I was in.

Before I could think further on this revelation, I realised I was hot. Not merely uncomfortably warm but so hot that my skin burned. Sweat dripped down my back and over my belly, leaving my hair damp. My mouth was dry and sticky. As we reached the opening, the feeling of dread surged again. I whimpered and Diarmuid's arm tightened around me. Ahead of us, Owain stopped, his large frame blocking my view.

"What is it?" Diarmuid whispered.

I tried hard not to tremble. Owain stepped aside so we could see. Another cavern, even larger than the last. Not far ahead of us, the floor dropped away into a yawning crevice, a smoky haze obscuring its depths. It stretched all the way across the cavern, an insurmountable obstacle between this side and the other.

If I could have spoken, I would have begged Diarmuid to never let me go, but he set me down on the rocky ground. I chided myself. I was forgetting who I really was. I, Brigit, should not be intimidated by these events. My mother would be ashamed. I gave myself a good shake then strode forward. I peered down into the depths of the crevice, holding my breath for the stench smelled like rotten eggs months. The crevice was exactly what it seemed from Diarmuid's arms: inconceivably deep, hot, and smoky. I stepped back from the edge and it was well that I did, for a wave of heat surged up and blasted my face. I stumbled back, eyes and skin burning. A massive tongue of fire followed the heat and a low grumble shook the ground, throwing me off my feet.

"What is it?" Owain asked. His face was ruddy and his shirt was drenched in sweat. He clutched Rhiwallon's limp body to his chest and I wished it were me there instead of her.

"There are tales of such places," Diarmuid said, "where the ground parts and shakes, where fire and flames leap up from below. Sometimes, the fire pours out like ale flows from an over-filled mug."

Yet within the boundaries of the fey lands, things might not be what they seemed. The heat on my face and the burning in my lungs seemed fierce and real but this might prove to be our exit if we trusted enough to ignore the illusion and walk over the chasm.

"What do we do?" Owain asked. "Can we go back?"

Diarmuid shook his head. "Not if I know anything about the

fey's rules. If we don't continue, they might well snatch Rhiwallon away again. We have to keep moving forward and let the fey take us where they will."

The rising steam shifted and we now saw a rocky bridge. Its tenuous span passed from one edge of the gaping hole in the ground to the other, stretching right across the cavern. There was no visible means of support and it would likely crumble the moment someone stepped foot on it.

Diarmuid nodded towards it. "That's our way out."

The words from Titania's rhyme already ran through my mind. *One may pass the fiery depths and only once may go.*

"A trap," Owain said.

Another ground tremor was accompanied by the rankness of rotting eggs. The stench wormed into my lungs and I felt like I was choking.

Diarmuid held his hand over his nose. "There's always a way through the tasks set by the fey. We have to think."

"One may pass and only once," Owain said. "Clear enough. Go. We'll wait here."

Diarmuid glared at him. "Nobody is staying behind. We came in here together and we leave together. We just have to figure out what we're missing. There's a way out."

The answer seemed obvious to me. Owain could carry all of us. His presence was no accident any more than mine was. But how could I tell them? Owain would listen but not understand. Diarmuid would understand but not listen. My tail drooped.

Diarmuid's face showed determination. He was considering crossing the bridge with the intention of seeking help for the rest of us. The ground trembled and grumbled, and I was nearly thrown off my feet. My mind spun as I slunk after Diarmuid and Owain. I couldn't think of a single way I might convey the solution. I had to stop Diarmuid before he stepped onto the bridge. I barked, short and sharp. They turned to look at me.

"What is it, girl?" Diarmuid asked, a distant look in his eyes.

Owain met my eyes. I held his gaze and he slowly nodded. "Bramble wants us to listen."

Diarmuid looked out at the bridge. "There's got to be another way around."

"Bramble knows it," Owain said.

"Huh?" Diarmuid shot him a puzzled look. "What? She's just—"

Owain cut him off, but I knew what Diarmuid had been about to say and my heart burned. "We need to listen to Bramble."

Diarmuid shook his head. "Owain, we don't have time for this. We've got one chance. There has to be another way across."

Owain still held my gaze and now he nodded at me. "Go on, Bramble."

Frustration mounting, I barked again. Why would the fey send me on this journey in such a useless form? Surely they foresaw this. They knew that at some point, I would desperately need to speak.

Diarmuid sighed. "I don't think now is the time—"

"Course now is the time." Owain's voice, although placid as ever, was underlaid with tension. "Bramble needs to tell us something and we need to listen."

Diarmuid opened his mouth to argue but Owain stood his ground.

"You're a bard," he said. "You must know tales where things like this happen."

"Things like what?"

"Folk trapped in other forms."

Diarmuid looked at him blankly and Owain motioned towards me. Diarmuid's mouth opened and closed. "She… I found her… She's just…"

My heart shattered into a million pieces. After all the time Diarmuid and I had spent together, all the secrets he had confided in me, he still had no idea. I had hoped that perhaps somewhere deep inside, he suspected there was more to me than there seemed. That he would understand once he finally let himself see.

Owain shrugged, adjusting his grip on Rhiwallon who still hung, unresponsive, in his arms. "P'rhaps I'm wrong. I'm just a simple man. Seems to me a bard would know more about these things than me."

Diarmuid eyed me closely and I met his gaze, not trying to hide the hurt flaring in my eyes. It wasn't like he would see it anyway. Owain would though. If his arms weren't full of Rhiwallon, he would have given me a comforting rub and some soft words. But it wasn't Owain I wanted to comfort me.

As Diarmuid looked me in the eyes — really looked at me for the first time — I saw his disbelief and yet also the tiniest spark of doubt. He was examining himself, wondering whether it was true, whether he might have missed some clue to my Otherworldly state. But mostly, he simply didn't believe. Eventually he shook his head.

"We don't have time for this." His tone was conciliatory. "The longer we spend in here, the stronger Ida becomes. Whatever you think Bramble may or may not be, what we need to worry about right now is finding a way out of here."

The look Owain gave him was the closest to disgust I had ever seen on the big man's face. Then he turned his back to Diarmuid and looked right at me. "Tell us, Bramble."

Diarmuid sighed and I knew he probably rolled his eyes but I tried hard to ignore both him and the hurt in my heart. How could I convey the idea of carrying us? A horse. Horses carry people. In my mind, I saw a horse stretch out its neck. It shook its mane and extended a foreleg before prancing around. I tried to copy its action but my body was all wrong. My neck didn't stretch elegantly like a horse's and I probably looked like I was shaking water off myself, not shaking a mane. When I extended one of my front legs, it didn't seem to bend the way I wanted it to and my prancing made Diarmuid raise his eyebrows as if I had suddenly lost my mind.

Owain nodded encouragingly. "Go on."

Diarmuid's eyes went blank. He wasn't even paying attention

any more. My heart plummeted. How else could I tell them? My gaze landed on Rhiwallon, still held firmly in Owain's arms. Even now, after bearing her for so long, he showed not the slightest sign of tiredness. That gave me an idea.

I trotted over to Owain and stood beside him, arching my back as if he was lifting me with a hand beneath my chest. He looked down at me and waited, his face patient. I stood up on my back legs, front paws resting on his knees like I did when I wanted to sit on his lap, and still Owain merely stared. Diarmuid wasn't even watching.

"Keep going, Bramble," Owain said. "What else can you show me?"

I voiced my frustration with a bark and Diarmuid glanced at me.

"She wants you to pick her up," he said absently, before turning back to contemplate the bridge.

I barked again — *yes, yes!* — and comprehension filtered into Owain's eyes.

"Clever Bramble!" he said.

I let my tongue hang out, panting a little.

"Don't you see, Diarmuid," Owain said. "That's the solution. We *can* all cross the bridge."

Diarmuid spun around. "What?"

"Bramble figured it out."

Diarmuid's face showed brief incredulity before he schooled it to politeness. Perhaps it was better I was a dog than a woman, for at least in this form I was under no illusion as to my future with Diarmuid. It simply didn't exist.

"I'll carry you across," Owain said. "All of you, all at once."

"One may pass the fiery depths and only once may go," Diarmuid said. He nodded slowly. "Yes, yes, it could work."

Owain smiled down at me and his plain face looked quite handsome. He might not recognise me for what I truly was but at least he knew I was more than I seemed.

"Well done, Bramble," Owain said.

"I suppose Bramble gave us the key, by asking you to pick her up," Diarmuid said. "We would have figured it out sooner or later."

I raised my lips and snarled at him. Diarmuid, of all people, should have been the first to know. Instead, it was Owain with his simple mind and his open heart who was willing to listen.

Diarmuid raised his eyebrows in surprise. He extended a hand towards me, his face cautious. "Bramble, take it easy, girl."

I snarled again and turned my back on him. I sat, the cavern floor warm beneath my rump.

"Leave her, Diarmuid," Owain said. "You can't fix it 'til you see the truth."

"See *what* truth?" Diarmuid asked, a frustrated edge in his voice.

"Look at her," Owain said gently. "Really look at her."

I didn't need to look back over my shoulder to know that Diarmuid didn't so much as even glance at me. His attention was already focused again on the bridge.

DIARMUID

MY SOUL FINALLY felt the truth of Owain's words even as my eyes saw only the familiar scruffy terrier. Shame and utter disappointment welled up in me as I turned back to face the bridge.

I was the bard, the one who knew the ancient tales. Here was one living an ancient archetype of tale and I had never even noticed. It should have been me who recognised Bramble first. Not Owain, whose occupation called not for delicate words, filled with symbolism and meaning and truth, but rather brute force and the delivery of blood and death. I heard Titania's words again: *One will bear another's coat until the final round.*

"It's Bramble, isn't it?" I said. "The riddle. The one who bears another's coat."

Owain barely glanced at me. He shrugged.

"So what is she?" I muttered, eying Bramble who sat with her back to me. "Human? Fey? Is she sent to spy on us or to aid us?"

Bramble huffed but didn't turn to face me. Owain scowled and shame coloured my cheeks. Bramble had never given me any reason to doubt her and, indeed, hadn't she deciphered the riddle's clue to crossing the chasm?

"We should go," I said. My mind was all awhirl and I didn't know what else to say.

In silence, the three of us stepped up to the place where the bridge began and my already-doubtful heart sank. The bridge was barely a handspan across, a continuation of the same rocky floor we had traversed for so long. It looked as if the living rock had simply grown and stretched from one side of the chasm all the way across to the other. There was no visible means of support and the rock was so thin it could not possibly hold even Bramble's slight weight.

Owain still carried Rhiwallon as easily as if she weighed no more than Bramble but was he strong enough to carry all three of us across? The bridge must be two hundred paces or more. And what if the tongues of fire rose up again? There would be no escape.

"I don't think this is possible," I said. "There must be another way across."

"You can climb onto my back. Bramble will have to sit on Rhiwallon." Owain's voice was calm and certain. He nodded towards the terrier. "Lift her up."

I was slightly reassured that Owain at least thought this would work. If I could have thought of another option, anything at all, I would have suggested it but my mind was blank. I felt a deep certainty that this was the solution Titania intended us to find.

Bramble trembled as I grasped her around the middle. If Rhiwallon panicked, she would knock Bramble right off her lap. Under other circumstances, I would have given Bramble a gentle stroke or said something comforting but I couldn't bring myself to do it. I released her abruptly, almost dropping her onto Rhiwallon.

With Rhiwallon and Bramble in his arms, Owain planted his feet wide apart and waited for me to gain purchase on his back, between his pack and Rhiwallon's bow. My first two attempts resulted in hard landings on the rocky floor. With both tailbone and pride bruised, my third attempt was more successful and I managed to clamber up high enough up to wrap my arms around Owain's neck. My legs grasped his waist tightly.

Owain shifted slightly, adjusting his grip on Rhiwallon. If he was nervous, he did not quiver, but was as sturdy as ever. He stepped right up to the chasm. I felt his chest expand as he took a deep breath. Then he placed one foot on the narrow bridge.

I held my breath, heart pounding wildly, as Owain leaned forward. His muscles tensed beneath me and he hesitated, testing the bridge's strength. The moment seemed to last forever. Finally, he stepped forward. Now that he had committed to the crossing, he had no option other than to keep going until he reached the other side. If not, he may as well throw us all over the edge right now. Over the chasm the heat was even fiercer. It flooded up from the depths, the air so hot it almost burned my face.

Owain strode confidently across the bridge, carrying four lives with every step. I kept my gaze locked on the far side of the chasm, not daring even the smallest glance down for fear I would panic and lose my grip. If I let go, Owain couldn't catch me, not without dropping Rhiwallon and Bramble, and they were both precious to him. Certainly more precious than I. I stared at the end of the bridge, praying with every step that Owain would have the strength to get us there.

Halfway across, he wobbled briefly before regaining his balance. I tightened my grip on his neck a little too much and his shoulders twitched as he started to gasp for air. I forced my fingers to relax and he was able to breathe again. We crept towards the end of the bridge with excruciating slowness. I was aware of every beat of my heart and of every breath Owain took. He laboured now, drawing in big gulps of air and his neck gleamed with sweat. My limbs began to shake with the effort of holding on and the heat made my head spin.

We were barely a dozen paces from safety when a roar shattered the air. Images flashed through my mind: griffins, harpies, banshees. Owain's foot slipped and he teetered. Moments passed and my heart seemed to stop beating as I clung to his back. In my mind, I saw the four of us plunging down into the chasm. The image was so vivid that it took several moments before I realised we weren't plummeting towards the bottom after all.

Owain continued, step by step, bringing us steadily closer to the other side. A muscle in my thigh developed a cramp and the prospect of waiting even another few moments became almost unbearable. It took every scrap of my willpower to hold on as Owain made those last perilous steps. As his foot touched solid safety, my leg began to spasm. Owain stepped off the bridge as I slid down his back and tumbled onto the rocky surface, landing mere finger widths from the edge.

He crouched with a grunt to deposit Rhiwallon, still insensible, on the ground. Bramble tumbled off Rhiwallon's lap, trembling convulsively, tongue hanging out as she panted. Owain sat, abruptly, beside Rhiwallon's prone form, his legs splayed out in front of him. His shirt was drenched with sweat and he raised his shaking hands to cover his face.

I rolled onto my hands and knees and scurried away from the edge, then lay on my belly on the warm rocky floor. Right now, it was all I could do to lie here. I could not have done what Owain did, even if I had the physical strength. Only the tremble in his hands now betrayed how terrified he had been.

"What was that noise?" I asked. "It sounded like..."

In truth, I didn't know what it sounded like but I didn't need to identify the creature to know danger lurked nearby.

And it made me think of another winged beast: the raven I had dreamed of for so many years. Ebony feathers, beady eyes, midnight-dark blood glistening on its beak. Perhaps as I drew closer to a confrontation with Ida, I also came nearer to discovering the meaning of the raven.

Bramble stumbled over to Owain. She licked him on the knee and gazed up at him. Owain met her eyes and it seemed some wordless communication passed between them. How could I have ever thought of Bramble as mine? I had often fallen asleep at night imagining myself roaming the fields of Silver Downs, creating my tales while Bramble ran at my side, jumping streams and scrambling onto rocks to find a sunny place to nap. It had been many days since I had considered trying to find her previous owner, but perhaps staying with me was never her intention. I had no claim over her. For reasons known only to her, Bramble had decided to journey with me this far. It was clearly Owain she was fond of. Owain she would depart with once this was over. Perhaps it was better that way for I likely wouldn't survive the coming confrontation with Ida. Still, it was like a little piece of my heart had crumbled away. I scrambled gracelessly to my feet, my thigh muscles still spasming.

"We should keep moving," I said. "I would prefer not to wait until whatever creature made that sound arrives."

Owain's hauled himself to his feet. He winced and held his shoulders oddly as he gathered Rhiwallon up again.

"Are you hurt?" I asked.

He shook his head but didn't meet my eyes. The roar came again, ringing through the cavern. Was it a sound of challenge? Of alarm?

"Let's go." I turned to the opening at the far end of the cavern. "Maybe this path will lead outside."

I stepped forward, feeling more alone than I had since the day I first found Bramble in the woods. Behind me, Owain followed, bearing Rhiwallon. Bramble trotted beside him. When I reached the opening, the tunnel stretched ahead of me, dark and ominous, smelling of damp and something I couldn't identify, like a cross between a wild boar and the new sparks from a tinder.

"Diarmuid?" Owain spoke quietly and I heard both hesitance and exhaustion in his voice.

I took a deep breath. "Let's go."

"We're right behind you."

We had been walking for only moments when I spotted light up ahead.

"I think the tunnel's ending," I said.

From the corner of my eye, I saw a flash of white near the ground. Bramble, moving ahead of me.

"Bramble, wait," I hissed. "It might not be safe."

A sniff of disgust.

I trudged faster. I could not let her go alone into unknown danger. Not now that I knew. We reached the end of the tunnel together and entered a small cavern illuminated by clean, white light. There were three doors.

Like the bridge, the doors belonged to this place, melding into the surrounding rock as if they had grown out of it. The doors were identical: smooth panels of wood stretching from side to side, arced at the top, their sides fitting cleanly into the rocks without hinge or latch.

Owain and I looked at each other. I was sure he, like I, searched the riddle for any reference to doors.

"How do we choose?" I asked. "Are we permitted to open each and look through or may we open only one?"

"More tunnels?" Owain asked.

"Possibly. Or other places."

I frantically searched my memory as I stared at the doors. Surely somewhere in my mind was a tale of mysterious doors in a fey tunnel but I could recall nothing useful.

"There doesn't seem to be anything in the riddle that tells us what to do," I said. "If this is another test, there will be rules. We just don't know what."

"Can't follow rules we don't know."

"No." My voice was curt, although I did try to temper my tone. "All we can do is choose one door to open and trust it will be the right one."

"How?"

We stared at the doors and at each other, neither wanting to make a choice that might send us into an even worse situation. Bramble, meanwhile, was busy. I had paid scant attention but now I noticed that she was sniffing each door again and again. She finally stopped, nose pressed to the base of the middle door.

"Bramble's chosen," Owain said. He adjusted his grip on Rhiwallon. Her head lolled backwards, her eyes still blank.

I didn't want to admit the truth only because I was disappointed that *I* hadn't recognised Bramble first. The fact that Owain saw through her disguise before me didn't make it any less true. It simply made it harder to accept.

"Bramble's choice," I agreed.

Bramble looked up at me and I saw, for the first time, the hurt in her eyes. I had let her down over and over. My recognition now did little to alleviate the pain I had caused but I hoped it might show I was finally willing to believe.

"Are you sure?" I asked her.

With her eyes locked on mine, Bramble nodded and I could no longer even pretend to deny the truth. Whatever Bramble might be, she understood my words.

"All right, then," I said.

I set my hand against the door. Its wood was smooth beneath my palm. I held my breath and pushed. The door swung open without the slightest sound or hesitation. Blinding light burned my eyes. Behind me, Owain muttered a curse. Squinting as my eyes adjusted, I gasped, for now I knew what manner of beast we had heard. Many a tale spoke of such places but I never dreamed I would see one with my own eyes.

Here, by my foot, a golden bracelet studded with crimson gems. There, a cunningly-carved chest overflowed with jewels the size of my fist: blood-red, sea green, the clear blue of a midsummer sky, and wine-dark purple. A silver sword, so finely-wrought it could not have been made by human hands. A golden helmet, splendid enough for a king to wear into battle. Everywhere I looked, priceless treasures were scattered across the floor and piled into mounds. As always in this strange underground place, there was no obvious source of light. It seemed the air itself shone white, illuminating the vast treasure stores and reflecting off them. But where was the owner of these treasures?

"Don't like this," Owain muttered.

I was instantly thankful he was not the type likely to become overwhelmed with greed. "The dragon won't be far away. We need to get out of here before it returns."

Rhiwallon stirred and moaned. Owain cleared some space, moving rare treasures out of the way with his foot, and gently set her down. Bramble leaned in, sniffing Rhiwallon's face. Rhiwallon lay still and quiet for a few moments. Then her eyes seemed to focus. She looked up at each of us in turn.

"Wh—" Her voice was hoarse and she stopped to lick her lips. "What happened?"

"You're safe now," Owain said, his voice gentle.

"There was a…" Rhiwallon's voice was stronger, although still halting. "An enormous…"

"We came to get you," Owain said. "It's dead."

"Are you sure?" Her face was a curious mixture of trust and disbelief.

"Dead," Owain confirmed.

"It won't come after you again," I said, feeling rather redundant.

"There was a… a *thing* standing over me when I woke up." Her voice was a little stronger now. "And then there were hands. They touched me, picked me up, so many hands. Then I was in a cave and it was tying me up. I thought it wanted—" She clutched both hands to her stomach and shuddered. "I thought it was going to kill me."

I wondered what she had been going to say before she stopped herself.

Owain raised a hand, as if touch her, but hesitated. He let his hand fall. "It's all over."

Beside me, Bramble whined softly, and almost without thinking, I rested my hand against her back. Exactly what manner of creature she was didn't seem all that important right now. What mattered was that we were all alive, and together. But that might not last if we didn't get out of here soon.

"We need to move," I said. "The dragon will return sooner or later and I, for one, want to be gone before then."

Rhiwallon started to sit up and Owain quickly reached out to help her. She waved him away and unsteadily climbed to her feet. "I'm really not in the mood for a dragon right now."

"I'll protect you," Owain said.

She looked at him for a long moment. "We'll protect each other. I'd like my bow back."

He handed her weapons over without comment and she strapped the belt around her waist, fumbling a little with the buckle. Once the quiver hung the way she wanted it to, she slung the bow over her shoulder. "How do we get out of here?" she asked in a voice that sounded almost normal.

All three of them looked to me. Why should it be me who led them? Surely any decision I made would only lead us astray. Look at where I had taken us so far. And yet they waited.

"We still haven't found the key," I said. "Perhaps the next door we need will be locked. It would make sense for the locked door to be the one leading from a dragon's lair. Of all of the caverns, this might be the one we need to leave the fastest, so of course it will be locked."

"I can carry you, if you need," Owain said to Rhiwallon.

She glowered at him. "I can walk."

"Don't touch anything," I said, feeling somewhat left out. "The tales tell that he who steals from a dragon's lair will pay dearly, usually with his life. And keep together."

We set off in single file, me first, then Bramble, Rhiwallon, and Owain at the back, scouring the treasures for anything that might be the key from the riddle. Our progress was slow and I was ever conscious that the dragon must soon return. Surely it had already scented us.

"This is impossible," Rhiwallon said. "How are we supposed to find one tiny key in all of this? It could be buried within any of these piles."

"It must be here somewhere." I straightened my shoulders and tried to act like the leader they seemed to expect me to be. "The riddles of the fey are never impossible. They want us to give up, to fail, but they have to allow us an opportunity to succeed, however small. So the key is here and it's somewhere we can see it, just as the riddle says."

"What happens if we don't find it?" Owain asked.

We hadn't yet discussed the possibility of failure. In a tale, the hero eventually succeeds at his task. He might fail the first time and perhaps the second, and the odds against him might seem insurmountable, but he always wins in the end. Except in my tales.

"I don't know," I said. "Perhaps we will have to stay here forever. We should have asked."

"Too late now," Owain said and I envied his simple practicality.

We traversed the dragon's lair step by step, passing countless mounds of treasures. Bracelets, rings and crowns. Shields, swords and a golden suit of armour. Box after box spilled over with brightly-coloured jewels. The dragon who possessed these treasures must be ancient indeed.

Behind me, Owain called out. "Diarmuid, wait."

I turned around and discovered I was some distance ahead of the others. "What's wrong?"

"Bramble stopped. She won't move."

Bramble was crouched down low to the ground, tail tucked beneath her rump, her whole body shaking. Of course it would be Owain who noticed her distress. It was never me.

"Bramble?" I asked. "What is it, girl?"

She looked around the cavern, gaze darting from place to place. It was as if she searched for something she could smell but not see.

"It's the dragon, isn't it?" I asked. "It returns."

Bramble met my eyes and whimpered.

Rhiwallon sighed. "Really not in the mood."

"We should hurry," I said. "We can still find the key and get out of here."

Even as I spoke, a bellow rang through the air. The dragon had returned.

39

IDA

I AM OUT of patience with the mortal man who has been my companion these last few days, although companion is hardly a suitable description. His overwhelming desire to please irritates me. He hovers by my side, waiting for the opportunity to do something, anything. At times, I tell him to go away and he does, but only briefly. Then he returns, eager as ever, apologising for whatever he believes made me send him away.

I can't help but compare him to the boy. The boy is tortured, with his dark thoughts and his twisted tales. But he is also aloof, reserved. He holds himself somewhat apart from others. He observes. He does not cling or fuss or smother.

I do not understand how mortals can commit themselves to another for a lifetime. True, their lives are fleeting but surely they grow tired of their mate, bored with endlessly repeating the same conversations, the same actions, day after day after day. Some choose to leave, to find themselves a new companion. But so many stay and spend the rest of their lives trying to convince themselves they are happy.

This mortal has been my companion for, what, three, four days? I grit my teeth every time he enters the room for I cannot bear to hear his whiny voice, full of flattery and hope. Today, I will tell him to leave, to go out to the woods and to remain there. And then I will be able to relax, to soften my tight muscles, to unclench my gritted teeth.

I shall choose another companion. There are plenty of fine men in this village. In fact, this morning I saw one who might be suitable. Lean and broad shouldered. Thick, red hair. Strong hands. He will be satisfactory. Pleasant to look at and not too annoying are my only criteria. There was a woman with him this morning, perhaps a little younger than he, small and dark-haired. She was clutching his hand and smiling up at him. A sister perhaps, or a wife. No matter. He will forget her quickly enough.

If only I could forget. But I know I will measure every companion against the boy. If I could forget him, perhaps I could be happy. I need to find a companion who does not force me to remember what I no longer have.

40

BRIGIT

A ROAR SPLIT the air and I froze, quivering, my belly pressed against the rocky floor. The dragon's scent overwhelmed me, a cross between some forest creature and a recently-extinguished fire. I felt it in my nose, tasted it on my tongue.

"Run!" Owain grabbed Rhiwallon's hand and scooped me up as he fled.

Clutched to his chest, I could feel his heart pounding. If Owain was scared, I was even more afraid. We darted around mounds of treasure, but surely running was pointless, for we had found neither the key nor the door to which it belonged. We needed time: time to search for the key, time to find the door, time to make sure we didn't break the riddle's rules. We could hardly do that while fleeing a dragon. Another roar echoed and I clung to Owain, heedless of how my claws dug into his arm. We were out of time, doomed.

Diarmuid yelled and pointed. "There, the door."

And there it was: a small wooden door, large enough for Owain to squeeze through but not big enough to admit the dragon. If we could find the key quickly, we might yet escape. Another roar, closer this time. The dragon's odour grew stronger and I gagged as it wormed into my lungs. It was worse than the rotten egg smell of the fiery chasm. My heart was almost bursting out of my ribs.

A swift eddy of wind flowed over us and a presence passed above. Then the dragon landed its huge bulk between the door and us. Its scales were bright golden like the sun and as it folded its wings, I glimpsed a ruby red sheen beneath them. Jagged teeth protruded from a long snout. Its eyes were startlingly human.

"Halt." The dragon's voice echoed around the chamber, repeating in a dizzying chorus.

We inched closer together and I was keenly aware that our only weapon was one small dagger. Owain's arm tightened around me and he wrapped his other arm around Rhiwallon's shoulders. We stood together, he and I and Rhiwallon, with Diarmuid slightly apart from us. I pitied him for not having Owain's strong arm around him too.

"Where are you running to in such a hurry?" the dragon asked, inspecting us each in turn.

We looked to Diarmuid. He hesitated, but then cleared his throat and straightened his shoulders.

"I apologise for disturbing you." The wobble in Diarmuid's voice betrayed his unease. "We wandered in here by mistake."

The dragon snorted and its eyes glinted with amusement. "By mistake, eh." Its voice sounded like rocks smashing together. I wanted to bury my face into Owain's shirt and cover my ears with my paws. "Humans don't enter my home by mistake. They come to steal my treasure."

"We haven't taken anything," Diarmuid said. "We didn't even mean to come in here but we thought we were probably allowed to open only one door and this was the one we chose."

That was my fault. But the other doors smelled of danger and dread. The door that led us here smelled of hope and the way home.

"Of course you chose that door," the dragon said. "You could smell my treasure. The scent of it leads people here, drives them half-mad with desire. They come in and paw through my treasure, pocketing what they will, and then they sneak out, thinking I haven't been watching them the whole time, thinking I haven't seen everything they did, noted every item they touched."

"If you were watching, then you know we didn't take anything," Diarmuid said. "We were looking for a way out of the tunnels. Nothing more. And we saw the door just before you arrived. In another few moments, we would have been gone."

"Aah, you saw the door, did you," the dragon said. "And how did you plan to unlock it?"

"There's a key," Diarmuid said. "We thought it might be here somewhere."

"So you did intend to steal from my treasure." The dragon's voice rose triumphantly. "I knew it. No human has ever entered my home without the intent of theft."

"We are here by the design of the fey," Diarmuid said. "The tunnels in this place twist and turn, leading wherever the fey want us to go. If we have been brought here by their design, and we face a locked door, surely they intend us to locate its key."

"The intent of the fey is no concern of mine," the dragon said. "It matters not what excuse you give for your presence. You have already admitted to entering my home for the purpose of stealing from me."

Diarmuid's face had that distant look that indicated he was mentally riffling through all the tales he knew. He stood up straight and looked the dragon in the eye. I admired his bravery, even as I trembled with fear.

"Then what solution do you propose?" he asked. "How do you intend to ascertain our guilt?"

"I already know your guilt," the dragon said. "I have no need for further proof."

"We are entitled to be offered a task," Diarmuid said. "Satisfaction of which would earn us our freedom."

The dragon eyed him and the amused glint turned dangerous. "You fancy yourself a druid, little human," it said. "Or a bard perhaps." The dragon's tone made it clear what it thought of either profession.

"I am a bard. And not only that, but I am the seventh son of a seventh son."

The dragon's face twitched. "And that holds some significance for you, it seems."

"It means I am destined to be a bard. In my family, the seventh son of a seventh son is always a bard."

"And be you a good bard?" the dragon asked.

Diarmuid hesitated and I held my breath, willing him to tell the truth. "No," he said finally. "My tales do not resonate with my listeners."

"And who do you blame for that, little bard? Yourself or the parents who cursed you to be bard by giving life to the seventh son of a seventh son?"

"The fault is none but my own. I might be a good bard one day, but I have much to learn yet."

The dragon looked Diarmuid up and down and when it spoke next, the sneer was gone from its voice.

"So, little bard, you snuck into my home with the aim of thievery. How do you intend to repay your debt?"

"Since we didn't steal anything, it seems to me we haven't incurred any debt," Diarmuid said.

His words made me quake for they sounded like a challenge. Indeed, the dragon seemed to draw itself up higher. Its gaze swept from Diarmuid to the rest of us.

"And what say you, friends of the little bard?" Its eyes bored into us each in turn. Me it lingered on and I felt horribly exposed. Could the dragon's gaze pierce this form I wore? "Well?"

Owain and Rhiwallon glanced at each other and it was she who spoke first.

"We had no intention of taking anything," she said and I admired the way her voice didn't even tremble. "We only wanted to find a way out."

The dragon made a low noise, perhaps a growl or merely a

clearing of the throat. "You entered my lair without permission. Surely, for that, you owe me something."

"What do you propose we owe you?" Diarmuid asked.

"Why, treasure of course," the dragon said. "If you each provide me with a treasure worthy to redeem for your intrusion, I'll allow you to leave."

"We don't have any treasure," Diarmuid said. "Because this is a place of the fey, we were not able to bring anything of cold iron with us. We have neither sword nor jewels nor anything else of value. The only thing I have, which you are welcome to if it pleases you, is this dagger." He retrieved the dagger from his boot and offered it on the palm of his hand.

"And my brooch," Owain added, fumbling in a pocket. He held out the small keepsake he had used to mark our progress through the tunnels. "You can have this too."

The dragon barely glanced at the offered items before it snorted. "Surely you jest. Look at the priceless treasures surrounding you. I have here riches worth many kingdoms. No human king possesses treasure to rival the value of mine. And yet you offer me a plain dagger and a scratched brooch?"

"We offer you everything we have," Diarmuid said. "Doesn't that make them priceless?"

The dragon tipped its head to one side, considering, and nodded. "I suppose it does, in a way, and yet your offerings are poor. None the less, I accept your treasures, such as they are. You may place them on the ground."

Diarmuid and Owain each set their item down. I had to remind myself to breathe.

"You have not redeemed yourselves," the dragon said.

"We have given you everything we have," Diarmuid said. "What else can we give?"

The dragon considered him. "You tell me. What else have you to offer, little bard?"

"Shall I tell you a tale?" An edge of desperation crept into Diarmuid's voice.

The dragon laughed and then coughed. Small puffs of steam escaped its nostrils. "You have already confessed your failure as a bard. Now you expect me to accept a tale as payment for your intrusion?"

"Then what do you want from us?"

There was a long pause. The dragon looked around its cavern and, for a while, almost seemed to forget we were there. Hope flared briefly and my tail curled up just the tiniest bit. Perhaps, while the dragon was distracted, we could sneak out. But we still needed the key.

"You will answer a riddle," the dragon said at length. "Four riddles, one each. For each correct answer, I will give leave for the one who answers to depart. How does that sound, little bard?"

I trembled. How could I answer a riddle while trapped in this form? I wished, for Diarmuid's sake, that I could be brave and tell him to leave me behind, but I desperately hoped he would find another way.

"Provided we can choose who answers each riddle and we are permitted to have one to answer for all, we accept," Diarmuid said.

"No," the dragon said. "Four riddles, four answers, one each."

I felt their eyes on me, Diarmuid, Owain and Rhiwallon. I tucked my tail between my legs and didn't look at any of them.

"That's not fair," Owain said.

"Fair?" The dragon pulled itself up to its full height. I hadn't realised until now how it had lowered itself down, presumably for ease of talking to us. Now it sat up on its haunches and stretched out its neck, glaring as it towered over us.

"What is fair about your intrusion in my lair? What is fair about forcing me to endure your stench? Do you have any idea how long the odour of humans lingers? It will be months before I no longer smell you every minute I am at home."

"And if we fail?" Diarmuid asked.

"Why, then, I eat you."

"We accept," Diarmuid said and my heart broke. He intended to leave me behind. "Ask your first riddle."

The dragon snorted but appeared mollified. It thought for a few moments. "What whispers and roars, inhabits several forms, and can be a source of both life and death?"

My heart pounded and I felt Owain holding his breath. I had no idea what answer the dragon expected. Surely Diarmuid was the only one of us who could answer such a thing. There was no hope for me anyway but if the riddles were all this hard, then we had already lost. I knew the moment Diarmuid had found the answer for his face lit up. My heart ached to see it and it was only in that moment that I realised how much I loved him.

"Water," he said.

"Water indeed, little human," the dragon said. "Very well, then, what is quieter than a whisper and yet louder than thunder?"

Diarmuid spoke quickly. "This is Bramble's riddle."

I held myself very still. I could hardly fathom his reason for this.

The dragon considered him for a moment and then turned its gaze on me. "Aah, you mean the creature who wears not its own form?"

I stared back at the dragon. How did it know?

"Yes, I feel your surprise, little one. It blazes from your eyes."

It was probably very old and knowledgeable. Perhaps it could even tell me of a way to escape this form. But I could not speak to the dragon, however much I might wish it, not unless it could read my mind.

The dragon turned back to Diarmuid. "How will she answer my riddle if she cannot speak?"

"She has already answered for you," Diarmuid said. "With her silence."

Of course, the answer was silence. My heart lifted and my tail curled. Maybe, just maybe, we could pass this test. Maybe Diarmuid didn't intend to leave me behind to be eaten by the dragon.

The dragon huffed and considered its next riddle. "What is

both welcomed and despised, liked and feared, a source of sorrow and a source of joy?"

"Death," Owain said immediately.

The dragon acknowledged his answer with a dip of its head. "What can make one both run and freeze, cry and scream, be thankful to be alive and wish one was dead?"

We waited. Rhiwallon was the only one who had not yet answered. To my surprise, she gave a faint smile.

"Fear," she said.

The dragon smiled, in as much as such a creature can. It nodded its huge head as it eyed us each in turn.

"Well done, little humans. You surprise me."

"Will you honour your bargain?" Diarmuid asked. "And allow us to leave?"

"A dragon never goes back on its word," it said, somewhat haughtily.

"And we can continue our search for the key?"

It hissed and its eyes flashed darkly. "You are arrogant indeed to think I would allow you to take something from my home."

"Then how will we unlock the door?" Diarmuid asked. "You have agreed to allow us to leave but we need the key."

"How you achieve your goal is of no concern to me," the dragon said. "Go back the way you entered if you cannot exit by the other."

"We can't," Diarmuid said. "That way will take us many days and we have neither food nor water."

The dragon shrugged and its tail twitched, much as an irritated cat swishes its tail before it extends its claws and swipes. "That is your problem. Not mine."

We looked at each other, Diarmuid, Owain, Rhiwallon and I. They all looked as empty of hope as I felt.

"May as well keep going," Owain said.

Diarmuid's shoulders slumped. "And then what? We sit and wait until someone else happens along?"

"Hurry up, little humans," the dragon said. "Linger too long and I may change my mind."

"Let's go," Diarmuid muttered. "We'll think of something."

I felt disheartened, almost despondent. But perhaps the door wasn't locked after all. The reference to a key might have been Titania's way of distracting us. I sat up straighter in Owain's arms. There might be a way out after all.

That hope lasted only until we reached the door and confirmed it was indeed locked. Had I been in my own form, I would have sat down and cried. Instead, I was struck by a powerful urge to lift my muzzle and howl. I swallowed my desperation and looked to Diarmuid. He traced the lock with one finger. It looked nothing like any lock I had ever seen.

"This reminds me of something," he murmured and his eyes were distant even as his hand lingered on the door. "The leaf, Owain, the red one."

Owain tucked me under one arm and fumbled in his pocket. He retrieved a scarlet red leaf and I remembered watching him pluck it from the floor after the fey had left. *Might be useful,* he had said. Now he stretched out his hand, leaf balanced on his palm, to Diarmuid.

Diarmuid glanced at it and nodded. "That's our key." He motioned towards the door. "You do it, Owain. You were the one who thought to keep it."

Owain stepped forward, his thick fingers holding the leaf with care. The lock was exactly the size and shape of the leaf and he gently slid it into position, placing the leaf flat against the door's surface. It unlocked with a click.

"Farewell, little humans," the dragon said from behind us. "Perhaps you might return another time."

We stepped through the doorway, Diarmuid first, then Rhiwal-lon, then Owain carrying me. I pitied the dragon left behind, lonely and surrounded by mounds of treasure.

41

BRIGIT

I WANTED TO howl when I realised that on the other side of the door was yet another green-lit tunnel. We had rescued Rhiwallon, crossed the fiery bridge, answered the dragon's riddles, and found the key. What more would be asked of us? I rested my head on Owain's shoulder with a heavy sigh.

We crowded into a tunnel, which was far narrower than the others we had traversed and barely ten paces long before it ended in another door. The roof was high but the width was exactly the size necessary for Owain to pass through and no more. He had just stepped through the doorway, when Diarmuid spoke.

"Owain, wait," he said. "Keep the door open."

By the time Owain managed to turn around in the too-small space, the door had closed with a soft thud. "Too late," he said.

"See if you can open it again." Diarmuid's voice sounded strange, as if he was barely controlling panic.

Clutched in Owain's arms, I could see that the door was blank and smooth.

"No handle," Owain said.

"What's the problem?" Rhiwallon asked.

"Push it," Diarmuid said. "Maybe it didn't close properly."

Owain pressed his palm to the door but even I could see that it had closed securely and the make of its frame was such that it could only be opened from the other side.

"Won't budge," Owain said.

We waited.

"There's no way to open the door at this end," Diarmuid said, at last.

"We're trapped?" Rhiwallon asked.

"There must be a hidden lever or button," Diarmuid said, although he didn't sound like he believed his own words.

Owain managed to deposit me onto the ground, then he began running his hands over the earthen wall. I pressed my nose to the base of the wall, searching for anything that looked different. I searched the floor also but found nothing unusual in the hard-packed earth.

"We must be missing something," Diarmuid said.

"Could it be up higher?" Rhiwallon asked.

We looked up. The roof of this tunnel did seem much higher than the others.

"But what would be the point in putting it out of our reach?" she asked.

"Maybe it's another test," Diarmuid said.

We craned our necks, eyes straining with the effort of trying to see something that was intended to be invisible. I worked my way methodically along the wall, starting from the edge near the dragon's door. Everyone kept getting in my way and obscuring my view, and I let out a loud yelp when Rhiwallon stood on my paw. She muttered an apology.

Owain picked me up and I wriggled around in his arms to gain a higher purchase. When he realised what I was doing, he held me up over his head. My tail quivered at being up so high but his hands gripped my ribs firmly so I tried to ignore my unease and focus on my task.

It was easier to scan the walls now that I had an uninterrupted view, but even so, I could see nothing unusual. I let out a frustrated growl.

"Keep trying, Bramble," Owain said. He squeezed past Rhiwallon, which was only possible if they both turned sideways, to let me inspect the far end of the wall.

"This is hopeless." Rhiwallon sank down to sit cross-legged on the floor. "Titania wants us to rot in here."

"Can't give up now," Owain said.

"Well, what are we supposed to do? We've checked every inch of that blasted wall. There's nothing there. We're trapped in here until she decides to let us out. And what if she doesn't?"

My stomach rumbled loudly, a reminder that it had been many hours since we had eaten. And it had been so long since we ran out of water that I wasn't even thirsty anymore. We were all exhausted and covered in muck from the dead beast. We couldn't go on like this for much longer.

My eyes were sore from straining so hard but I kept searching. There had to be a way out of here. The fey wouldn't lead us here for no reason. I checked the last section of wall, right above the door that would lead us somewhere else, but there was nothing. I sighed and Owain started to bring me down. But just as he moved, I spotted something. It was the shallowest of depressions, just a slight dip in the otherwise smooth wall, and I only saw it because I was on exactly the right angle.

I gave a wuff and he froze.

"Do you see something?" he asked.

I barked and he held me back up high again.

Whatever I was looking at was almost out of my sight and certainly out of reach. Even if Owain were to lift Diarmuid, he wouldn't be able to reach it. But how could we check whether this was the key to opening the door if we couldn't reach it?

"I can't see anything," Diarmuid admitted.

"Me either," Owain said. He continued to hold me up over his head and I kept my gaze fixed on the indentation, fearful of not being able to find it again if I even so much as blinked.

"I think I see something," Rhiwallon said. "It might be nothing though and it's too high up."

"I could lift you," Owain said.

"I still wouldn't be able to reach it."

I was close to despair. We were hungry and thirsty and tired, and now it seemed the final key we needed was positioned deliberately far out of our reach.

"Could you push it with an arrow?" Diarmuid asked.

Rhiwallon shook her head. "No, it's easily three times my height. I couldn't even get close. Unless…" She tipped her head to the side, still considering the indentation.

Owain's fingers were beginning to dig into my ribs uncomfortably. I wiggled and he lowered me, clutching me to his chest once more. Now that Rhiwallon had also seen the indentation, I was less afraid of not being able to find it again. She stared up at it, one hand on the quiver at her hip. I understood where her thoughts were heading and my heart thudded faster. It could work. Slowly, Rhiwallon drew an arrow from her quiver. With the other hand, she reached for her bow.

"That's impossible," Diarmuid said.

Rhiwallon shrugged. "I'll just keep shooting until I hit it. I need some room though. And watch for the arrows as they fall. An injury is the last thing any of us needs now."

Owain and Diarmuid moved to the other end of the tunnel. Rhiwallon nocked the arrow and drew it back, lifting the bow to aim.

Diarmuid was right: it *was* an impossible shot. But I had seen Rhiwallon take down a running hare with a single arrow that pierced right through the eye. As she took aim, I held my breath. She released the arrow and it sprang up, almost too fast for my eyes to follow. The arrow knocked the wall and vanished.

"What happened?" Owain asked.

"Where did it go?" Diarmuid said.

Rhiwallon's face was pale. "It disappeared as soon as it hit the wall."

A long moment of silence followed her words. I was so very

tired. After all we had been through, it seemed unfair that we should encounter such a charm now.

"How many arrows do you have?" Diarmuid asked, at last.

"I carry five," she said.

"Four left," Owain said.

Rhiwallon nodded. "Four left." She took another arrow from her quiver. "Might as well get on with it."

I couldn't quite see the indentation from my perch in Owain's arms but the first arrow had been close. Under other circumstances, I had no doubt that Rhiwallon would have hit her target. But the tunnel was dimly lit and she was shooting on an extremely steep angle to a tiny target far above her head. Close would not be good enough.

Rhiwallon nocked the arrow and aimed. Once again it hit very near to the indentation and silently disappeared. She immediately took out a third arrow, set it in place, and fired, all in the time it took me to draw a single breath. Again, the arrow disappeared. Rhiwallon hissed.

"You can do it," Owain said.

Rhiwallon turned and shot him a glare. Diarmuid opened his mouth and she glared so hard at him that he simply closed it again. The fourth arrow missed also. Her face was red now, although I didn't know whether it was with frustration or anger.

With a deep breath, she set the final arrow in place. The world seemed to slow around me as I watched her exhale gently, her gaze fixed on her target. She raised the bow and the arrow and they were like extensions of her arms. I followed the arrow's trajectory. I couldn't tell whether it had hit its target. If it hadn't, it was close. Very close. I held my breath and prayed.

Slowly, ever so slowly, the door in front of us rumbled open and light flooded the small tunnel. Diarmuid and Owain cheered and even Rhiwallon looked pleased. I barked in appreciation, and then we hurried through the door before it could close again. We stepped out into sunshine scented with spring.

42

DIARMUID

THE SUN HOVERED low over the horizon, its light soft. Dawn perhaps? Snow still remained on the ground although patches of grass peeked through in some areas. How much time had passed in the outside world? I breathed in deeply, rejoicing in the feel of fresh, cool air filling my lungs.

For a while, we just stood there, letting the sunlight soak into our skin. Rhiwallon stood with her hands clasped over her stomach. The empty quiver hung from the belt around her waist. Owain's face was tight and his shoulders hunched. Bramble's tail and ears drooped. My fingers itched to stroke her hair but I no longer felt I had any right to touch her. Not until we figured out what manner of creature she was.

Unless I was much mistaken, we emerged from the mound in the same place we had entered it. The paths of the fey could appear to lead in one direction when in reality going another. If we went back inside, we might not find the original path we took but something entirely different. I had no desire to find out.

"Why so morose?" I asked. "We did it. We rescued Rhiwallon, made our way through the tunnels, answered the dragon's riddles, and found a way out. You should be pleased."

"We barely got out," Rhiwallon said. "The dragon would have gladly eaten us."

"No it wouldn't." I didn't feel quite as confident as I sounded. "Dragons enjoy company. They love riddles. It would have kept us alive as long as we kept talking."

"She," Rhiwallon said. "The dragon was a female."

"How do you know?" I asked.

"I just know. She was sad too."

"Lonely, most like," I said. "Dragons lead solitary lives. She will probably think of us for years to come."

"Last dragon I ever want to see," Owain said.

"I'm sure it will be." I was only half-listening for already my mind had turned to Ida. Was there still time to stop her? Or had she already killed everyone in Crow's Nest and moved on? How exactly does one go about destroying such a creature? And would destroying her also kill me? I would never fall in love, never marry, never bed a woman. I would never say goodbye to Eithne or learn whether Caedmon still lived or whether Grainne was injured. I would never find out who Bramble really was.

I had no choice, though, for this was my fault. Ida came from my head, from my evil thoughts, and I had to be the one to destroy her. I hoped I was brave enough. I hoped it wouldn't be very painful when I died.

As we slowly began to make our way back to the campsite, Owain stumbled and then let out a yell.

"My axe!"

He picked up the axe he had left behind when we entered the mound. I soon found the dagger he had loaned me. His other dagger was there too and eventually we found the lamp. It had rolled down a slight slope and rested at the bottom in a snowy ditch.

Clutching our weapons and the lamp, we staggered back to where we had made camp so many days ago. My legs were shaky, my stomach growled and I was thirsty enough to drink a river. When we reached our camp, everything was just as we had left it.

The oxen grazed nearby, ignoring us. Maybe — just maybe — fewer days had passed out here than within the fey mound. I might still have time to stop Ida.

We filled our water flasks from the stream and eagerly gulped down every last drop. Never had water tasted so sweet. My stomach was so empty it hurt but I couldn't eat with globs of the dead beast still all over me. It had dried, hard and crusty, and my clothes were stiff with the stuff. I waded into the icy stream and scrubbed myself all over with a handful of sand, letting the cold waters cleanse me. By the time I was finished, my skin was raw and I was so cold I couldn't feel my toes.

While I was bathing, Owain and Rhiwallon had built up a fire. They took turns to bathe and even Bramble returned wet and shivering. Rhiwallon dried her off with a blanket. Then we ate. The bread was stale but the cheese was sharp, the dried meat smoky, the apples sweet and only a little too soft. As I ate, the fog lifted from my brain. It was a wonder I had been able to think clearly enough to answer the dragon's riddles while I was so hungry.

Our meal finished, we prepared to leave. There was no need for discussion about whether we should rest first. Without knowing how much time we had lost in the fey tunnels, the only thing we could do now was get to Crow's Nest as quickly as possible.

Owain climbed into the front of the cart and Rhiwallon and I settled ourselves on blankets in the back with Bramble's basket tucked in between us. Bramble was still damp so I tucked an extra blanket around her. She sniffed at me before tucking her nose into the blanket but the noise didn't seem quite as haughty as usual.

As we set off with a creak, I looked back towards the mound. Far beyond it, past an expanse of snow-covered hills, stood the lonely figure of a dragon. I raised a hand in farewell and it seemed the dragon dipped her head in response. Then she rose up on enormous wings and sailed away towards the rising sun.

Nothing of note happened for the rest of the day. The oxen

trudged along, tireless as always. Rhiwallon and Bramble slept. Sometimes I dozed but mostly I simply sat there. I should have used the time to plan but I found I no longer cared. In two days I would face Ida, if she was still in Crow's Nest. In two days I would try to destroy her. And in two days I would likely die. There didn't seem to be much point in planning. Melancholy gripped me for the first time since the start of my journey. It wrapped around my shoulders, clouding my head, as familiar as an old friend.

We halted an hour or so before night fell, and made camp beside a small stream. Rhiwallon didn't offer to hunt and we all knew she had no more arrows anyway. She built a fire and Owain cooked a meal of porridge and flat bread. I tried to help but mostly just got in the way. Bramble sat close to the fire.

The heady scent of our first warm meal in days wafted through the campsite and my stomach grumbled. The sky darkened as we ate, burning tongues and fingers in our haste. Hot porridge sank down into my stomach, warm and comforting and filling. The melancholy eased just the tiniest bit. The moon rose and it looked much the same as it had the night Rhiwallon was taken, a waxing crescent still a few days away from its darkness.

I slept soundly, waking only once. Owain sat by the fire, a blanket wrapped around his shoulders and over Bramble, who slept on his lap. I missed her warmth against my legs.

We packed the cart the next morning with the quiet speed of folk well accustomed to travelling together. We would reach Crow's Nest tonight and tomorrow I would face Ida. I walked beside the cart for a while. Long walks across the length and breadth of Silver Downs always gave me room to create my tales so perhaps walking would also help me find a solution to the problem of Ida. I thought of, and discarded, a dozen possibilities. Threats, weapons, dire warnings. I doubted any such thing would work. As we drew steadily closer to Crow's Nest, I still had no plan and failure seemed increasingly certain.

43

DIARMUID

W E REACHED CROW'S Nest shortly before dusk and claimed a well-worn bedchamber in an inn called The Midnight Traveller. The bedclothes were thread-bare, as was the rug, and the door didn't quite close. Nevertheless, the floor and furniture were dust-free, the dresser bore both an oil lamp and an almost-new candle, and I was thankful to not be spending another night outside.

The dining room was full of the heady smells of fresh bread and good soup. My stomach grumbled in eager anticipation. The pub's dilapidated appearance belied the quality of the cook's meals for the food was just as good as the aroma promised.

"Well, Diarmuid," Owain said as he broke off a large chunk of bread and soaked it in the thick barley soup. Brown droplets splattered his shirt as he lifted it to his mouth. "What will you do?"

Wiping my bowl clean with the last of the bread, I felt their eyes on me. Even Bramble, delicately lapping at her bowl, waited for my response.

"I'll think of something," I muttered.

They waited. I was very much aware of the other patrons

slurping their soup, crunching crusty bread, and asking for more ale.

"I thought you had a plan," Rhiwallon said. Her bowl was mostly untouched for she ate little enough to leave a sparrow hungry. "I thought you knew what you were doing."

I had never said I had a plan, but I suddenly found it hard to meet her eyes. "I have no idea what to do. I know how to fight a little but not against a creature like Ida. Physical strength will not be the solution; if it was, I would have no fear for Owain is surely stronger than any three men. I think this will require cunning and craft and trickery of some sort. But exactly what, I have no idea."

"Have to find her first," Owain said.

"And she may not want to be found," I said.

"Do you think she knows you are coming?" Rhiwallon asked.

"Probably. She knows how I think, how I react, as intimately as I myself do. She knows I will come after her. She probably already knows exactly what I will do. And she will know how to escape me."

"And if you fail?" Rhiwallon's voice held a challenge and she looked me right in the eyes. "What then?"

I stared down into my empty bowl and despair flooded through my body. "I don't know. I don't think anyone else can stop her. It has to be me."

They waited, three pairs of eyes fixed on me. Owain and Rhiwallon's faces were still fatigued from our time in the fey tunnels. Bramble's ears were lowered, a certain sign she was unhappy.

"She will destroy us all," I said. "One village will not be enough. Once there is nothing left there to amuse her, she will move on to the next village. Then the one after that, until she has destroyed everyone and everything."

"But why?" Rhiwallon asked. "Why would she want to destroy everything?"

I shrugged. "She is evil. There is no reason for what she does other than that she wants to."

"If she knows you so well," she said. "Perhaps you also know her."

A small glimmer of hope rose within me. "Perhaps."

In an attempt to change the topic, I ordered another round of ale. I could not voice my most secret fear about Ida: that I had created evil because *I* was evil. We sat in silence for some time, sipping our drinks. I was absorbed in my thoughts when somebody slammed half a dozen mugs down onto our table.

"Hello there," said a cheery voice. "Mind if we share your table? I'm buying."

Owain tipped his mug at the two men who stood beside us. "Sit down, friends. It's a mighty thirsty night."

The men settled themselves at the other end of our table. Mugs clattered as the speaker passed them around. He had shaggy dark hair, ruddy cheeks and an air of merriness. "I'm Braden," he said. "This here is Drust."

Drust barely glanced at us. He was a skinny man with hunched shoulders and red hair. A mist of misery hung over him as he toyed with his mug.

Owain introduced us. I wanted to plan for tomorrow, and enjoy the company of my friends on what might be my last evening, not make small talk with strangers. But the inn had filled while we were eating and our party of four was using only half the table. I could hardly tell them to go away, but Owain didn't have to be quite so friendly.

"What brings you to Crow's Nest?" Braden asked.

I froze. I couldn't explain my journey to strangers. Owain and Rhiwallon didn't offer any explanation either. The silence stretched a little too long and eventually Braden laughed.

"No matter, friends." He drained his mug in little more than a swallow and reached for another. "You don't want to talk about why you're here, that's fine with me. Must be a secret quest, eh? Off to save the world?"

We all chuckled and if my laughter was hollow, I doubted Braden noticed.

"Drink up, Drust," Braden encouraged. "Not much point dragging you here to drown your sorrows if you won't drink."

Drust lifted his mug and took a half-hearted sip. "Happy?"

"Drust here's mourning the loss of his brother," Braden said.

"How did he die?" Owain asked.

"He's not dead," Drust said. "Yet."

"Is he ill?" Rhiwallon asked.

Drust shook his head.

We waited, confused, and eventually Braden elbowed Drust. "Go on, you'll have to tell the whole story now. They'll hardly believe it but it makes a good tale."

Drust sighed and fiddled with his mug.

"All right, then," Braden said, clapping him on the back. "You drink and I'll tell them. Drust's brother has been charmed by a witch. What do you think of that?"

I froze.

"A witch?" Owain's tone was cautious.

"Anything she says, he does," Braden said. "He's completely enamoured."

"What makes you think she's a witch?" Rhiwallon's voice was sceptical although she shot me an uneasy look.

"She's been making a name for herself here," Braden said. "If she tells you to do something, you do it. People say it's like they forget everything other than the need to obey her. She's made folk around here do awful things. So many families ruined. And now she's got Drust's brother."

"He doesn't *see* her." Drust's voice was barely more than a whisper. "I mean really see her. He sees the lovely figure and the long hair and those innocent smiles. He hears the sweet whispers and tinkling laughs. But he doesn't see what she does, how she destroys everything."

"Can no one convince her to leave?" I had to know what they had tried.

"Nay. Everyone's too scared to go near her," Braden said.

"Nobody wants to draw her attention. People are fleeing rather than chance be her next victim."

"Have you tried to reason with your brother?" Rhiwallon asked. "Tell him he's been charmed?"

"I've only been able to speak to him once," Drust said. "His eyes go blank and he seems to stop listening as soon as I mention her."

"I suggested we hit her over the head and drag her away somewhere," Braden said. "But Drust won't be in on that."

"We wouldn't even get near her," Drust said. "She would know before we arrived."

"We don't know that," Braden said. "Not for sure."

"I don't want to be her next target. Not even to save my brother."

"Where did she come from?" Rhiwallon asked.

Both men shrugged.

"She simply turned up one day and never left," Braden said. "We thought at first she might be one of the fey. But then things got nasty and what reason could they have for such a thing? We lead quiet lives here. Nothing of interest to them."

"My brother has never wronged anyone," Drust said. "He's a good man."

"Drust here's given up. He's mourning his brother as if he was already dead."

"I don't see that there's anything else I can do," Drust said.

"Drink up then," Braden said. "There's a plan for you."

Braden changed the topic then and I stopped listening. Maybe they weren't talking about Ida. Maybe some other woman here was bewitching men and making them do her bidding, heedless of what chaos she caused. Somehow I doubted it.

We finished our ales and retired, leaving behind the two friends who were well on their way towards becoming exceedingly drunk.

As we left, I turned back to Drust. "What's your brother's name?" I asked.

He looked up at me blearily. "Davin," he said. "His name is Davin."

44

IDA

E LIVES. AT last, I feel him moving towards me once again. I still cannot explain his disappearance, and his reappearance is just as sudden. I hardly know what to think. My hands tremble and my heart stutters within my ribcage. His companions come too but not my beast. Perhaps he has killed it. That surprises me, for the beast in his tale did not die.

I am under no illusions as to his purpose, however I might wish it to be otherwise. He comes to destroy me, and that, I suppose, is as it should be. That is what the hero in one of his tales would do, or try to do at any rate.

I created him, one could say. All that he is today is because of me, for I whispered his every thought to him. Without me, he probably hardly knows who he is any more. He was a boy of ten summers when I flared to life in his head. He was hardly old enough to know his own name, let alone his mind. I influenced the man he grew up to be.

We shared his head for nine summers. When his brother went off to war, I told the boy he had no destiny of his own, not like his brother. When his brother handfasted, I told the boy he would never do the same since he couldn't even speak to a woman. He always believed me. His emotions fed me, fuelled my power. Jealousy, discontent, misery, loneliness. They bled into me and drip by drip, my power grew. So I continued to whisper and he passed his youth in a daze of dispirited emotion, until the day I was strong enough to leave.

Perhaps once I left, he realised his thoughts had not been his own. It matters not whether he understands. All that matters now is that he comes for me. He will not succeed, of course, for my power grows every day. The more I cleanse this town, the stronger I become. I fear nothing, not even the queen of the fey. I could crush her, if I chose, crumble her into dust like last summer's bloom. But I have nothing to prove. Not to her, not to the boy, not to anyone.

My current companion does not have a mind like the boy's. I tolerate his ingratiating presence only because I crave company. After sharing the boy's head for so long, my own thoughts are lonely. So I allow this mortal to stay here in my house and he amuses me somewhat, although already I tire of him. It is of no matter. There are companions aplenty here and I shall find myself another soon, as I did last time.

45

DIARMUID

ORNING DAWNED, COLD and clear. When I drew back the curtains, the sunlight was so brilliant it danced off the window pane. It seemed unfair such brightness should be darkened with what I must do today.

Breakfast was steaming porridge, creamy and thick with plump grains. My stomach threatened to refuse even such scant amounts as I forced myself to swallow. I had too many regrets, too many things left undone, unsaid for this to be my last meal.

Bramble lapped her porridge, her pink tongue swiftly emptying the bowl. My fingers itched to stroke her soft hair and I allowed myself to do so for the first time since I had discovered her secret. She stopped eating to gaze up at me with that unblinking stare. How I wished I knew what she was thinking when she looked at me like that. If only I had taken the time to notice she was more than she seemed. Even as a friend, I was a failure.

Owain finished his meal and turned to me. "Diarmuid, you have a plan now?"

The porridge turned to dirt in my mouth and I swallowed with difficulty. "I need to find Ida."

"And then?" Rhiwallon asked.

I couldn't meet their eyes. "I don't know. I'll talk to her, I suppose. Try to convince her that what she is doing is wrong."

"She won't listen," Rhiwallon said.

"I know. But I don't know what else to do. I don't have any idea how to destroy her."

"You need a plan," Rhiwallon said. "You can't go into something like this hoping you'll figure it out as it happens. She's probably already planning what she will do."

"I know." I pushed away my porridge. I couldn't eat any more of it now. "But I don't know how to stop her, how to destroy her. I've been trying to come up with a plan the whole way here, but I have nothing. I think my tales are the key but I don't know how they work. Not every tale comes true."

"Which ones did?" Rhiwallon asked.

"Only the one about Ida." I felt somewhat silly at the admission.

"Only one?" she said. "That's it? You've come all this way, just because of one tale that was probably a coincidence?"

"Every seventh son of a seventh son in my family is a bard who can bring his tales to life. But I don't know how the power works."

"How did they deal with it?" Rhiwallon asked. "The ones before you? Your father?"

"I never asked. I've never even heard him tell a tale. He stopped because they came true. I think he might have killed his brothers with a tale. That's all I know."

"Had you asked a few questions before you left home, we could have used that information today," Rhiwallon said.

Her words stung. "I don't have any choice now. I have to find her and destroy her. That's what I came here for. It's too late to worry about what I should have done." I hesitated, staring down at my empty bowl. I didn't want to say these next words but I had to. "You should all stay here. It might be dangerous." I corrected myself. "It *will* be dangerous."

"We will stand with you," Owain said and Rhiwallon nodded. A soft grunt from Bramble indicated her agreement.

"I can't ask that of you." I could have wept tears of gratitude and sorrow as I looked around the table, meeting their eyes: plain, simple Owain, a large man with a heart to match; Rhiwallon who glowered at me from across the table and who even now kept her secrets close; and Bramble who gazed at me with fear in her eyes. Would I live to discover the truth about her? Would I have the opportunity to repay their faith? I swallowed hard. "No, you have come this far with me but I need to go on from here alone."

"Pish," Owain said. "We're going with you."

And that was that. I didn't have the strength to argue further, not today when I must face Ida and could well lose my life.

"Where do we start?" Rhiwallon asked. "How do we find her?"

"I can find her." I was suddenly confident. "If she knows me better than anyone else, then I also know her."

This was what I had forgotten all along: I knew Ida. I had created her. She knew nothing but what I had given her.

As we left the inn and strode down the street, smoke curled up from chimneys to linger in the air. I tasted it on the back of my tongue, sweet and sharp, filling my lungs and nostrils with its pervading presence. A plump orange cat sunning itself on a doorstep glared a challenge at Bramble as we passed but she barely deigned to look at it.

We reached a corner. Ahead, the road looked much the same. To the left, a birch tree, bright with new leaves, sheltered the path, and I knew.

"This way."

I followed the branching path past the birch tree and it felt right. A deep certainty centred in my bones. Soon enough we stopped in front of a cottage. It was prettily presented with white-washed walls and a thatch roof.

"This is it," I said.

"How do you know?" Rhiwallon asked.

"I just know. I feel it. She's here."

Owain stared at the front door, a furrow between his eyebrows. "What now?"

"We go in," I said. "She already knows we're here."

As we approached the door, it opened, seemingly of its own accord. Bramble stopped, sniffing the air.

"Like I told you," I said. "She knows."

I didn't need to call out, to ask where she was. Unerringly, I led my companions through the front passage, across the kitchen, and down the hallway.

We found her in a sunny back room with serviceable wooden chairs and a long workbench. The room was still and quiet, and despite the chill morning, the hearth was empty. Ida sat on a chair, hands folded in her lap, her gaze fixed on the doorway as we entered. Sunlight danced over her blonde hair and her plain white dress. She was simply waiting. Her eyes met mine and she gave a small smile.

"So," she said. "You come at last."

"You knew I would."

"Of course."

"Do you know why?"

The small smile became dazzling and I understood, briefly, why so many did as she requested.

"You want to destroy me. I know you, Diarmuid. I know your lofty goals of educating the simple man, teaching him compassion, honour and nobility beyond what his poor mind can comprehend. That's why people never understand your tales. Don't you know? They can have no possibility of understanding the concepts you try so hard to instil in them."

Her words cut through me and yet it was a distant hurt. It seemed so long ago that my biggest problem was that nobody liked my tales.

"What about you?" I asked. "Do you understand those concepts? Honour, bravery, loyalty. Surely you know of these from my tales?"

Ida tittered, covering her mouth with a delicate hand. Beside me, Owain gave a small sigh and I stiffened. Could Ida turn him on me? She hadn't looked at him once. Her attention, as far as I could tell, was solely on me. I resisted the urge to step away from Owain. If I could not trust him, then I could trust no one.

Ida's eyes, wide open and summer-sky blue, were fixed on mine and her voice was coy. "What do you hope to achieve with such a question?"

"What do you know of the world?" I asked. "The world is dirty, dark, messy, filled with blood and hopelessness and death and despair. Why would you want to leave my head to live in the world?"

"Oh, dear boy," she gasped, laughing again. "I know so much about the world and it's all thanks to you. Every tale you told, I heard it. Every lesson you tried to teach your hapless audience, I absorbed it. But your mind, although a fascinating place with all of your agonies and tortured thoughts and hopeless dreams, is not nearly as good as being out in the world. You merely told tales. I bring them to life."

Behind me, Rhiwallon hissed. Owain shifted his feet and I felt like a traitor even as I tensed, wondering whether he would attack me. Bramble stood with ears alert, her eyes suspicious.

"You could hear my tales?" I asked.

"Not just your tales, my dear, but your every thought," Ida said.

My mind went numb. I had suspected Ida would remember the conversations we'd had but I never suspected she had been listening in on my thoughts. Could she still do that, even though we were now two separate beings? How could I defeat her if she knew everything I thought? As I stood speechless, Ida turned her attention to my companions.

"Oh, you naughty boy," she said with another tinkling laugh. "You have brought all of these friends into my house and you haven't even introduced them. Let me see, who have we here?"

She turned first to Owain. "Oh my, such a strong man," she

said with a simper. "A simple man, honest, hard working. Not much else to you, is there?"

Owain sighed again. I would have glared at him had I dared take my eyes off Ida.

Next Ida fixed her gaze on Rhiwallon. "You are an interesting one. Do they know the truth about you, I wonder? Do they know from what you run? No, I think not. I cannot imagine the boy would harbour one such as you if he knew the truth."

There was no time to wonder what she meant for Ida looked now to Bramble. My heart pounded and in my mind, I whispered *no, no, leave her alone.*

"Oh." Ida's tone was surprised. "Does he know?"

"Ignore them," I finally managed. "They mean nothing to you."

"Oh but they do." She arched an eyebrow at me. "For they mean something to you, don't they? Who would have thought you would find such a collection of friends. Such an *interesting* collection."

"They know nothing," I said, trying not to think about how much they meant to me. I willed my mind to be calm, blank, thought-less. "They barely even know why I'm here."

I wilted a little under the direct stare of Ida's cold blue eyes. "And why are you here?" Her voice was steely. "Do you really come to try to destroy me, here in my own house?"

"Is this your house? Or did you charm it away from someone?"

Her chin jutted out and her eyebrows narrowed as she glared at me. My chest began to tighten and in just a few moments I could barely breathe. Choking as I fought to draw in air, I met Ida's gaze and she smiled, a slow, calm smile hinting at secrets only she and I knew.

Sweat trickled down between my shoulder blades. My feet wouldn't move. I tried to speak, to ask for help, to beg Ida to stop, but nothing came out other than a strangled gasp. I couldn't breathe.

Bramble whined and, somehow, I managed to tear my eyes away from Ida and look down at her. She stared up at me, her gaze showing me her kindness, her goodness and her wisdom. Suddenly I could breathe again. Bramble's doing? I had no way of knowing. I fell to my knees, sucking in deep breaths. Ida continued to stare at me, sending more tendrils of power winding around me. I didn't dare look at her. It seemed she had no power over me unless I met her eyes. Now there was only one thought in my mind. *Run.* I fled and my companions were right behind me.

Her laugh followed us, trickling like water over stones. As we reached the front door, I heard her voice as clearly as if she stood beside me.

"What a silly boy you are."

The door slammed behind us and I ran. Rhiwallon and Bramble were at my heels but Owain soon lagged behind. I halted beneath an old oak tree whose skeletal limbs stretched up to the sky, waiting for spring's new leaves to cloak them. I was horribly aware of how close we still were to Ida. Could she control us from a distance or did she need to see us for her charms to work? Owain was gasping for breath as he reached us.

I knew I should say something, thank them for going with me, even if we had failed, but there were no words in my head. I was empty, drained. I had nothing left. I had lost and Ida would continue to destroy Crow's Nest, one life at a time.

"What do we do now?" Rhiwallon asked.

"Go home, I suppose." I stared at the houses around us, although I barely saw them. Houses looked the same everywhere we went. Stone or whitewash. Thatched roof. Herb garden. Vegetable patch. Raven sitting on a low stone fence, head cocked quizzically as it watched us. Chimney with a plume of smoke curling up into the blue sky. How could the sky be so blue on a day like this? Didn't it know that I had failed? That countless people would die because I couldn't stop Ida? Despair flooded my limbs, making them too heavy to move. I would stand here until my bones crumbled into dust. I had failed.

"That's it?" Owain asked. "You're done?"

"I tried. What more can I do?"

Bramble glared so fiercely that I had to look away.

"We travelled all this way with you," Rhiwallon said. "We stuck with you through those blasted tunnels and through cold, wet days on the road. We stood with you in her house. Because we believed you were going to stop her. You created something that should have never existed. We believed you when you said you would destroy her. And now you're running away."

"What would you have me do? I tried but you saw what she's like. You felt her magic worming its way into your head and under your skin. She will turn us against each other, twist us to her will. This is what she does, what she has done to the people here. What can I do against that?"

"Seems you could do more than run away," Owain said.

Shame raced through my limbs and coloured my face. "You felt her power. I could tell. It was working on you."

Owain shrugged and his face was open and guileless. "Yeah, I felt it. She wanted to control me. She nearly did."

"What stopped her?"

"You ran away before she fully had me. I followed."

I turned to Rhiwallon. "What did Ida mean when she asked whether we knew the truth? Who are you running from?"

Rhiwallon's face paled a little and she looked away. "That's my business, not yours."

"If Ida knows about it, she can use it against you. I'd say that makes it our business too."

"It's not," she said, fiercely. "You think everything is about you, Diarmuid, but it's not. This has nothing to do with you."

"P'rhaps you should tell us," Owain said. "Diarmuid's right. If she knows, she can use it."

She looked up at him for a long moment but it was Rhiwallon who looked away first.

"You'll judge me," she said. "I don't need that."

"I won't," he said. "You have my word."

There was another long pause before she spoke. "I'm carrying a child. I'm not sure whether the father knows. I don't have any way of contacting him, don't even know his real name. But if I can get far enough away, maybe he won't be able to find me. And he won't ever find out about the baby."

"Why don't you want him to know?" I asked.

Rhiwallon's face was calm and her voice held nothing but determination. "If he knows, he'll take the child. And I won't let him. It's as much mine as it is his. More, even, for he isn't the one who has to carry the babe for nine months."

"Why would he take it?" I asked and was rewarded with a withering glare.

"For a bard, Diarmuid, you really don't know much, do you?"

"What does that have to do with it?"

Before she could respond, Owain answered. "Because he's fey. The father."

Rhiwallon nodded, chin held high.

"So the beast…" I said.

She shrugged. "He might have sent someone, or something, after me. More likely, he's completely forgotten about me and moved on to the next poor girl who swoons at his pretty face and fancies herself in love with him."

"I thought the fey were trying to delay my journey." I felt like an idiot even as I said it.

"Maybe," she said. "Or maybe it was me they wanted all along. It doesn't matter now anyway. We got away, and now we've got your creature to deal with. Once this is all over, I'll keep moving. The further I go, the less likely he is to find me."

"I don't think you can run from the fey," I said. "The tales tell—"

Rhiwallon turned her back on me and walked away. "Thank you, Diarmuid," she said frostily over her shoulder, "but I think *your* wisdom is probably the last thing I need."

Despite all our days of travelling together, despite the frantic search through the land of the fey, nothing I knew about her was true. I had thought Owain was the one Fiachra warned me about, the one who wouldn't be what they seemed. Then I had thought it was Bramble. Could it be that he had meant Rhiwallon all along?

Owain and I looked at each other in silence, neither wanting to be the first to speak. Bramble leaned into me, her body warm against my leg.

"Did you know?" I murmured to her. "Did you see through her?"

Bramble blinked at me. I leaned down to rub her ears and she gave a little sigh, leaning her head into my hand. At least I had Bramble. Bramble and Owain. These were my true friends right here.

46

BRIGIT

I HAD GUESSED half of Rhiwallon's secret, but it had never occurred to me that the fey were involved in this too. The men we saw at the inn were clearly human but perhaps the one who had hired them was fey. I had never believed in coincidence or chance. If Rhiwallon was running from someone, and we happened across men searching for someone, the two were connected in some way, even if she wasn't the one they sought.

I wondered now at the time we had spent in the tunnels. Was that an attempt by the fey to capture Rhiwallon or, perhaps, her child? Or did the delay have some other role in Titania's plans? If she had nothing to do with Rhiwallon's abduction, she had given no sign of it but that might be a part of whatever game she played.

Owain seemed unperturbed. The woman he had claimed as his responsibility carried another man's child but his eyes were calm and considering. No doubt he was already making and discarding various plans. He wanted to save her. He *needed* to.

In my own form, I could have eased the sickness Rhiwallon experienced most mornings and could have helped her deliver the child. Perhaps Mother could do even more, for she had much arcane knowledge. She might know a way to shield Rhiwallon from the fey. My chest tightened and my throat felt thick. I had often wished my abilities would disappear along with Mother's expectations for me, leaving me free to chase adventure and danger. I had wished them away too freely. Here was a woman — a friend, of sorts — who needed the aid I could have given her and I was as powerless as if I had no ability at all.

It seemed strange that the Sight had never shown me Rhiwallon. I had seen Diarmuid and Owain and myself. I had recognised Ida the first moment I saw her in person. The white hair, the cruel smile. But the visions had never shown me Rhiwallon. I could only wonder why.

The three of us stood in silence for some time. Owain seemed absorbed in his thoughts. Diarmuid's eyes were downcast, mouth wobbling a little, shoulders slumped. He smelled of defeat.

"So…" Owain said at length, after Rhiwallon had stormed off. "What now?"

Diarmuid didn't look at Owain as he shrugged. "Now I go home and admit I failed."

Silence stretched again. I looked between Owain and Diarmuid. I waited and, sure enough, Owain finally found his next words.

"Just like that?"

"Huh?" Still Diarmuid didn't look at him.

"You're giving up?"

Diarmuid hung his head. "I tried. I really did. I thought I could… I don't know, *do something*. Convince her, persuade her. But she's too strong."

"She'll keep killing people."

"You don't think I know that? What she's doing is my fault. I have to live with that. But I tried. I couldn't stop her. What more could I have done?"

Another long pause.

"Seems to me," Owain said. "Instead of asking what you could have done, maybe you should ask what to do next."

Had I hands instead of paws, I would have applauded. Instead

I was struck by an urge to bark long and loud, but I restrained myself. Owain was a fine man and if Rhiwallon couldn't see it, then she didn't deserve him.

"You think I should try again?" Diarmuid asked.

"That or give up," Owain said. "And we've come too far for that."

"But what else can I do? You felt her power. How can I destroy something like that? Talking to her is of no avail. She will never be persuaded to stop."

"Hit her over the head. Like Braden and Drust said. Tie her up. Might be able to talk sense with her then."

I had forgotten Drust. Had his brother, Davin, been somewhere in the house while we were there? Should we have tried to rescue him?

"We need to surprise her," Diarmuid said at length. "She won't expect me to return."

"Need to strike fast," Owain said.

"Surprise is as good a weapon as any."

I contributed a bark of agreement.

Diarmuid tentatively stroked my shoulder. He had been odd with me ever since he realised I was more than just a dog. Often he would stretch out a hand to touch me but then pull back at the last moment. I gently touched my nose to his hand. He might be a fool sometimes but he was still *my* fool.

"What do we do about Rhiwallon?" Diarmuid asked.

They looked at each other in silence. I read the same answer on each of their faces but neither wanted to be the one to say it.

"I don't know whether we can trust her," Diarmuid said, eventually.

Owain studied his hands. "Don't know. Hope so."

"Maybe she shouldn't come with us next time. Just in case. She has been lying to us the whole time."

"Protecting herself."

"But how do we know she's not still lying? That she wouldn't betray us if she thought it would save her? She helps Ida and Ida helps her to hide?"

Owain shrugged. "Either she'll betray us or she won't. Not much you can do 'bout it either way."

47

DIARMUID

W HAT WOULD CAEDMON say if he was here? He was born to be a soldier, one who fought and delivered death. I had never thought less of him for it. It was simply not the path I had envisioned for myself. But perhaps to defeat Ida, I needed to become a soldier too.

"How would I do it?" I asked.

"Cut her throat," Owain said. "Messy but quick."

I tried to picture myself standing over a bound woman, knife in hand. Owain would hold her steady. There would be blood. Would she feel pain? Would she scream? Beg for mercy? My stomach contracted and I pushed the thoughts away.

"I'll find some rope," Owain said. "When we go back, you distract her. I'll get behind her and grab her. Then you tie her up."

"Then I… kill her?"

He looked me right in the eyes. "Has to be done, Diarmuid. I can do it, if you can't."

I swallowed, hard. "It has to be me. I have to be the one to stop her."

"I'll get the rope," he said and left.

Bramble and I waited beneath the oak tree. The street around us was quiet and empty, unusual for this time of day. Perhaps folk were staying inside, away from Ida's attention. My hands shook. Today I would kill a woman. No, not a woman. She wasn't human. I had to remember that. I also had to remember that she might be able to read my thoughts. I couldn't think anything I didn't want her to know. I definitely shouldn't think about our plan.

When Owain returned, he had a length of rope wrapped around his waist, beneath his shirt. He was such a large man that the extra bulk was barely noticeable. My small dagger was already in my boot. Would it be enough to slit a woman's throat? No, she wasn't a woman, no matter how much she looked like one. She wasn't even real.

There was nothing left to say. Owain clapped me on the shoulder, nearly knocking me off my feet. Bramble met my eyes with a solemn gaze. I wished my feet would sink down into the earth beneath me and root themselves there. But step by step, we returned to the house Ida had made her own.

The curtains were drawn and there was no sign of habitation. But she was there. I felt her sense my arrival almost as clearly as if I could see her. She lifted her head, as if scenting me, and turned her face towards where we stood. Despite the walls between us, it felt as if we locked eyes.

"Oh, silly boy." Her voice was a mixture of surprise and disappointment. "You're not really going to try again, are you?"

"Let's go," I said to my companions, gritting my teeth and trying to look confident, despite my quavering voice and shaking knees. I laid my hand against the smooth panels of the door and pushed. It stayed firmly shut. I tried the handle but it seemed to be locked.

"Let me," Owain said.

I stepped back.

He lowered his shoulder and slammed into the door. It splintered with a groan and swung open, wobbling on loosened hinges. Owain started to enter but I stopped him with my hand on his arm.

"It should be me," I said. "I should be the one who goes first."

He met my eyes and for a moment I thought he would argue. Then he stepped aside. The interior was dimmer than before, a strange thing since the sky was clear and the sun had yet to lose its morning harshness. Yet inside was the murkiness of late afternoon when the border separating one thing from another becomes harder to distinguish and one must squint to make out the details of a thing. The air here was colder than outside and I shuddered as a chill danced down my spine.

Ida was in the kitchen, a scene of apparent domesticity. She wore a wide apron, the ties wrapped several times around her slender waist. In front of her, on the workbench, was a large pot, a bunch of herbs and a freshly-skinned hare. The wood stove was lit but I felt no heat from it. The knife flashed as Ida chopped carrots and turnips.

"Boy," Ida said and her tone was entirely pleasant. "Whatever are you doing here?"

She spoke as if she had expected me to be gone for the day and I had instead returned home early. I felt wispy tendrils of power snaking out from her and wrapping around my mind. My thoughts wandered. I shook my head and steeled myself against her power.

"You know why," I said. "I'm here to stop you."

"What on earth are you talking about?" Ida trilled a silvery laugh. "I'm merely making soup. And you, my boy, are being extremely rude. Aren't you going to introduce me to your friends? I suppose there will be enough soup for us all. I'll add more vegetables to make it stretch."

Where was Owain? Why wasn't he inching around behind her, ready to grab her so I could tie her up? I suddenly realised what I was thinking and turned my thoughts instead to the ocean. I felt the motion of the waves in my mind and let my thoughts drift with the movement of the water.

Owain stood beside me, gazing at Ida, open-mouthed, his eyes seeing nothing but what she wanted him to.

"Stop it," I said to Ida. "I know what you're doing."

Her eyes were wide and innocent. "You know you're a silly boy sometimes. Now, who are your friends? I think there's one fewer than last time. Where is the pretty girl? My oh my, I suppose you boys must fight over her. Such a pretty little thing."

Beside me, Bramble shifted and growled, so softly as to be almost inaudible. A rush of relief flooded me. Owain might succumb to Ida's charms but not Bramble. But without Owain, I didn't have the strength to hold Ida down. I would need a new plan. I tried not to stare at the knife in Ida's hands. Tried not to picture myself pressing it to her throat. *Waves on sand, erasing footprints, leaving behind shells and rocks in their place.*

"Do you live here alone?" I asked, stalling.

She smiled but there was no warmth in it. "Oh no, I have a companion. A fine young man. He is not presently here but you may meet him if he returns."

Ida finished chopping vegetables and started on the hare. She removed the limbs with a couple of expert slices and began stripping the flesh from the carcass. Beside me, Bramble whined and, for a moment, I saw her skinless form there on the chopping board, her body being divested of flesh in preparation for Ida's soup. Then I blinked and the world shifted and Bramble was by my side again. I restrained the urge to touch her, to reassure myself she was really all right. The more Ida knew about my friends, about how much they meant to me, the more danger they would be in. Even thinking about Bramble might put her in danger. *Seagulls flying above the waves, dipping and soaring with the wind.*

But Ida already knew. Of course she knew. She stared at Bramble even as she continued to strip the hare's carcass. "What a sweet creature," she said. "Is she yours?"

I hesitated. If I said yes, Bramble might be in even more danger. If I said no, perhaps she would think Bramble didn't belong to anyone and add her to the cooking pot with the hare.

"Yes," I said at last.

Bramble's huff was both immediate and expected.

"She's darling," Ida said. "Her spirit fairly blazes from her eyes, but then I expect you know that, don't you?"

"She's just a dog." I carefully kept my voice casual and thought of restless waves. "Not terribly obedient but she's company."

Bramble's head instantly turned to me and now indeed her spirit did blaze from her eyes. I wanted to beg her to understand but I looked away and didn't let myself think about how I was trying to protect her. Several soft thuds came as Ida finished chopping the hare and threw the pieces into her cooking pot. She lifted the pot and turned towards the stove. This was our chance.

Owain stared at Ida as she placed the pot on the stove and stirred the contents. I kept my mind blank, not letting myself think about how this was the moment in which Owain was supposed to act. I waved at him, trying to catch his attention without alerting Ida, and finally, reluctantly, he looked at me. I raised my eyebrows and tipped my head towards Ida. *Waves and currents. Swirling sand and frothy water.* Owain's face was expressionless, his eyes empty. Ida finished stirring and set down the spoon.

Beside me, Bramble uttered a soft growl. Slowly, the fog cleared from Owain's eyes and, finally, it seemed he actually saw me. Ida turned back to us, wiping her hands on her apron. At the other end of the house, a door opened and closed.

"Ida, my love, are you here?" a voice called.

"Of course I'm here," Ida snapped. "Where else would I be, you silly man?"

Heavy footsteps along the hall. My palms began to sweat. I pictured an enormous beast of a man, as broad as he was tall, and fierce. When the man entered, I swallowed my surprise. He was rugged, yes, and of muscular physique. But he was no larger than average and had a face which, under other circumstances, I might have described as kind. I saw echoes of his brother in the shape of his forehead and his chin.

"Ida, is everything all right?" Davin asked, scanning us each in turn. I could not hold his gaze but looked at my feet. I did not want him to see an intent to murder in my eyes.

"Everything is fine," Ida said. "My dear friend has come to visit. And, look, he brought some friends."

Davin eyed me, as if waiting for me to contradict her. *Fish swimming, deep beneath the surface.* I said nothing.

Ida fluttered her eyelashes at Davin. "My dear, you are home earlier than I expected." For all her soft words, her voice was waspish. "Did I not tell you to take your time?"

"But I did not want to leave you for so long," Davin protested. "It is not good for you to be alone so much and it is not seemly either."

A shadow crossed Ida's face and she turned her back on him. "Will you stay for lunch?" she asked me. "The soup will be ready in a while."

"No." I meant to say something further but unease was building within me. Those few moments while she stirred the pot might have been our only chance.

"Oh, what a pity." Ida pouted.

Davin frowned. "Why would you want other company, my love? Am I not enough?"

"No, you silly man," she said. "You're boring. You never talk about anything interesting. In fact, I'm growing quite tired of you."

There was barely time for a look of disappointment to cross Davin's face before Ida turned to Owain. Bramble barked once, a brief warning.

"Kill him," Ida said with a nod towards Davin. "Do it for me."

Owain's eyes were glazed and his face blank as he drew a dagger from his boot. It took him only four steps around the bench to reach Davin.

Davin looked disappointed, rather than fearful. "My love, you cannot mean this."

"Oh but I do," Ida said with a vicious smile. "And you would please me by not resisting."

"Owain—" I started, but I was too late.

Davin's eyes were still locked on Ida as Owain raised the knife and stabbed him in the heart. Davin staggered and blood ran down his chest but he never took his eyes off Ida. I was too stunned to move until something splattered on my face. When I wiped it, my hand was covered in blood.

Owain pulled his knife from Davin's chest. Davin swayed for a moment before crumpling to the floor. He gasped and tried to lift an arm towards Ida. Even as he died, his gaze was fastened on her.

Ida merely nodded and turned back to the stove. "You may leave now."

I couldn't take my eyes off Davin's body. A pool of blood seeped around him, slowly stretching across the wooden floor. When I finally looked away, Owain was gone. Even now, he obeyed her.

Bramble barked and there was urgency in her voice. She was waiting by the door. I stumbled after her. As we left, I glanced back. Ida stirred the contents of the pot on the stove. She looked calm and unperturbed. To see her, nobody would know that a man lay in his own blood beside her.

Bramble barked again and finally I followed, a sudden chill wracking my body. The sun was bright and warm as we exited the house. It soaked into my skin although it didn't ease the chill. I had failed again and, this time, a man had died.

I stumbled along, seeing nothing and aware only of Bramble's presence at my side and the pain in my ankle until we caught up to Owain. He was standing in the middle of the path, staring at the bloody dagger in his hand.

"Diarmuid." His voice was full of anguish. "What have I done? Tell me, what have I done?"

"You killed a man, Owain." The words were bitter on my tongue. "And he didn't even raise a hand to defend himself."

"No," he said and then lifted his head and screamed to the sky. "No."

I left him there and headed for the inn. First Rhiwallon, then Owain. Would Bramble be next? Would I stand in Ida's house as each of my companions betrayed me in turn? I suddenly realised I was alone. Bramble had stayed with Owain.

In my mind, I saw Fiachra. He sat at a desk, a sheaf of papers spread out in front of him. *I will be watching you on your journey,* he had said. *If you have need of me, call and I will come if I can.* He had not told me how but somehow I knew. *Fiachra,* I screamed silently, holding his image in my mind. *I need you.*

Fiachra seemed to lift his head and look right at me. "I am coming, Diarmuid," he said.

My mood lifted slightly as I hurried to the inn. Fiachra would be there, waiting. He would know what to do. There would be another way to destroy Ida. I burst into the inn, my eyes searching the common room. He would be there, I knew it. But there were only two men there and neither was Fiachra. My heart sank. Even Fiachra had abandoned me. I stumbled towards the staircase that led up to our room.

"Ho there," the innkeeper called. "Can I get you something, friend?"

"A bath," I muttered. "Send up water."

If he noticed the blood on me, he said nothing.

I was relieved to find our bedchamber empty. I didn't know where Rhiwallon might have gone but at least she wasn't here. A boy brought a bucket of water and I washed thoroughly. Blood swirled in the bowl, leaving it muddy-red. I pulled off my clothes and left them in the corner of the room. I would not wear them again. Even if the blood splatters came out, they would always remind me of the day I watched my friend stab a man to death.

As I dressed, heavy footsteps announced Owain's arrival. My stomach twisted. How could I face him after what he had just done? I kept my back to the door and finished buttoning my shirt.

"Diarmuid." Owain's voice was tormented.

Despite my intention to not look at him, I did. His face was pale beneath splashes of blood. My sympathy surged at the horror in his eyes but I ruthlessly squashed it down.

"She made me do it." His voice pleaded with me to believe. "It was a charm. I would never do such a thing. I've never killed a man without a contract."

"You're a killer." I spat the words at him. "No wonder you do what you do for a living."

I pushed past him and left. He didn't try to stop me. Bramble waited behind him in the hallway. I met her eyes and the disapproval I saw there made me feel even worse. The last thing I needed was to be judged by a dog.

I stormed down to the common room and ordered an ale. I intended to drink until I fell off my chair. Then perhaps I might forget, if only for a while, what a failure I was.

48

DIARMUID

I MIGHT HAVE expected one of my companions to join me in the common room — Bramble perhaps — but, hour after hour, I sat alone. I lost count of how many ales I drank. At some stage, I must have told the innkeeper to keep them coming because as soon as I finished one, the next would appear beside me. Eventually he brought me a bowl of soup.

"You need to eat, my friend," he said softly, depositing the bowl by my elbow. "Too much ale without food is not good for a young man." He didn't wait for a response.

I intended to ignore the meal but the savoury scent hit my nostrils and my stomach growled. The room had been bright and almost empty of patrons when I sat down. It was now more than half full. Lamps drove back the encroaching darkness and a small fire blazed in the hearth. I must have sat here for hours, noticing nothing but my own miserable thoughts.

My one remaining friend was Bramble but she had stayed with Owain. Owain the killer. Owain who had stabbed to death a man who never even raised a hand in his own defence. My stomach churned abruptly and the soup came back up, splashing into the nearly empty bowl. The innkeeper appeared promptly at my side.

"I'll take that," he said, reaching for the bowl. "And I think perhaps you've had enough ale for today, my friend. How about you go upstairs and get some sleep?"

"Do you have any spare bedchambers?"

"Sorry, we're all full up tonight." If he wondered at my request, he didn't ask. "You're welcome to sleep in the barn though."

I found an unoccupied corner in the hayloft. I had left my blood-splattered coat in our bedchamber but I found a horse blanket that didn't smell too strongly. I wrapped myself up and burrowed into the hay. My head spun and my stomach churned. I vomited twice more although I managed to avoid the hay. The loft smelled like sickness and sour ale as I pulled the blanket over my face and fell asleep.

I felt thoroughly wretched when I woke. My head throbbed, my stomach still churned and my mouth tasted bitter. The loft reeked, making my stomach roll and empty itself yet again. I washed outside in a horse trough, the water cold and none too fresh. The early morning glare burned my eyes and my head throbbed even harder. I stumbled into the inn.

I sat at a table in a gloomy corner, far away from the windows and the brightness of the fire, and massaged my throbbing temples. Then suddenly I realised somebody sat across from me. Bitter comments welled on my tongue as I looked at Fiachra: about how long he had taken to arrive, how he should have warned me that all of my companions would desert me and I would fail. But I said nothing.

"I told you this would be harder than you expected," Fiachra said.

"You should have told me everything you knew. I could have been more prepared."

"It is not my place to tell you what may or may not happen. I cannot foretell the future. The choices you make are your own decision."

"I think you know more than you pretend to."

He didn't respond.

"What do I do now?" I asked.

"What do you think you must do?"

"Must you answer everything with a question? Why can't you tell me what to do?"

Fiachra merely looked me in the eyes, his face as implacable as ever. "This is your quest, Diarmuid. Is it finished?"

"How can I ever finish? I can't match her power. She is turning my friends against me, one by one."

It wasn't until I said it that I realised I no longer blamed Owain. Ida had charmed him, like she charmed everyone else who carried out atrocious deeds at her instruction. Still, I didn't want to face him. I couldn't bear to look in his eyes and see my friend and know he had killed an innocent man.

"Tell me about your journey," Fiachra said.

The words began to spill from me and I told him everything. About finding Bramble and how we had almost died in the woods. Owain rescuing us. Finding Rhiwallon. The journey through the tunnels and the beast and the dragon. How I had tried and tried again to defeat Ida. How I had failed.

"So you intend to give up," Fiachra said. There was no judgement in his tone but I squirmed at his words.

"I'm not exactly giving up," I said. "But I have no other options. Ida is too powerful."

"You have power of your own, Diarmuid."

The tiniest flicker of hope flared. "My tales?"

He looked at me and waited.

"But how could telling a tale defeat *her*?"

Still he said nothing.

Slowly, awkwardly, my thoughts came together and I discovered I already knew the answer. "She came from inside of my head. Her strength, her power… it all came from my words. So perhaps I could defeat her with a tale, if I knew how they worked."

It sounded ridiculous. Whatever power I might have, surely Ida was far stronger. And the one time I had deliberately tried to make a tale come true — in the fey tunnels — it didn't work. I picked at a splinter poking out of the table. It dug into my thumb and a bead of blood formed. I stared down at the blood with disinterest. The pain was nothing. It could be someone else's hand for all I felt.

"Perhaps the aim is not to defeat her," Fiachra said. "Perhaps you need to mend the breach that is broken. Restore that which should not have been divided."

"Do you mean I need to send her back into my head?" My stomach suddenly felt hollow and my chest tightened until I could barely breathe. "I can't. Even if I could somehow get her back in there, I can't live like that. Knowing she's in there. Knowing she's watching everything I do, listening to everything I think."

"You've lived like that for years already, Diarmuid."

"But that was different."

"How?"

"I didn't know she was there. I didn't know she was alive."

"Why does that matter?"

"I don't want to live like that."

"Ida is your responsibility," Fiachra said evenly. He rested his arms on the table, looking completely at ease.

"But how would I even do it? Do I tell a tale about a muse who comes to life and is returned to the bard's head?"

Fiachra shrugged.

"Can I wait until tomorrow?" I asked. "I can't go back yet. I need… time. To prepare."

"Time for more people to die?"

"You didn't see what happened yesterday. It was awful. Davin didn't even raise a hand to stop him. He just stood there."

"Remember, Diarmuid, this is what she does. She charms folk into doing what she wants, and they have no choice but to obey."

"Surely they could resist. Surely there was a part of Owain's mind that was still his own. He could have stopped if he wanted to."

"Have you asked him?"

My cheeks burned. "No, I haven't spoken to him. Not since… Not since we argued."

"Owain is your friend, Diarmuid. He acted on Ida's will. This is her fault, not his."

"I can't risk taking him with me again. What if she orders him to kill me? Would he do it?"

"Perhaps. It seems to me that the people she charms have no control over their actions."

"Will you come with me? Surely she couldn't charm you."

"I cannot interfere. I can only advise, and only because you asked me to. What you choose to do, and how you do it, are your decision alone."

"You would leave me to go to my death rather than interfere?"

He looked at me evenly but didn't answer.

"So I'm on my own," I said, bitterly. "All of my companions have deserted me and I'm left to face Ida alone."

There was a huff from the floor and Bramble glared up at me. I hadn't even realised she was there. As I met her gaze, the tightness in my chest eased a little.

She huffed again, then looked to Fiachra. He met her gaze and they stared at each other silently for the longest time. Eventually, he nodded.

"Your task has been great, little one, but it's almost at the end. You need to be strong a little longer."

Bramble dipped her head, as if in thanks.

"I guess we should go then." I felt like I had been excluded from a private conversation. "Might as well get this over with."

"Eat first," Fiachra said. "This is the day you either complete your quest or fail entirely."

I suddenly realised I was famished. The innkeeper brought new bread and steaming bowls of porridge. I set a bowl on the floor for Bramble and then ate with gusto.

Fiachra didn't speak again until I had eaten my fill. "I can teach you how to deal with Ida once she is back inside your head. It will be different this time, for now she knows what it is to be alive. She will resist, and you must be prepared."

"But once she is back in my head, she won't be able to resist any more, will she?" Fear clenched my stomach and already I regretted having eaten.

"She has power now that she didn't have before. She may continue to fight and you need to learn how to fight back. Now, close your eyes. Picture a box. Can you see it? It need only be small but you must see it clearly."

I concentrated on the blackness inside my mind and, slowly, a wooden box formed. I focused, ensuring all of its edges and corners were clearly defined.

"I see it."

"Good, hold the box there. You need to be able to see it, even when you open your eyes. This is where you will put Ida. As soon as you see her in your mind, open the box and push her inside."

"How do I push her?"

"With the force of your mind. It may help to exhale, quickly and strongly, at the same time. Push her into the box and replace the lid. Then you must hold the lid in place."

"How long do I hold it?" I looked into his dark eyes and he stared back at me, waiting for me to find the answer for myself. "For ever. I will always have to hold down the lid so she can't escape."

"It will be hard at first but, after a while, you will hardly need to think about it."

"What will happen if she gets out of the box?"

"I can't answer that. She may have the power to influence what you say and do. She might even be strong enough to take over your body. To make it hers."

"Could she force me into the box?"

"Perhaps."

I realised I was holding my breath and slowly let it out. I had always known I might not survive my quest but I had never anticipated living with Ida in control of my body, watching helpless and trapped while she carried out her terrible deeds.

"I don't think I can do this."

"This is your decision, Diarmuid, and yours alone. I cannot tell you what you must do. I can only advise you to listen to your heart. What does it say?"

I didn't want to answer but he waited patiently, his face calm and his hands relaxed.

"I have no choice," I said at length. "She is my fault."

"Be strong, Diarmuid. As soon as Ida is back inside your head, you must get her into the box. She will be confused and disorientated for a few seconds and that is your chance. Once she regains her senses, she will fight you."

"I guess I should go then."

Bramble immediately stood. I looked down at her, a scruffy terrier not even as high as my knees. "Are you sure you want to come with me? It will be dangerous."

She glared but didn't deign to huff.

"I know you want to help, but I... I might not be coming back again. I can't promise to look after you."

She stalked over to the door and waited. Somehow, the knowledge that I wouldn't be alone eased my fear the tiniest bit, even if my sole companion was a small terrier who may or may not turn out to be one of the fey.

49

DIARMUID

OON BRAMBLE AND I stood yet again on the doorstep of Ida's stone cottage. I carried no weapon except for the dagger in my boot, yet I felt strangely calm. I looked up at the bright blue sky. A single cloud drifted lazily. This might be my last view of the sky. I took a deep breath, letting the cool air fill my lungs. Perhaps my last taste of the air outside of Ida's house. This was it. I would find a way to force Ida into the box, or die trying. I had my tales and, if that failed, I had my dagger. I would not live with her controlling my body. I would kill myself first.

I knew better than to ask Bramble again whether she was sure she wanted to accompany me but there was something else I needed to say. I crouched down beside her.

"Thank you." I stretched out a hand to stroke ever so gently the silky hair on her chest. I wanted to touch the torn ear and run my fingers over the red scar on her shoulder and flank, but I didn't. Hair was already growing over the wounds and in a few weeks they would no longer be visible, except for the damage to her ear. "You've been a good friend to me. I had hoped you might come back to Silver Downs once this is all over. But if something happens to me in there, get out straight away. Go and find Owain. He'll look after you if I can't."

She blinked at me, just once.

"I know you understand me, even if I don't know what sort of creature you are."

Bramble extended a paw and touched me gently on the cheek.

"I hope I get a chance to find out who you really are."

She looked towards the door.

"You're right. Let's get this over with."

I stood, wincing slightly at the pressure on my injured ankle. The door had been mended since Owain broke it down and it didn't resist us this time. The hallway was dim and silent, a memory of days spent in a fey tunnel. Nothing existed outside of this moment, just Bramble and I walking along the dimly-lit hallway, past a rack of coats and scarves. Past a pair of men's boots standing tidily against the wall. Past closed doors that led to other rooms. Lonely accoutrements of someone else's life. I took a deep breath. The house smelled of herbs and furniture wax and fresh bread.

I could feel Ida. She was in the back room where we had found her on our first visit. I had feared she might be in the kitchen with Davin's body still lying there, his blood staining the wooden floor, his limbs stiff and eyes blank.

Doubt started as a quiver in my stomach. I hesitated and Bramble looked up at me, a question in her eyes.

"Perhaps I shouldn't do this," I said. "She's happy here. Free." I turned back towards the front door. "She won't hurt anyone else if I leave her alone. She just wants to live, in a real body, in the real world."

My feet already carried me back through the doorway. "It was a mistake to come here. I see now that things aren't as bad as I thought."

Bramble barked once, short and sharp, and Ida's influence drained away. Anger and shame warred within me. Anger that she would try again to control me and shame that I had allowed it so easily. This was what it felt like to be one of her victims. I hadn't even recognised what she was doing. Her thoughts had seemed as natural as if they were my own.

I clenched my fists and strode back down the hallway, Bramble at my side. I would not let Ida send me away. This would be our final confrontation. The culmination of my quest. One way or another, this meeting between us today would decide both of our futures.

Ida sat in the back room, in the same wooden chair as on our first visit. She wore a plain white dress, the skirt covered with a white apron. She looked innocent. Harmless.

I caught myself this time before the thoughts could control me. Now that I knew she sought to influence me, it was easier to recognise when my thoughts were not my own.

We stared at each other in silence. It was still somewhat strange to see her in front of me. A figment of my imagination made real. She didn't look quite as I had imagined. I hadn't given such a hard glint to her eyes or such a cruel twist to her mouth. Those features were hers alone.

I fidgeted, growing impatient as the silence lengthened, and finally it was I who spoke first.

"You know why I am here."

"Of course." Her tone was entirely pleasant, as if we were discussing something of no more consequence than the weather or what I ate for breakfast. "And you know I won't allow it."

"I can't let you continue doing this. You're my responsibility. I brought you into this world, even if I didn't mean to."

"Poor boy. Such a burden on you, isn't it. Such terrible powers. Such responsibility for one so young."

Her words wormed into my brain. They burrowed, trying to elicit self-pity. At my feet, Bramble growled softly. I clung to the sound, letting it too seep into my mind, and it eased Ida's hold.

"I didn't ask for this ability." My voice sounded strong. "I didn't know what I was doing when I created you. I didn't know I could do such a thing. But I did it, and I take responsibility for it."

"What do you intend to do about it, Diarmuid? How strong are you? And where are your companions? They seem to be deserting you, one by one. Look at you now, standing there with nothing but that creature at your side."

"My companions have been through much for me. They have travelled a long way, even through the realm of the fey, because they believed in what I intended to do."

"They never believed in your quest, Diarmuid. Each chose to accompany you for their own selfish reasons. You were a way for them to achieve what *they* wanted, not what you wanted."

"That's not true."

"Isn't it? Think about it. The girl is running away from the father of her child. You provided a disguise for her escape. Who would think to look for one such as she amongst a small party of friends travelling together? And the man, he flees his own demons. A wife who hates him, a career that allows him to indulge in his desire for murder. We all saw what happened yesterday. He could barely stop himself from bathing in poor Davin's blood."

"Stop it. You're twisting it all. Everything you say is only part of the truth. They are my friends."

Ida's stare flickered down to Bramble and my breath caught in my throat. *Not her,* I thought before I remembered that I must not think anything I wouldn't want Ida to know. *My mind is an ocean. Restless waves. Impatient currents.*

"You know this creature is not what she seems." Ida's voice was light and her eyes sparkled as if she was sharing a joke. "But do you know exactly what she is? Have you ever wondered how she came to be in such a form? It is a punishment, surely, and a grave punishment indeed to be taken from your own form and forced into another. What secrets does this creature, the last of your companions, hold?"

"Leave her alone." My voice was less steady now. "She's done nothing to you."

"Oh, but she has. She's comforted you, aided you. Look at her now. She desperately wants to speak, doesn't she? But she can't, except with barks and whines and growls. Do you wonder what she might say, this fiery little companion of yours, if she could speak? Shall we find out?"

My heart stumbled and my eyes locked with Bramble's. I saw fear in them, but also hope.

"Please," I said. "Don't do anything to her."

I didn't need to look at Ida to know she smiled. "Oh I'm not going to do anything to her. I'm going to undo what has already been done."

50

BRIGIT

A RUSHING WIND filled my ears. The world blurred, fading and twisting as I fell. My body felt wrong. Stretched. Contorted. Too big. I wanted to tuck my tail between my legs and howl.

The scents were gone. I couldn't smell Diarmuid or Ida or the lingering traces of Davin's death. The only odours left to me were bread and furniture polish. Without my sense of smell, I was blind. I whined but the noise sounded wrong. My mouth didn't work properly and my teeth were the wrong shape. My tongue was too small in my mouth. And my tail, where was my tail? I crouched on the wooden floor, confused and shaken. When I tried to speak, actual words came out. My voice was croaky and my mouth numb.

"D-Diarmuid?"

I reached for him as I stumbled to my feet. Hands. Long fingers, a scar on my wrist where I had burnt myself through carelessness in the kitchen. My own hands. I looked down. Legs, feet shod in boots. I stood on human legs. I wore the same work dress as the day the fey girl had taken my form from me. With shaking hands, I touched my face, my hair. My heart leapt. I touched my injured ear. It felt misshapen, twisted.

Diarmuid backed away from me, bumping into the wall.

"Diarmuid?" Words felt wrong. I had become so accustomed to Bramble's barks and whines, whimpers and growls. A dog can express such a variety of emotion within the limits of its speech.

"What are you?" Diarmuid whispered.

I took a step towards him and stumbled. My legs shook but slowly I remembered how to walk without the certainty of four legs. I moved closer to Diarmuid, wanting to be near him. I wanted his arms around me. I wanted him to pick me up and hold me to his chest, where I could feel his heart and smell his scent.

"Don't," he said. "Don't come near me."

I stopped, confused. "Diarmuid? What's wrong?"

His mouth twisted and his face was a furious red. "I don't know who, or what, you are, but don't come any closer."

My heart shattered. My chin wobbled and tears seeped into my eyes. I blinked them away. I would not cry in front of him.

Ida laughed, a soft, tinkling like wind chimes. "Oh my. Look at your little dog now."

Diarmuid glared at her. "Are you satisfied? You've taken all of my friends from me, one by one. What's next?"

Ida smiled coldly and her hands gripped the arms of the chair so hard that her knuckles were white. "What did you expect from me? Gratitude? You kept me locked inside your head for all those years. You owe me something for that."

"I owe you? I created you. Without me, you wouldn't exist."

"And what a fine existence it was. Trapped in your head, witness to your every thought and emotion."

Ida looked at me and I froze. *Please don't turn me back into a dog.* Had I still been Bramble, I might have whimpered. As Brigit, I stayed silent and looked her in the eyes. I was strong. My mother raised me to be confident, capable, a wise woman.

"My dear, you would be horrified if you knew even a tiny bit of what goes on inside his head," Ida said. "I've seen his true nature. You might think you know him but you see only as much as he wants you to. He won't show you the darkness inside."

"I know a little more than you think," I said and although my voice was hoarse and scratchy, the words were even enough. "Who do you think he confided to night after night? Why, the dog, of course. The dog knows everything."

51

DIARMUID

S HE WAS PERHAPS a year or two older than me and wore a grey dress with scuffed boots. Her dark hair was coming loose from its bun and wisping around her face. This was the woman I had seen from time to time, the one I had hoped to find the courage to speak to. The one I had thought of when Caedmon asked whether there was someone he should meet while he was home.

I backed away. My legs were weak and my face hot. Secrets I had shared with her flashed through my mind. She knew every-thing about me, things I had never said to another person, things I had said only because she was just a dog. I never expected to one day be face to face with a person — a woman — who knew those secrets.

She was strong, this woman who used to be Bramble. Ida was sending out her power, trying to weave a hold around her, but if the woman noticed, she didn't show it. At first she held herself uncertainly, as if still figuring out what form she inhabited. I recognised the moment she realised she was human again, the moment she decided to fight. She straightened her shoulders and stood tall. Then she glared at me and I saw Bramble in those wide, unblinking eyes.

"You needn't worry," she said in a voice that sounded unused to human speech. "I'll keep your secrets. But first we need to deal with her."

I turned back to Ida. It was time to be strong but, expectedly, I found myself pitying her. This would be the end of her freedom, here in this room with its workbench and its sturdy chairs. This was where her tale ended.

"Ida, it's time to finish this," I said, gently. "I'm going to tell you a tale. It's about a bard who brings his muse to life. Somehow, she draws from him enough power to escape out of his head, and she goes off into the world. But something is wrong with the muse. She is dark, twisted."

"She is what she is," Ida said, "because everything she knows comes from the bard's head."

Her power swirled around me, seeking, burrowing. I pushed it aside and concentrated on my story.

"When his muse leaves, the bard knows he has done something very wrong and is determined to make things right again. So he goes in search of her, and when he finds her, he tells another tale, a new tale about how the muse returns to the bard's head. And as he speaks, his muse, just like the one in his tale, is drawn back inside of him."

I waited, bracing myself for the intrusion. But Ida continued to sit in her chair, an almost bored look on her face.

"What's wrong?" asked the woman who used to be Bramble. "Why isn't it working?"

"I don't know," I said through gritted teeth. How could it not work? Even Fiachra thought this was what I needed to do.

"Think," not-Bramble said urgently. "Think of when you created her. What was different about that tale?"

Ida laughed. "Have you *still* not figured it out? We are in for a long day, aren't we?"

"Ignore her," the woman said. "Focus."

I cast my mind back, trying to ignore the welling panic. When I told my very first tale, the one in which I created Ida, it had been the night before Caedmon was leaving to become a soldier. I remembered that the days ahead without him had seemed long and empty.

"I was lonely," I said. "Despondent. I was afraid that Caedmon might never return. And afraid he would return changed."

"How is that different from when you told other tales?" the woman asked.

I hesitated but as the words started to flow, the pieces came together and I began to understand. "I am nervous before I tell a tale, anxious that my audience won't like it. But once the tale begins, I am calm. All other emotion disappears. The words flow from somewhere deep inside of me. That first time, I didn't know that folk would hate my tales. I was fully focused on the tale, on my words, on how I felt. My feelings are the key."

"Try it," the woman said. "Let the emotions fill you and over-whelm you, then tell your tale."

Perhaps she was right. I had nothing to lose if she wasn't.

Ida laughed. "You're never going to figure it out at this pace."

I blocked out her words, closing my eyes and taking a deep breath. I thought about the reasons for my journey, my desire to make up for what I had done. I thought about the journey itself and what we had gone through to get this far. I thought about my friends, one by one. Owain, a killer by trade but a kind, gentle man who had saved both my life and Bramble's. Rhiwallon, a woman fleeing the man she feared would take her child. And then there was Bramble. My smallest companion. The one who had lain beside me night after night while I poured out my fears and my hopes. The one who had stood beside me as we faced down the fey, a dragon, and Ida. The one who was really a woman, trapped in another form, and I never even realised. And now here I was, alone. Betrayed by my companions, one by one. None of them was who I thought they were.

A warm hand grasped mine and held it firmly. No, not alone. I still had Bramble. In a different form, perhaps, but still, she was here.

I began to tell my tale again and this time I let my emotions infuse my words. I wove all of my hope and horror, heartbreak and happiness into the tale. I let myself feel — really feel — the devastation of realising that my tales were responsible for such awful things. I opened myself to the hurt and abandonment of Caedmon leaving to become a soldier. I felt the jealousy I had hidden away when he handfasted. My resentment that he had everything: a destiny, a career, a beautiful wife. My envy at his confidence, his ability to talk so easily to women, his bravery.

I felt the horror of climbing up the rock pile to rescue Rhiwallon and being pursued by the beast that had stolen her away. The terror of facing the dragon, the awful hopelessness of realising that our fate would depend on the ability of each of my companions to answer a riddle. The frustration of knowing I had gotten us into such a situation but that I would need help to get us back out.

All of these emotions welled up inside of me, filling my heart and my limbs and my head, until I thought I would either burst or lose my mind. I poured it all into my tale. It was still a dark tale but now there was also hope. There was wonder and beauty and love. It was unlike any tale I had ever told before.

As I reached the end of the tale, where the muse is drawn back into the bard's head, I opened my eyes. Ida still sat in her chair but her face was pale and her eyes wide. She gripped the arms of the chair, her knuckles white and straining. I could feel her struggling, still trying to control my thoughts, still trying to influence Bramble. Her power had little strength over me while the woman who used to be Bramble held my hand, but still she tried.

My mind began to fill with a presence both strange and also instantly familiar. I kept my eyes on Ida as she faded, her essence drawn back into my head. I said my final words. The tale was ended. For the first time in many weeks, I saw her in my mind. Her delicate figure, the translucent skin, her long white hair.

Ida began to writhe and scream. I closed my eyes and concentrated. I imagined the wooden box, its lid already open in preparation. Recalling Fiachra's instructions, I exhaled and somehow *pushed* at Ida, shoving her in the direction of the box. At first she didn't seem to notice. I managed to push her right up against the box before she realised what I was doing. Then she fought me. I clenched my teeth and blood filled my mouth as I bit my tongue.

As Ida struggled, the pain was as real as if she beat a hammer against the inside of my brain. My head pounded but I fought to ignore the pain and stay focused. Already my legs trembled and I panted from exertion. No matter how hard I pushed, Ida was always a little bit stronger. Then she was gone and instead I fought a black raven that somehow seemed to be both inside my mind and right in front of me. Wings beat against my face and sharp claws raked my arm. There was something inside my mind that I recognised as my self, my own essence, and it was being pushed towards the box. Panic grew, sharp and nauseating.

"Fiachra," I screamed. "Help me."

Then he was there with me in my head.

"This is *your* mind, Diarmuid," he said. "*You* control what happens in here."

His presence calmed me, focused me. I resisted, pushed back, managed to get away from the box. The raven disappeared and Ida returned. We grappled, struggled, fought. Then, so suddenly that I wasn't even sure how it had happened, Ida was in the box. I slammed down the lid.

The box trembled and I held the lid secure. My mind-self had hands now and they gripped the lid so tightly that the edges cut into my fingers and my own blood stained the wood. Surely the box would break apart from the force of Ida's anger. But, somehow, it held and gradually her resistance lessened.

Eventually I thought I could probably make my way back to the inn while still holding down the lid. Fiachra was gone. I hadn't even noticed when he left.

I opened my eyes to find the room dark. The woman who used to be Bramble was curled up on the chair in which Ida had sat. She looked at me, a question in her dark eyes.

"Don't speak," I said. I finally noticed how my legs trembled and sweat dripped down my back. "I can't..."

We left Ida's house. I barely noticed the dark skies or the empty streets as I stumbled back to the inn. Beside me, Bramble was silent. All of my attention was focused on the box. Ida had settled for now but it was likely a trick to lure me into thinking she had given up. As soon as my attention wandered, she would spring from the box and take over my mind. The possibility of being trapped and helpless in my own body kept me focused, despite my fatigue.

Owain and Rhiwallon were in the common room when I reached the inn. I didn't look at them, couldn't risk being distracted by talking to anyone. I focused on the stairs, making my way up them with such single-mindedness that I hardly noticed when I crashed right into someone. He swore at me and Bramble muttered a soft apology, tugging my arm to lead me away. I reached our bedchamber and collapsed onto the bed, my weary body sinking into the softness of the straw mattress. Exhaustion flooded my limbs, making them heavy, and my concentration wavered.

Suddenly Ida sprang out of the box. Again, I grappled with her, pushing her back. She gained the upper hand and I gritted my teeth, pushing harder. This was my mind and I would *not* be a prisoner in it. I eventually managed to confine her again. By that time, my hands trembled and I was dizzy with exhaustion. Then someone sat beside me on the bed, someone who smelled like sunny days tinged with lavender. A hand gently touched mine and the scent of fresh bread filled my nostrils. Something pressed against my lips and when I opened my mouth, a small piece of bread was deposited in it.

I hadn't realised how hungry I was. I kept my attention on Ida's box and when I opened my empty mouth, more bread appeared. Bramble didn't speak as she fed me, piece by piece. Once I had eaten my fill, she held a mug to my mouth and cool ale trickled down my throat.

I moved from the bed to a wooden chair. All through the night, I kept my attention focused on the box. Ida struggled for a while but eventually she stopped. Perhaps she slept, or perhaps she wanted me to think she slept.

Bramble, Owain and Rhiwallon took turns to sit up with me through the night. From time to time, someone would hold a mug to my lips or offer me some bread. I ate and drank to maintain my strength, feeling neither hunger nor thirst. Ida stirred occasionally, pushing at the lid for a while but then settling again.

When eventually I was sure I could keep part of my attention on the box, I opened my eyes. Daylight filled the bedchamber. Bramble sat cross-legged on the bed. Owain and Rhiwallon were absent.

"I think she is contained." I yawned. I was exhausted and drained, both physically and mentally.

"Does she still fight?"

"Sometimes. Mostly, she's just waiting."

I stood and stretched. My back was stiff and my legs cramped from spending the night in the wooden chair. Ida moved, cautiously, testing my attention. She found the lid of her box securely fastened and sank back down into stillness.

"There's water here if you want to wash," Bramble said.

I nodded, too exhausted to speak if words weren't necessary.

"I'll wait downstairs," she said.

I pulled off my shirt, which was stiff and sticky, and washed the sweat from my body. The shirt reeked but my spare was still covered in Davin's blood.

The common room was mostly empty of patrons. My companions were gathered around one table and a sole man sat at another. He was hunched over, almost asleep, a mug of ale by his hand. He looked like he had been there all night. The scent of yesterday's mutton still lingered in the air, mixed with the stench of stale ale.

"Thank you," I said. "I couldn't have done this without you."

"Is she really back in your head again?" Rhiwallon asked. She held herself stiffly and didn't look at me. I couldn't tell whether she was still mad at me or afraid.

"She's still fighting but I'm learning how to keep part of my attention on her. It's getting easier."

I turned to Bramble. "Who are you? How did you come to be a dog?"

"I was stubborn," she said with a hint of a smile. "I refused a task from the fey and that was my punishment."

"What was the task?"

"A journey. They wanted me to go somewhere but wouldn't tell me where or why."

I hesitated. Was the journey she took the one they intended? She guessed where my thoughts led.

"Yes," she said. "I think this is where they meant for me to be."

"Why?"

She shrugged. "They have their own reasons, and are unlikely to share them with me. It doesn't matter. They achieved their aim."

"What was that?"

She shook her head and a faint blush tinged her cheeks. "It doesn't matter."

"What is your name?" I asked. "Your real name? I can't help but think of you as Bramble."

"Brigit. But I don't mind Bramble. I've become quite used to it."

It was hard to think of her as Brigit when I saw Bramble every time I looked at her. Brigit's eyes were much like Bramble's, and like Bramble, her emotions flared from them. I hadn't often stopped to think about what she was feeling before, but I could read her eyes now: hope, confusion, and something that looked a lot like hurt.

The innkeeper brought bowls of porridge. I barely tasted my meal, focused as I was on Ida's box. Perhaps if I concentrated on it all day, I would be able to maintain my focus long enough to sleep for a while tonight. I suspected, though, that it would be several days at least before I could safely sleep.

I hardly knew what to think of the fact that Bramble was really a woman. Brigit. I tried not to think of the many confidences I had shared with her as she lay beside me at night. My cheeks were hot and Owain gave me a strange look but he didn't speak until he had finished his porridge.

"Well, Diarmuid." He pushed away his empty bowl. "What now?"

"I suppose we go home," I said.

Rhiwallon made a strangled sound and buried her face in her hands. Owain leaned close to murmur something to her.

"What's wrong?" I asked.

A sharp kick bruised my ankle.

"Idiot," Brigit hissed.

Belatedly I remembered Rhiwallon's secret. "I'm sorry," I said. "I—"

Another kick and Brigit glared at me. I stopped talking and ate my porridge in silence. Other patrons wandered into the room, some in pairs or groups and some alone. They ordered meals or ale and chatted with their companions. It was strange to see the world continue in such an ordinary fashion. After last night, it seemed everything should be different somehow.

"Where is your brother?" Brigit asked. "The druid?"

I shrugged. "He has probably left, gone back to wherever it is the druids live."

"He's very knowledgeable," Brigit said. "He taught me much."

I waited but she didn't elaborate.

After the meal, we returned to our bedchamber to gather our belongings and start the journey home. I was right behind Bramble — Brigit — as she opened the door, and I saw what she saw: the room was gone.

We walked into an enormous cavern. And we weren't alone. The last time we confronted the fey, there was a multitude of them. This time we faced only the king and queen.

52

DIARMUID

BRIGIT STEPPED FORWARD. With a sigh, I followed. Rhiwallon and Owain were close behind me. It might have been the same cavern in which we had last encountered the fey, for the cavern walls were composed of layers of orange and brown and red rocks, and the ceiling arched up high out of sight.

Oberon looked grave but there was a hint of something about him that suggested he might be more compassionate than she. Titania stood stiffly with her hands on her hips. Her long dark hair flowed unrestrained down to her waist. She wore a scarlet dress that swept the floor of the cavern and dipped so low over her chest that I averted my eyes, blushing. Titania looked at me, eyebrows raised, but said nothing.

"Why are we here?" I asked finally, tiring of her silent game and too exhausted to care about being polite.

"To account for yourselves, of course," Titania said. She looked at us each in turn, eyes lingering on Brigit. "So, you have found a way back to your own form."

"It was one of your kin who stole my form from me," Brigit said and although her tone was respectful, it also contained a clear challenge.

Titania's mouth turned up into something that might have been a smile if her face wasn't so cold. "You refused an instruction. We made you comply."

"What right do you have to give me any instruction? Had she told me why she wanted me to go, I would have gone. You have no right to demand and expect me to obey."

"Mortals are stubborn and stupid. There is no point trying to explain something you can't understand."

"You could have given me a chance to understand."

"It matters little whether you understand or not." Titania's glare was icy. "You have done what we wanted. The reason is of no consequence."

"It mightn't matter to you but it does to me," Brigit said. "Nobody should be forced into another creature's form. To have to learn how that body works, how it responds. To have everything they know about the world suddenly taken away."

Titania glared at Brigit. "You are stubborn, just like your father. You had better be careful if you don't want to end up the way he did. You came too close this time. Cross me again and it will be worse for you."

Brigit looked like she wanted to say more but Titania dismissed her with a slight lift of her chin and looked towards Rhiwallon.

"He suspects you are with child," Titania said. "He knew there had to be a reason you ran."

Rhiwallon paled but she straightened her shoulders and stared back at Titania. "Do you intend to tell him where I am?"

"He hasn't asked me."

"Was it his beast that stole me away? Or yours?"

Titania barked a laugh. "That beast was no fey construct. We have no need to conjure such a creature. If he knew where you were, he would have simply taken you himself."

"Then where did the beast come from?" Rhiwallon asked. "And why did it take me into your lands?"

Titania lifted one slender shoulder in an elegant shrug. "It should not have been able to access my realm. The one who made such a creature is powerful indeed, but you should ask your own companions for the answers to your questions."

She turned to Owain then and looked him up and down. Owain stood silently, waiting for her to finish her slow inspection.

"You chose a strange path," Titania said and her tone was almost friendly now. "But you should choose your friends with more care. When she discovers your secret, she will turn on you."

She gave Owain no opportunity to speak but turned instead to me. I quailed a little. Ida stirred, perhaps sensing a momentary lack of attention, and I redoubled my focus on holding the lid securely on her box.

"Bard," Titania said. "Your quest is complete."

"So it would seem." I was pleased my voice sounded strong and confident despite how I trembled inside.

"Mortals are not meant to have power such as yours. But your line is strong and determined. Unnecessarily stupid at times. I shall make the same offer to you that I have made to every seventh son of a seventh son in your family. I can remove your ability. I can take it away from you so you never bring your words to life again. You can be free to tell your little tales without fearing the consequences."

"Why would you do that?"

"My reasons are my own and they need not concern you." Titania's voice was impatient now. "Do you accept or not?"

"What will you give me in exchange?"

"What will I give you? Why would I give you anything? I have made an exceedingly generous offer to remove a troublesome ability. I needn't give you anything in exchange for making your life easier."

I hesitated, sorely tempted. If Titania were to take my ability, I could be a bard again. And this time, I would study my craft. I would not be so proud about telling the learning tales my audience despised, but would create tales of beauty and wonder, courage and heroes. But if I retained my ability, I could never tell another tale.

"If you want something from me, you must offer something in exchange. You cannot take my ability, but I can freely give it to you. And I do not intend to do that unless you offer me something of equal worth."

All pretence of a smile faded from Titania's face and I trembled as her face twisted in fury.

"You stupid mortal. Do you think to bargain with me? I have already been generous with you. I have given something of immense value, to you at least, but it seems you are too stupid to realise it. I shall not give you anything further in exchange. You will give me your ability in payment for what you have already received."

I didn't bother to ask what she meant. "Then I decline your offer."

"Foolish man. Why are the bards of your line so stupid? I make this same magnanimous offer to every one of them and they all refuse."

I held my tongue for none of the responses that came to mind were terribly polite. But now I knew that Papa too had rejected Titania's offer.

"Go then," Titania said. "Stupid mortals. You have no idea how good I am to you."

I blinked and the cavern was gone. We again stood in the doorway of our bedchamber. The hallway stretched behind us and the murmur of voices and the crash of plates rose from the common room.

"Well, that's that." Brigit sounded as dazed as I felt. "She could have at least left us closer to home."

53

DIARMUID

I TRIED NOT to look at Brigit as we prepared to depart The Midnight Traveller. Clearly the task she had refused had something to do with my quest. But why was Titania so interested in my journey? Did she know I couldn't succeed without Brigit? And if so, why did she care?

As we hauled our packs out to the cart, the oxen snorted and seemed as keen as we were to be off. The day was bright and sunny and perfect for travelling. The snow was melting a little more every day and the wrens and robins had appeared from wherever they had spent the winter.

It was hard to concentrate on keeping Ida's box closed while doing other things, perhaps harder than I had expected. I clung to Fiachra's belief that it would become easier with time. Could she still hear my thoughts? Was she also witness to everything I said and did? Now that I had some small understanding of how my ability worked, I was beginning to realise why Ida was what she was. If indeed everything she knew came from my head, then all she knew of the world was from my tales. I had never told a tale where the hero succeeded because of his courage or where light triumphed over dark. Never had my tales culminated in a happy ending or the banishment of evil.

Caedmon had tried to tell me. The night we had sat up late in front of the fireplace after his betrothal party seemed like a lifetime ago. Was he still alive? Or had I killed him with that poorly-chosen tale about the soldier who was beaten to death by his new bride's menfolk? And what of Grainne? Did I harm her too?

How many others had I hurt? All because I had presumed to tell tales that would teach my audience to be better than they were. Why had I thought it was my place to do such a thing? Over and over people told me they wanted to hear of heroes and love and happy endings but I resolutely continued to tell my dark tales of danger and injury.

It was just as well I had already resolved to never tell another tale. I couldn't be trusted with them. I would never forgive myself for the havoc Ida had wrought, but at least I had been ignorant of my ability back then. I no longer had such a defence. And if there was any possibility that Ida still listened in on my thoughts, then I had to be very careful to only think such things as I would want someone else to know. Perhaps the right kind of thoughts could change her. Perhaps I could insure against the possibility that she might escape again. I could teach her honesty, courage and humanity. If she knew more of light and beauty, perhaps things would be different next time. Owain's voice intruded on my thoughts.

"I'll go settle the account," he said.

Brigit quickly offered to go with him and I was left alone with Rhiwallon for the first time since our encounter in the barn. I caught her glaring at me as she tossed a pack into the cart. She wore her travelling clothes today: long pants, her freshly restocked quiver hanging from a belt, and her red hair tucked up under a scarf.

My cheeks immediately heated and I ducked my head, pretending to search for something in my pack. The air felt thick with our silence. Suddenly Rhiwallon stomped over to stand right in front of me where I couldn't pretend I didn't see her.

"I wouldn't have betrayed you," she said, crossing her arms

over her chest. "I can hardly believe you would think that. I thought we were friends."

Surprised, it took me a few moments to think of a response. "I couldn't be sure. Her power was strong. She charmed Owain and he's the toughest man I know. I thought she would try to turn each of you against me. And I thought…"

"Say it." Rhiwallon's tone was withering.

"I thought that if she offered to protect you, to hide you, you might help her in return."

"She's evil, Diarmuid. She needed to be stopped. I knew that just as well as anyone did. I wouldn't have traded my own security against stopping her. I didn't come this far just for my own benefit."

"You didn't?"

Rhiwallon's glare became even frostier.

"But you didn't even believe me. I thought we just happened to be going in the same direction."

"It's a hard thing to believe when someone you barely know tells you they've brought a creature of their imagination to life. I partly believed you, just not completely. Not until I saw her. When I stood face-to-face with her and felt her power, then I believed. But by then you had stopped believing in me."

I hung my head, thoroughly ashamed. "I'm sorry. I don't know what else to say but I'm sorry about the way I treated you. That I didn't believe in you. And I'm sorry about that night in the barn." I finished in a rush. "You deserved better than that. Caedmon set it up and he wouldn't listen when I tried to tell him no."

Rhiwallon's smile was gentle and for perhaps the first time, I didn't feel like she was mocking me. "I understand. But does she know?"

"Who?"

"Brigit."

"Of course not. I've not told anyone."

"But you'll tell her sooner or later, won't you?"

"No, never."

"It's not a secret you can keep if you intend to build a future with her."

My mouth fell open and I stammered. "What- Why- I don't know what you mean."

Rhiwallon rolled her eyes. "It's obvious, Diarmuid. Anyone who has eyes can see the way you feel about her."

"Do you think she knows?"

"Probably, but she's waiting for you to make the first move."

"But what would I do?"

"Just tell her. Tell her how you feel."

"I couldn't."

"Then the two of you will part ways and you'll probably never see her again."

"Is there nothing else I can do?"

"It's time to be a man, Diarmuid. If you want her, you're going to have to tell her."

I swallowed hard and stared down at the ground. "What will you do now? Where will you go?"

Rhiwallon shrugged. "Away from here. As far as I can. Somewhere he will never look. Where even Titania won't be able to find me if he thinks to ask her."

"I wish you luck," I said. "I hope you find somewhere safe."

"Thank you, Diarmuid." Rhiwallon tossed the final pack into the cart and climbed in after it. It seemed the conversation was over.

54

BRIGIT

A S WE LEFT Crow's Nest, things felt strangely familiar and yet at the same time, they were so different that I wondered how I had ended up in such a situation. Once again I shared the cart with Diarmuid and Rhiwallon. Only this time, instead of being tucked into a cozy basket with a blanket that Diarmuid had wrapped snugly around me, I sat with my back against a pack and the edge of my thighs touching Rhiwallon's.

Diarmuid sat on the other side of Rhiwallon. That didn't surprise me. He would hardly want to be in a situation where he might accidentally touch me. I hardened my heart. He had hurt me enough. It was time to remember who I was: Brigit, wise woman. Or intended to be a wise woman, at least. What would Mother say when I finally arrived home? Had she been worrying about me or had the Sight showed enough for her to make sense of my strange journey?

We spoke little as the cart rumbled along and the day passed with us each absorbed in our own thoughts. My heart lifted a little at each sign of spring's approach: young shoots of grass in a sunny patch where the snow had melted, tiny new leaves on birch and beech, pale yellow catkins on hazels. The only sign of human habitation was a trail of smoke from an unseen chimney. The oxen moved slowly, pulling the cart with unusual reluctance.

We were midway between towns as the light started to fade from the sky. Owain directed the oxen away from the road and halted beside a row of shrubby birch that would provide some cover from overnight winds. I clambered out of the cart, my legs stiff after hours of sitting. Diarmuid, Owain and Rhiwallon quickly fell into their usual routine of setting up the camp. I hesitated, unsure how to contribute for as Bramble I had not been expected to do anything other than curl up in my basket and watch.

"You could make some tea," Rhiwallon said, her tone almost friendly. She had seemed almost as startled as Diarmuid to see me in my own form for the first time. Owain, on the other hand, had greeted me with a firm hug and a complete lack of surprise.

"Tea," I said. "Good idea."

A search of the area around us elicited a handful of sage and thyme. Diarmuid had already made a ring of stones for a fire pit and built up a pile of dry twigs and dead leaves. Rhiwallon had just started the fire and was tucking the flint back away in a pocket. I emptied a flask of water into a pot and nestled it amongst the blazing kindling.

Rhiwallon returned with a pair of hares before the water had even boiled. For a moment, I felt like Bramble again, curled comfortably by the fire, watching as Rhiwallon skinned and gutted the hares. As Bramble, I was always hopeful she might offer me the innards and was always disappointed when she tossed them into the fire. As Brigit, I could make a decent enough meal of the innards if necessary although I preferred the roasted meat, smoky from the fire and dripping with hot juices. Rhiwallon chopped the hares into chunks, skewered them on sticks and arranged them around the flames.

Diarmuid sat on a blanket and began removing his boots.

Should I sit next to him or on the other side of the fire? The stiffening of his shoulders indicated he had noticed my nearness but he feigned intense interest in his boots. That made up my mind. If Diarmuid wanted to pretend I didn't exist, I would sit right next to him. He said nothing as I sat on the blanket, but he edged over a little to give me room. I waited a minute or two but he obviously didn't intend to speak.

"Do you still see the ravens?" I asked.

Diarmuid started and, for a brief moment, actually looked directly at me. His face was pale and haggard with deep shadows around his eyes. He hadn't slept since he had captured Ida.

"I- What- How do you know about that?"

I shrugged and looked away into the fire. It had been more of a lucky guess than anything else but Diarmuid wouldn't know that. I was being stubborn, as usual, for what good could come of forcing his acknowledgement? But my obstinate heart wanted to know that he saw me and as a woman, not a terrier.

"The ravens are still there," he said, at last. "Everywhere I look, I see them. They are Ida, or they are from her. I suppose it doesn't matter which. Either way, they are intended to remind me that she watches me. She's always watching."

"Is she secure?" I asked.

"She's locked away as securely as I can. Whether it will be enough, I don't know."

"What will happen if she gets loose again?"

He plucked a handful of grass and shredded it restlessly. "Fiachra said she might be able to take over my body. Maybe she won't want to, though. Maybe she will want to leave again. Fiachra thought that if she became strong enough to escape again, I might not be able to restrain her. And all of this will have been for nothing."

"It's not for nothing," I said, surprised at how fierce I sounded. "You did what you had to do, regardless of what happens in the future. Maybe that's enough for now."

"Do you think so?" Diarmuid looked at me with shining eyes. "Do you really think I've done enough to make up for what she did? The people she killed. The lives she ruined. The families she destroyed. They haunt me."

"Of course they do," I said, trying to soften my usual no-nonsense tone. "That means you care. There would be something wrong with you if it didn't haunt you."

"But I can never make it up to them."

"No," I said. "You can't. But what you can do is ensure she never gets loose again."

Diarmuid nodded but made no further reply. Rhiwallon began fussing with the roasting chunks of hare, turning them so they didn't burn. Fat dripped from them and sizzled in the flames, sending up an aroma that made my mouth water. Owain returned from taking care of the oxen and eased himself down onto a blanket on the other side of the fire. Such a familiar scene from our days of travel and yet at the same time, now so strange.

I missed Bramble with an intensity that surprised me. The steady balance of four paws. The pleasure of a wagging tail. The acute hearing and sensitive nose. The sniffs and barks and growls that she communicated with. The simplicity of needing nothing more than a meal, a warm basket and a kind hand to stroke your back. The freedom of returning an affectionate caress with a nuzzle of the head or the press of nose against skin.

The sun had completely disappeared, leaving us in darkness except for the glow of the fire. Rhiwallon began passing around the sticks of skewered hare. For a moment, I hesitated, expecting Owain to cut the meat for me and drop it into my bowl. Then I remembered and reached for a stick. The meat was sweet and tender. When I was finished, I tossed the stick back into the fire and watched it crumble into ash.

The herb tea was ready and I wrapped a cloth around my hand to remove the pot from the fire. I portioned the tea into mugs and handed them around, then returned to my spot on the blanket. I wrapped my fingers around my mug, relishing the warmth as I waited for the tea to cool a little. Normally, I would either sit on Owain's lap or curl up in my basket and it felt strange to sit in front of the fire in my human form.

"Tell us a tale, Diarmuid," Rhiwallon said, her tone studiously casual.

Diarmuid flinched and shook his head. "I don't tell tales anymore."

"But you know how it works now, don't you?" she asked. "You figured out how to make them come true."

"To an extent," he said. "But there might be more parts to the puzzle. Other ways to bring them to life. I won't risk it."

"Then tell the right sort of tale," I said. "One that won't hurt anyone if it comes true."

Diarmuid's gaze flicked up to meet mine ever so briefly. He was tempted, I knew. It must hurt to feel like he couldn't tell tales anymore. After all, he had always expected barding would be his livelihood once he became accomplished enough. What would he do now?

"Try it," I said. "Keep your emotions in check, watch what you are thinking, and tell only a tale that won't hurt anyone. Learn how it really works."

If I was honest with myself, I wasn't encouraging Diarmuid solely for his own benefit. I wanted to hear a tale, something grand and adventurous. I had now tasted three of the four things I had always wanted. Danger, mystery, adventure. I had yet to experience romance but I could live with three out of four. My appetite wasn't dampened in the slightest. True, they weren't what I had expected. Instead of adventure being a glorious thing where I was filled with courage and fire and recklessness, it was wet and cold, dirty and hungry, and sometimes miserable. There were times I didn't know whether I would live through it. But it was also exhilarating and fabulous. My skin tingled and my feet itched to start walking, go somewhere, have another adventure.

But I couldn't. It was time to resume the life intended for me. Time to go back to possets and charms, potions and cures. But perhaps the tales of a good bard might give me adventure and mystery and danger once more.

"I don't think so," Diarmuid said, at last. "Not tonight anyway."

55

DIARMUID

I AVOIDED BRIGIT as best I could on the journey home although I was always conscious of exactly where she was. Each night as I wrapped a blanket around me and stared up at the stars, I missed having Bramble's warm body beside me. The ache inside of me seemed much larger than the absence of a dog. From time to time, I considered approaching her but my cheeks heated at the very thought and I didn't know what I wanted to say anyway. It just seemed there was something between us left unsaid.

The four of us travelled together as far as Tors. Owain and Rhiwallon intended to branch off from there, heading to a larger town some days travel away. Although neither he nor Rhiwallon mentioned an intention to stay together, it seemed that was the case. I was sad to part ways with them. Owain wrapped me in his big arms, almost crushing my ribs with his hug. Rhiwallon surprised me with a quick kiss on the cheek. I blushed fiercely, remembering that the last time she had kissed me, my hands had explored her bare breasts. Brigit gave me an odd look.

Brigit took Rhiwallon aside and spoke to her quietly. She handed Rhiwallon a small packet and they hugged. I couldn't be sure but I thought Rhiwallon might have been crying.

"What did you give her?" I asked later.

Brigit's face was shuttered. "Nothing you need be concerned about."

Brigit and I departed from Tors on horses purchased at Owain's expense. One day, when I had money of my own, I would pay him back. The horses were somewhat old and not terribly fast but they were quicker than travelling on foot. We spoke little as the day passed although Brigit seemed to spend an awful lot of time glaring at me. I spent the hours concentrating on Ida's box. I caught myself questioning every thought, wondering whether it was my own or hers. I still didn't know whether she could hear my thoughts but in case she could, I was ensuring there would be nothing that would give her any power over me. How much of what I had thought was myself had really been Ida?

Despite everything, I found it hard to wish Ida away entirely. She had been my constant companion since my tenth summer, but I did regret bringing her to life, and I regretted that I hadn't tried to learn about my ability earlier. I realised I was sinking down into melancholy and quickly changed my line of thought. I couldn't afford to linger over thoughts like that anymore.

As we drew closer to home, the landscape became more familiar. The snow on the distant hills was melting and grass had started to grow in the fields. Birds circled high overhead, too high up to tell what species they were. I could smell just the faintest trace of a familiar scent that I had always associated with home.

We reached the start of the woods stretching all the way to the edge of Silver Downs and Brigit reined in her horse.

"There is where I leave you," she said, with another glare in my direction.

I stammered something incoherent. She rode away without another word.

"Wait," I called.

Brigit turned her horse and came back. She paused in front of me, one hand holding the reins, the other on her hip, her eyes flashing. I recognised that look.

"Why are you angry at me?" I asked.

"For a bard, you don't seem to know much." Her horse stomped and snorted, as eager to be away as she.

"What's that supposed to mean?"

"How could you not know, Diarmuid? You were *surprised* when you saw me."

"I didn't know you were…" *A woman*, my mind supplied. *The very same woman I was trying to find the courage to speak to all those weeks ago.* "Human."

"What exactly did you think I was then?"

I must have looked like a fool, my mouth opening and closing uselessly. "I don't know," I said, eventually. "I just knew you were something else. Something more."

"And yet Owain had to point out even that much to you." Brigit's tone was bitter. "I would have thought all those tales might have taught you something."

"They did. I just didn't expect to find something straight out of a tale right in front of me."

Brigit gave me an incredulous look. "What has this whole journey been if not something straight out of a tale? You create a creature in your mind that somehow comes to life, one of our party gets abducted by a beast that most certainly shouldn't exist, we spend days searching bewitched tunnels, and answer a dragon's riddles. Is this not exactly like a tale? Even without what happened to me?"

"Well, yes, but…" It was clear there was nothing I could say that would make this better.

Brigit rolled her eyes.

"You could have tried to tell me," I said. "Why didn't you?"

My feelings were a confused mix. Hurt that the little terrier who had been my companion for weeks was not what she seemed to be. Surprise that she was really this fierce creature who glared at me until I wanted to sink into the ground. Amazement that it was really a woman with whom I had shared my darkest secrets and deepest hurts. Hope that perhaps, despite everything, there might be a tiny chance of a future for us.

"Why didn't I tell you, Diarmuid?" Brigit's tone rang with sarcasm. "Do you know how many times I tried? Every time I communicated with you, I was hoping you would realise I was no ordinary dog. And you know what? You never noticed. You were too busy being wrapped up in yourself and your quest. The noble bard who releases evil into the world and goes on a heroic journey to redeem himself and humanity."

"You make me sound pathetic. But I *did* release evil into the world and I *did* have to do something about it."

"Yes, yes, I know." Brigit sounded tired suddenly, as if all of the fight was gone out of her and there was nothing else left. "You know what, Diarmuid, just go."

My heart fluttered anxiously. If I left now without saying what I needed to, I would never have the courage to try again. I took a deep breath as she started to turn her horse around. "Brigit, there's something I need to say."

She paused but didn't turn around. I took a deep breath. I had to do it.

"No," she said.

"But I have to—"

"I'm not interested." Her voice was calm and indifferent. "Whatever you want to say, it can go unsaid."

"No, it can't." I surprised myself but suddenly I couldn't leave without knowing I had at least tried.

She turned back to face me and I was struck by the lack of emotion in her face. She didn't care. Despite all we had been through together, Brigit didn't care about me. I flicked my horse's reins and fled. There was no point saying anything. She was right. There was nothing left to say. At least I hadn't humiliated myself by telling her that I thought I loved her. My eyes filled with tears and I dashed them away with an impatient hand. This would not be the homecoming I had hoped for, returning with Bramble, or Brigit, at my side.

Of course it won't be, Ida said. *You didn't really think it would be anything like you imagined, did you? Oh, poor little Diarmuid, you really did. What a shame.*

I ignored her taunts and redoubled my focus on keeping her box secure. Ida fought back, briefly, but seemed to have little fight in her yet. That would change. She would regain her strength and it would be harder to keep her locked away. But I would become stronger too, Fiachra had said. And with time and practice, it would be easier to keep Ida in her box. Maybe one day I would hardly even know she was there.

56

DIARMUID

THE SUN WAS already sinking by the time the horse brought me in sight of the Silver Downs lodge. Lamp-light shone from the windows and I could just make out a stream of smoke from the chimney against the red-streaked sky. My family would be sitting down to eat soon. If I hurried, I might be home in time for dinner.

I anticipated a raucous greeting with my brothers crowding around and Mother fussing over me. There should be news by now of whether Caedmon had arrived safely at the campaign front and I would finally learn whether Grainne had been injured.

Would they find me changed? I didn't know how to account for my journey. Ida had been defeated, that was obvious. But they would expect she had been destroyed. How would I explain I had made her a part of me again? They would see only evil when they looked at me, Ida staring out through my eyes.

By the time I dismounted, my hands were trembling so hard, I could barely hold the reins. I led the horse into the stable and busied myself with rubbing her down and filling the grain and water bins. I knew well enough what Papa would say if he discovered I had gone inside without tending to my horse.

I approached the lodge, my heart pounding. Never before had

I been nervous about entering my own home. Ivy was creeping up over the grey stone again now that the frosts had passed but otherwise the lodge looked the same as ever, from the outside at least.

As I reached the front door, I hesitated. What if it was locked? Should I knock? Wait for someone to come out? There was no reason for anyone to come outside until morning. I turned the knob and the door swung open with the smallest creak. A flood of warmth and *home* rushed out over me. Dinner, the smoky scent of a fireplace, a faintly astringent smell I had always associated with the house being cleaned. I was home at last. I strode in and made my way to the dining room.

Fiachra was the first to notice me as I stood in the doorway. He inclined his head very slightly towards me, almost a *well done* motion, and I nodded back. Next to him was Mother. She half stood as I entered and then paused with a hand held over her heart. She looked tired and worn and I regretted that I had caused her grief. Beside her sat Papa, reaching out his hand to her. He looked older than I remembered.

On Papa's other side was Eremon with Niamh beside him. The children were absent, likely already put to bed and watched over by a servant. Eremon's face was grave but Niamh was pale and her eyes wide. Eremon wrapped an arm around her, as if to protect her.

My eyes stung and for a moment I thought I might cry in front of all of them. Then Ida stirred. I slammed the lid back down on her box and locked away my emotions. My brothers were all there, all except for Caedmon. It was Eithne who was missing, her and Grainne.

"Where's Eithne?" I asked.

Mother blanched and fled the room. Papa rose but Fiachra stopped him with a hand on his arm and a few soft words. Papa slowly lowered himself to his seat while Fiachra followed after Mother.

"What happened? Where's Eithne?"

Silence stretched while my brothers all looked towards Papa. His mouth opened but nothing came out.

"She's gone away for a while," Eremon said finally.

Away? Eithne never went away. The look on Papa's face told me this was not the time for questions about my sister.

"Is there enough dinner for me?" I asked instead, sharpening my focus on Ida's box as she stirred again.

"Of course, son." Papa seemed relieved that this at least was a question he could answer. "Come, sit."

There were several spare chairs and I chose one next to Marrec. He said nothing, only passed me a bowl of new potatoes. I never expected him to say much and it was comforting to find that Marrec, at least, was the same as ever.

Someone handed me a platter of mutton and I served myself a large portion. The meal tasted exactly as it always had. The meat was juicy, the vegetables crisp and fresh — a far better meal than I had eaten for weeks.

There was silence at the table as we ate. Neither Mother nor Fiachra returned and Papa merely picked at his meal. My stomach clenched and my appetite fled. I caught the eye of Sitric, who sat opposite me.

"Have you started scribing yet?" I asked.

He flinched and almost dropped his mug. "Yes. It's… fine." He swiftly crammed a spoonful of potatoes into his mouth.

As I looked around the table from brother to brother, they all avoided my eyes, and I finally realised what was wrong. They were scared of me. Scared that whatever had happened to Papa's brothers would happen to them too. I pushed away my half-eaten meal and stood, almost knocking over the chair in my haste.

"I'm going to get some sleep," I muttered.

My bedchamber looked the same as ever, a little dustier perhaps and somewhat musty. I flung open the window and leaned out, taking a deep breath of the evening air. The sun had fully set now and everything was shadows and darkness. Nobody had asked about my journey but perhaps Fiachra had already told them.

I took another deep breath of cold air and the faint scent of fire tingled in my nose. The moon was full, shining white and cold. Far beneath my second floor window was hard earth, grassy but devoid of rock or fence. I leaned out a little further. Would I die if I fell from this height?

A knock at the door interrupted my morose thoughts just as Ida roused. Fiachra didn't wait for an invitation. By the time I had closed the window, he was leaning against the wall.

"They're afraid of me, aren't they?" Bitterness edged my voice.

He met my eyes evenly. "They fear what they don't understand."

"I'm still me. This has always been a part of me. They just didn't know before."

"You need to show them."

"Haven't I already done enough?" I disliked the whine in my voice but was too tired to conceal it.

"In a way, you've done too much. And they fear what else you can do."

"Can she hear everything I say?"

"Does it make any difference?"

"I suppose not. Where is Eithne? And Grainne?"

"Eithne has her own destiny to fulfil. And she has gone to do it. Grainne too has her fate. They are together and, so far, they are safe enough."

"But where are they?"

He didn't look away but I knew he wouldn't tell me.

"Is there any way to get rid of her?" Perhaps speaking Ida's name would have no effect but there was a chance, a small one, that it might give her strength. I would never again speak her name.

"In truth, Diarmuid, I don't know."

57

IDA

OW DID HE trap me in here? I am stronger than he, yet here I am. Is this to be my world now? Confined to a plain wooden box somewhere inside Diarmuid's mind? I cannot survive like this. Not after I have become accustomed to the smells and sounds and sensations of the world outside. In here I can feel nothing. Not the gentle kiss of the breeze in my hair or the warmth of the sun on my arms. Not the crunch of ice under my feet or the wetness of water against my skin.

I am strangely weakened. I used so much energy to fight him that it seems there is nothing left. I am smaller, shrivelled, drained.

Before, I could roam his mind. Explore his thoughts and feelings. Now the box in which he has contained me blocks almost everything. I can still, if I concentrate, hear his thoughts, feel his emotions. But it is muted, distant, and it takes all of my energy.

Time passes. Or perhaps it doesn't. I sleep or maybe I stop existing for a while. When a little strength returns, I try to claw my way out of the box. But he too has grown stronger and he holds the lid down with a strength I can't yet match.

So I am trapped. But I will bide my time and conserve my strength. When I am stronger, I will escape again. And this time I will destroy him before he can contain me again.

58

DIARMUID

O VER THE NEXT moon I found it difficult to fit back into my old life. Mother tried to pretend she wasn't afraid and my brothers grew more relaxed around me. I took long walks across Silver Downs, trying not to think about Bramble's absence, and spent my days learning how to function while still keeping Ida's box securely closed. I could finally sleep for a couple of hours at a time, although it was always a restless sleep and I came awake with a start every time, heart pounding as I wondered whether Ida had escaped. I didn't tell any tales, didn't even let myself think any.

In the late afternoons, I sat in Eithne's herb garden as the sun slipped behind the tree-shrouded horizon. Blooming shrubs filled the air with sweet fragrance and often a lone warbler continued to sing long after the rest of his flock had bedded down for the night.

Lost in my thoughts one afternoon, I didn't notice Papa until he sat beside me on the wooden bench. I said nothing and it was some time before he cleared his throat.

"You've had a difficult time, son," he said.

"I did what I had to."

Papa stared down at his hands and I waited.

"We hoped not to have a seventh son. You were unexpected. Agata was taking herbs to prevent a pregnancy."

I nodded, biting my tongue. There was so much I desperately wanted to ask.

"I didn't intend to pass on this curse." His voice broke a little.

"It's not a curse," I said. "It is what it is."

"As soon as I realised what I could do, I stopped telling tales. I've never told another since."

"Titania?" I asked.

He nodded, meeting my gaze only briefly.

"Why didn't you tell me? If I had known, I could have been prepared. I would have been more careful." Anger began to roll inside of me and Ida stirred. I breathed deeply to calm myself and she subsided again.

Papa kept his gazed fixed on his weathered hands and sighed heavily. "I tried, once, but you wouldn't listen."

"You should have tried harder."

"I know." A long pause. "At first, we thought… We thought that if we said nothing, if we let you determine your own future, perhaps you would choose a different path. You might have been a scribe like Sitric, or a farmer, or a craftsman. We hoped… *I* hoped the tales might not sing to your blood the way they do to mine."

"I would have done things differently had I known. Told different tales." I didn't even try to mask the bitterness in my voice. "Nobody *had* to die."

"We made a mistake. I know. The day you announced you were a bard, my heart sank down into my boots and it's stayed there ever since. But by then, we had spent so many years pretending you wouldn't be a bard, we didn't know what to say. We hoped the curse had ended with me, that since it had been so many years since I last told a tale, somehow you would be free of it. And when you first started telling your tales and nothing happened, we thought you were safe."

We sat in silence for some time.

"Did you figure it out?" he asked at length.

"Emotion," I said. "That's what brings the tale to life. When I tell a tale while I am filled with emotion, it comes true. There might be other ways but I've not explored them. I don't intend to either."

"I should have known. It explains… It explains what happened for me."

"Your brothers?"

He closed his eyes. And I knew. He didn't have to say it.

"That was the last tale I ever told," he said. "I knew about my — our — ability. My father warned me long before I was old enough to tell a tale. He never told a single tale himself. He was too afraid. His own father had died when he was merely a babe and his grandfather was already dead. It was his grandmother who told him and she knew very little, only that there was a strange ability passed down from seventh son to seventh son. There was nobody left by then who knew how it worked.

"I didn't believe him at first, just as you didn't believe me. And for a long time, nothing happened, so I felt safe. I became confident, cocky even. Thought my father had been mistaken.

"I had argued with my brothers. They were jealous of the bard son who seemed to do nothing all day while they were busy making a living, supporting the family, supporting me. I didn't have any great renown so I contributed no income from my tales. My eldest brother, Eremon — your brother was named for him — he said he would no longer support a brother who did not contribute to the family coffers. I was bitter. Jealous they all had destinies that allowed them to contribute. Angry they weren't prepared to be patient while I learnt my craft.

"The tale I told was based on the Children of Lir. I spoke of a bard who cursed his six older brothers and turned them all into swans. The brothers remained swans for three hundred years and then they returned to their original forms, still the same age as they were when they changed."

My heart stumbled. "So your brothers… they're still alive? Still swans?"

"I saw them change." Papa's eyes held the most terrible sadness I had ever seen. "It was the first time one of my tales came true, and the last tale I ever told. They flew away and never returned. I hope... I hope they are alive and safe and that they will return one day. I deeply regret I will not be here to tell them how sorry I am."

"Have you tried to find them?"

"For many years, any time I saw a swan, I spoke to it, apologised. There was never any indication the swan understood. Whether any of them were my brothers, and whether they still retained any part of their human mind to understand my words, I'll never know. But in my tale, the swans returned and became men again. I pray that my brothers will also return, whole and sane."

"Do you think they will come home?"

He shrugged. "Where else would they go? As long as Silver Downs belongs to our family, it is still their home. Your brother, Eremon, knows, and he will ensure his heir also knows. The knowledge will be passed down from father to son and when three hundred years has passed, I trust that my brothers will be welcomed home as family."

Papa said nothing for some time after that. Occasionally he passed a hand across his eyes, as if to sweep away tears. Eventually he continued.

"Our father died shortly after. He couldn't live with the loss of six sons. So Silver Downs came to me, and I've kept myself busy ever since, running the estate the way Eremon would have. I wasn't supposed to be the heir and I had to learn fast. And that's what you need to do now. Find something else and learn it. Just because you were meant to be a bard, doesn't mean that's all you can do."

"But I don't know who I am if I'm not a bard."

"You'll figure it out," he said. "Trust me, son. There's something else out there waiting for you."

59

DIARMUID

A FEW DAYS later, a messenger arrived. He was a rugged man, travelling on a sturdy horse. Both man and beast looked well accustomed to lonely journeys across the country. Papa took the man into his study and closed the door. They remained in there for only minutes before Papa showed the man to the kitchen and then returned to his study alone. He didn't come back out again until dinner time and then his face was grave and grey.

My stomach was growling at the smell of soup thick with spring vegetables. But Papa looked solemnly around the table and my insides went cold.

"A messenger came today," he said. "From Caedmon's commanding officer. Caedmon did not return to the campaign front."

My stomach clenched. For a moment I couldn't breathe, couldn't see. I clutched the table, my knuckles white in clenched fists.

"We mustn't think the worst." Papa looked everywhere but at me. "Perhaps he has been delayed. He may have fallen ill and stayed somewhere to recover."

"Then why would he not send a message?" Eremon asked. "Either to us or to his officer?"

"Perhaps he is so ill," Marrec said.

"That he doesn't recall who he is," finished Conn.

Eremon shrugged and looked away. It was clear he didn't agree but was reluctant to argue. Of all my brothers, he was the most like Papa in that regard. Only now I understood why Papa held his words in such tight reserve.

We all pretended to be busy with our meal after that. The soup curdled in my stomach. Mother stared intently into her bowl, stirring her soup but seemingly eating none. Her face was composed but the knuckles on the hand gripping her spoon were as white as mine.

Another life ruined. If I hadn't told that wretched tale about the soldier and his wife, Caedmon would have made it safely back to the campaign.

"Where are Eithne and Grainne?" I asked, suddenly desperate to know. "Are they safe? Is Eithne… is Eithne well?"

Silence. Mother continued to stare into her soup but now her hand shook. My brothers looked to Papa and it was clear nobody would tell me if he didn't. Papa put down his spoon.

"They have gone away," he said, finally. "On a journey, of some sort. Exactly what, we don't know. Fiachra said only that they will return if they can."

"Did he say nothing further?" I asked.

"He hinted that someone — something — might pursue them, and it was better if we knew no details."

"Was Grainne injured?" I stared into my soup, ashamed to ask, but I had to know.

Papa looked to Mother and it seemed this answer was hers to give. Mother's chin wobbled and she nodded slowly.

"Badly?" My voice cracked.

"She was…" Mother's voice failed. She licked her lips and tried again. "She was beaten. She refused to say who did it. She was still recovering, still fragile. She was not fit to undertake a journey and Fiachra knew."

"So why did she go?"

"The journey was Eithne's," Papa said, "and we know no more than that. Grainne went with her, out of love and friendship."

I had not known Eithne and Grainne were so close, but then I knew very little of Grainne. I had been too mired in my own discomfort with women and my jealousy towards Caedmon to get to know her. But I knew Eithne and I remembered the man who had attended Caedmon and Grainne's handfasting, the one who stood off in the trees and did not mingle with our family and friends. Now that I knew more about the fey, I recognised the pale skin and blood-red lips. Who was he to Eithne? Did he have something to do with this strange journey of hers?

All this talk of journeys made me think of Brigit. She had never said why the fey had wanted her to go with me, only that whatever their aim was, it had been achieved. Did I dare hope that their aim had been to bring the two of us together? What purpose could the fey have for such a thing? But if their aim was achieved, did that mean she cared for me?

Staring into my soup, I saw not vegetables and broth, but Brigit's face, or rather, a meld of Brigit and Bramble. It was as Bramble that I first loved her and I couldn't not see the shaggy white terrier any more than I could not see Brigit herself. I had tried to forget and slide back into my old life but I wasn't the same person as the one who first set out to find Ida. I could no more forget Brigit than I could forget Ida.

If it were true that I had killed Caedmon, I would regret that for the rest of my life. I would regret also that Grainne had been injured so grievously but I could no longer affect those events. However, the way I had left things with Brigit was something I could still change, if I chose.

It seemed I faced a new decision. I could stay in a world I no longer belonged in, or I could seek out a new life for myself.

It took me until morning to decide what to do.

60

BRIGIT

I KNEW DIARMUID was coming for the visions showed me. I recognised the gentle hill he rode up and the stand of silvery birch he paused to rest his horse beside. I knew the day's eye bush there in a hollow and the rock that looked like a giant frog. The thought of seeing him again made me want to run in circles and bark madly. For how long would my first reaction be that of Bramble rather than Brigit? Perhaps some lingering sense of Bramble would stay with me forever.

The Sight showed me myself, throwing my arms around him and weeping, although I knew not whether it was with joy or grief. Of course, I resolved there would be no embracing or weeping. I would greet him coldly, somewhat disdainfully, hear him out and then send him on his way again. Anything I might have once felt for Diarmuid was gone. I had had my taste of adventure, mystery and danger, and would learn to be a good wise woman, like I was supposed to. Perhaps I would never have the romance I once desired but one cannot have everything. I had achieved three of the things I once wanted more than anything else, and if my heart beat a little faster at the thought of Diarmuid's arrival, and my breath caught in my throat, it was of no consequence, for he meant nothing to me. Truly.

I searched the visions for clues as to when he would arrive. The birches still bore patches of winter bareness. The day's eyes were only just beginning to bloom. I examined the bush near our front door. It was a tight mass of buds with few flowers unfurling. He would come soon.

Diarmuid's arrival would almost be a relief for the visions had tormented me all night. I had slept little and by mid-morning couldn't keep my attention on the task at hand. I knocked over a bin of flour and smashed a jar of preserved berries before Mother sent me out to work in the garden.

The sun was warm on my arms and spring was everywhere I looked. In the trill of the swallow, in the pale new shoots of garlic and onion, in the clear sky wearing nothing but a single cloud. My mood lifted as I lost myself in my work, pulling weeds, thinning some early carrots, and turning over the soil in preparation for planting the cabbages. At length, I paused to rest and stretch my aching back. It was then that I saw the horse and rider.

They were still some distance away, far enough that I could only make out the shape of a body on horseback. But my soul knew it was Diarmuid and already my heart beat a little faster. I could almost feel the tail I no longer had begin to wag. I wished I was not wearing my oldest dress, entirely suitable for gardening but perhaps not what a woman would choose to wear as she faces one who might, under other circumstances, have been her husband. I wished I did not have dirt up to my elbows and all over my apron but then I hardened my heart. I had no need for nice dresses and frippery, for Diarmuid meant nothing to me. I would give him the courtesy of hearing him out and then send him on his way. No weeping. No embracing.

I caught myself touching my damaged ear. Bramble's fight with the boar had left that ear twisted and misshapen. The skin was thickened and still tender. I often found myself touching it in moments of uncertainty. It reminded me of the tenacity of a little dog who refused to be a boar's breakfast and the memory gave me strength. If Bramble could escape the boar, I could face Diarmuid.

I returned to my chores and tried to forget the approaching horse. But I felt him draw steadily nearer. He was still some way off when he reined in his horse, pausing for so long that I expected him to turn and leave. But soon enough he was right in front of me, silhouetted against the sun. I wiped dirt-covered hands on my apron and squinted up at him.

Diarmuid dismounted. His face was schooled to what he probably thought was blankness but his eyes were full of hope. They showed anxiety too. He was uncertain of his welcome.

Good, I thought. *You will get no welcome here.* I stifled the urge to lift my lips and snarl.

"Bramble," he said. "I mean, Brigit."

My resolve softened ever so slightly, for his closeness made me feel like Bramble again, unsure of my own form and my mind. Craving his presence and his touch. Wanting nothing more than for him to see me as I really was. Well, this was what I really was. Covered in dirt and with my hair in disarray, this was me.

"Diarmuid," I said.

He hesitated and his gaze darted around as if looking for escape. He was uncomfortable, a contradiction as ever: the bard who could tell a tale to a roomful of strangers and yet couldn't speak to a woman without blushing and stuttering. Not that it mattered how much he blushed and stuttered because this woman didn't have the slightest interest in him. If my fingers longed to reach out and touch his face or stroke his hair, that didn't mean anything. If I craved the touch of his hand on my ear or my neck, it was merely a lingering memory of being Bramble. I crossed my arms across my chest, lest I accidentally reach out for him.

Resolve fluttered across Diarmuid's face and he straightened his shoulders.

"Bramble. Brigit." He took a deep breath and tried again. "Brigit, I came to apologise."

"For what?" *My heart is hard, like rock. I will not bend like a willow, like a weak woman.*

"For... for everything. For not seeing you, not listening to you. For taking you for granted. For letting you think I didn't w-want you."

"Right from the start you were trying to shove me off onto someone else." My tone was hard with accusation. "You wanted to leave me at Owain's house."

"I was trying to do what was best for you." His eyes begged me to believe. "I didn't know what was ahead of me and thought you would be safer if you stayed with Owain. You seemed to like him. I thought you would be happy there."

"So you thought you had the right to make decisions for me?"

"You were a dog. Or, that is, I thought you were. You were already special to me. We needed each other those first nights in the woods. Neither of us would have survived alone. I thought you belonged to someone who lived nearby and that if you stayed with Owain, they might find you. And if they didn't, I knew Owain would take good care of you. And that's all I wanted. To protect you."

What I wanted was to throw my arms around him and never let him go, but I held them stiffly to my chest, sternly forbidding them to move. I would *not* fall for his sweet words.

"I didn't need protecting."

"Brigit, you were half dead when you found me. I didn't think you would survive the night."

"I would have gotten through somehow. I didn't need you to come sweeping in and rescue me."

"All right, then, I'm sorry." There was a hint of frustration in his voice. "I'm sorry I saved your life. I'm sorry I didn't leave you to bleed to death in the forest, sorry I tried to protect you. I'm sorry for everything."

He ran a shaky hand through his hair and turned back to his horse. "I'm sorry I disturbed you today. You don't have to worry about it happening again. You won't see me again." He grasped the reins and set a foot in the stirrup.

My heart stirred and myriad images flashed through my mind:

Diarmuid tenderly washing the blood from my paw. Cupping his hand and filling it with water so I could drink. Lifting the blanket so I could curl up next to him, his warmth holding the freezing night at bay. Wrapping his arms around me at night as he prattled endlessly while I wished he would shut up and go to sleep. He was the reason the fey had sent me on such a journey. I could be stubborn and let him leave, or I could let him in.

"Wait," I said.

Diarmuid turned back to me so quickly that his foot caught in the stirrup and he almost fell. He said nothing, but at least he waited.

My mouth went dry and my knees started to shake. I didn't know what to say. Yes, there were probably things I needed to apologise for but my mind was as blank as his face. So I did the only thing I could. I threw my arms around him and wept. Diarmuid didn't hesitate. He wrapped his arms firmly around me.

"Bramble—" he started.

"Ssh," I said, wiping away tears. "It's all right."

"I might not have seen what you really were but I loved you from the first moment I saw you. You were covered in blood and barely able to stand and yet you held your head high as you stumbled towards me. A scruffy little beast so full of courage."

There was only one answer I could give. "Diarmuid, I suggest you shut up and kiss me."

"Happy to oblige," he said.

As his lips met mine, a warm tingle raced through my whole body. I didn't know why the fey wanted us together but clearly this was what they intended when they ordered me to journey to an undisclosed destination. If only I had known.

61

DIARMUID

I KISSED BRIGIT and my heart sang. When we finally drew apart, she took my hand.

"Come inside and meet my mother," she said. "I suspect she knew you were coming today."

"How would she know such a thing?"

"The visions," she said, as if that explained everything. "Mother is a wise woman. She has trained me for the same career."

"You're a wise woman?"

"Not yet but I'm learning. I could have helped you much on your journey, had I been in my own form."

"You helped enough."

My legs trembled with sudden nerves as we approached the stone lodge. It was smaller than the house at Silver Downs but looked cosy and sturdily made. The front door opened and the woman who stood there had the same sharp nose as Brigit and the same hair that refused to be restrained. The apron over her work dress was smudged with evidence of the day's chores. She smiled at me and her eyes shimmered with tears.

"You come at last," she said and hugged me fiercely. "I'm Treasa."

I stiffened and awkwardly hugged her back.

"You recognise him," Brigit said. She sounded unsurprised.

Treasa raised a hand to rest it against Brigit's cheek. "Brigit, my dear, I knew he was for you the first time the Sight showed him to me and that was long before your birth."

"How much—" I stammered. "That is, do you know—"

"I know enough," Treasa said, kindly. "What the Sight didn't show, Brigit told me. And now you must carry the consequences with you. It must be very difficult."

It was the first time anyone had shown sympathy for what I had done and my eyes burned. I quickly blinked away the tears.

"It was difficult at first but I'm growing more used to it every day. She doesn't seem very strong yet but Fiachra, my brother who is a druid, says she will regain her strength in time. I don't know whether I can keep her contained for ever."

As I spoke, Treasa led us into the kitchen. She took three mugs from a shelf and added a scoop of something from one container, a pinch from another, and a sprinkle from a third, then filled them with water from a pot on the wood stove.

"Is there any other option?" Treasa set the mugs on the well-worn table and motioned for me to sit.

I pulled out a sturdy wooden chair. Bramble sat close beside me, her hand still tucked in mine.

"No," I said. "There is no other option. If I do not keep her contained, she might take over my body or she could escape. And I don't think I could restrain her if she got away from me again."

"We do what we must," Treasa said. "And that is as it should be. Now, your tales. Do you still tell them?"

I inhaled the spicy scent rising from my mug. "I will never tell another tale. I can't, now I know what I can do."

"Brigit said you only recently discovered the key to your ability."

"I'm not taking any chances. What if I'm wrong? Or what if I'm right but there's more to it? I can't put more lives at risk."

"So what will you do?" Brigit asked.

"My brother Sitric needs an assistant. He has more work than he can manage. I'm going to Maker's Well to work with him. He says there is enough scribing work for us both to make a living, good enough to support a family."

Treasa nodded and swirled the tea in her mug. "Yes," she said. "That will be suitable."

"Where is the rest of your family?" I asked Brigit. "Your father?"

I wished I hadn't spoken for a cloud quickly settled over both Brigit and her mother.

"You don't need to tell me," I added quickly.

"You should know," Brigit said. She leaned across the table to grasp Treasa's hand. Treasa lifted her chin defiantly, a gesture I recognised from Brigit.

"I can tell him, Mother," Brigit said, softly. "You don't need to do this. Diarmuid, my father was killed. Murdered."

I inhaled a sharp breath. "I had no idea. I wouldn't have asked…"

Brigit smiled grimly. "We don't know who organised it, although we have our suspicions." She and Treasa exchanged a look. "Father had upset a certain person. A very wealthy and powerful person. We suspect he arranged for Father to be killed."

"By someone like Owain?"

"By someone exactly like Owain." Brigit's voice was milder than I might have expected.

I looked from Brigit to her mother. Treasa didn't look as accepting as Brigit did. "You don't think…"

Brigit shrugged. "I don't believe in coincidence."

"I don't know what to say."

"I've made my peace with it. If it was Owain, he was doing his job. I don't blame him, I blame the man who hired him."

Our conversation was interrupted by laughter, which preceded four girls who all looked much like Brigit. They swarmed into the house, rosy-cheeked and with hair flying every which way from their adventures.

"My sisters," Bramble said with a suppressed smile. "Clidna,

Sulgwenn, Keena, Myrna. Don't worry about which is which. You'll never remember and they all look much the same anyway."

"Brigit!" one of the girls exclaimed. "Mother, she is so rude to us."

Treasa said nothing and they didn't seem to notice. Brigit pursed her lips and grinned at me when the girls weren't looking.

I stayed a little longer and then left with the excuse that I wanted to be home before dark. In truth, the noise of Brigit's sisters made my head spin and it was difficult to concentrate on Ida's box. They were loud and vivacious, constantly teasing and arguing and shouting. Sometimes all four of them would burst into laughter at the same moment while I was left wondering what had happened. Perhaps it was me they found so amusing. I would have to get used to them for they might one day be my sisters.

My heart was light as I clambered up onto my horse and headed back to Silver Downs. I hadn't dare let myself anticipate how Brigit might greet me but when she had been cold and a little disdainful, it had seemed no more than I deserved.

I still saw Bramble every time I looked at her and perhaps I always would. It seemed that Brigit had come to terms with what had happened to her and it wasn't fair of me to cling to Bramble but, still, I missed her warm body beside me at night. I missed the way she pressed her head into my hand when I rubbed her ears. I even missed the disdainful sniffs she gave when she thought I was being a fool.

Someone else I missed was Caedmon. As much as I hoped we might still receive a message from him to explain his delayed return to the campaign, I was certain I had killed him with my ill-considered tale. All because I had let myself be consumed by jealousy and bitterness.

I would probably never tell another tale but sometimes I let myself hope that one day I might be brave enough to try again. I kept remembering what Brigit had said about telling the right sort of tale. If Ida ever got away from me again, she would need to know about honour and bravery and integrity. If I ever told another tale, that was the kind I would tell.

But for now, the pain of losing Caedmon and the agony of knowing that I was responsible for Ida's actions at Crow's Nest were still too raw. I would live with that for the rest of my life but maybe one day, I could try again. If I ever had sons, I would want to be able to pass on the knowledge of how our ability worked. I wondered how Brigit would feel about seven sons.

62

DIARMUID

A FEW EVENINGS after my visit with Brigit, I went out to Eithne's herb garden after dinner. Sitting in the garden my sister loved so much made me feel closer to her, even if she wasn't here. I still didn't know where she had gone. Fiachra wouldn't tell and it seemed nobody else knew the details. How my chronically ill sister would handle any sort of journey, I didn't know, and I lacked the courage to ask. Grainne had been still healing when she and Eithne disappeared on their mysterious journey but at least Eithne wasn't alone.

As I sat on the little wooden bench, which was still warm from the afternoon sun, peace seeped into me for perhaps the first time since I had told the tale about the soldier and his bride. Maybe for the first time since my tenth summer.

The herb garden was mostly still bare for without Eithne, nobody had thought to plant it for the new season. A couple of spiky bushes had survived, rosemary perhaps, and something that I thought might be mint but the rest of the garden contained only bare earth beneath melting snow. Even though little remained alive after the winter, the air still bore traces of the scent of herbs.

I should re-plant the garden for her. Tomorrow perhaps. Eithne would have saved some seeds and I figured that as long as I could find them, I could manage the task.

I didn't notice Papa's arrival until he stood right beside me.

"Mind if I join you?" he asked. His face bore a few more wrinkles than it used to, probably due to all the grief his wretched children had caused of late.

I moved over to give him room and he eased onto the bench with a sigh. I continued to look out over the garden, breathing in the herb-scented air and keeping my thoughts calm. I had found that the calmer I was, the less Ida was interested. She typically only stirred if I was anxious or angry or upset. So I was trying to be more placid.

"It's a gift, you know," Papa said. "I know it mightn't seem like it right now, and it took me many years to see it as such. Why it was granted to our family, I don't know."

"Titania seems to have taken great interest in us."

"Aah, Titania." Papa made a noise that might almost have been a laugh. "She was furious with me. Did she offer to take your ability away?"

I nodded. "I refused."

"As did I," he said. "And many others before us, from what I gather. Titania lives in hope that one day one of our bards will be foolish enough to agree. That's what makes me think it is supposed to be a gift. The fact that she wants it so much."

"Who do you think might have granted it?"

Papa shrugged and rubbed his stubbled chin. "One of the fey, I assume. Many generations ago."

"Maybe it was intended as a curse." Bitterness edged my voice and immediately Ida stirred. I smoothed out my feelings, pushing the bitterness away, and she settled again.

"I don't think so, given how desperate Titania is to reclaim it. I've always regretted that I didn't take the time to learn how it worked. Part of me died the day I stopped telling tales and a little more of me died every day since then. Don't let that happen to you, son. You're the first one in several generations who has a chance to learn how to use the power properly. Make it count."

"I don't know if I can. Caedmon…"

"Learn from your mistakes," he said, fiercely. "Don't stop telling tales. You can pass the knowledge on. Future generations of this family will benefit from whatever you learn."

"Perhaps," I said. "Would you want to learn too?"

"No, son, my time for telling tales has passed. It's up to you now. You're the bard of Silver Downs. The tales, and their power, lie with you."

Papa might not be a bard any more, but even so, I felt the power of his words. They lodged securely in my mind and refused to let go. Could I be the one to really understand this strange power of ours? Could I be the first to pass down the legacy in full, not just the gift but also the knowledge of how it worked?

For the first time in many months, snippets of a new tale began stirring in my mind. A fragment of words, a brief image. So the tales were still there after all and they still called to my blood. Perhaps I could be a bard again one day after all.

ACKNOWLEDGEMENTS

Thank you to my wonderful beta readers, Megan Grey Walker and Hannah Ivory Wright. Your insightful feedback gave me the confidence to finish this story.

Thank you to David Farland for teaching me everything I know about description and for advice when I didn't know what direction to take an early draft of what would eventually become *Muse*.

Thank you to my awesome editor, Meghan Pinson. Without you, this book would be nothing like it is today. Thank you to Deranged Doctor Design for a beautiful cover. I'm beyond thrilled. Thank you to Nick Hawkins for proofreading.

Thanks also to everyone who has read this far. I started this manuscript at a time when I wasn't sure I wanted to continue writing and it led me here. I hope Diarmuid and Brigit's story fills your heart the way it does mine.

And, finally, thank you to my family for supporting me through this journey. To Neal for all of the many hours you've tiptoed around the house, being quiet while I wrote. To Muffin and Lulu who are always convinced I can't write if they aren't there right beside me, guarding me. To Frehley, who really couldn't care less as long as I stop writing to feed her on time. And to my angel Bella. I miss you every day.

ALSO BY KYLIE QUILLINAN

The Amarna Age Series

Book One: *Queen of Egypt*
Book Two: *Son of the Hittites*
Book Three: *Eye of Horus*
Book Four: *Gates of Anubis*

Tales of Silver Downs Series

Prequel: *Bard*
Book One: *Muse*
Book Two: *Fey*
Book Three: *Druid*
Epilogue: *Swan*
(A mailing list exclusive)

See kyliequillinan.com for more details
or to subscribe to my mailing list.

ABOUT THE AUTHOR

Kylie writes about women who defy society's expectations. Her novels are for readers who like fantasy with a basis in history or mythology. Her interests include Dr Who, jellyfish and cocktails. She needs to get fit before the zombies come.

Her other interests include canine nutrition, jellyfish and zombies. She blames the disheveled state of her house on her dogs but she really just hates to clean.

SWAN – the epilogue to the Tales of Silver Downs series – is available exclusively to her mailing list subscribers. Sign up at kyliequillinan.com.

SNEAK PREVIEW - FEY

W HEN I AM ill, my dreams are filled with things that aren't really there. Some of these things I have really seen, like the power of a fire as it rages out of control and the might of a winter storm that strips branches from beech trees and thatching from houses. Others I have never viewed with my own eyes. They probably came from the tales my bard brother told. Titania, queen of the fey, glowering at me. Tiny beings no larger than my thumbnail, human-shaped but with wings. A creature, in appearance nothing more than a rock, but clearly sentient. I longed to see these beings but I could never hope to live a normal life, let alone one in which I might actually meet such creatures.

The images repeated one after another but eventually they returned to the boy. Always the boy. He appeared to be around my own age, although the fey can seem any age they choose. His milky skin and crimson lips shouted his fey heritage, and his dark hair was roughly cut as if he cared little about the result. Blue eyes stared at me, never blinking or looking away, just watching, considering. Unusual eyes, for a fey. He stood silently in the corner of my bedchamber and watched as I drowned in fevered dreams. Sweat soaked my linen nightdress and my damp hair stuck to my cheeks.

As the fevers subsided, the dreams disappeared and the boy with them, and I once again became aware of my surroundings. It was always startling to emerge from the dreams and discover that time still had meaning.

I lay in my bed, staring up at the knotted ceiling. I turned my head to see sturdy wooden furniture now coated with a thin layer of dust. Thick green drapes shielded the window. A hand-knotted rug lay in front of the fireplace. The air smelled stale and old. Mother sat beside my bed, her eyes shadowed and her face pale.

"Welcome back, Eithne," she said.

I struggled to sit up but my limbs were weak and I collapsed back down onto the bed.

"How long?" I asked. My voice was hoarse and my mouth tasted dry and bitter. Mother hesitated but I knew she wouldn't lie to me.

"Nine days," she said.

Her words chilled me and eventually I realised I was clutching my woollen blanket so hard that my knuckles had gone white. I forced my fingers to relax and straighten the blanket. Its wool was coarse and prickly.

"It's never been that long before," I said.

Mother nodded.

"It's getting worse, isn't it?"

I needed to hear it, to know that it wasn't all in my head. Like the dreams, no matter how real they seemed.

Mother sucked in a breath. She looked away, towards the window where the drapes were tightly drawn, hands smoothing the skirt of her work dress.

"You can say it," I said.

She looked back at me and her dark eyes glistened. "Yes, Eithne, it's getting worse. We always knew the illness might progress but I had hoped you would have a little more time."

I inhaled deeply, steadying myself. I knew what was ahead of me, had known since I was old enough to understand the truth. She had never tried to shield me from it. Death was the end of the journey for each of us. It just came sooner for some.

"There's never enough time though, is there?" I said, too fatigued to hide the bitterness in my voice. "We are always too young to die."

Mother swallowed hard. "Always too young, my darling." She avoided my eyes as she gathered up the pitcher and mug sitting on the small white table beside my bed. "I'll take these to the kitchen. I'll be back in a little while, to sit with you."

"I would like that."

I knew she was leaving because she needed to compose herself, not because the pitcher needed to be returned to the kitchen immediately. We had servants who could undertake such a task.

I stared up at the ceiling as Mother closed the door. I traced a crooked crack with my gaze and tried to pretend I couldn't hear her crying. Death had ever loomed present for me, from the day I first struggled out of my mother's womb, eager to be born and far too early with the birth cord wrapped tightly around my neck.

A sickness of the blood, the wise woman said when I told her about the recurrent fevers and chills. The days where I couldn't keep down even the thinnest of broths. Nights where my blood boiled within my veins. No cure, she said. Even the druid could only shake his head and say he was sorry. When one lives with the idea of death every day, one becomes somewhat used to it. At least I saw fabulous things in my dreams. They let me feel like I had lived just a little.

***

Enjoyed this sample? *Fey* is available now at your favourite retailer.